Home Before Dark

Home Before Dark

CHARLES MACLEAN

HODDER &
STOUGHTON

Lyrics from 'Jambalaya' by Hank Williams & ... Sony/... V
Acuff Rose Music. Administered by Sony/ATV Music Publishing.
All rights reserved. Used by permission

First published in Great Britain in 2008 by Hodder & Stoughton
An Hachette Livre UK company

1

Copyright © Charles Maclean 2008

The right of Charles Maclean to be identified as the Author
of the Work has been asserted by him in accordance with
the Copyright, Designs and Patents Act 1988.

All characters in this publication are fictitious and any resemblance
to real persons, living or dead, is purely coincidental.

A CIP catalogue record for this title is available from the British Library

Hardback ISBN 978 0 340 95149 1
Trade Paperback ISBN 978 0 340 95150 7

Typeset in Plantin Light by Hewer Text UK Ltd, Edinburgh

Printed and bound in the UK by CPI Mackays, Chatham ME5 8TD

Hodder & Stoughton policy is to use papers that are natural, renewable
and recyclable products and made from wood grown in sustainable forests.
The logging and manufacturing processes are expected to conform
to the environmental regulations of the country of origin.

Hodder & Stoughton Ltd
338 Euston Road
London NW1 3BH

www.hodder.co.uk

For Jeremy and Jamie

There will be days, maybe not now but in the months and even years to come, when she happens to be on your mind and the phone will ring and without thinking you'll pick up, wondering if this could be her calling to let you know she's all right.

You don't stop worrying about your children when they grow up and leave home. You don't stop even after they're not there any more to worry about and never will be again.

If there is an end to wishing you could turn back the clock, or to hoping you will wake one morning to discover it was all a bad dream, I haven't reached it yet. Acceptance is harder to find, I suspect, grief more difficult to resolve, when your family has been violated. Since Sophie died we haven't been the same. The murderer doesn't just murder his victim, he murders a little part of the family as well. He murdered a little part of Laura and me that night.

I dream about him, our murderer and yours – a human being with no conscience, no regard for the value of another's life, who is indifferent to the pain and havoc he leaves in his wake, who isn't human, at least not in my book, yet is still walking around free, still living his life.

I had advice for them, insights I felt it might be appropriate to share with others, strangers, whose lives he destroyed. As if my own experience had allowed me a unique understanding of what they must have been going through. I felt so sorry for them. I felt and still feel what happened was partly my fault. And I wondered if I should write. I wanted to write.

Something held me back me though.

Florence

When the telephone rang, Sam Metcalf was sitting, as she preferred to sit, cross-legged on the floor in her underwear, listening to Maria Callas pour heart and soul into Catalani's 'Ebben? ne andro lontana' and thinking she should have got out of this damned life a long time ago.

In four days she was leaving Florence, flying home to Boston on a one-way ticket. Her stripped-down apartment in the Oltrarno – its ochre walls bare of pictures, most of the furniture gone, a cardboard city of boxes and packing cases ready to be shipped – looked like some Third World departure lounge, but Sam still felt the wrench, giving up a place that held so many memories.

She removed her earpiece.

There was nothing to keep her here. Federico hadn't been in touch for almost a month and she neither expected nor wanted to hear from him again. And yet – Sam closed her eyes – you never knew, the prick might feel like saying goodbye.

The phone kept ringing, starting to get on her nerves. Any normal person would have realised by now that she wasn't home. But what if it was important?

She dried her eyes, her plump knuckles briefly dislodging the frame of her glasses, then squinted up at the kitchen clock, a gloriously tasteless fixture above the ancient gas stove – its familiar face, laminated in years of cooking grease, was a reproduction of the Angel Gabriel from Leonardo's *Annunciation*.

2

Eleven minutes to twelve.

She would remember the exact time of the call.

Getting up on her knees, Sam looked around for the phone, followed the lead across the floor and retrieved it from under a pile of papers. She couldn't help herself.

Her hand shook a little. Please . . . please God, don't let it be Federico.

'*Pronto*?'

'Yes, hello . . . is this Sam? Sam Metcalf?'

She let out her breath in stages.

It was a young voice, friendly sounding, American accent, no one she recognised – her prayers, disappointingly, had been answered.

'Who wants to know?'

'I was given your number by a mutual acquaintance. Ed mentioned you were leaving town soon, and I wanted to talk to you about Sophie . . .'

'You knew her? Wait a minute. Who is this?'

'Yes, ma'am, I had that privilege.' He gave a deep, slightly theatrical sigh. 'An angel if ever there was one . . . Sophie spoke, and I saw *all* the colours of the rainbow.'

Something was wrong here.

'Look, Mr . . . I'm sorry, who did you say gave you this number?'

'Think of me as Ward,' he said softly, inflecting the name upwards to sound like a question.

'Think of you as what?' She felt like laughing.

'Sam, you and I never met, but . . . I believe we both know why I'm calling.'

The first jolt of alarm went through her.

'What the hell are you talking about?'

'Just that it might be better – after what happened to poor Sophie – not to go stirring up the past. Nobody knows about any of this. Let's keep it that way.'

3

Again his voice lifted the statement at the end into a question mark.

Suddenly she knew, oh Jesus, her skin prickling – it was the call she'd been expecting, dreading, for so long now she thought he'd forgotten.

'What do you want?'

'I'm sure that it's what *she*'d want,' Ward went on quietly, 'looking down on this situation from above . . .'

Sam hung up, slamming the receiver into its cradle.

A minute later, the telephone rang again.

She hadn't moved. She stood staring down at her bare arms, which were folded over her belly, hugging herself, rocking, unable to stop.

It rang five more times.

In the dreams she'd been having, the caller always rang off before she could answer; she'd wake up, covered in sweat, one arm flung out towards the silent phone. Now that he'd finally got in touch, Sam had a feeling the dream would never recur.

It was, in some kind of way, a relief.

PART ONE

I

'Are you sure you want to go through with this?' Laura asked.

'Am *I* sure?'

'Everything is going to remind you of her.'

I turned towards my wife, but for a moment couldn't speak. She sat staring ahead. 'Well don't say I didn't warn you.'

We were parked just off Borgo San Frediano, across from the entrance to the atelier. The heat in the taxi was stifling.

'We're here now, we might as well go up,' I said, trying not to let my impatience show. I was already late for my next appointment at the *Questura*. 'I didn't come back to Florence because I want to forget.'

She retaliated sharply, 'And I didn't come here to sightsee.'

I had suggested to Laura that while I was occupied with the police later, she could always go and look at the Fra Angelicos in San Marco.

'Sweetheart . . . it'll be all right. Just let's get this over with.'

I climbed out of the cab and held the door for her.

Her anxiety about meeting Bailey Grant and looking at Sophie's drawings was understandable. Eleven months ago, when I'd collected our daughter's portfolio from the studio, I'd found that being shown her work (so much of it unfinished) was like losing her all over again. Laura couldn't face coming with me then. Now she was going to find it harder – a lot harder.

I hadn't told her everything.

The drawings had only turned up recently. One of Sophie's fellow students had discovered a folder and a sketchbook while cleaning out the lockers in the cast room. Bailey had

7

written to say the work it contained was quite remarkable, but also somewhat disturbing. His words.

While I paid off the taxi, Laura stood in the narrow doorway under the shade of a torn green awning. It was nearly midday, I felt the sun branding my neck.

'I don't remember it all looking so . . . squalid,' she said.

The volatile fug of oils and turpentine thickened as we climbed the steep marble stairs from the street. Waiting for us at the top stood a slim young woman in jeans and a black T-shirt; she was carrying an armful of small mirrors.

'It's a long way up,' she said in English. 'I'm India, by the way, Mr Grant's assistant.' Her auburn hair was cut short like a boy's. I hadn't seen her before. 'You must be . . . Sophie's parents.'

I nodded and without another word she led us back through a warren of hot dusty rooms lit by tall windows. The place had been a church before it was converted into a studio complex. Through an open door we caught a glimpse of a life-drawing class in progress, the students hushed in concentration.

I took Laura's arm and gave it a squeeze.

When we first brought Sophie here to see the studio, she was only eighteen and still uncertain about coming to Italy to learn how to draw and paint. 'This place gives me the creeps,' she'd said with a shudder, 'it's like an art cemetery.'

I didn't listen to her when she claimed to be afraid of Florence, afraid of being overawed, destroyed by its beauty. I tried to persuade her that developing her artistic talent was a better way to spend her gap year than backpacking through Africa or lying on a beach in Thailand. In the end the choice had been hers, but I regret . . . no, it's more than regret, I blame myself for influencing her decision. I even told her – I can hear it now – that she would be 'grateful to us some day'.

These things will haunt you forever, if you let them.

India pulled back the blackout drape that hung across the doorway of Bailey Grant's private studio and said, 'They're here.'

He was standing at his easel, palette and brush in hand, Ry Cooder on the stereo. I got the impression he had hurriedly taken up the stance – a template of the artist at work – the moment he heard us coming. With his flowing grey locks, white linen jacket and faded blue jeans, Bailey cultivated the image of the hip maestro.

'Where shall I put these?' India was still clutching the hand mirrors.

He didn't answer but went on dabbing with growing intensity at the canvas on his easel. I wasn't altogether surprised to see that it was the same painting – a lurid, life-size calvary in the manner of Titian – that he'd been working on the last time we met. His gift was for teaching.

'Where shall I put these?' India repeated. I noticed her portrait, a small delicate head, leaning against the wall. 'You did *ask* for them.'

'Anywhere.'

She set them down noisily on the only uncluttered surface, and left.

'Two seconds . . . and I'll be with you,' he said.

Stepping back at last, he surveyed his work and sighed. Then, taking one of the mirrors and facing away from the canvas, he held it up to frown over his shoulder at what he'd done.

'"*Il vero maestro*", Leonardo called it – the true master. Gives you a different perspective, a fresh eye,' he explained as he joined us. 'The mirror doesn't lie. How are you both?'

We shook hands. His was damp with sweat and it occurred to me that our being there together might be making Bailey nervous. This couldn't be easy for him either.

We had found no fault of any kind with the atelier over

Sophie's death. Bailey had written us a moving letter of condolence, but he hadn't seen Laura since it happened. For her he reserved a grave little smile of unspoken sympathy.

We talked awkwardly about this and that: the sultry weather, the tourist problem, the scholarship my wife and I had endowed in Sophie's name.

'Can we just get on with it?' Laura said.

He looked embarrassed for a second, then nodded and led us over to an old leather sofa under the window. On a coffee table lay the dark green folder that Laura's brother, Will, had given his niece for her last birthday. It was engraved in gold with her initials SL. I glanced at Laura, but her face gave nothing away.

Deftly tying his hair back with a rubber band, Bailey opened the folder and began to leaf through the drawings. They were mostly of plaster casts of antique and Renaissance statues. It was academic work, clearly of a high standard; I can't say that I recognised it as Sophie's.

'Early days, but already you can see evidence of real talent,' Bailey enthused, holding up a charcoal sketch of a Roman mask. 'Her *sfumato* – the smoky transition from light to shadow – is remarkably accomplished for a beginner. Sophie was driven, you know. She had that passionate fury in her eye when she drew . . .'

'Bailey,' I stopped him, 'we're a little pushed for time, you mentioned a sketchbook.'

'Ah yes, the sketchbook.' He put the drawing back on top of the others and closed the folder. 'We were just looking for it before you arrived. It seems to have gone temporarily astray.'

There was a moment's silence.

'What do you mean?' Laura frowned. 'You don't have it?'

He fiddled with the ribbon-ties of the folder. 'It was on the desk in my office upstairs. I saw it there last night. We only discovered it was missing an hour ago.'

'Well, I expect there's been some mistake,' I said. The atelier had a reputation for being disorganised.

'I'm sorry, but I find this unacceptable.' Laura flew up from the sofa, walked around the coffee table and stood over Bailey. 'Why couldn't you have just *sent* us the drawings? We've come all the way out here to Florence . . . for what? So you can tell us Sophie showed "promise"?' Laura is the calmest person I know, but she can be formidable when roused. 'And now you've *lost* the sketchbook?'

Under her stony blue gaze, Bailey wilted. 'I'm sure it'll turn up.' He rubbed the back of his neck. 'How long are you staying in town?'

'We fly home the day after tomorrow,' I intervened.

'Since we're obviously never going to see them,' Laura said acidly, 'would you mind explaining what was so special about these drawings?'

Bailey looked at me before answering. There was no conspiracy to hide anything from my wife. I just thought it best not to worry or alarm her until we could all look at the sketchbook together, and then decide what, if anything, should be done.

I nodded for him to go ahead.

'The drawings are of a house,' he began hesitantly. 'Pen and ink, mostly interiors, they're minutely, even obsessively detailed. There are one or two human figures, but insubstantial, more like effigies than real people . . .'

Laura interrupted. 'What house? The villa where Sophie was lodging?'

He shook his head. 'It's a white clapboard Colonial, with a porch, the kind you get in any affluent American suburb. Inside, things are much as you'd expect, only in miniature. The mood is bleak, shut-in, heavy with menace. The sense of scale and the tension comes from the doors and windows, which allow surreal glimpses of our own full-size world. It's like being trapped inside a doll's house.'

Bailey paused to let this sink in.

I looked at Laura. Her face was expressionless.

'There's a drawing of the kitchen, for example, which shows the back door standing ajar. Across the threshold lies a shadow – the windows are dark, as though the shadow has fallen over the whole house. What you see outside is a sliver of trouser-leg and part of what looks like a giant sneaker.'

Laura bit her lower lip. She looked down at her hands. Watching her, I could tell she was struggling to keep her composure. 'I suppose you think this tells us . . . reveals things about Sophie's state of mind?'

'The drawings speak for themselves,' Bailey said. 'I have no idea what it signifies, but some of them do seem oddly prescient.'

'If that's the case . . .' She fell silent, my poor wife. I could see the tears welling up. When she spoke again, her voice was trembling. 'Why didn't she *call*? Why didn't she talk to some-one?'

'Come and sit down, Laura,' I said quietly.

2

The day we lost Sophie was the day we said goodbye to the future. With immediate effect all her tomorrows were cancelled, and so many of ours that when we looked ahead we realised life as we knew it had really ended.

Laura and I found it hard to talk to each other. There are no adequate words and if there were you wouldn't want to use them. We took refuge in the comfort that family and friends bring, we gave each other succour, yet we remained two people locked in separate rooms of misery and despair. It may be every parent's nightmare to lose a child, but you wake from the nightmare. That's when the worst part begins.

Every morning the pain of loss is there, waiting to flood back in with returning consciousness. I grew to hate that brief dawn of forgetfulness before it did. The visceral ache gets less but never really goes away.

It's not that you have to go on living, it's the fact that you do.

In the early days, at the mercy of strangers, we let ourselves be guided through the world of officialdom like bewildered refugees. It makes a difference, of course, when things go wrong abroad, if you have money. We were shown nothing but kindness by the Florentine authorities, particularly the *Questura*, the Italian state police. This may sound like ingratitude, but I should have been less trusting.

I took a liking to Andrea Morelli, who headed the investigation into Sophie's murder. He had an easy-going charm, seemed steady rather than brilliant, but cut a reassuringly solid figure. His promise to bring 'whoever did this terrible thing' to justice defused for a time my own longing for revenge.

I convinced myself that we were in good hands. There was no reason to think that Inspector Morelli's sympathetic manner, the sensitive way he handled Laura, his understanding of sophisticated lives, made him any *less* competent or determined to find Sophie's killer, but I'm pretty sure now he knew from day one that he'd landed a case he wasn't going to solve.

Our daughter was beaten and strangled to death on a night in April, the twenty-seventh to be exact, when the temperature dipped unexpectedly below zero. She'd been in Florence for six months and had just e-mailed us to say she was loving her second term at the atelier. Another couple of weeks, she'd have been twenty.

We'd arranged for her to lodge at the Villa Nardini, where her room looked out over the formal gardens. In the '*boscos*', an area deliberately left to grow wild, there's a semi-derelict grotto, and it was there that her body was discovered by the family dogs on their morning rounds. Why Sophie, who hated the cold, had gone into the garden late at night remains a mystery.

There was little physical evidence. Nothing to indicate whether she had an assignation, or was followed and forced inside the grotto. No tracks or fingerprints were found, no fibres, no bodily fluids, saliva, skin or hair samples, from which DNA could have been extracted. Forensic tests established that Sophie's murderer didn't assault her sexually (which was some small comfort). She was knocked unconscious, then strangled.

The fact that he was careful, meticulous even, in the execution of a crime that is usually associated with ungovernable passions, Morelli believed suggested that Sophie was murdered by somebody she knew.

However brutal, he insisted, it was not an arbitrary act.

The investigator's office was on the sixth floor of the Questura building on Via Zara. A small cell-like room with a combed ceiling, it barely had space for a desk and two chairs. Under the high window, a cluster of framed diplomas and family photographs, haphazardly arranged, lent the only personal touch.

'I can understand your frustration, Signor Lister,' Morelli said, as he shut the door behind us and gestured for me to sit. 'Believe me, I share it.'

'In other words,' I said flatly, 'you're no further forward.'

14

He smiled. 'We've made some progress since your last visit.' His lightly accented English was close to faultless. 'We've widened local enquiries to a five-kilometre range. We're concentrating now on the immigrant population. It takes time.'

'How many people have you got working on the case?'

Morelli leant back in his chair and crossed his legs. A balding thirty-four-year-old Genoan, short but robustly built, he had a glow of health about him that I'd come to resent. I imagined him working on his golf handicap, or his suspiciously uniform tan, when he should have been finding Sophie's killer.

'It varies, but I can assure you, Signor Lister, this is still an active investigation. We're taking computers at random from internet cafés all over Florence, examining the harddrives. The Computer Crime Squad in Milan is building a profile, which should give us a better idea of who we're looking for.'

None of this was new. 'What evidence is there that Sophie was stalked online?'

'If we had evidence, he'd be in custody by now. But we're almost sure that's how he got into her life. Cyber-stalkers are often isolated, emotionally void individuals. The immigrant fits the profile because he may be experiencing stress or culture shock and suffering a sense of loss of his culture of origin.'

'Andrea, it's been over a year, you don't even have a suspect.'

He reached for the phone on his desk, keyed in a couple of numbers and asked in English for the Sophie Lister file. 'We haven't given up hope.'

I shook my head. It's not what you want to hear from someone in charge of a murder investigation. Not when the victim is your child.

Morelli had found nothing so far to support his theory that Sophie knew her murderer. Her teachers and friends from the atelier, her landlady, the other lodgers at the Villa Nardini, all confirmed what she had already told us – she was too busy with her work to get romantically involved. No one remembered seeing her with a stranger, or noticing any change in her behaviour. There'd been no suspicious types hanging around the villa or the atelier in the Oltrarno.

If Sophie felt threatened, or was aware that she was being stalked, she never spoke of it to anyone. I kept thinking about Bailey's description of the drawings, wondering how long she had lived in fear. Why *didn't* she tell us? Laura had been right to ask. I just wasn't sure I wanted to know the answer.

Sophie was religious about keeping in touch, calling home on her mobile once or twice a week and e-mailing the family (mostly her brother, George, to whom she was particularly close) on a regular basis. She had a laptop with her in Florence, but couldn't hook up to the internet from her lodgings – the Villa Nardini made few concessions to modern times.

Like many students, she used internet cafés to go online, surf the Web and conduct her e-mail correspondence. It was in one of these brightly lit anonymous places, as common in Florence as pizzerias, that the police believed she may have encountered her killer.

'I don't think he met her online,' Morelli said. 'At least not in the conventional way. I think he saw her first in the real world, then maybe afterwards they started talking and formed an online relationship.'

There was no electronic trail. Even with their limited resources to carry out an investigation in cyberspace, the *Questura* had established that much. Sophie didn't frequent chat rooms – or if she did, it wasn't under the screen-name she had registered with MSN. There were no recorded conversations in the archives of the main service providers. I'd also done some research of my own.

'How would he have found her?' I asked.

'Let's say he spots her on the street, in a shop or restaurant – she was, after all, striking – and follows her to an internet café. She sends some e-mails. He waits until she leaves, then slides into her seat and gets her details from the computer terminal she's just been using. Or maybe he shoulder-surfs her as he walks past her screen, and memorises her e-mail address.

'Later he contacts her online, a casual friendship develops, and she responds in the innocent belief that he's far away, in another town, even another country . . . while, all along, he's sitting across the room or at the next terminal, observing her.'

The investigator paused and our eyes met as he smoothed a hand over his polished head. 'He uses the internet to gain personal information about her, then begins a combination of online/real-world stalking. One day he just turns up in her life and identifies himself as the person she talks to online.'

There was a knock at the door and his secretary entered. She handed a file to Morelli, then left again without even a glance in my direction.

He opened the folder and withdrew some photographs. 'Remember these?'

The glossy prints he spread on his desk were of a chalk outline in the paved floor of the grotto chamber. It had been drawn around Sophie before her body was removed from the scene.

I nodded. I had no idea what was coming.

He leaned forward and picked up one of the prints. The diagram, a map of the last place on earth she occupied, still filled me with revulsion and anger. I was never shown photo-graphs of Sophie's body.

'The victim's position is interesting,' he said. 'She didn't fall, she was laid out on her back, her arms folded across her chest. It was done with care by someone who had a desire to show respect.'

I frowned. 'You mean remorse?'

'Signor Lister, what I have to say you may find a little shocking. I mean tenderness . . . *amore*. Her killer was possibly in love with her, or considered himself to be in love. The chief delusion of the cyber-stalker often concerns romantic love and spiritual union rather than sexual attraction.'

'Tenderness,' I repeated calmly, though I was seething. Perhaps any father would have reacted as I did. 'Is that why he knocked her unconscious before he strangled her? Is that how it goes when you love someone, Commendatore? Tenderness!'

I could hear my voice rising.

Morelli pressed his palms together. He took a deep breath and went on, 'With this type of individual, when his attentions are rejected, love turns to violence very quickly. Sometimes in an instant.'

'You expect me to feel sorry for him?'

'He may also have believed that your daughter returned his feelings. In his eyes, you understand, they would have been the "ideal match".'

This was all just guesswork. He really didn't have a clue.

'Studies indicate that violence is more likely where the victim and stalker were formerly in an intimate relationship.'

'What are you saying? That they were lovers?'

'I think that is unlikely.'

I was glad that Laura wasn't with me. She would have hit him.

'I know how hard this must be for you.' He was watching me intently. 'If it had happened to one of my children . . . I would be the same.'

'Are you suggesting that Sophie brought it on herself?'

He shook his head. 'She may unwittingly have encouraged him. Possibly flirted with him online in the belief that it was harmless and safe.'

'Why is it that you people always end up blaming the victim?'

'Signor Lister.' He lifted his hands. 'This has not been an easy case.'

Past tense. They'd already filed her away. He'd as good as admitted it.

There was a short heavy silence.

'Do you think Sophie knew she was in danger?' I asked. I already had the answer, but sometimes those are the best questions to ask.

Morelli made a steeple with his fingers and tapped them against his chin. 'I think . . . yes,' he said gravely, 'she may have known.'

An image floated up of Sophie aged five or six playing for hours with the doll's house that's still in her room at home. I'd intended telling him about the sketchbook, the drawings that seemed to foreshadow her murder, but since I had nothing to show I decided not to mention it.

He rose to his feet, bringing the interview to an end.

We shook hands and Morelli promised to keep me informed of any new developments. It was obvious he didn't expect to be getting in touch soon. The best I could hope for was a cold-case review perhaps years from now. I was being asked to accept that Sophie's killer might never be brought to justice.

I had one more question to put to him.

'Did you ever talk to a friend of Sophie's called Sam Metcalf?'

'Metcalf?' The investigator seemed anxious for me to leave now. He was probably thinking about lunch. 'I don't recognise the name.'

19

'Apparently Sophie used her place sometimes to go online.'

'Leave it with me, I'll look into it.'

'She's flying home to the United States next week. For good. I'm seeing her tomorrow. I could let you know what happens.'

'By all means,' Morelli said, as he walked me to the door. He stopped and put a hand on my shoulder, so that I had to turn to face him. 'This individual, the perpetrator . . . the truth is, Signor Lister, for all we know he could have come from the other side of the world to kill your daughter . . . and then returned there.'

I felt like reminding him of his immigrant theory, but then I thought, what if the sketchbook had in fact been stolen from the atelier? Could one of the drawings have identified her killer?

'Or he could still be here,' I said, 'in Florence.'

3

Laura and I sat sharing a bottle of wine on the terrace of our hotel, a former monastery set among its own olive groves in the Viale dei Colli. A degree or two cooler in the hills, it still felt oppressively hot. We had the garden to ourselves and all you could hear was the soporific murmur of doves and the splashing of a downhill water chain that linked a series of fountains and reflecting pools. It was peaceful at the Villa Arrighetti, almost too peaceful. I would have preferred a hotel in town.

I wanted to feel closer to the crowded streets and piazzas

where I knew Sophie had walked, the places where she'd hung out. I didn't care about Florence's infernal reputation in summer. But Laura insisted on getting away from the locust swarms of tourists, the heat, the traffic, the noise. She was on a different kind of pilgrimage to mine. We all have our own ways of remembering, our own paths of escape.

At around two thirty Laura went inside to lie down. We had arrived late the night before and she had complained of not sleeping well. I ordered an espresso, made some calls, then followed her up to our suite: two high-ceilinged, sparsely furnished rooms that opened onto a pillared loggia. The luxury was there but understated. I looked in the bedroom and saw that Laura was asleep. Helping myself to a cold beer from the fridge, I took my laptop out onto the balcony.

It was now almost ten to three and I felt a coiling sense of anticipation, a not-unpleasant tightness in my stomach. I logged on to the internet and listened to a Mozart piano concerto while I checked my e-mail.

There was nothing from Sam Metcalf. I took that to mean that the meeting was still on for tomorrow. I hadn't intended telling Investigator Morelli about Sam – she'd asked me not to say a word to anyone – but I felt bound to let him know that his department's investigation hadn't been as thorough as he claimed.

I'd encountered the same apathy in London. The way our own police handled things had been depressingly inept. After Sophie was murdered, two Scotland Yard detectives were sent out to Florence to assist the *Questura*. Home again a month later, they described their trip as an agreeable waste of time. I complained and the case was duly referred to the Police Complaints Authority. All I really wanted was to challenge the official view that Sophie's killer was unlikely ever to be caught.

And yet, as time went on, and the weeks and months became a year, I gradually sank into that state of inertia people try to dignify by calling 'acceptance'. I'm not the type to dwell on the past, I believe in getting on with life. But grief has its own trajectory and pulls you along. The pain doesn't fade, it goes somewhere else or lies dormant for a while, and then it comes back when you least expect it.

Laura had found some comfort in her religion after Sophie died. As a non-believer, I didn't have that option. I buried myself in work – sixteen-hour days, endless meetings, constant travel. I didn't want to have a single waking moment when I wasn't fully occupied. I've always been a grafter (Laura claimed she didn't notice the difference), but since the murder I'd lost my enthusiasm for doing deals and making money – money we didn't need. I just kept going and going.

After talking to Bailey and Morelli, I realised that even if I could learn to live with what happened (being in Florence again had awakened some strong emotions), I would never lose the sense that as her father I had failed Sophie, let her down.

At three o'clock exactly I tapped in a password for the instant messaging service I use. 'Adorablejoker' wasn't online. I clicked on her screen-name and typed 'you're late', which a touch of the return key transferred to the dialogue box.

templedog: you're late

There was no response. She must have left for work already.

I sat staring at the screen, resigned to the fact that I'd missed her or that she'd simply forgotten, when suddenly her name showed in bold and the button face beside it lit up with a smile, indicating: 'I am available'.

adorablejoker: no, *you're* late . . . i was on my way out

templedog: I can't stay long

aj: so what else is new?

td: hold on, lighting a cigarette

aj: put it away

td: blowing smoke in your eyes

aj: i swear to cheese . . . get that shit away from me

td: just a couple more drags and I'll put it out

aj: sure you will

td: damn . . . hold on a sec

I could hear laughter. I glanced back through the double doors into the bedroom and saw that Laura was awake. Sitting up in bed, pointing the remote at the TV.

There was little danger of her coming onto the balcony, and if she did I only had to hit the minimise button and the dialogue box would vanish. I had nothing to hide, but I didn't feel at that moment like explaining 'adorablejoker' to my wife.

td: unfortunately I have to go. When will you be on again

aj: i dunno, it may be a while

td: sounds ominous. I enjoy our conversations

aj: you need to break the habit, mister

td: what's that supposed to mean?

aj: i have to go down to DC

td: oh really, what for

aj: visiting a friend. i'll be gone a couple of weeks

I stubbed out my cigarette. Still listening to Mozart, I looked up from the screen, squinting against the harsh sunlight as I let my gaze follow the avenue of cypresses that ran down the hill between the olive groves. I imagined her sitting by the window of her studio apartment in Brooklyn – a world away.

aj: he's just a friend. married, two kids
td: look, it's okay . . . you need to get out more
aj: it's not what you think, you know
td: I don't remember saying what I think. I'll be pretty busy myself
aj: well then . . . i'm gonna let you go
td: have fun in Washington
aj: yeah . . . i gotta run

I started to type something, just to have the last word, but Jelena was gone. The little yellow icon beside her name had faded to grey.

It was nonsense, of course – we'd been chatting online for a few months, all perfectly innocent and above board – but I *had* felt a twinge of resentment, even jealousy, which caught me by surprise. I scrolled back and re-read what she'd said about going to visit her 'friend' in DC. I had no business feeling anything at all.

I waited another few moments in case she changed her mind and decided to come back online. Then I logged off and sat staring out over the top of the balcony at Florence – the same view of rooftops and towers and verdigris cupolas dominated by the pink hump of Brunelleschi's dome that I keep pinned up on the board in my London office and I expect always will. A card from Sophie wishing me a happy birthday, it had arrived a week after I learnt she was dead.

When I heard the news, I was in the middle of the biggest, most important deal of my life – it was a gold-mining venture in Australia I'd been lucky enough to scramble aboard. We had just finished signing the papers and were at the shaking-hands stage when I was called to the phone. In a jubilant mood, I barely caught the murmured phrase 'on the line from Florence . . .' yet I knew instantly, in the pit of my stomach, I knew something had happened to Sophie.

You don't really formulate your worst fears until the words are spoken. I remember oddly the smell of the perfume Joy, which Laura uses, clinging to the receiver. It was reassuringly familiar . . . for a split second I thought, no, all's well. Then I heard the confirmation that turned my moment of triumph and every moment of triumph, or failure for that matter, to ashes, to nothing. Forever.

I stood up and walked to the edge of the balcony and looked down into the hotel grounds, trying to ignore a feeling of restlessness, almost apprehension. It may have been thinking about Sophie that brought it on, or wondering if I'd ever hear from 'adorablejoker' again, or the more immediate worry that tomorrow's meeting with Sam Metcalf would turn out to be another dead end: I wasn't sure of the reason. Then I realised that I was being observed.

Our loggia couldn't be seen from the garden, but at the end of the cypress avenue, the other side of some old iron gates that give onto the Viale Galileo Galilei, I could just make out a figure standing motionless and gazing up towards the villa.

I swung around, almost knocking over my beer – Laura had just wandered out onto the balcony. I said something to her, and she smiled. When I looked back down the hill again the figure was gone.

4

At the turn of the stairs, Sam Metcalf paused, leaning out from the rail and looking up through the balusters to check the landing above, before she climbed the last flight. It was a precaution she always took, ever since coming home from a party late one night to find a stranger waiting for her there. She counted herself lucky he'd only wanted money. Sam felt in her jeans pockets for her key.

Outside her apartment, she pushed the door all the way open so that she could see there was nobody lurking in the hall or the kitchen. Then, still wary, stood and listened for any unfamiliar sounds, straining to hear over the music.

The Iranians in the apartment below were playing Sheryl Crow's 'All I Wanna Do' at full volume. At least she knew she wasn't alone in the building.

It was broad freaking daylight . . . what could possibly happen?

She had to psych herself up before she could walk into the apartment, dump her stuff, then, armed with a small knife taken from the magnetic rack in the kitchen, look through all the rooms. They were exactly how she'd left them.

A storm of honking rose from the street under her windows. She came back into the hall and kicked the front door shut. Leant her back against it, eyes closed.

She let the music soothe her, waiting for that line she liked about the sun coming up on Santa Monica Boulevard, when Sheryl's 1990s hymn to laidback LA suddenly cut out. In the silence it left she could hear a car's engine idling.

A moment later, the Iranian couple's door slammed and there was a clatter of heels on the stone stairs. From the street a hoarse male voice bellowed '*Vaffanculo!*'

Then, as the car moved off, the telephone rang.

In the kitchen, Sam glanced at the Leonardo clock above the stove and went on fixing herself a cup of coffee, trying not to think about where she should have been thirty minutes ago. She wasn't picking up, not for anyone.

Clearing a space for her laptop, she sat down at the table and waited for the phone to stop ringing. She knew she should have called Sophie's father, told him she couldn't make the meeting, made up some excuse. The last shrill note resonated through the empty apartment. She took a sip of coffee and scalded her lips.

Shit . . . Her hands wouldn't stop trembling.

'Nobody knows about . . . any of this. Let's keep it that way.'

The voice had been seductive, fresh and faintly husky, like a young Bill Clinton's. It was the insinuating Midwestern lilt, the question mark at the end of a sentence where none was needed that had creeped her out, leaving her in no doubt as to what would happen if she talked.

Last night, at her friend Jimmy's house in Fiesole, she had been too afraid to confide in him. He'd have insisted on her going to the *Questura*. But what could she have told the police? That she'd received a vaguely threatening phone-call from an unknown person she thought might be a murderer? Sam had lived in Italy long enough to know the police wouldn't offer her protection. They'd probably just withdraw her *permesso*, stop her leaving the country.

She'd lain awake until four a.m. trying to decide whether or not to keep the appointment at the Trinità bridge. She hated the idea of letting Sophie's family down – felt doubly guilty because she should've told them what she knew a long time ago – but she couldn't take the risk now.

She wasn't prepared to die for people she'd never met.

It wasn't as if she'd been all that friendly with Sophie. The girl had come up to her after a British Council lecture, claiming to be interested in early Renaissance ceramics. Sam, whose field it was, had taken her under her wing. A sweet kid, beautiful, talented, innocent, and yet – Sophie Lister had turned out, disappointingly, to be keener on using her place for going online in private than learning the secrets of the Della Robbia workshop. They barely talked.

Sam switched on her Toshiba. She used to think about the dead girl's fingers having touched the keys, afraid her bad karma would rub off on her, as if it were something you could catch like a virus; but she was over that now.

It was the website she'd come across last week while weeding her Favourites List – a website that could only have been left there by Sophie – which, she believed, had contaminated the machine.

Sam went in the bedroom to pack.

She was booked on a train to Venice, leaving Santa Maria Novella at five forty – less than two hours from now. Having failed to get a flight out that afternoon, she'd cancelled her airline ticket to Boston and used the fifty per cent refund to buy a rail pass across Europe. She hadn't told anyone, not even Jimmy, she'd changed her plans. It was safer that way.

She wasn't sorry to be quitting Florence. She'd fallen in love with the city aged nineteen on a Study Abroad programme and ended up calling it home for nearly a decade. But she saw herself now turning into what she despised, a perpetual student, staying on year after year, completing one course in fine arts, and then another, kidding herself that it wasn't only about Federico.

At twenty-eight, still attractive with her vellum-white skin, sheaf of dark curly hair and blue eyes – she called it her Jewish colleen look – Sam had days when she worried that he had stolen her best years. She'd known too many lonely, washed-up, middle-aged American women, who'd come for the art and the sex and had to settle for working in bookshops or as tour guides or teaching English at one of Florence's billion or so language schools. Even if her life hadn't been in danger, she felt she was getting out just in time.

Sam frowned and listened.

The faint ticking came from her travel clock on the bedside table. She folded it into its green lizard-skin case and dropped it in her overnight bag, then sat down on the bed with a sigh. She knew she should strip the mildly disgraceful sheets, she just didn't have the energy. A rumpled fold of cream silk caught her eye. From under the pillows, she pulled out a nightshirt that she hadn't worn for the past couple of weeks. In hot weather she always slept naked.

Wait a minute. The act of slipping a hand between mattress and pillows had triggered a memory of her and Federico. Jesus . . . wait just a goddamn minute.

She pulled back the pillows, then jumping to her feet tore the sheets from the bed. She moved the bed out from the wall and yanked the mattress to the floor. It was gone, no mistake, she'd have remembered packing it – her vibe wasn't there.

She thought hard, trying to recall the last time, searching for an innocent explanation. Unless Federico . . . but the sonofabitch had given her back his key weeks ago, the same day he dumped her and, with a predictability that made her ashamed for him, returned to his Florentine wife and children.

Her stomach heaved. She ran to the bathroom and stood over the basin until the nausea passed. Catching sight of

29

her reflection in the mirror, Sam saw that her eyes were almost black. Fear had dilated her pupils till only a thin corona of blue was left. She needed to take something . . . she knew she still had some Valium somewhere. Her white face moved sideways as she slid open the door to the medicine cabinet.

Behind it, on the glass shelf, lay her 'silver bullet'.

'Oh God, no,' Sam breathed, as she took down the vibrator and with trembling fingers slowly revolved its chrome shaft. Then almost dropped it. Fixed to the base was a little red heart-shaped appliqué sticker she had never seen before.

She walked back in the kitchen and picked up her cell phone. Her hands were shaking so hard she had to key four or five times before she got the number right.

Ward must have come for her last night, and left a keepsake.

5

'There's something I haven't told you,' I said.

Her lips pursed as for a kiss, Laura leaned forward to blow on a forkful of risotto that was too hot to put in her mouth.

'I was supposed to meet someone earlier, a friend of Sophie's called Sam Metcalf.' I hesitated. 'I kept the appointment, only she didn't show up.'

Laura lowered her fork.

'I think she stayed away because she's afraid.'

'Does it make you feel better, Ed? Is that why you keep doing this to me?'

Her voice grew loud suddenly, as if she'd forgotten we were in a restaurant. The terrace of the Villa Arrighetti was busier than yesterday, the other tables mostly occupied by elderly couples who talked in hushed tones.

'A week ago,' I went on, ignoring some curious looks we were getting, 'I received an e-mail from this girl. It said she'd found some stuff on her laptop left there by Sophie that she thought might be of interest. Apparently Soph used her computer sometimes to go online.'

'Why did she contact you?' Laura was instantly sceptical. 'Why not the police?'

'She was in Boston at the time of the murder. She knew nothing about it until she got back to Florence a month later. I'm not sure that she *didn't* go to the police.'

'Did you talk to Morelli about her?'

'I brought up her name, he didn't react. Sam asked me not to tell anyone.'

'You don't think that's a little odd?' Laura frowned, then added, 'And why wait so long to get in touch?'

'Look, all I know is what she said in her e-mails . . . we've never spoken.'

She blew on her food again, swallowed a mouthful of rice. 'You know . . . this is really delicious.'

'Can we stay on the subject? It's important.'

'So bloody important you felt no need to tell me about it until now.'

'I didn't tell you because I didn't want to get . . . your hopes up.'

I had been planning to tell her, but only after I'd met the girl and decided whether the information she had was significant. Same as with the sketchbook, I wanted to avoid upsetting my wife over nothing

31

'My hopes?' Laura smiled and shook her head.

'Anyway, I did speak to you about her,' I said quietly; the last thing I wanted was an argument. 'I asked you if you'd ever heard Sophie mention anyone called Sam.'

'Maybe you thought you did.'

'I want justice for her, Laura. Is anything wrong with that?' She didn't answer, her pale unsparing eyes resting calmly on mine. 'Well . . . *is* there?'

It wasn't that Laura had no interest in seeing Sophie's killer caught. She just didn't want things to drag on indefinitely. As I said before, we deal with loss in our own ways. She was seeking a different kind of peace.

She kept staring at me as she took a sip of wine. 'Try not to be late this evening. You *are* going to be there, aren't you?'

'What do you think? Of course, I'll be there.' I wasn't looking forward to the requiem mass she'd arranged to have said for Sophie (who never set foot in a church, if she could help it) at San Miniato, but I knew Laura needed my support.

Our main courses arrived just then. She'd ordered *carpaccio*, I'd chosen the roast lamb with rosemary. We ate in silence, enjoying the food. It's an odd uncomfortable truth, but loss doesn't dull the appetite.

Laura had changed for lunch into a light summer dress and done something different with her hair, which is sandy blonde and very fine. When we first met she used to favour the Alice band and striped shirt with the collar turned up look – she's come a long way since then. I told her how good she looked.

'Were you thinking of taking a siesta?' I asked, when we'd left our table and were walking slowly back across the terrace.

She sighed. 'I might lie down for a while.'

At the foot of the stone staircase that leads up to the villa's *piano nobile*, Laura turned to me and said in a low, feeling voice: 'Let it go, Eddie. Leave the past alone. Nothing you or anyone can do is going to bring her back.'

A friend offering sensible advice.

The moment we got inside the door of our suite, I locked it. Laura stood waiting by the window, against the light. She didn't move away when I came up behind her. I took the initiative, but I've no doubt it was what she wanted to happen.

There was urgency, then the shared pleasure of release. Perhaps I felt sorry for her, or for both of us, perhaps she took pity on me, but we came out of our separate fortresses and for a while forgot. Laura and I hadn't made love to each other for months. I find it difficult to write about this.

I don't want to keep saying that I loved my wife . . . I did, but even before Sophie was murdered things had not been brilliant between us. During the first days and weeks after it happened, I depended on Laura to get through. We clung to each other, literally clung to each other, but when that no longer brought comfort, when the drug stopped working, we retreated into ourselves, and grew further apart.

We didn't talk, not about what we'd just done.

Laura got up from the bed and went into the bathroom. Naked she looked vulnerable and somehow very English. She had a nearly perfect figure, yet she moved awkwardly without clothes on. I told her I had some work to do. She turned and smiled at me from the bathroom door, her lavender-blue eyes unnaturally bright, and I felt a stab of unspecific guilt.

There was love still, on both sides, only it was dying a little every day.

⋆   ⋆   ⋆

33

After taking a shower, I went out onto the loggia with my mobile and laptop and checked to see if Sam had left word. There was nothing.

The next half-hour or so was taken up with business. I dealt with my e-mails, then spoke to the London office on the phone. The company I own, Beauly-Lister, pioneers developable 'land with a view' in the world's most desirable, which usually means unspoiled, locations. Our sector rivals worry about return on cost of capital, land prices and margin growth. We start from the premise that a magical view is like a great work of art, almost but not quite beyond price.

I let Audrey, my assistant, know what time our flight got into Heathrow tomorrow morning so that the car could be there to meet the plane.

While we were still talking, I received an incoming-mail alert from Sam Metcalf, and hurried Audrey off the phone.

What Sam had to say was disappointingly brief.

Look, I made a mistake . . . there's really nothing to discuss. Please don't get in touch with me again. I'm sorry, Sam.

The e-mail came with an attachment which I opened at once. It turned out to be another couple of lines of text. I wondered why Sam hadn't simply added them to her original message. It was as if she'd had a change of heart.

You can try this, she had written, I came across it while weeding my Favourites list. Like I said, I think your daughter left it on my comp.

There followed, on a line by itself, the address of a website:

34

The graphics took a long time to download. I hadn't any idea what to expect. I was nervous that something might be revealed about Sophie that I didn't want to know. I felt a wave of sadness at the thought of her having had secrets.

There was no home page as such, no titles welcoming you to the site, no tags or text of any kind, only a counter in the bottom left-hand corner. It clocked me as the 572nd visitor. The domain name, *homebeforedark*, suggested something vaguely apocalyptic, perhaps to do with religion or New Age music. I was way off.

As the central image formed, mystified at first by the back-drop of trees, lawn and picket fence, I felt a growing excitement: for what was slowly taking shape in front of my eyes was a building, a white American Colonial house in a suburban setting.

I almost called out to Laura to come and look.

I wanted to know if she'd 'get it' too, make the same connec-tion I'd instantly made with the 'clapboard doll's house' that Bailey Grant had described so vividly from his memory of Sophie's sketchbook.

It wasn't hard to see in the stylised design of the pillared mansion on my screen where Sophie might have found her inspiration. The graphics had that hyper-real, 3-D-ish look of a virtual building which, like any doll's house, can be entered and explored room by room.

This couldn't be coincidence. I looked back into our bedroom and saw that Laura was napping. I didn't feel like disturbing her.

There were no instructions on how to navigate the site. Access was certain to be protected, but that didn't mean it wasn't worth eliminating the obvious. Moving my cursor to the gate in the picket fence, I double-clicked on the latch –

with no result. I tried the US-style mailbox; the flag was in the up position, which looked promising, but again nothing happened. I followed the path up to the dark-green front door and clicked on the brass knocker.

A standard pop-up box appeared at the bottom of my screen asking for username and password. I entered a couple of random combinations, then gave up. I could have used George's help – my fifteen-year-old son was into 'gaming' and nimble at reading visual clues. Laura had wanted to take him out of school and bring him with us to Florence, but for a number of reasons I'd vetoed the idea.

I dialled Bailey's number at the atelier. A girl, who wasn't India, answered and said she would see if he could be disturbed. Then put me on hold, activating a loop of the Eagles' 'Hotel California'.

While I was waiting, I moved the cursor slowly across the façade of the house. The windows were all shuttered, giving the place a deserted, rather forbidding aspect. I clicked on each of them in turn until suddenly the shutters of an attic dormer swung back, revealing a half-open sash window. I let out a whoop, thinking I'd found a way in, but the window wouldn't budge. Behind it was only blackness.

'So this is what you call work. I've often wondered.'

Laura, a towel wrapped around her, was standing by my side looking over my shoulder at the screen. Absorbed in my task, I hadn't heard her come up behind me.

'You recognise it?'

Just then the Eagles cut out and I held up a hand.

'Mr Lister, I've got good news . . .'

I didn't let Bailey finish. 'And I have a question. The clapboard house in Sophie's drawings . . . front door, left lower panel, is that a cat-flap?'

There was silence from the other end.

'How could you possibly know?'

I looked up at Laura. I wanted to hug her.

'Bailey, say Sophie's killer knew about the drawings – was there anything inside the house he might have seen as a threat to himself?'

'You'll have to judge for yourself. We found the sketch-book.'

I turned to Laura. 'Did you hear what he just said?'

She nodded coolly, her gaze held by the screen. I was still taking in the significance of all this when I felt her touch my arm.

'If you like,' Bailey was saying, 'I can bring it along this evening.'

'Isn't that someone trying to reach you?' Laura asked, pointing to a blue flashing message icon on the taskbar of my laptop.

'Here, you talk to him,' I said and handed her my mobile. 'This could be the girl . . . Sophie's friend.'

I knew it wasn't Sam Metcalf, but the blue light kept flashing and I had to divert my wife's attention.

6

Two rings, then it stopped.

When it rang again, she snatched up the receiver.

'It's me, Jimmy.'

'Wait.' Sam went over to the window and looked down into Borgo Stella. He was on the stoop immediately below, talking into his cell; she could see the top of his head, Raybans set jauntily among blond curls, and the shirt he had on earlier with the wide magenta stripes. He stepped back off the sidewalk and, holding out his arms, called up to her, '*E Samantha, ti amo.*' Jimmy always had to act the fool. '*Amore e 'l cor gentil sono una cosa . . .*'

She leant out to check both ends of the street.

A girl in jeans walked past carrying a single sunflower over her shoulder like a fishing pole, the base of the stem wrapped in silver foil. She could hear Puccini's 'Nessun Dorma' coming from an open window somewhere, the big notes struggling to soar above the traffic. Nothing else stood out. The reassuringly familiar smell of resin wafted from the furniture restorer's workshop two doors down.

'Okay,' she said and hung up.

She went back out to the hall and buzzed Jimmy in. Her building didn't have CCTV or an intercom, which was why she'd insisted he call first. She wouldn't unlock the door until she heard his voice outside, and could check through the fish-eye that he was alone.

'You look a little rough,' he said right off the bat.

'Thanks.' She'd done her best, rinsed the red from her eyes, pinned back her hair, even put on make-up, but Jimmy knew her.

He swept past her into the hall. She bolted the front door behind him, then turned and saw him standing there, waiting for her. She stumbled into his arms. 'God'm I glad to see you, you have no idea.'

'Hey, hey, hey. Take it easy.'

She was shaking.

'You're later than you said. We need to get going.'

'Get going? Where?' He blinked at her. 'You mind telling me what this is about? Has that scumbag been messing with you again?'

Jimmy was never a big fan of Federico.

She pulled away from him, shaking her head. All she'd said on the phone was that she was in trouble, she needed his help. It was Jimmy all over that he hadn't hesitated, and that it took him damn near an hour to get here.

'There's been a change of plan. I'm leaving today, I'm booked on a five-forty train to Venice.'

'Whoa, girl, what about tonight . . . the party? You cannot *not* be there.'

'Just tell people . . . I dunno, tell 'em I got news from home. I had to get back for a family funeral. You'll think of something.'

'Come on, Metcalf, you can do better than that. This is me, Jimmy. What the fuck's going on?'

Sam smiled and touched a hand to his face. She felt uneasy about involving him.

She'd known Jimmy Macchado since they were at college together. After graduating from South Bend, Indiana, they'd lost contact for a while; then bumped into each other again by chance in Florence – he'd just arrived to start a job at the New York Film Academy on Via dei Pucci, teaching cinematography – and renewed their old friendship. A year ago he'd moved out to Fiesole, but they stayed close, getting together or talking on the phone most days.

Jimmy was the one person in Florence she could trust.

'Look, I need you to take me to Santa Maria Novella. All you have to do is make sure I get on the train.'

'You're crazy. I'm not moving until you level with me.'

She chewed her lip, debating.

She turned and went in the living room, navigating a path through the packing cases to the couch. He followed and helped her clear a space so they could sit down together. She took his hands, searching his eyes.

'You can't talk to anyone about this . . . I mean it, Jimmy.'

He drew a finger and thumb across his lips. 'Zipped.'

'Remember Sophie, the English kid who was murdered?'

'How could I possibly forget?'

'I got a call yesterday from the man who killed her.' Sam waited for a reaction, but Jimmy just looked at her. 'He warned me not to stir up the past.'

'What? Wait a minute, back up the truck. You *know* her killer?'

'Only by sight. But he knows who I am.'

'So that's why you came over last night. Why didn't you say something?'

'Because I was too goddamned scared . . . Jimmy, I think he's been here in this apartment.' Her voice cracked a little.

'Okay, calm down, just tell me what happened. When did you see him?'

'About ten days before Sophie was killed. It was late evening, I went to draw the curtains and noticed a man standing across the street. Youngish, early thirties I guess, average height, okay-looking – I didn't pay much attention. Just assumed he was

40

waiting for someone. But then he looked up and our eyes met. Something about his expression made me step back.

'Don't laugh, but I thought *I* had an admirer. It never occurred to me that he might be waiting for Sophie. I didn't think anything more about it until I got back to Florence and heard what had happened.'

'Did you report this to the *Questura*?'

She shook her head. 'I started to make the call, I felt guilty enough, but then I figured if the man I saw was responsible for Sophie's death, he knew where I lived, what I looked like. How could the cops stop him coming after me?'

'But he didn't, did he?' Jimmy said. 'You never saw or heard from him again – until yesterday, right? So why does he wait a year to threaten you? Why now?'

'How would I know? I should have got the hell out of Florence then. If it hadn't been for work, I would have done.'

'You stayed because of Federico, don't kid yourself. Did you tell *him* about the call? Did you tell anyone else?'

Tears filled her eyes. 'No, no I didn't.'

Earlier, when she realised she needed help, he'd been the first person she wanted to call. In a weak moment she'd even started to dial his number. What stopped her was knowing that she would go to pieces if Federico refused.

'Samantha, honey,' Jimmy said softly. 'What's going on? Talk to me.'

She was wondering whether she should ask him to deliver her laptop to Ed Lister's hotel. The Toshiba didn't have a case and she'd wrapped it in clear bubble wrap and buried it in her L.L. Bean book bag – it was out there in the hall with her backpack and suitcase. Sam hesitated.

'I can't . . . Jimmy, believe me, you don't want to get mixed up in this. It's too dangerous. We have to go now or I'll miss my train.'

She could guess the reason Ward had come back. He

must've found out somehow about the files on her laptop – files Sophie had left behind that possibly could identify him, and which he would do anything to recover.

7

The white clapboard house vanished from the screen, leaving behind the text of Sam Metcalf's abrupt e-mail asking me not to contact her again. I replied anyway, thanking her for the information and enquiring about the username and pass-word to the *homebeforedark* website. No reference to her change of heart, no pleas to reconsider her decision – I kept it short and to the point. I thought that was my best chance of preserving the fragile link between us.

The messenger light had stopped flashing. I'm not sure if Laura had noticed my reluctance to respond, or even realised that I hadn't. She was basically allergic to computers. Smiling at something Bailey was saying to her on the phone, she seemed to have lost interest. I felt relieved when she turned away, my mobile to her ear, and wandered back through the French doors into the bedroom.

I pulled up my contact list and saw that 'adorablejoker', the girl from Brooklyn I knew only as Jelena (she saw no need to tell me her full name) had left a brief message, but was 'currently offline' – or using the invisible mode. I thought for a moment then started to type. She didn't let me finish.

adorablejoker: can't talk . . . running out the door.
templedog: didn't you just message me?

42

aj: i got like 45 minutes to get to Penn station

td: what did you want to say?

aj: it's not important . . . all right, last night, i dreamt you were in some kind of trouble, something to do with Florence, with your daughter . . . is everything ok?

That gave me a jolt.

I hadn't mentioned to Jelena that I was in Italy, or said anything about following up leads on Sophie's murder. Her intuition at times registered borderline ESP. She claimed it was her island blood; her maternal grandmother came from Martinique.

td: everything's fine

aj: you're not at home are you?

td: in Florence . . . with my wife. We fly back tomorrow

aj: it's true then

She knew about our loss. She rarely brought up the subject, but whenever I did she'd listen quietly. Her sympathy came across always as warm and genuine, not overdone. Ironically it was because of Sophie that our paths had intersected in cyberspace. After she was murdered, I'd wasted soul-destroying hours wandering through chat rooms, hoping to pick up a trail that would lead to her killer. In one of the rooms – I don't remember its name – I bumped into Jelena.

The very first online conversation we'd had, six months ago, I warned her that I was grieving for a child who'd been murdered; but I didn't dwell on it and I avoided going into too much detail. I'd said nothing to her, for instance, about the possibility that Sophie met her killer on the internet.

I didn't want to scare her away.

td: we're over here collecting some of Sophie's things. We had to come back . . . There's a mass being said for her this evening.

43

aj: i understand. i wish i could say a prayer for her

td: you don't need a dispensation

aj: but it's inappropriate . . . Ed, something feels wrong . . . be careful

td: you worry too much. I'm not in any kind of trouble

aj: what's your sign again?

td: very funny . . . don't you have a train to catch?

aj: yeah and i'm desperate to get out of here. you keep talking to me

td: no, other way round

aj: stop fucking lying

After Jelena – or 'Jelly' as she preferred – went offline, I sat for a moment staring at the picture of her I'd pulled up onto my screen. It was a head and shoulders shot – the only likeness she'd sent me of herself – and showed a skinny, brown-skinned mop-headed girl in an olive-drab T-shirt with a faded hand-printed logo of The Clash across the front. I hadn't told her that I'd worked with the band in the early 80s when I was living in New York and involved in the music business. I didn't want to seem as if I was trying to impress her. Besides, it dated me.

She looks absurdly young, absurdly pretty. Head to one side, chin down, she's gazing straight at camera with canted almond eyes (she also claimed Indonesian and Dutch ancestry) that sparkle with mischief and a 'show-me' attitude; she has a full curved red mouth you can see wouldn't stay still or suffer fools for long. From one low-resolution digital image I couldn't tell if she was strictly beautiful (she insisted she had the features of an ant), but it was a face you had to look at, and that I couldn't look at without wanting to smile.

'Eddie!' Laura was calling to me from the bedroom. 'We're going to be late.'

I closed the file, then shut down my laptop.

Sooner or later, a girl as bright and attractive as Jelena was bound to meet somebody (I half-suspected she already had)

44

and that would be the end of our unorthodox but harmless friendship. She was twenty-five years old, I was forty-six, a family man – and the differences only began there.

There was nothing shady going on between us. In the real world, I'd have put money on a middle-aged businessman enjoying private conversations with a woman young enough to be his daughter being up to no good. Maybe I had a blind spot where Jelly was concerned. But, as far as I was concerned, she was just a charming cipher, a ghost at the other end of a computer terminal.

In her company I escaped reality for a while. It was that simple.

8

Without Jimmy's help, Sam would never have made it.

Arriving at the station just after five thirty, he carried her bags for her as they fought their way across Santa Maria Novella's triumphal concourse – she hadn't bargained on a local soccer game swelling the rush-hour crowds with over-excited fans – and out onto the track for the Venice Express.

Jimmy, pouring sweat, tickets between his teeth, helped her board the train and find her reserved window-seat with only minutes to spare.

'Trust you to pick the observation car,' he gasped.

She looked out the small grimy windows and pulled a face. An old woman in widow's black nodded politely from the seat opposite. Sam smiled at her and sank down onto the banquette with a sigh.

She felt giddy with relief. She glanced up at Jimmy who was trying to find room for her suitcase on the rack, when the train suddenly jolted forward.

'Forget about that. Go, or we'll both end up in Venice.' It had crossed her mind to ask him to keep her company. 'I'll come to the door. I got something for you . . .' She shooed him away.

The moment his back was turned Sam unzipped her suitcase. The silk robe lay on the top. She'd bought it for Federico – that didn't matter now. She wanted Jimmy to have the robe, but there was no way she could give it him wrapped only in tissue paper. She'd thrown away the elegant box it came in to make more room in her case.

Sam hesitated, then emptied the contents of her L.L. Bean book bag onto the table. She transferred her laptop to the suitcase, covered it with clothes and zipped the lid.

Asking the old lady to keep an eye on her stuff, she ran down the aisle with the distinctive white and black book bag.

'Oh my God,' Jimmy went, as she handed it over, 'just what I've always wanted . . . what is it?'

Sam laughed and leaned down from the carriage steps to kiss him on the mouth. 'I owe you, *you*, big time.'

She could see the guard walking up the track slamming doors. There was nobody else on the platform. Jimmy took a peek inside the canvas bag and whistled. 'This must have cost a small fortune . . .'

She heard the clatter of heels. A woman ran past.

'If it's the wrong size, you don't like the colour, whatever . . . you can always change it . . . you know the store on Via Tornabuoni.'

'What about this?' He held up the bag. 'I'll mail it to you.'

The door slammed shut. As the train began to shunt

46

forward, Jimmy walked along beside her carriage. She caught the chirruping first bars to 'O Sole Mio' and smiled as she saw him reach for his cell phone and consult the display. Sam felt another twinge of guilt at the thought that she might have exposed her friend to danger, but as far as she could tell they weren't followed. She was going to miss him.

She mouthed through the window, 'Look after yourself.'

Then Jimmy stepped back, gave a little wave and slid from view.

9

After dark the main gates of the Villa Nardini are closed and the family use a less conspicuous entrance in the ivy-covered perimeter wall on Via Rucellai. I got there at seven. The Nardinis were away, but I had their permission to go anywhere I liked in the house and grounds. Coming home from a party, Sophie had let herself in this same door the night she was killed.

I'd run the sequence countless times in my head. Her murderer sees his chance and steps out swiftly from the shadows – I noticed a magnolia tree across the street that shaded the pavement. There were plenty of places he could have hidden.

But was that really how it happened? Wouldn't she have screamed, struggled, tried to run for it? Morelli believed she let 'the perpetrator' into the grounds because she knew him. Via Rucellai is a quiet, well-lit residential street with a boutique hotel on the corner and a retirement home for nuns over-looking the villa's garden.

No one saw or heard anything.

My hand had hardly touched the bell when the nail-studded oak door swung inwards. Rutillio, the old *portiere*, stood framed in the doorway; his long secretive face, caught by the light in half profile, might have been a detail from a Renaissance painting. A gentle soul, who'd been kind to Sophie – I'd spotted him at the requiem mass earlier – Rutillio had broken down when giving evidence at the inquest. He greeted me with a sombre, '*Buona sera*, Signor Lister.'

I was glad I didn't have enough Italian to make conver-sation as I followed him across a cobbled forecourt, lit by a string of lanterns, and out onto the terrace. The formal garden lay ahead, stretching away into a reservoir of private darkness.

It was a warm, starless evening. Rutillio handed me a torch and, thanking him, I took the way he indicated around a huge chalice-shaped fountain and down some steps into the parterre. I'd no interest in the house.

When we came before, I'd helped Laura pack up our daughter's room and I didn't need to see it again. Sophie was always telling us she would have preferred to live some-where less grand, so she could experience the 'real' Florence. Sometimes I wonder, if we'd let her find her own level, whether she would still be alive today. We weren't over-protective parents, but her mother . . . no, we *both* felt that she'd be safe here in this haven of privilege and tranquillity.

On that visit Laura told me about a dream she'd had of wandering through the villa's reception rooms (all herringbone parquet floors and gilt chairs lined up along the walls) throwing open one set of double doors after another, calling Sophie's name, searching for her. She insists now she had this dream

48

weeks before the murder. I'm not sure if her memory can be relied on. She certainly never spoke to me about a premonition . . . but then I didn't always confide in her either.

She knew I was coming here tonight. I would have liked Laura at my side, but wild horses couldn't have dragged her back to the place where our angel was taken from us. The kill site, the police called it.

A procession of classical statues, time-worn allegorical figures on marble pedestals, loomed up in the light of my torch then fell back into darkness as I walked down the central avenue, the gravel crunching under my shoes. It's not known if Sophie came this way that night. The labyrinth of paths, laurel hedges, and medulla-shaped borders didn't yield a single clue as to which route she took, or how her killer entered and left the grounds.

The last time I was here the police refused to let me enter the grotto, the scene of the crime, because it was still being examined by Forensics. I'd just come come from identifying Sophie's body at the mortuary and I remember standing in front of the *limonaia*, the colonnaded shelter where lemon trees are kept in winter, and staring into that dank cordoned-off opening, the white-suited figures creeping about inside like maggots, and being overwhelmed by a sense of utter devastation, unable to comprehend *why* this had happened.

I hadn't returned to lay Sophie's ghost, or to try to come to terms with her loss (I knew I wasn't going to find peace or 'closure', a word so false it makes me angry every time I hear it), but the image of the grotto had become embedded in my consciousness. It was like a black hole, a decaying star at the centre of my existence into which I sometimes felt everything was disappearing.

I needed to bear witness in some way to the absolute wrong

that was perpetrated here on my own flesh and blood . . . I saw this as something left undone.

Yes, I took it personally.

Outside the *limonaia*, I stopped and looked back, raking the beam across the shadowy rooms of the garden. It had been laid out long before the villa itself was built, to conform with some now-forgotten symbology – its hidden meaning, Sophie told me once, supposedly to do with 'a secret trail leading from the darkness of ignorance to the light of wisdom'. I wasn't into Renaissance gardens or the occult, but the murderer could have been.

Taking the path I remembered leading into the *boscos*, the unkempt corner at the far end of the garden, I soon came on the mound of the grotto. It had been formed originally to look like a natural cave with rusticated boulders piled around the opening. A couple of straggly cypresses stood sentry outside.

I lit a cigarette to steady my nerves. Now that I was here, I felt a reluctance – repulsion is closer – to enter the place. I had to force myself over the threshold of what I saw desolately as the mouth of hell. I felt afraid for *her*.

The torch cast my shadow ahead of me, picking up the carved stone benches either side of a pedimented doorway. Beyond lay the circular chamber with domed ceiling and flagstone floor where Sophie had been discovered by the Nardinis' dogs, a yapping posse of Jack Russell terriers.

Just inside and to the left of the doorway the chalk outline tracing her body was still clearly visible. Somebody had neglected to wash it away. I could understand why not many would want to come down here after what happened. But I wasn't prepared for that vivid diagram, for the stillness, for the scene to be so . . . fresh.

She looked as if she was sleeping.

50

The walls of the grotto were smooth and plain apart from a stone rosette at the apex of the dome. An iron grille incorporated into its design covered an air shaft that I imagined would also admit a little light by day.

Advancing to the centre, I sank down onto my haunches, then slowly revolved the beam of the torch through 360 degrees, exploring the floor and sides of the chamber; there was nothing, not even a dead leaf or a cobweb. It was as if the place had been swept clean, leaving only the chalk diagram.

I lay the torch on the ground pointing in its direction.

At the requiem, Bailey had told the mythical story of the first drawing, about a young girl who sees her lover, a soldier, asleep by the fire and longs to preserve his beauty. Taking a charred stick from the embers, she traces his shadow thrown onto the wall of the cave by the firelight and so makes permanent his presence in the world.

'A simple act of love,' Bailey had said, 'but in her instinctive urge to make a mark, to record and so stay the fleeing moment lies an antidote to the human condition.'

I knelt forward and put my hand inside the chalk outline. I felt the stone flags . . . they would have been colder on the night. One theory, supported by the bruising, was that the killer struck her from behind somewhere in the garden, then carried her in here and strangled her. He would have had to have been strong.

In his valediction, Bailey pointed out that we should be grateful for the life of a young artist who 'drew like an angel' and left something of herself behind in her work. I disagreed, but liked him for saying it. After mass we stood on the steps of San Miniato looking out over Florence. Laura was crying, just barely holding it together, and I had my arm around her. Bailey came up to us and I was afraid he would want to talk, but he simply handed over Sophie's sketchbook and left.

I didn't have time to do more than leaf through the drawings on our way back to the hotel. Even a quick glance confirmed what I already suspected: that they were inspired by the white house in the website Sam Metcalf had found on her computer. A page had been cut out from near the front of the sketchbook. Bailey couldn't say whether this was recent, but he assured me that no drawings were missing.

I switched off the torch.

In the pitch dark, the rise and fall of my breathing, magnified by the sepulchral acoustics, reminded me of a sleeping animal, or something heavy being dragged in effortful stages across the floor. The crypt had an earthy, not unpleasant smell.

The truth is I could never face up to the reality of Sophie's murder – it was partly why I had to come here. I wanted to replay the sights and sounds of what was done to my child in this dismal spot. I wanted to confront the demon. I tried to imagine her state of mind . . . there was a shield in the way. Oh Jesus fucking Christ, you have to *know* how scared she must have been.

I began to shiver although it wasn't cold.

I remembered the last time I saw Sophie, we were standing on Via del Moro outside the restaurant where Laura and I dined last night. We'd had an argument, nothing major, and she seemed a little down. I almost asked her if everything was all right, but Sophie brightened and the moment went past. This was only a week before it happened, when it seems certain she was already being stalked.

Why didn't she say anything to me? Why didn't I pick up on the fact that she was afraid? I've asked myself often enough. At the time I was preoccupied with work, under pressure, putting the finishing touches to the deal that made me rich enough never to have to worry about money again. She may have felt I was too busy to bother with her problems – I find that hard to bear.

I reached a decision then, right there in that hell-hole where the horror caught up with her, which was as binding as a solemn oath. After fourteen months, I didn't need to analyse my pledge or question its legitimacy. The police, who'd achieved nothing in all that time, had as good as admitted defeat, closed the case. The rage against injustice which I'd suppressed for long enough had distilled into cold clear resolve. I've always had drive, the voice inside you that will never, never let you give up, but from now on, I decided, I would devote all my energy and resources to avenging Sophie's death.

If it took the rest of my life I was going to find him.

I'd heard something: a soft, dry whirring sound that seemed to come from above my head. Resisting the urge to snap on the torch, I held my breath and listened. The whirring noise stopped, but for a moment longer I thought I could hear breathing that I knew wasn't mine.

By now my eyes had adjusted to the blackness. I was conscious of a faint glow around the vent at the top of the dome. It came from a tiny segment of the night sky that had just grown darker. A shadow had passed over it as if someone had moved their head into the opening and was looking down at me through the rusted grille.

Careful not to make any noise, I reached for the torch that lay on the floor beside me and closed my fingers around the handle. Then, in one swift movement, I swung it upward and, aiming at the centre of the ceiling, hit the switch.

The beam sprang onto the target. Blinking at the sudden brightness, I squinted along the shaft of light. I can't be sure of exactly what it was I saw glinting back at me from behind the grille. Possibly the lens of a camera, or a pair of glasses, or a refracting eye . . . it had a metallic bluish tint.

The next instant it was gone.

It took me at most thirty seconds to scramble from the grotto's inner chamber to the top of the mound. There was no one there. My heart still racing, I shone the torch all around, throwing the beam into the undergrowth, up into the trees – it revealed nothing unusual, no movement anywhere this end of the garden.

Searching the bushes on the mound, I found the outlet for the air-vent easily enough. It was capped by a heavy stone cowl. The ground round about showed no sign of having been disturbed.

Yet I knew I hadn't imagined what happened, I knew I'd seen *something*.

Just then I heard the explosive chatter of a *motorino* starting up the far side of the perimeter wall on Via della Scala. I wheeled around, swinging the light up to the top of the wall, when my mobile went off in my pocket like an alarm clock.

Laura! I'd promised to call her before seven, and it had gone clean out of my head. I answered without waiting for her to speak.

'Sweetheart, I'm sorry . . . I'm on my way now. All well?'

There was a long pause.

'All well here. How you doing?'

It was a man's voice, husky, lilting.

'Who is this?' My first thought was that somebody was with Laura, but that made no sense. There was a sudden dull thump from the other end of the line, followed by incoherent mumbling.

I glanced at the mobile's display screen, it was empty.

'You know what?' The sing-song voice had a strained quality, as if the caller was exerting himself. His breathing came hard. 'This isn't . . . a real good time . . . not right now.'

'I think you must have a wrong number,' I said.

'Take it easy, Ed.'

'Wait, who *is* this?'

But the line was already dead.

10

Ward tasted a mouthful of the pappardelle and nodded. '*Molto buono* . . . excellent,' he said to the waiter who'd brought the plate to his table and insisted on waiting for a verdict, '*mille grazie, signore.*'

He wanted to be left alone now to enjoy his food.

The home-made pasta and *sugo di cinghiale* complemented each other perfectly. He drank some wine and chased the rich musky flavour of wild boar to the back of his throat. He was relieved it hadn't triggered, as sometimes happened when he was in a 'feeling' mood, an explosion of colour. The cuisine here was spectacular enough, he didn't want the experience blown off by a firework display.

He was sitting where she sat that evening with her father.

He thought of asking the maitre d' about the tall quiet English couple who dined here last night. Same table? Ward was curious, but couldn't risk drawing attention to himself. If Ed and Laura walked in off the street right now – he'd checked there was no reservation in the name of Lister – he wondered how it'd feel. Would they recognise him, or sense his presence? Would he somehow give himself away? The idea of observing them at close quarters excited him.

It would be like Sophie bringing him home to meet her folks. The only reason he chose this place – one of the few authentic Tuscan restaurants in Florence where the menu wasn't limited to white beans, offal and steak – was because he wanted to feel close to her again.

He cleaned the last of the dark sauce on his plate with a piece of bread and put it in his mouth, then licked the small graze on the knuckle of his thumb. He knew he was playing a dangerous game coming back to Florence.

Last night he'd carried out a quick search of Sam Metcalf's stripped-down apartment, working around but not touching the tiers of boxes and packing cases in every room – a laptop wasn't an item anyone would choose to ship.

He wasn't sure if he'd been right to warn her. He'd called Sam from the airplane, out on the tarmac, as soon as the seat-belt signs were switched off. When she realised who he was – that was a moment to savour – he'd heard fear tint her voice. It triggered one of his episodes, keeping him in his seat long after the other passengers. So far a simple phone call had achieved the desired effect. She'd lost her nerve about meeting up with Ed Lister. But the potential for trouble was still there – he'd been left with a situation that could easily get out of control.

He'd seen Sam Metcalf just once, from a distance. Ward never forgot a face. The snapshot of her he'd found in the bathroom (her arm around some greaseball at the top of Giotto's bell tower) matched the one in his head.

How well, he wondered, did she remember him?

Where he'd screwed up was assuming the laptop was in the tote bag Sam gave her friend at the station. He should've noticed from the way he held it that the weight was different; but he was too far away. Plus Jimmy walked funny.

He'd followed him down Via Tornabuoni, cruising the windows of the designer stores, staying just close enough to move in quickly if it became necessary. Ward knew all about shadowing people. When he saw the subject dive into

Ferragamo, he felt certain it was to meet Ed Lister and hand over the laptop, but a passing glance through the window revealed Jimbo, swathed in a Hugh Heffner-style silk robe, admiring himself in the floor-to-ceiling mirror.

The canvas bag at his feet.

His main course arrived – veal escalope *al limone* served with baby leaf spinach. He was going to be sitting up on a train half the night, he didn't want to feel stuffed. He looked at his watch: five to eight. He asked for the coffee and his check to be brought at the same time. Then, as the waiter turned away, he called him back.

'And, *signore*, a slice of your chocolate *torta* . . .' He shrugged and gave a self-indulgent little smile. 'What the hell.'

It was in an empty courtyard off one of the narrow back streets behind the Piazza Antinori that he caught up with Jimmy Macchado. He was halfway in the door of the apartment when Ward called out, 'Hi, you don't know me . . .' Stepping from the shadows with his hands up, big friendly smile. 'But when I passed you just then, I thought, hey, seen that face before. Aren't you a friend of Sam Metcalf . . . ?'

They'd taken it from there. Small world, fellow Americans abroad, dear old Florence, everybody knows everybody . . . and so on. He found it came naturally to him playing the flirtatious straight guy – hesitant, sincere, butch-lite – practically irresistible to Jimmy's kind.

His mistake, the dumb schmuck, was going on about how he'd love to invite him in, only it wasn't his place . . . he was just cat-sitting for a friend. Had to water the plants too, every other day, for a month.

By the time Ward got to see that there was nothing in the tote bag but the desperate-playboy robe, it was too late to let him go.

The voice, lime-green against the blue rhombus that turned slowly between his ears, kept asking the annoying question, why?

Jimmy was begging for it, that's why.

C'mon, you can do better than that.

You really want to know?

You're dying to tell me . . . what didya have to kill him for, Ward?

He was getting lime-green needles now. He picked up a spoon and began working his way methodically through the chocolate cake.

He couldn't let him go because, one, the little cocksucker'd seen his face. Two, it was obvious that Sam had told Jimmy everything. And, three, the added bonus, he'd given him an address for her in Venice – a small hotel on the island of Burano.

He didn't want to talk about this any more.

Ward slung his rucksack over one shoulder and set off down Via del Moro. It had been hot and stuffy in the restaurant and he was glad to breathe the slightly fresher air of the streets. He crossed to the opposite sidewalk and lingered for a moment in an unlit doorway. It was here that he'd witnessed, it seemed like only yesterday, Sophie and her old man saying goodbye for the last time.

The word goodbye had taste and weight . . . it felt like something oily slipping through his fingers. One day he hoped to tell Ed about the love he felt for his daughter. Try to make him understand that he and Soph were meant.

At the corner with Via del Sole, he looked back again and saw that a black Mercedes cab had pulled up in front of Garga. He waited to see who would get out.

It wasn't the Listers. He continued on his way, making a

nostalgic detour that took him past the Badia, the church where Dante supposedly first set eyes on his Beatrice. He had left himself plenty of time to walk to the railroad station and still catch the night train to Venice.

Venice

II

'Notice anything going on in this one?' I asked Will.

The sketchbook lay on the table between us, open at an exterior view of the house. I drew his attention to an attic dormer with the shutters thrown back revealing a half-open sash window.

The same dormer I'd seen come to life on the *homebeforedark* website.

'You may need a magnifying glass,' I said.

Will gave me a disparaging look over the top of his glasses, then pushed them up onto his forehead and bent low to examine the drawing.

'Isn't that someone standing there,' he said, 'a figure behind the casement?'

I nodded. 'What was Sophie's state of mind when she drew this?'

He sat back in his chair, considering. 'You say the drawings are based on a website this friend of hers claims Sophie left on her laptop?'

'A virtual house. I haven't seen inside yet, but the façades are identical.' I'd explained to Will about Sam Metcalf and our aborted meeting in Florence. I'd heard nothing more from her.

'This really isn't my field, Ed.'

'I wasn't asking for your opinion as a shrink.'

Besides being Laura's brother and one of my oldest friends, Dr Will Calloway is a senior consultant in psychiatry at the Maudsley Hospital. He put his hands together in a prayer shape. 'Yes, you were.' Little smile. 'I get a sense of reined-in emotions, issues of flight or concealment, fear perhaps – that comes across quite strongly. Doesn't stop the drawings, of course, being the product of Sophie's own imagination.

He pushed a plate of sandwiches towards me. Laura and I had left Florence early that morning and I'd called Will on the way in from Heathrow to ask if he could meet me for lunch. We'd ended up ordering from the hospital cafeteria.

'What if it was a real house,' I said, 'an actual place?'

Will turned to another drawing, an interior, that showed two empty chairs facing an ancient cabinet TV in the corner of a bleak-looking lounge. The picture on the miniature screen was the famous scene from *Breakfast at Tiffany's* where George Peppard kisses Audrey Hepburn in the rain. I suspect Sophie had added the tiny image as a personal touch. The movie was a favourite of hers.

He closed the sketchbook. 'I'd like to borrow this, if it's all right with you. I want to show these drawings to a colleague. We need an objective opinion.'

Will was silent a moment. He'd been particularly fond of his niece. Then he said, with a sigh, 'My guess is she knew she was going to be murdered.'

'So what did you want to talk about that couldn't wait?'

The question, though I was half expecting it, caught me off guard.

'Will, for Christ's sake . . .' I'd been describing what happened last night in the grotto at the Villa Nardini. Brushing aside his observation that I was distraught, full of anger, possibly in a hallucinatory state, I insisted there *had* been

62

someone up on the mound peering down at me through the vent. I didn't imagine it. Or the call to my mobile. 'I think I actually spoke to Sophie's murderer.'

He smiled. 'I know you, normally you'd have gone straight to the office.'

'You're not listening. I'm almost sure it was him.'

'Did you call the police? Your friend, Morelli?'

'What would have been the point?' I'd told Will earlier about my discouraging visit to the *Questura* and how it made me realise finally that it was down to me now to get justice for Sophie. 'Don't worry, I'll follow this up. I'll find him.'

He nodded slowly. 'How's Laura, by the way?'

'She's fine, fine, I think Florence did her good. The requiem helped.'

'And how about you? Aside from your . . . ordeal.'

I took a bite out of a sandwich, tuna and sweetcorn. The conversation was taking a predictable turn. Before we left, I'd told Will I had hopes of our trip bringing Laura and me closer together.

'We're surviving,' I said, answering his next question before he could ask it. 'I won't pretend it's any better than that.' I drank some coffee. I wanted to smoke. Will, imperturbable, knew how to wait.

'There's nobody else . . . in case that's what you're thinking.'

He was aware that we were having problems, and that Sophie's death had widened the cracks. I don't know if Laura ever spoke to him about our marriage (somehow I doubt it), but I did from time to time. Will was scrupulously careful not to get involved or take sides. 'Never even crossed my mind.'

He'd introduced me to his sister the spring of 1983, when we all happened to be in New York together. Laura was over visiting friends and I'd just come back for another bite of the

Apple after a disastrous debut a few years before had forced a hasty withdrawal. Will, who was doing his doctoral thesis at Columbia, helped with my rehabilitation, gave me a place to stay until I got on my feet and put me in touch with all the right people, including my future wife.

As he once said himself, he had a lot to answer for.

I looked around his neat, antiseptic office, the NHS-green walls relieved only by his patients' art offerings. Maybe I was prompted by the therapeutic setting, or by an uneasy conscience, but I never intended to bring up the subject of Jelena.

'I need your advice, Will, and this time I don't mean professional advice.'

'You just hate to part with money.' He was deadpan behind his owlish, horn-rimmed glasses. 'Fire away.'

'I met someone . . . in a chat room on the internet.'

Silence. Then he burst out laughing. 'For Christ's sake, Ed.'

'I was hoping that's how you'd react,' I said evenly.

'I can't help it . . . it's just so perfect. The last person in the world I'd expect to hook up with an online chick. Is she legal?'

'Maybe this is not such a good idea.'

As a rule I keep things pretty close to my chest. But if I ever feel the need to unload I can depend on Will to take the piss. Which isn't a bad arrangement, if you're prone (as I've been told I am) to taking yourself too seriously. After Sophie died, I opened up to him – as a friend, not as a shrink, though his understanding of the psychological effects of loss did no harm. That was different.

'Why do I get the feeling you're being defensive?'

He meant it as a joke, but I couldn't really see the funny side.

'Until a year ago,' I retaliated, 'I had hardly any experience

64

of the internet. I used to warn Sophie about the dangers without really understanding what they were.'

Will slouched down in his chair. 'I'm sorry, Eddie.'

'When the police admitted they hadn't the resources to hunt for her murderer in cyberspace . . . well, I know more now.'

'Remember you telling me. No stone unturned.'

'I told you I was posting bulletins on MySpace and writing on Facebook walls asking for information. What I *didn't* tell you was that I began trawling the Net using Sophie's old ID, pretending to be her, hoping the stalker might respond.

'In the end I found it too painful, but I went on haunting the chat rooms, looking for someone who might have come across Stormypetrel – Sophie's screen-name. I'd talk to anybody, approach total strangers and start telling them her story – I know, it sounds pathetic, but it helped. At least I felt I was doing something.

'Anyway, that's how I got talking to this girl. It wasn't a pick-up, Will. She lives in Brooklyn, she's twenty-five, single, teaches kindergarten . . . oh and she plays the piano – surprisingly well. She doesn't think she has a hope of being accepted, but her dream is to study music at the Conservatoire in Paris.'

Will was looking at me, not saying anything.

For a moment it was as if his sister was sitting there. There's a strong family resemblance. He has her candid, light blue eyes, a Calloway feature; though Will's dark-haired and sturdily built, as opposed to willowy blonde. They have a certain way of tilting the head, the same appraising smile – emotional detachment, a coolness at the centre, is another family trait.

'We got on right away. She's bright, she makes me laugh.'

'Have you met her? Seen her on cam? Spoken to her?'

I shook my head.

'But I take it you know what she looks like?'

'She sent me a photo . . . reasonably attractive.'

'How can you be sure it's her?' He sighed. 'Does she know you're married? How old you are? *Who* you are? You didn't give her your real name, did you?'

'Look, I really don't think she's interested in my money.'

'Then she can't know how much you're worth,' he said drily. 'So what's the attraction? Sex, I suppose. But for her?'

I didn't mind being grilled by Will. It was probably what I wanted: someone to ask the awkward, obvious questions. He needed to get one thing straight, though.

'This is *not* about sex.'

Will lifted an eyebrow.

'We just seem to hit it off in some mysterious way.'

He groaned. 'Ed, I see a lot of patients who are involved in online relationships. They all "hit it off in some mysterious way". Strangers project their daydreams and fantasies onto each other. It's called affective transference. But don't underestimate the seductive power of a wishful e-mail. Cyber affairs can cause havoc.'

'It's not even close to being an affair. I can walk away from this any time, just hit the delete switch . . . And so can she.'

He looked sceptical. 'Have you told Laura?'

'What for? I'm not playing away from home. You know I'd never do anything to hurt Laura. I said there's no one else and I meant it.'

'Then why are you telling me?'

'Her life is so different to mine half the time I might as well be talking to somebody from another planet. And yet it feels . . . I don't know, I feel I can be myself with her.' I shifted in my seat. 'She helps me to forget.'

'The analogy is opening up to a stranger on a train, someone you know you'll never meet again.' It was the doctor speaking now. 'You've had a rough year of it, Ed. It's not hard to see why this happened. Only you're wrong if you think there can

66

be intimacy without strings. I don't like to preach, but the person you should be . . .'

I cut him off. 'Then don't.'

'You asked my advice.' Will took off his glasses and rubbed his eyes. I was braced for his midlife crisis lecture, but all I got was a warning. 'She could be setting you up for blackmail, some kind of scam. Think what would happen if this came out.'

'If what came out? It's not even an issue,' I said calmly.

'You're flying blind, Ed. People find not what they want on the Web, but what they wish for: that's why it can be dangerous. *Just remember you can't see the expression on her face when she's typing to you.*'

Will glanced at his watch, then leaned back in his chair and put his hands behind his head. 'Your fifty minutes are up. I have other patients to see.'

'Very funny.' I made a one-fingered gesture.

'So what are you going to do?' he asked as he walked me to the door. 'How are you going to find this person?'

For a moment I thought we were still talking about the girl.

In the car, on the way from the Maudsley to my office, I booted up my laptop and checked my mailbox again. I'd sent Jelena a message earlier asking if she'd arrived safely in DC. Her reply was short and breezy – you didn't have to see the expression on her face to know that the friendliness was genuine.

Will had got her all wrong.

adorablejoker: Well, hi right back at ya! I'm doing ok. slept the whole way on the train – could've used some company. it's hot as hell down here. looks like I'll only be gone one week instead of two. I gotta go now. take it easy, Ed. jELLY

Take it easy, Ed? I smiled.

I'd lain awake half the night rewinding and playing back in my head those same words from the conversation on the mound. Trying to picture the circumstances of the sinister thuds and mumblings I'd overheard.

I wrote myself a memo: Phil to ask his diagnostic people at Secure Solutions is it possible to trace a call made *to* a mobile phone when the number has been withheld? If yes, when can I expect a result?

The only person in Florence I'd given my number to (apart from Bailey) was Sam Metcalf. I wasn't sure if there was a connection, the call could have originated anywhere, but I could see now why Sam might have had cold feet and asked me not to get in touch with her again: she was afraid *one of us* was being watched.

'Take it easy, Ed.' Had I really heard that hoarse 'Ed', or could the last, upwardly inflected syllable have been an 'eh'? 'Take it easy, eh?' I'd told the caller he had a wrong number. But, either way, I felt sure contact had been deliberate.

I sat back, lit an unfiltered Gauloise and, gazing out at the rain-slick streets of Olympia, turned up the volume on Bob Marley's 'One Love'. I thought about Jelly deliquescing in the sultry heat of Washington DC. It was a dangerous contrast and the music didn't help. I found myself wishing I was over there with her.

Take it easy, Ed . . . Had to be coincidence.

12

Leaning over the bridge, Sam aimed her camera at the illustrated wake left by the vaporetto. Wanting to get the way the lemon sky heaved and shivered on the surface of the canal; the façades of houses that rippled along its banks until they dissolved into shadow. You had to be an artist like Turner, she thought, to capture the nuances of light, the broken reflections . . . the timeless aspect of Venice.

A figure in a black shawl appeared on the landing-stage, giving the picture the focus it needed. Sam hesitated, and got off a shot just as the next herd of sightseers strayed into her viewfinder.

When she looked again the landing-stage was empty, the light gone from the water . . . well, sugar. She moved on before anyone could ask her directions to San Marco, or what part of the US she was from. One thing about digital – you could always edit out the aliens later.

On the other side of the bridge, she crossed a small, tree-shaded square and ducked into a church that from the outside looked like an ordinary house with shuttered windows. Its dark, stone-scented interior felt deliciously cool. She sank down on an empty pew in front of the altarpiece, an insipid ascension attributed to Veronese, which you had to feed coins into a light-box to illuminate.

Sam just wanted to take the load off.

She was staying out on Burano, fifty minutes by vaporetto from the centre of Venice – a schlep, if you happened to forget your credit card or needed to run back (as she had just done) for a shower and to change clothes. Not that she was complaining: the secluded little island felt like sanctuary and her room at the Albergo Zulian, a modest hotel in a row of bonbon-coloured fishermen's houses recommended by Jimmy Macchado, had a view over the Lagoon.

She'd called Jimmy yesterday to let him know she'd arrived safely. And then again this morning. So far she'd heard nothing back, which sucked – the SOB could at least have thanked her for the robe – but was not that unusual for him. Sometimes he'd hole up at the house in Fiesole and go 'off the air' for days at a time. He'd mentioned having a backlog of scripts to read this weekend.

She looked at her watch: just after seven, plenty of time to get to the restaurant.

Unlike Jimmy, an old Venetian hand, Sam didn't know the city well. She'd spent the past two days sightseeing, discovering for herself the shimmering glory of the place: it had helped keep her mind off things. Revived by the salt air and strong clear light of the Adriatic, she was starting to unwind.

What happened in Florence – the creepy phone-call, the suspicion someone had been in her apartment, her own almost hysterical reaction – now seemed remote and unreal, like a dream she had to make an effort to recall. Unpleasant though it had been, the episode had allowed her to close a door on the past. The compulsion to look over her shoulder was just about gone.

Then, last night, a chance encounter had given Sam's still fragile sense of security a boost. At a chamber concert in the Chiesa San Bartolomeo, she'd found herself sitting next to a couple from Princeton who turned out to know her parents. Balfe and Fern Rivers were 're-doing Europe', and when they heard that Sam was on her way to Paris, had insisted she drive up to Vienna with them. She found their company

70

numbingly dull, and Balfe had a louche gleam that could turn out to be a problem; but she saw the advantages and didn't hesitate.

Dinner tonight was with them, and some Italians they knew.

She took off her glasses and rubbed the lenses on the hem of her silk shirt. Then rose and with a token bow, still polishing her glasses, walked slowly down the aisle. At the back of the church, starting to fill now for evening mass, she noticed a woman in a black shawl who reminded her of the figure on the landing-stage.

As she drew closer, Sam put her glasses back on and saw that the woman was in fact a young girl – pale, sickly looking. Over the bench next to her was draped an empty black rucksack that she'd mistaken, in her myopic state, for a wrap.

In the tangle of winding alleys and dilapidated squares behind the palazzos of the Grand Canal, it's easy to become disorientated. Sam threaded the labyrinth, her MP3 player tuned to a local rock station, letting instinct guide her. There were enough people around not to have to worry about getting lost. As long as she kept the setting sun at her back, she figured, she couldn't go far wrong.

The *osteria* was in Cannaregio, near the northern quays, not far from Campo Mori. She'd looked it up on the map before leaving the hotel, then in the rush to catch the vaporetto had managed somehow to leave the map behind.

As she wandered deeper into the *sestiere*, glimpses of the Salute's great white dome flying above the rooftops grew less frequent until Sam could no longer rely on it to get her bearings. She asked an elegant couple for directions; the man smiled and made a flat-handed, chopping gesture: '*Avanti dritto, sempre dritto.*'

A block further on, 'straight ahead' was open to interpretation.

She thought of calling the restaurant, but she'd jotted down the name and telephone number on the back of the map.

Jimmy, of course, had a theory about getting around Venice. 'Where you're going,' he'd told her in the taxi, 'does not depend on which path you take. In Venice, there are *fabulous* things on every path. Don't worry about the path you choose taking you to your destination. Your destination will find you.'

Sure. Sure it will.

She crossed another bridge into a square paved with herringbone tiles; she noted the church with its seventeenth-century Baroque façade, the pharmacy on the corner. There were two exits: Sam chose the *calle* that looked least deserted.

She started down it; the radio playing Foo Fighters' 'All My Life'.

It had been one of Sophie's favourite songs. Yesterday Sam had found a message from the dead girl's father on her cell urging her to call him. She felt badly about erasing it. But there was no way now she was getting back in touch.

One thing still bothered her: how did 'Ward' know she'd contacted Ed Lister and that they were planning to meet? He must have somehow intercepted her e-mail; or, if he lived in Florence, maybe monitored her phone-calls – it was possible he'd been keeping his eye on her since before the murder.

Sam had on her Prada sandals, white Capri pants and a gold silk shirt tied at the waist. In Florence, she'd learnt to dress to avoid attracting attention; here, she didn't mind if she turned a head or two – it had been a while since she felt good about the way she looked. She could feel sweat trickling under her arms.

About halfway along the footpath, she saw a glimmer of water ahead that by her reckoning shouldn't have been there. Then, around the next bend, the *calle* ended abruptly in a terrace with crumbling classical pillars looking out over a wide, luminous expanse to the islands of the Lagoon. It was like stepping up onto a stage. Feeling exposed and slightly bewildered, Sam removed her earphones so she could appreciate the serenity of the view. Somewhere a child was crying.

The sun had just gone and she stood watching the light drain from the long reaches of sea and sky, wondering if her decision to leave Italy was the right one. She'd become accustomed to being surrounded by beauty. She gave a shiver at the thought of relocating to Pittsburgh, where she'd applied for a job on the curatorial staff of the Sands Taylor Museum. She lifted the back of a hand up to her forehead.

Earlier she'd spoken to her mother, who was almost incoherent with excitement that her baby was finally coming home.

Oh, Federico, she murmured, closing her eyes. This was home.

He'd been in the house behind Piazza Antinori for almost an hour before he opened the door to the fridge, hoping he might find a cold beer, or maybe something to eat.

The job had only taken five minutes. He'd gone straight up to the bedroom and removed the small painting in the ebony frame from the wall above the bed. Then wrapped it in newspaper and put it inside the plastic shopping bag he'd brought with him. Bad Feng Shui, he remembered the old fart saying, to hang a picture over a bed.

There was some other stuff, watches, gold cufflinks, a Moroccan dagger he fancied, but Guido had warned him to touch nothing.

He knew the house well enough not to have to turn on lights. He sat in the gloom, dreaming about the new life that lay ahead.

Until a couple of weeks ago he'd worked as a waiter at a restaurant near Santa Croce, where he'd been eyed up by the

Englishman he knew as Daniel, the owner of the house. He'd come to two parties here and after the last one his host had invited him to spend the night. He'd taken the three hundred Euros Daniel had paid him for his services and, while the older man slept, an impression of his house keys.

Before they had sex, Daniel had told him he wanted to see more of him when he returned from a business trip to Phuket. He'd weighed the earning potential of an arrangement with the portly old queen against his cut for stealing the painting, which Guido had assured him was worth at least a million.

Gianni Arcangeli was seventeen and wanted a Porsche.

He'd arrived at the house around six thirty, which was about the time Daniel's American friend, Jimmy, came every second day to water the plants and feed the cat. He knew he'd been there yesterday – he'd watched from the alley as he'd entered the house with another man, but hadn't bothered waiting to see them leave. There was little risk of his returning this evening.

If anybody asked, he was doing Jimmy a favour. He'd even put out some food for Cesar, before settling down to wait upstairs in the sumptuous all-white *salone* that smelt of dried flowers. His instructions were to stay until after dark, when there'd be fewer people around in the courtyard. He soon grew bored, then hungry.

The kitchen was on the ground floor. Its bare stone walls and high ceiling with exposed beams reminded Gianni of his uncle's farmhouse in the Val d'Elsa, only this place had been given the designer treatment. The fridge was an American import, a side-by-side stainless steel Sub-Zero 600 Series, the best money can buy. It stood almost seven feet tall. He remembered it being well stocked.

Winding a dishtowel around his hand to avoid leaving prints, he reached for the handle, noticing only now that the trays and shelves from the fridge were piled up on a nearby worktop. It crossed Gianni's mind he was about to be disappointed.

He pulled open the door to the Sub-Zero. A lurid light sprang into the room and instinctively he reared back. Folded into the space normally occupied by provisions was the fully clothed body of a man, one bent knee pulled upwards like a dancer's against his blackened windpipe. He barely had time to take in Jimmy's blond curls, the striped shirt, the shades hanging askew, before the corpse which had been held in place by the fridge door lurched forward onto his shoulder.

The boy screamed as the ice-cold face, a mottled orange and blue colour, brushed his cheek in a grotesque parody of a social kiss. His breath came in short panicky gusts, as he tried to wrestle Jimmy back into the fridge. When he'd got all the stray limbs tucked inside, he slammed the beautifully engineered door shut and leant against it like someone battling to keep out a wintry blast.

For a minute or two he couldn't move. Tears ran down his face. All he could see in the shadows were Jimmy's bulging eyes and obscenely poking tongue. Then he heard something scrunch under his foot and, still sobbing, knelt to pick up Jimmy's crushed, ice-cold sunglasses. He'd seemed like a nice person too.

He knew the mess he was in – he wouldn't be able to take the painting now. He needed to leave right away. Tell no one, not even Guido, he was ever here.

It wasn't until he was out on the street, trying to kick-start his *motorino*, that Gianni noticed he'd cut his finger on a piece of broken lens.

Dusk doesn't linger in Venice. By the time Sam Metcalf had made her way back from the waterfront to the Rio della Sensa, it was fully dark. Crossing a humpback bridge to a square lit by lanterns, she thought for a heartening moment she'd found the *campo* near the restaurant. Then, with a dismal flush of recognition, she took in the herringbone tiles, the elaborate church, the corner pharmacy . . .

She'd been going round in a circle.

Close to tears, Sam felt ready to quit and head home, when it occurred to her to call Jimmy Macchado. He knew every bar, café and trattoria in Venice. She tried him first at the Fiesole number, then keyed his cell. He wasn't picking up on either.

She set off dejectedly down the second *calle* that led out of the square and kept going until she came to a junction. Stopping under a street lamp, she checked the display to make sure she had the right number before trying Jimmy's cell again.

She heard it ringing, ringing . . . and then with a frown she slowly lowered the phone, puzzled by a brief simultaneous chitter of electronic birdsong that seemed to come from one of the lanes whose entrances lay ahead.

Sam stood very still, listening. She could have sworn she'd heard close by the opening bars of 'O Sole Mio', Jimmy's kitsch, maddeningly chirpy ring-tone.

Her heart was beating fast. There was nobody else in sight. What if the sonofabitch was *here* . . . in Venice? She knew how he liked to kid around, spring surprises.

'Jimmy?' Looking up at the houses, she repeated his name, louder.

There was no reply, no movement at the windows, nothing.

She put the phone back to her ear, and instantly realised her mistake. Jimmy's voice-mail had cut in – what she'd heard was the musical intro to his recorded message. She'd forgotten it was the same dumb jingle.

She let go her breath, feeling like an idiot.

'Hey, it's me,' she said wearily. 'I know you're there, so please pick up . . . *come on*, man.' She paused, giving him the chance.

'Listen, I'm lost. I am *totally fucking lost*. I followed the path, just like you said, all that Zen bullshit . . . I need you to talk me out of here.' She gave him her vague destination and her present position – the name of the *calle* she had started down was 'The Alley of the Blind', which figured – then added: 'If you get this in the next few, call me, with a map.'

She flipped her cell shut. Unless she heard from him, and she didn't hold out much hope, Sam planned to make her way back to the Fondamente Nuove and get the next boat out to Burano. She would call the Rivers from her hotel and explain.

The alleys and byways of Venice, the arcane circuitry of the city, can play tricks with sound. Hearing someone coming towards her, or so she thought, Sam waited for the echoing footsteps to materialise. Then had to press herself against the wall as a stout woman weighed down by shopping bags overtook her from behind with a muttered '*Buona sera, signora.*'

Uncertain which of the two lanes ahead to choose, she watched the woman take the left-hand fork, and decided to follow. Around the next corner, Sam saw her guide twenty yards ahead turn into a doorway under a balcony supported by carved stone angels. By the time she drew level, the ancient door had already slammed shut; from its Judas window a square of light fell on the shopping bags left in a heap outside.

Sam was wondering why – maybe the woman dumped them to answer the phone, or see to a child – when she felt her cell vibrate against her hip, alerting her that she'd received a text message.

Son of a gun . . . Jimmy.

CAN'T TALK NOW . . . IN A MTG, BUT HERE'S WHAT TO
DO: TURN AROUND, GO BACK TO THE LAST Y, THEN TAKE
THE OTHER BRANCH. U WILL COME TO A PASSAGE THAT
RUNS ALONG RIO DELLE GATTE. FOLLOW TO ARCADE . . .
TXT ME WHEN U GET THERE. IT'S CLOSER THAN U THINK.
CIN CIN! J.

She laughed out loud and, relief sweeping over her, texted
him back: THANK YOU, JEEEEESUS!

Then started to retrace her steps,

His directions were easy to follow. The footpath by the
stagnant, foul-smelling *rio* looked singularly uninviting. On
either side of the water, decrepit houses, their windows mostly
dark or shuttered-up, drew closer together as she walked
beneath a narrowing hatchway of star-flecked indigo sky, the
path soon reducing to a point where two people couldn't
pass. But Sam had faith in her navigator.

She remembered someone, maybe Jimmy, saying, check:
if you can hear your own footsteps, it means you're on a
dead-end street.

She could hear own breathing, it was that quiet.

Her cell phone vibrated. Sam gave a start, almost dropping
the damned thing as she fumbled to get the flap open.

ARE U THERE YET?

She answered: YEP, YEP.

GO ON TO THE END> MAKE A SHARP LEFT>U CAN'T SEE
IT YET, THERE'S A SLIT BETWEEN THE HOUSES . . .
SHORT CUT!

Sam frowned. Something felt wrong. Ten, fifteen yards
ahead of her, the water course plunged under the arcade and

78

the footpath she was on stopped altogether. How could he know how far along it she was, or what she could or couldn't see? If Jimmy was fooling around, playing with her . . .

She hesitated, then keyed:

CAN'T GO ANY FURTHER.

Sam waited, not moving.
There was a long pause before he replied:

SEE THE CUT?

Still Sam didn't move. She let her eye travel on ahead beyond the last house on her left, then slowly track along a hoarding in front of a demolition site. Where the arcade cut across the hoarding at right angles, she could make out a line of deep shadow that might have been a passage.

U'LL FIND OSTERIA AL BACCO ON THE OTHER SIDE.

That was it, of *course*, the name of the restaurant!

YOU GOTTA BE KIDDING . . . SWEAR THIS ISN'T A JOKE?

Jimmy knew what she'd been through in Florence. It was absurd to think he'd deliberately set out to trick her or play stupid games.

HAND ON MY HEART, GIRL . . . AND BTW, LOVE THE ROBE!

She stood staring at the area of shadow, at the black water of the *rio* that glinted where it hit a hidden reef before it disappeared into the tunnel. She took a couple of steps forward, then suddenly was filled with certainty that someone was hiding there. A feeling of dread sent a cold skin-prickling rush down the back of her neck.

She froze, her eyes fixed on the dark passage-mouth, wondering if whoever was waiting could see her. This had nothing to do with Jimmy. He couldn't possibly know . . . But there wasn't time to explain. Every instinct was telling her to go back, get out of there, turn and run, *now*.

Sam didn't move. She couldn't make herself look away.

She thought she saw something stir in the shadowy entrance to the cut. Overcome by a helpless, almost sensual feeling of inertia, she delayed long enough to key in, fingers trembling:

ON MY WAY. THANKS FOR HELP. TALK LATER, S.

She waited a few more seconds, wanting to be sure. If there was someone there and they were going to make a move it would have to be now.

She turned around and, the image of the dark cut still fixed on her retina, walked quickly back along the path until she reached the corner. She stopped and looked behind her. No sign of movement. A light came on in one of the windows.

She almost laughed aloud with relief.

Then in the sudden brightness she saw something that glinted on the ground, ten, fifteen yards back along the path, where she'd been standing. Instinctively, her hand flew up to her face – she'd dropped an earring.

Sam knelt to take off her sandals, debating whether to go back for it. As she rose, clutching the shoes, a shadow detached itself from the black passage-mouth.

She turned then and ran, ran like hell.

The restaurant found her. She couldn't say otherwise how she got there. Emerging from a long winding *calle* into a busy, well-lit square, Sam recognised her new friends sitting at an outside table under a blue and white awning. Out of breath, her heart still pumping, she tried not to let them see her until she'd pulled herself together.

But Balfe Rivers was already on his feet, waving and smiling at her. 'Over here, Sam! Look who's here everybody!'

Sam felt the blood from a pebble-cut squelch between her toes as she walked over to join them. Balfe took her arm and guided her to the only empty chair at the table. 'You had us all worried.'

'I'm sorry, I got . . . lost track of time.'

'You look like you could use a stiff one, honey,' Fern said drily.

13

It was the first party we'd given at Greenside since Sophie died, and we were all three of us a little on edge. Laura had seized on George's sixteenth birthday as an opportunity to open up the house again, invite a few neighbours over, as well as his friends, and make a start at getting back to normality, or something like it.

We stood together on the front steps and greeted the first arrivals. It was a warm June evening and the house, an impeccable early-Georgian mansion of pale granite that's been in my wife's family for centuries, looked magical all lit up against the dark sweep of the downs. Laura had observed the Calloway party tradition (inherited from her Virginian grandmother) of placing a hurricane lamp in every window of the house. A string quartet played Bach on the terrace.

At that point we were hardly speaking to each other.

Earlier, while getting dressed, we'd had an argument about the present I'd given George for his birthday – a toffee-apple-red Yamaha Warrior quad bike.

'You heard what happened?' She was at her dressing table, putting the finishing touches to her make-up. 'He nearly turned the bloody thing over.'

'He swerved to avoid the dog,' I countered, fiddling with my cufflinks. I'd got back from London with less than twenty minutes to shower and change before the party. 'Everyone says he was never in any real danger.'

'It's tempting fate and you bloody know it. You *promised* to be here.'

I tried to persuade Laura that losing Sophie and the fact that our son was all we had now were not valid reasons to think he was any more at risk than any other boy his age. I don't believe in being over-protective. But she was his mother.

'If anything ever does happen to him . . .' She didn't finish, just stared at me in the mirror, her coruscating blue eyes judge and jury.

'You know why I had to go up to town,' I said quietly. 'It was important.'

I'd arranged to meet Phil at Secure Solutions and deliver the SIM card from my mobile phone in person. I wanted to make it clear that I regarded tracing the call I received on the mound at the Villa Nardini as a priority.

'Whatever you do, Ed, is always so "important". But what about George? Your family? What about *us*?'

'You're all that really matters to me,' I said.

The Yamaha provoked the outburst, but I felt it was coming anyway. I dislike rows. I grew up listening to my parents having at each other on a daily basis and swore never to repeat the tedious, emotionally draining pattern in my own marriage. Although Laura and I argued, we usually managed to remain civil under pressure and avoid wounding fights. There were lapses, of course, but something else had got into her that night. She accused me of neglecting our 'only child', never being at home, using work as an excuse to avoid my responsibilities – I was surprised by the depth of the resentment and even bitterness that rose to the surface. I think only some instinct for self-preservation, or perhaps fear of the irrevocable, prevented her from saying what was really on her mind. The nearest she got was when she turned suddenly and shouted at me,

'You are not *present* in this marriage, Ed!'

Taken aback by her onslaught, and its unhelpful timing, I was aware that there was more than a little truth in what she was saying.

My defence was simply to switch off. But when we could no longer delay going down to meet our guests, I said to her, 'Can we talk about this another time? It really isn't fair on George, or kind to Sophie's memory. If we want to make this a wonderful evening for *them*, we need to present a united front.'

'You're good at that sort of thing. I'm not,' was her answer.

I don't think anybody noticed the tension between us. Friends, especially those who knew and loved Sophie, still handled us with care and made allowances. We spent most of the evening apart, and then I spotted Laura across the dining room, alone for a moment and looking elegant but forlorn in a new silver-grey Nina Ricci outfit she'd bought the last time we were in Paris.

She turned and walked through the door that leads onto the terrace. Lifting a couple of glasses of champagne from a passing tray, I drew a deep breath and followed. I caught up with her before she reached the parapet, and handed her a glass.

'It's a success, Laura,' I murmured. There were other

couples out here enjoying the night air, sitting at tables over-looking the lake. The temple had been floodlit for the occasion, the path around the shore lined with flickering torches.

She shrugged. 'Apart from the fact George can't stand the music.'

As if on cue, a wave of sound surged up from the marquee as the band got loud suddenly with the feel-good classic, 'How Sweet It Is'. Drums and bass echoed around the downs like rolling thunder. I was responsible for the music.

'It doesn't seem to be stopping him from having a good time. Maybe you would like to dance?'

'Don't think so, not right now.'

We stood there a while longer. People came up to us and murmured their compliments about the evening. I noted that Laura, in spite of what she'd said, played the part of gracious hostess effortlessly.

'I'm going inside then,' I said at last. 'I have to call Phil ... he's working late tonight,' I added, answering a question she hadn't in fact asked. 'I'll use the phone in the library. Twenty minutes.'

'I doubt if you'll be missed.' The lights on the water shivered to the grimy beat of a Christina Aguilera cover. I pretended I hadn't heard what she'd said.

'Don't worry, I'll hold the fort.' She smiled, then added in a brittle tone, 'You know what would be nice, Ed? If you didn't always have to look like you'd rather be anywhere in the world except here.'

I shrugged and turned away. The constant sniping was starting to get to me. The fact was that lately I'd been making an effort to spend more time at home with my wife and family. I suddenly felt resentful, not just of Laura, but of all these people who'd invaded our home. The driveway had been turned into a glinting river of expensive cars; I could just make out a huddle of chauffeurs leaning against their glossy chariots, gossiping, cigarettes glowing like fireflies in the dark.

Looking up at the house, I noticed now that, although there was a lamp in every window, one was unlit – only Sophie's old bedroom had been left dark. It struck me as something more than an unfortunate oversight.

She was right, I didn't want to be here.

Four minutes till midnight.

There was no real urgency. In Washington DC, coming up to seven, it'd still be light out . . . as if that made any difference. I was seized by the irrational thought that if I hurried I might get there in time.

I cut through the crowd, clearing a path. The long, stone-flagged hallway dissolved into a blur of flushed and grinning faces. A blonde in a too-tight gold dress, one of our office managers who'd helped organise the evening, playfully captured my arm.

'Hey, you!' I blew her off, kept moving.

I was almost to the stairs when something made me look back.

Laura had followed me indoors and, from the far end of the room, was observing my progress. She did her amused-smile, little-finger-wave thing and I had no choice but to smile and wave back.

In the library, I closed the door and walked over to my desk. Picking up the phone, I dialled the number Phil had given me, then sat down at the computer.

While I waited for him to answer – I wanted to know if he'd made any progress with tracing that call – I logged on to the internet.

My chances of finding Jelly online were remote, but I pulled up my friends list onscreen, planning to drop her a note, then drew a short convulsive breath.

adorablejoker: hey . . . how ya doin?

templedog: I don't *believe* this

    I left a message on Phil's voice-mail asking him to call me back, then put the phone down.

td: I'm . . . this is so weird, I mean, I just had a feeling . . . where are you?

aj: still in DC

td: at your friend's house?

aj: library, in the comp room

td: the Library of Congress?

aj: sure, where else can a girl rest her feet after a hard day's shopping?

td: you know the odds against our bumping into each other . . .

    I'm not sure if it was the coincidence that threw me, or the exhilaration I felt at seeing her. After taking a moment, I lit up a Gauloise.

aj: you aren't upset with me?

td: should I be? What's your address in Brooklyn?

aj: hmmm . . . kinda wish you hadn't asked that

td: why? afraid I might show up on your doorstep?

aj: i'm just not that kind of girl

td: I wanted to send you something

aj: save your money, mister . . . hey, feel like taking a trip?

td: okay, where to this time . . . Marrakesh, Samarkand, Venice?

aj: what were you going to send me?

td: you'll never know

aj: boo . . . so, in your mind, where are we?

td: Venice, one of my favourite hotels in the world, the Cipriani . . .

aj: i dunno . . . streets full of water. i told you i'm scared of water

td: hold on . . . phone

At the same moment I picked up the receiver I heard loud whispering in the passage outside the library. A young girl I knew vaguely as somebody's daughter put her head around the door and, seeing me at my desk, dissolved into giggles.

'Shhhh . . . there's someone in here.'

'Thanks for getting back, Phil,' I said, looking now at my son, George, who was standing behind the girl in the doorway, both obviously a little the worse for wear. I couldn't help wondering if Laura hadn't sent him up to check on me.

'Sorry, sorry,' he slurred, grinning. 'Dad, this is . . . Clarissa.'

'Here's where we are,' Phil started in without preamble. 'I told you we had a mole at your phone company. He's been able to trace the network the call came from, but that's as far as he can go.'

'Nice to meet you,' I mouthed, my hand over the receiver, 'hope you're having fun,' and waved amiably at George, who retreated with his arm around the girl's neck.

'Your caller uses Uno. Now we have to find someone there to tell us which of their subscribers originated the call. More difficult, but we're working on it. None of this is legal, so it's going to be expensive.'

'I don't care how much it costs, I just want his name.'

After I hung up the phone, I took a sip of champagne, got up and walked over to close the library door, which George had left wide open.

aj: still there?

td: I'm sorry . . . I have to go now

aj: i know, you need to get back to the party, mister

td: wait, *wait just a minute* . . . I don't remember mentioning any party

aj: well you did. you told me . . . it's your son's birthday

td: no, seriously, there are 150 people here. how did you know?

aj: i can 'feel' you sometimes, the situations you're in, what's on your mind. like right now, you're thinking . . . your wife must be wondering where you are

td: I was actually trying to picture the expression on your face when you typed that. It's important, Jelly. *How* did you know about the party?
aj: Don't you ever listen? YOU TOLD ME

I decided to check later to see if she was right. I had archived most of our conversations. There was a pause, a longer pause than usual, before she continued.

aj: anyway, i'll be back in new york tuesday
td: good, we'll talk about it then. Look after yourself
aj: i'm in the library of freaking congress . . . what can happen?
td: I was just thinking, maybe we could get together for a drink sometime
aj: well, *don't* think it, ed . . . and don't you dare say another word

I sat for a moment, staring at the screen, trying to imagine her at a computer terminal in the Thomas Jefferson Building on Capitol Hill. There was something thrilling about Jelly being in a place I knew reasonably well: it connected our footprints in the real world, brought us a degree closer. I'd meant what I'd said about getting together. I wanted to meet her now.

Before returning to the fray, I poured myself another glass of champagne, then opened the music files she'd sent me and sat back, eyes closed, listening through my headphones to her playing the piano.

I'm no judge of musical talent (I was on the money side of the business), but Jelena clearly had a gift and I hoped to encourage her. She'd refused point-blank to let me interfere, which was understandable. I couldn't see the harm, though, in letting someone who really knew their stuff hear her play. I'd already made a few discreet calls, which resulted in my getting an appointment at the Conservatoire for the day after tomorrow. I planned to be in Paris anyway.

What I told Will about our relationship was the truth: Jelly and I were friends, nothing more. But over the last few days, I don't know how or when exactly it happened, something had changed. Nobody could have been more resistant than I was to the idea of becoming involved. My life was complicated enough, the last thing I needed was to get caught up in some half-baked internet romance – I didn't even buy that it was possible to fall for someone on a laptop screen. But I couldn't get her off my mind. Looking back I can see now that there was a gradual, almost imperceptible escalation, an upping of the stakes – and that somewhere along the line, crazy as it may seem, I'd fallen.

14

After he was gone, Jelly deleted the floor-plan and images from the website of the Library of Congress that she'd pulled up onscreen while they were chatting. Just to get a feel for the place. She lingered over the view from an upper window in the Jefferson Building. A wintry scene, looking out across the Court of Neptune fountain to the Capitol and down the snow-covered Mall, it was pretty enough to make her want to visit Washington some day.

She hit 'close' and signed off with a little sigh. What if it occurred to Ed that the library wouldn't be open this late on a Saturday? She'd just have to bluff her way out of it. She went over to the counter so she could pay what she owed. She could hear somebody in the back office, a man's voice, talking on the phone in Arabic.

She tried to imagine what Ed was doing right now. She

could picture the country mansion, the floodlit lawns, dancing . . . but couldn't see him at all.

'That'll be fifteen.'

The real world drifted back into focus. It was the Moroccan guy, Hassan, the one she couldn't stand, waving his hand in front of her eyes like he was trying to bring her out of a trance. 'Hello?'

'I almost fell asleep waiting.'

'Be fifteen dollars.'

'*What?*'

'You had coffee and Danish, you were online two hours.'

'You are kidding me, right? I didn't even leave work till after five.'

'Fifteen, sugar.'

'Fuck the sugar shit.'

She slammed down ten on the counter, then, seeing he was still giving her the hard stare, grudgingly, another five. Hassan was always dogging on women; but he'd done it to her for the last time.

She presented him with her middle finger and a sweet smile, turned on her heel and stalked out into the heat and traffic of Flatbush Avenue.

There was a mini-mart on the corner and she had to dive in there to get a soda, or die of thirst. Her plan had been to go around to her mama's place after work so she could practise the Schubert piece on her piano for Monday's lesson. Only it was a ten-block hike and she was meeting Tachel at seven – damn nearly that now.

It would have to wait till tomorrow.

She went by the house most days to practise and more often than not stayed to dinner – the lure of her mama's cooking sometimes giving her the extra motivation she needed to keep up her music. Jelly dreamed of one day owning her own piano – not some cheap upright, but a fine old instrument like the Chas M. Stieff baby grand she'd grown up with which had a tone modern pianos couldn't touch.

She walked slowly on, listening to the Andante on her MP3 player, following the score's intricate phrases in her head, knowing exactly when to turn the imaginary pages. It was her fingering that needed work – exercises, scales . . . not playing around on a goddamned computer. She was still mad at herself for blowing the fifteen bucks – half the money she'd set aside to pay Mrs Cato, her piano teacher.

In a roller-coaster mood, Jelly felt light-hearted one moment, down the next. She'd only stopped by the cyber-café to check her e-mail, but then the man had shown up, they got talking and somehow she'd lost track of time. Shit, the whole point of pretending she'd gone away to DC was to give herself a break from the Ed situation, which any fool could see wasn't healthy.

She unplugged her earphones and smiled. She'd spotted Tachel a couple of blocks ahead, standing at the entrance to the subway, trying to keep her distance from some Jamaican kids playing loud dub-mix on the stereo of an old TransAm parked at the kerb. A tall, dark-skinned woman, generously upholstered and proud of it, 'T' had on tight white jeans and a fuchsia halter-top, accentuating a rack that was already like see-what-happens-when-you-pray-for-boobs. She looked sizzling hot.

As she caught up with her friend, Jelly did a little Caribbean dance-hall routine on the sidewalk, laughing and acting crazy. She wasn't sure why but the scene struck her as funny and beautiful.

'What the hell's wrong with you?'

'Just happy to see you, I guess.'

Tachel rolled her eyes. 'What kept you? We're gonna be late for the show.'

'I was playing piano at Mama's, forgot the time.'

It surprised Jelly how easily the lie rolled off her tongue. She'd been friends with Tachel since high school and they could say almost anything to each other. She hadn't gotten around to admitting she was still chatting to the English guy she'd told her about early on, who wouldn't leave her alone, who was becoming more persistent, who wanted to get face to face now in real time – afraid T would laugh at her – but neither of them had ever managed to keep any secret for long.

She knew the best solution would be to delete Ed Lister, just take him off her buddy list. Only she couldn't quite bring herself to do it. She felt sorry for him on account of his tragic loss and, though there was really nothing she wanted from him – Ed had brought up Paris again, hinted at being able to help with her musical career – she enjoyed hearing about his glamorous millionaire life.

She told him she was going to succeed by her own efforts, or not at all.

While they were on, she'd checked out the Hotel Cipriani in Venice. She liked the look of the suites, even if they weren't huge and the site didn't show bathrooms.

Tachel shot her a suspicious glance. 'If I didn't know better, I'd say you were seeing someone.'

Jelly just shook her head, afraid a verbal denial, even though it was the truth, would come out sounding all wrong. T could read her like a book.

'Well, if it ain't love,' her friend observed as they descended into the stifling gloom of the subway, 'then, girl, you need to get laid.'

They could hear the rumble of an approaching train.

'Oh shush.' Jelly, hand on hip, took a last look round above ground. 'It's nothing that a pack of batteries won't fix.'

The Jamaican boys and their rusty TransAm were gone,

rolled up into the sunset that was dragging its gaudy ass like a carnival float down Ocean Boulevard.

'By the way,' Tachel announced as the doors of the Manhattan-bound D hissed open, 'guess who's back in town? Asking about you.'

Paris

15

Sam Metcalf had locked herself into a cubicle in the station washroom so she could be alone. Sitting on the toilet fully clothed, laptop on her knees, she was peering at the image that filled the screen. A classic vacation shot, taken two hours ago in Vienna's Stadtpark, it showed Fern and Balfe Rivers blithely assuming the waltz stance in front of the city's monument to Johann Strauss.

They made an unlikely couple: Balfe, tall, handsome in a hawkeyed, Sam Shepard kind of way; Fern, little and dainty, with a scrunched-up face like a Pekingese. But Sam wasn't looking at her travelling companions, or at the gold-painted statue of the composer chinning a violin under an arch adorned with twirling nymphs. Her attention was riveted by a figure in the background.

Sam slid the cursor over the tour group standing in shade on the far side of the monument and zoomed in on a blurred human form moving away from the edge of the group. It was the furtive stance that had caught her eye. At 200 per cent, the image fragmented into unreadably large pixels; she pulled back to 150, settling for a pointillist effect. A male figure, half hidden by the statue's pedestal, head turned aside, out of focus . . . she couldn't see the face.

Something about him, though, looked familiar.

On their leisurely drive through Northern Italy and into

Austria, Sam had taken tons of photographs, downloading them each evening into files labelled 'Treviso', 'Padua', 'Asolo', 'Graz' – all the places they'd stopped to explore along the route.

She pushed her hair back out of her eyes and clicked on the first album and selected the 'carousel' mode. She didn't have much time. The overnight train to Paris left in thirty-five minutes and the Rivers would already be starting to fuss. But if someone *was* following her, hiding in plain sight – she felt her gut clench and release as the slides flickered past – there was a remote chance that she'd caught him before on camera.

If he really was there at the Stadtpark just two hours ago, it raised the question she didn't want to think about: where was he now?

There had been no specific incident, nothing you could pin down, but ever since arriving in Vienna yesterday Sam had felt tense and ill at ease. Vienna was where she and the Rivers were due to part company – they were driving north through the Alps; she was travelling on to Paris by train.

She had gotten used to being looked after by the earnest, good-hearted American couple. Semi-retired academics, they reminded her a little of her own parents. Balfe had an irritating habit of calling her 'kid' or 'kiddo', but it was a generational thing and she'd been wrong about the louche gleam. He was harmless.

Last night, as a farewell treat, they'd taken her to Mozart's *Don Giovanni* at the State Opera House and, transported by the singing, the sets, the sumptuousness of the production, Sam had had a simple revelation – she really didn't want to go home to the USA. She'd come to Europe to learn about art, and discovered that what was missing from America was the layered understanding they had here of how *life* should be lived – but it was too late now to change her mind.

Supper after the opera was at Landtmann's, which Balfe told her had been a favourite haunt of Sigmund Freud's. Outside the landmark café, Sam checked to make sure there was nobody watching from a parked car, or lurking in the shadow of a doorway across the street. In a heightened state of awareness, she saw the bland, jovial faces of the Viennese as sly or even sinister, felt their eyes everywhere.

She'd left the Toshiba locked in the hotel safe.

'What better place to celebrate our last night,' Balfe said, gallantly holding the door for her, 'with H.L. Metcalf's daughter!'

She managed a weak smile. Her dad was a psychiatrist.

The slow, precise ceremony of dining at Landtmann's, with its marble tables, velvet banquettes and Viennese worthies reading newspapers under the floor-to-ceiling windows, only increased the tension. Fern asked her if anything was wrong, and she nearly burst into tears. She wanted to confide in them about the Florence murder and her fears of being pursued, but she held back. She already felt guilty enough about using the Rivers as a shield, taking advantage of their kindness. When Fern suggested over their *Schlagtorte* and *mélanges* that she and Balfe change their plans and travel on to Paris with her by rail, it seemed to come out of nowhere, and was like an answered prayer.

In the morning, she gratefully let them upgrade her ticket from a couchette to a first-class sleeper so they could stay together.

Sam glanced at the clock on the computer's toolbar. Eight twenty. They would be on board the train by now, fretting. The serial trawl through her photos had produced a couple of possible sightings, nothing definite.

Then she saw him. She halted the carousel at the market square in Asolo. Still no face. But she was pretty sure it was the same guy. Sam stared despairingly at the shadowy figure onscreen a second longer before starting to shut down her laptop.

Under the visor of her hand, she saw the door-handle of her cubicle being slowly turned from outside and felt a wave of nausea rush over her.

She gave a choking cough.

A woman's voice muttered, '*Entschuldigung.*' Sam heard footsteps moving away – she hadn't heard them approach – then the door of another cubicle bang shut, two, maybe three doors along from hers. It was nothing, she told herself, just bad timing.

Fear made her want to pee. She closed the lid of the Toshiba, and tugged down her jeans. The relief she felt was only momentary. There was no escape from her instincts: she knew now she was being followed.

Her first thought was to go to the police. She'd noticed a booth marked *Polizei* in the station's main concourse. But the reality of dealing with blockish Austrian officials, trying to make them understand, daunted Sam. What proof did she have that anyone was stalking her and, even if she was able to persuade them that a couple of fuzzy images amounted to a threat, without a description, what could they do?

Maybe it *was* all in her imagination. She remembered the panic she'd gotten into when she was lost in the *calli* of Venice. Maybe she was flipping out again over nothing. She decided to call Jimmy. He'd texted her at the restaurant later that evening to say he was going down to the Amalfi coast for a few days and would be in touch when he got back. She'd heard since then from a mutual friend in Florence, who'd spoken to him more recently. Jimmy sounded like he was having a good time, he'd reported, a little drunk maybe, but fine . . . he had Chuck Berry's 'You Never Can Tell' going full blast in the background.

Listening to old rock and roll? Jimmy? She'd laughed.

She keyed his cell number. No service.

Sam rode the escalator to the station's upper level, her laptop in a shopping bag securely wedged between her ankles. Rising up through the atrium, she scanned the crowded concourse below, feeling as exposed as if she'd walked out of the washroom naked. A modern concrete and glass structure, the Westbahnhof boasts huge triple-storey windows that let in panoramic views of the city. She realised she could also be seen from the street.

He's here somewhere, she thought, watching.

Ten minutes before the train was due to leave, she made her way back to the entrance to Track 14, where she'd left the Rivers with a porter to handle the baggage and help them find their sleepers.

The blue and white liveried engine of the EuroNight express was standing at the buffers. It gave out a low steady hum as Sam set off on the long hike down the platform. The sleeping-car section of the train curved out beyond the protection of the station roof into the thickening dusk. She measured her progress by the hazy pools of light that fell at intervals from overhead lamps.

Small groups hovered around the last open doors of the ordinary carriages; the platform ahead, except for one or two wagons-lits attendants, was almost deserted. She heard someone moving up fast behind her and had to fight the urge to look over her shoulder.

The running steps fell back and halted. Another train door slammed.

Her heart thumped against her ribcage. If he let her leave

Vienna, she told herself, she would be safe. She thought about Sophie and the way it must have felt when she realised there was no escape.

She wished . . . wished the hell now she'd never got in touch with the girl's father, never got involved. At the sight of a payphone further along the platform, Sam hesitated – her instinct was not to call Ed Lister, not to trust her cell – then she reached for her address book.

She wasn't sure what made her change her mind.

She just knew she had to tell *someone*, and Ed was the only person in the world who would believe her story.

16

The stilted first notes of 'Dreaming' from Robert Schumann's *Kinderszenen* filled the white audition room. I stood by the window looking out over the futuristic, slightly run-down Cité de la Musique campus, hands behind my back.

'*Trop fort, trop fort, pardon.*' Lucas Norbet reached for the dials of the stereo system, and lowered the volume.

'She's never had any formal tuition,' I offered, sounding almost apologetic. 'You can tell . . . she lacks confidence. Nerves. I'm sure you take all that into account.'

'But the opening bars *should* be slow, Monsieur Lister . . . len*tiss*imo!'

He gave me a reassuring smile, then scribbled something in a notebook. Late fifties, blue grapey eyes, a child's flawless skin, he looked with his trademark shock of snow-white hair exactly like a music professor should. As the Schumann began to flow, he leant back in his chair and stared at the ceiling.

For the next half-hour Lucas went through the repertoire, which Jelena had reluctantly let me download from her files. If I'd told her I was planning to share them with the tutor for admissions at the Conservatoire National Supérieur de Musique in Paris, she would almost certainly have refused. But her ambition, her dream, was to study here. I just wanted to open a few doors.

There was a black grand piano in a corner and I imagined Jelena sitting at it, head tilted to one side, long slim-fingered hands moving over the keys. As we listened to her rendition of Scott Joplin's 'Fig Leaf Rag', a huge grin slowly spread across Lucas's face. Somehow hearing her play in the presence of another brought her to life, and I felt my heart swell at his undisguised pleasure.

The last piece on the CD was Beethoven's 'Bagatelle in A Minor', 'Für Elise' and it was obvious from Lucas's expression that he'd had to sit through this particular 'favourite' once too often. A few bars in he paused the track.

'May I ask, Monsieur Lister, what age is your god-daughter?'

'She'll be twenty-six in September.'

'Ah, I feared as much.' He gave a deep theatrical sigh. 'We don't take anyone for piano who's over twenty-two at the start of the school year. Some of the less popular instruments yes, but piano is permanently oversubscribed.'

'I thought I explained,' I said evenly, 'that she was . . . grown-up.'

Lucas shook his head. I couldn't tell whether we'd hit a genuine snag, or if this was a tactical move. The melee of voices and instruments from the practice rooms, a kind of musical Babel, seemed to grow louder and more dazzlingly virtuoso.

'If she has her DFS or equivalent diploma, we do an "improvement" course for mature students up to the age of thirty.'

'She has no qualifications.'

He frowned. 'You know what puzzles me? In New York, you've the Juilliard, the Brooklyn Academy of Music, many other excellent schools. She could get a scholarship. Why does she want to come to Paris?'

I wasn't sure I knew the answer, but I elaborated on the little Jelly had told me about her childhood – growing up poor on Martinique, father never around, being taught to play piano by a grandmother she adored, who encouraged her dream of studying at the best school in the world . . . and so on.

'You say she wants to be a music teacher?'

'She's young enough to be idealistic.'

'*On sait jamais*,' he said, looking at me. 'I heard something there, particularly with the Scott Joplin. She could go further.'

'I would like to help make that possible.'

Lucas got up and removed the CD from the stereo; taking his time, he put it back carefully in its case, then placed it on the desk between us.

'We do, occasionally,' he said at last, 'admit an exceptional student who doesn't fit all the admissions criteria. Usually they are endowed by an institution.'

He kept his gaze on me while he spoke. I'd made Lucas aware of the foundation Laura and I had recently set up in Sophie's memory to give talented but poor artists and musicians the opportunity to develop their skills. I'd also explained to him that there was no connection between the charity and my wish to enable Jelena to fulfil her ambitions – he understood this to be a private matter.

'In your god-daughter's case . . .'

I can't remember exactly how he put it. The French are

past masters at this kind of delicate manoeuvre. A donation to the school's endowment fund, I was given to understand, would secure my 'god-daughter' an interview and formal audition, if not an automatic place. We had a deal, though I don't believe we could have come to an understanding if the girl hadn't had genuine talent.

'The instrumental test before a jury can be gruelling,' he said, I imagine just to cover himself.

I wrote out the cheque (the zeros ran a fair way to the east) and handed it over, stressing the importance of confidentiality – I told Lucas that nobody must know, particularly the girl herself, that she had a benefactor. I asked him, unwisely perhaps, if I could rely on his discretion.

He glanced down and I saw his eyes widen.

'One small detail, Monsieur Lister.' Lucas touched my shoulder as we stood waiting for the lift. 'How are we to make contact with your god-daughter?' He gave an embarrassed smile. 'I don't know . . . her name.'

That made two of us.

'She'll contact you,' I answered, and the doors slid open.

After leaving the Cité de la Musique, speeding along the Avenue Jean-Jaurès in a taxi, I dialled home then almost at once rang off – I'd forgotten it was an hour earlier there and Laura, who likes to keep to her routines, would be out walking Jura, Sophie's old black Lab. I pictured them on the path she always takes up onto the downs behind Greenside.

This was Tuesday, three days after George's party.

In Paris on business – Beauly-Lister has an office in St-Germain where I usually spend a day or two every week – I'd flown over that morning to look at a disused warehouse in the once unfashionable part of town east of the Marais. The views from the upper floors of the warehouse turned out to be disappointing. The agent tried to convince me that overlooking the backs of the railway yards at Bercy or being able to read the number-plates of cars on the Boulevard Périphérique were selling points. I just thanked her and left.

The taxi dropped me off in Montmartre around seven. With time to kill, I went for a stroll in the quiet streets to the north of Sacre-Coeur. The sky had cleared after the rain and the air felt fresh and smelled of lavender and wood smoke.

I was in a reasonable mood, pleased with the way the meeting with Lucas had gone. In a few hours, Jelly was due back .in New York and I was looking forward to 'seeing' her again – so much so I could hardly think of anything else. There was no question of my telling her the good news. But then I really didn't want anything out of this. Just knowing I'd put the wheels in motion was enough.

As I walked down the steeply stepped rue Utrillo, enjoying framed glimpses of the city spread out below, I remembered a corner café that had a genuinely local feel and decided to stop for a bite to eat. I sat down at an outdoor table and ordered a *pression* and the *assiette de charcuterie* with an endive salad. I wanted something light and simple, and to get it over with.

After I'd finished, I lit a cigarette and tried Greenside again. I let the phone ring half a dozen times – it was now eight thirty, Laura was either taking a bath or had gone out to dinner. I was about to hang up, when I got a call-waiting signal.

I clicked over. 'Ed here.'

'There are some things you need to know.'

'Who is this?'

'I don't have much time.'

I felt my chest tighten.

'Hold on.' I had never heard Sam Metcalf's voice before.

There had been no response to the message I left on her mobile, no reply to my last e-mail. Frankly, I'd given up hope of her getting in touch again, but I knew at once it was her.

'Please, don't put me on hold.'

'Only for a second,' I said calmly, 'I'm on the other line. Let me just get rid of this call.'

'No, there isn't *time* . . . listen.'

Rucksack slung over one shoulder, Ward stepped up onto the night express and walked along inside the carriages, bending his head now and then to look out through the windows onto the platform.

He needed to be sure Sam was on board when the train started moving.

He found his couchette in the fourth carriage, glanced in the compartment he had no intention of using, and kept going until he'd almost reached the sleeper section. He could see her now, standing more or less opposite talking on a payphone. In the corridor, he took up position just inside an open carriage door so that he could jump off the train if at the last moment she chose to let it leave without her.

He could tell from her body language that she was still undecided.

Sam glanced up at the station clock. She had three and a half minutes to make Ed Lister understand. She spoke low and fast.

'I'm sorry about Florence. It wasn't safe to meet. I had a phone-call warning me that if I talked to anyone . . . he was watching.'

'Who was?'

'The man who killed your daughter.'

'I see. So why are you talking to me now?' Ed sounded

cautious, almost suspicious. 'What made you decide to change your mind?'

'I know I'm being followed.'

There was a silence. 'Where are you?'

'For the next two minutes, Vienna. Then I'll be on a train, I'm getting the overnight express to Paris. Remember I told you Sophie liked to come round and use my laptop? I think there may be some other stuff on the hard drive that could help the police find her killer . . . I want you to have it.'

'How did you know I was in Paris?'

'I didn't . . .' Sam was taken aback, but the coincidence of his being there felt like a sign her luck was turning. 'It's a miracle, okay? My lucky day, Ed. What the bejesus does it matter?'

'All right, I'll meet you. Tomorrow morning when?'

'Nine forty-eight, Gare de l'Est. I'll try to e-mail you from the train . . . just in case. I have photos somebody needs to see. I think he may be in a couple of them. It's how I found out he's been following me.'

'If you're worried,' Ed said, 'make yourself known to the guard. Did you book a sleeper or couchette?'

'Sleeper. First class,' she shot back, feeling the buzz of imminent departure.

'Lock the door. Try to stay around people.'

'I'm travelling with friends. I'll be okay. My train's about to leave.'

'Sam, wait. You sent me the address of a website. I can't get access without the username and password.'

'Tomorrow,' she said. 'Just please, please be there.'

'*You* be there . . .' She cut him off.

With only a minute left, Sam picked up the shopping bag and started across the platform, then hesitated. If she was right, he was already on board. What if she happened to miss the train? She could leave the laptop in the phone booth and then walk away, just get the hell out of here. There was a chance he wasn't watching. And if he was, she felt sure it was the Toshiba he really wanted.

Along the track she could see Fern Rivers waving at her from the only open door on the train. She was shouting something, but her voice didn't carry over the rising din of the engine.

Sam watched as the uniformed guard, in a slow deliberate gesture, as if he were moving underwater, put the whistle to his lips.

She felt a light touch on her shoulder and spun around.

'Time to go, kid.' Balfe was there, smiling at her.

17

It was almost eight-thirty when I got back to the Place Vendôme. I walked through the lobby of the Ritz Hotel wearing an expression I like to think makes me invisible. The concierge on duty tried to catch my eye, but I kept going and took the lift up to the third floor. I was in a hurry to get to my laptop. The call from Sam Metcalf had left me wishing I'd made more effort to find her before now.

I always stay at the Ritz when I'm in Paris. It would cost less to rent a flat near my office in St-Germain, but I have an arrangement with the hotel that suits me better. Hemingway once wrote that the only reason for *not* staying at the Paris Ritz is if you can't afford it. I doubt he would recognise the joint since it was struck by the Al Fayed wand. The opulence and vulgarity that stalk the hushed mirrored halls are overpowering, but I hardly notice any more. I like grand hotels. It's an indulgence, but one that pays dividends.

I poured myself a stiff whisky and sat down at the desk.

The e-mail from Sam Metcalf was waiting in my inbox – a single line directing me to her webpage. Under a photo of a pretty, plumpish woman in gold-rimmed glasses, blue-eyed with a lot of dark curly hair, there were the usual deliberately vague biographical details, and a link to an image file of 'My Vacation' snaps.

I counted eleven photographs in all, mostly crowded street scenes, taken in different locations. The shots were arranged serially by date and time under the headings of towns. Some featured a dank-looking, middle-aged couple (Americans, going by their clothes). In two images, using a drawing tool, Sam had ringed an indistinct figure in the background. In a third, a shot of a cobbled pedestrian street, she had put a question mark over a blurred shadow in a doorway.

Seeking more definition, I imported the snapshots she'd marked to Adobe Photoshop and played around with the images. There was very little to work with: nothing resembling a face (the head always turned away), no identifying features – it was a man, but height, skin colour, hair, clothing: all were indeterminate. The only possible connection I could see was that in one, *maybe* two photos, the highlighted figure was carrying what looked like a black rucksack or shoulder bag.

I took a sip of Scotch and leant back, reflecting on how little I actually knew about Sam Metcalf. On the phone, her voice had a built-in quaver that I found worrying – it sounded like hysteria was never far below the surface. I didn't doubt her explanation for breaking off contact in Florence. If she had been warned not to talk by Sophie's killer, it was good enough reason to feel afraid. But paranoia has a habit of feeding on itself. If these photos were meant to be evidence that he was now shadowing her through Italy, it wasn't over-whelming.

Reaching for the mouse, I clicked on Sam's photo to enlarge the image, so I could study her face. Hardly a reliable guide, but all that was available to me. I recognised a serious person, sensitive, ardent, smart . . . she didn't *look* crazy.

Yet I wouldn't have bet on Sam Metcalf not turning out to be a flake, one of those lost souls who hunger for attention, thrive on drama for its own sake.

After a quick shower, I got dressed again in a clean shirt, pair of old jeans and loafers. Then I checked my computer in case Jelly had got back from DC early. There was no sign of her yet, but while I was online an envelope fluttered into my tray – I'd received another e-mail from the train.

Ed, hope you got the photos ok . . . There are more, but I haven't had time to upload them. First impressions?

I came across these while tidying my files. The username for *homebeforedark.net.kg* is Boundary7. The password's Levelwhite. Any problems try switching them around and/or alternative spellings.

The train is a dream. After boarding (with seconds to spare) I was served iced champagne! Off to dinner now in the restaurant car. Don't worry, panic attack over. I'll be fine. Looking forward to tomorrow – Gare de l'Est, 9.48 a.m.

Good luck, Samantha

The bright, too-confident tone only confirmed my view of Sam as a neurotic, but at least she'd calmed down. I acknowl-edged her e-mail with a brief reply, then went straight to the *homebeforedark* website. Good luck? She must have meant with accessing the site, but it struck me as an odd way to sign off, in the circumstances.

Waiting for the graphics to load, I felt a growing sense of anticipation. The virtual house was hardly complete (trees, lawn and picket fence materialised first) before I dragged my mouse up the garden path and 'knocked' on the front door.

The box asking for username and password appeared at the bottom of my screen. I typed in the combination Sam had given me and instantly, with a mellow 'evening bells' chime – this felt almost too easy – the dark green door swung back.

On entering the house, the first thing I noticed was that the interior didn't reflect the building's elegant Colonial façade. Behind its airy, white-pillared porch, lay another, less wholesome world. As I walked (whenever I moved the cursor across the floor I heard footsteps, mine) through the dim, unwelcoming lobby into an even gloomier hall stuffed with heavy Victorian furniture, I realised that the layout and décor seemed familiar. Everywhere I looked there were details I recognised from the drawings in Sophie's sketchbook.

So she *had* been here, inside this house. The proof was all around me. I thought about Sophie navigating the website, possibly afraid . . . but afraid of what?

I heard a door slam.

Involuntarily, I glanced up. In the mirror over the desk I could see behind my back the door to my hotel room. It was locked, but the sound had been realistic enough to give a moment's doubt. Onscreen, using the cursor, I wheeled slowly around and saw that the front door of the virtual house had banged shut behind me.

I found myself now in a long dark hallway with closed doors to left and right and a passage crossing it halfway down. Ahead, the far side of a round mahogany hall table, a chandelier hung over an ornately carved staircase that rose to the first floor. I clicked on the doors in turn, but they wouldn't open. I tried to enter the passage, climb the stairs; nothing happened. A light switch turned the chandelier on and off. But that was the only interactive mechanism I could find.

I had no idea what I was looking for, or what to expect. The carefully wrought interior of the house, the attention to detail, the realistic graphics and sound-effects were of a higher quality than most video games. But what was the purpose here?

I poured myself another drink, lit a Gauloise and waited.

Presently I realised I could hear music. Very faint and hesitant, as if somebody was practising the piano in a room at the far end of the house, going over the same notes again and again. I strained to catch the tune, but couldn't make it out.

Then, abruptly, the muffled tinkling ceased and, from nowhere, the figure of a woman appeared at the top of the staircase. Dressed in black, her hair scraped back in a bun, the grim-faced avatar might have been modelled on the housekeeper in Hitchcock's *Rebecca*. As I watched, the virtual 'Mrs Danvers' floated down the stairs and came gliding stiffly towards the hall table. She placed something on a silver salver, then, passing to the right, vanished along the passage.

She had left a card, which, when I clicked on it, generated a pop-up window in the form of an engraved invitation.

your company is requested
at a reception
live webcast
12 midnight

I barely had time to take in the message before the window closed, the dark hallway dissolved and I found myself back on the sunny porch outside the house. I tried 'knocking' again with my cursor, but the dark green front door, its brasses gleaming, remained shut.

What kind of reception, I wondered? Who would I meet there?

The formal invitation sounded harmless enough, but I was aware that 'live webcast' often has an erotic connotation. The nether regions of the Web seethe with party sites that cater for unusual or extreme sexual tastes. A few are creepy, most just silly, all sadly predictable. The idea that Sophie might have been interested in bondage or S&M dungeons seemed to me as far-fetched as it was distasteful. From what I'd seen so far, *homebeforedark* appeared to be about something different.

In her drawings, particularly the interiors, Sophie evoked a sense of menace I hadn't picked up from the website. Fear permeates the house in the sketchbook, and it feels real. The virtual experience was like visiting the set of a creaky old horror film. But that didn't rule out something having happened here to scare her.

I sat staring at the white mansion. I had a long time to wait – assuming the invitation wasn't a trick – before I could get back inside what I felt nearly certain was the domain of the man who killed my daughter.

I got up and went over to the bar to freshen my drink. I was thinking about Jelly, trying to imagine what could be holding her up – she should have been back at her apartment by now – when the phone rang.

The receptionist (I'd asked front desk to screen my calls) told me she had Phil from Secure Solutions on the line. He'd rung earlier when I was out.

'You'll be glad I caught you, Mr L. We have a result.'

'Hold on a second.'

There was music coming from the white house on my screen.

I lowered the phone. As before, it was somebody practising the piano, going over the same notes again and again. I turned up the volume on my laptop speakers and got it this time. A tinkling melody, mournful, sweet, yet with a dark undertow – instantly recognisable as the opening bars of Beethoven's 'Für Elise'.

I felt a little jolt of alarm. 'You believe in coincidence, Phil?'

Earlier that evening, at the Conservatoire, I'd listened to the familiar seesawing motif on Jelly's CD and couldn't get the tune out of my head.

18

Andrea Morelli was standing on the balcony of his hotel room, a towel wrapped around his waist, staring bleakly out over the moonlit Bay of Sorrento. The famously romantic view seemed to mock his affliction, adding insult to the worst injury any man can sustain and expect to live, though no longer as a man. He leaned his elbows on the rail and, pressing both fists to his temples, groaned aloud.

'Come back to bed, *liebchen*,' the girl called from the room. Her name for the moment escaped him. 'I have an idea to try something.'

'In a minute.' He cleared his throat and said, 'Give me a minute.'

His humiliation, he reflected, was as deep as the Mediterranean . . . deeper, it was oceanic. He'd never failed with a woman before, not even his wife.

'Okay, no problem.' It was Gretchen. He'd met her in the hotel bar after returning from the conference in Naples. A beautiful young Czech physiotherapist from Marienbad, she was Morelli's idea of perfection – tall, blonde, well toned, the sports-girl type. And nice with it.

She'd just smiled and told him it couldn't matter less, these things happen . . . which only made him feel worse. Beautiful, warm, willing – it was hardly her fault.

'You need to learn to relax,' she said.

They were on the bed, trying again, Gretchen's idea starting to work, when his mobile rang. Home number. He scrambled up, leaving her with a surprised expression on her face and, holding a finger to his lips, took the phone out onto the balcony. No towel this time.

He might have seen the funny side. Morelli prided himself on his sense of humour, which he knew was a rare commodity among Italian men, but it failed just as miserably as his dick had to rise to the occasion.

Only Maria would choose this of all moments to remind him to buy a birthday present for their youngest daughter. He reassured her, told her he loved her and got off the line. Almost immediately, the phone rang again. He debated whether to take the call. He'd given the detective covering his desk while he was away specific instructions not to disturb him unless it was important.

'Yes, Luca?' he asked wearily.

He listened to what Luca Francobaldi had to report and his spirits sunk even lower. It wasn't his night.

'Maybe he intended eating him,' he said when he heard where the body was found. The younger detective laughed. 'I'm not joking. You speak to the owner yet?'

'We're still trying to find him. He's on holiday in Thailand.'

'Perfect. How long was the body in the fridge?'

114

'Since the weekend. Forensics say the low temperature makes it hard to estimate the exact time of death. They found some blood on the kitchen floor.'

'What about your informant? Think you'll hear from him again?'

'The kid sounded pretty scared. I suspect he may know something about the attempted robbery, so I doubt it.'

Morelli scratched his chest. 'You said there was no ID on the body?'

'None, but I'm about to talk to the neighbours and the woman who cleans the house. There's an American who's supposed to come and feed the cat. The animal was starving. I'll call you back if I get a lead.'

He considered this for a moment, then glanced through the door at Gretchen. She was sitting naked on the bed in a double lotus position, Holy Christ . . . rubbing herself.

'Luca, I'm . . . a little busy right now.'

'You said to keep you informed if there was a crisis.'

'You call this a crisis?' He looked down and saw that his own was over. 'A frozen popsicle in the fridge of a *culattoni-*loving Englishman, Luca, does not constitute a crisis.'

'Okay, okay, sorry to disturb you. Good night.'

Morelli snapped his mobile shut, took a deep breath.

'*Liebchen!*' Gretchen's eyes widened as he entered the room.

'Does the name Jimmy Macchado mean anything?' Phil asked.

'Not offhand.' I tried to think.

The name, any name, seemed like a momentous development.

'He's the subscriber. Domiciled at Sixteen Via Belvedere, Fiesole. The call he made to your mobile last Friday originated in Florence. Since then Jimmy's been on the move. Do you want a list of his calls?'

'I want everything you've got.'

'I thought you might. We got unrestricted access to the network's logging system, but there isn't much. Saturday, he was in Venice. He made three calls that evening to the same mobile. On Sunday he rang the Hotel Marini near Asolo from somewhere in northern Italy. Then Monday, that would be yesterday, he turns up in Vienna . . .'

'The railway station.'

There was a slight pause. 'You're ahead of the game, Mr L. Sleeper reservations office at the Westbahnhof. The call was made at six thirty-nine p.m., local time.'

'Shit.' I closed my eyes. 'Anything else?'

'That was his last showing. Jimmy's been off the air ever since. We tried to reach him. The SIM card's no longer in service.'

'What was the mobile he called in Venice?'

'Hold on . . .' He read out a number I began to recognise halfway through as Sam Metcalf's. 'You want the subscriber's name?'

'It's okay,' I said grimly, 'I already have it.'

A pulse had started to beat in my head. I needed to warn Sam at once, tell her she was right about being followed, and that there was a high probability the man had boarded the EuroNight express in Vienna.

While still talking to Phil, I keyed Sam Metcalf's number on my mobile. An automated voice said her Vodaphone was 'currently switched off'. I brought up Sam's last e-mail onscreen. It was sent at 8.46 p.m., which meant she'd been in the dining car for the last ten minutes or so. She would be safe there. I just hoped she was with others and that they lingered over dinner.

'Phil I have to go. I may need to get back to you.'

'You know where I am.'

I hung up the hotel phone, hit redial on my mobile. This

time I got a 'No Signal' message. The express would be more than likely in the mountains by now.

It was doubtful she'd have internet connection either, but I e-mailed Sam anyway, advising her that the murder suspect – possibly using the name Jimmy Macchado – was on the train. I urged her to contact the attendant or guard immediately and make sure she was never at any time alone.

Then I called the front desk and asked them to get me the Sûreté.

19

Ward waited for the corridor to empty before knocking softly on the door of 21/22. He'd seen Sam leave the compartment five minutes ago when the old couple, all spruced up, came by to take her to dinner. But he needed to be sure: she might've forgotten something, or slipped back for another reason.

He knocked again, this time putting his ear close to the panelling.

'Yes? Who is it?' a female voice answered. '*Que voulez-vous?*'

He jerked his head back sharply. What the hell? Somebody was in there . . . not Sam. He could've sworn he'd overheard the Rivers promise her she wouldn't be sharing. He listened to her stable companion rustling around.

'Just a minute.' She was coming to the door.

He had to think fast. This wasn't in the plan. It had the potential to complicate things. He looked up and down the corridor. Still clear. He could easily make it to the corner without being seen. He hesitated for a half-second.

What do we do now, Ward? It's make-up-your-mind time, buddy.

'Ma'am, I'm sorry to disturb you . . .' The words just came right out. 'This is Balfe Rivers.' He paused, trying not to sound rushed. A wagons-lits attendant had appeared at the far end of the car. Ward kept his back turned. 'My wife and I are travelling with Sam Metcalf. We're dining together in the . . . restaurant.'

There was a click and the door cracked a few inches – a soft hazel eye giving him the once-over – then opened wider and he saw a big blonde girl, clutching the lapels of a black kimono to her chest.

'Okay.' She seemed dazed, as if she'd been napping, but now she caught the look of urgency on his face. 'Is everything all right?'

'Fern, my wife, isn't . . . feeling well.' He tried to affect Balfe's snobby Ivy League drawl. 'Nothing to worry about, Sam is with her . . . she just asked me to get some Tylenol from her bag. We usually carry an ample supply, but we . . . ran out.'

The girl nodded slowly, then, accepting it, broke into a big friendly smile. She was a little heavy but not unattractive.

'No worries. Come on in and help yourself.' She sounded Australian or Kiwi or something. 'I'm Linda, by the way.'

She retreated towards the window to let him enter and share the narrow space. She had a T-shirt on under the kimono and not much else judging from her thick bare legs. He shut the door behind him and quickly glanced around, taking in the twin bunks, the ladder, baggage racks, a mirror on the door leading to the toilet. He kept his hands in his pockets, his rucksack slung over one shoulder.

There was no sign of the Toshiba.

It was possible Sam had taken it with her to the restaurant. He'd only caught a glimpse of her leaving the compartment. But if not, it had to be here somewhere. He noticed the window blind wasn't pulled. He could see the lights of a small town hurrying by behind his and Linda's reflections in the dark glass. Where would she have hidden it? He wanted to ask which bunk was Sam's.

Linda stood, not saying anything, big ass swaying in the window.

'Sam said the medication is in the bag with her laptop.'

'You mean like a plastic shopping bag?' Linda looked puzzled. 'She had the bag with her when she went out.'

'You sure about that?'

'I'm positive.' She frowned. He saw doubt flit across her open good-natured face. 'Shouldn't you be like . . . older?'

'I don't know. Should I be?' He tried on the charm.

What's wrong with you? We need to get this over with, man.

'It's just that she told me she was meeting some friends of her parents . . .' Linda gave a little laugh. 'Would that be you?' But her voice betrayed her.

She tried to sneak her eyes past him, as if he wouldn't notice she was looking for ways of escape. He really didn't have a choice.

It would go fast now. 'You mind if I use the bathroom?'

'*What?* Look, I think you better leave, mate.' She moved towards the door, but he was barring the way. 'Right now. Get out or I'll . . .'

'Maybe I should, ' Ward said, reasonably, as he removed his hands from his pockets. You could hardly tell he was wearing gloves the latex was so fine. He pulled the shower-cap over his hair, checking in the mirror and tucking away stray wisps.

'What on earth are you *doing*? Please leave . . . oh God!'

'I'm sorry.' His arm shot out sideways.

He liked the way that little whimper sounded coming from such a strapping girl: aqua and blue, swimming-pool colours. One hand clamped her mouth, the other her throat. Her kimono fell open.

'I can't leave you like this, Linda.'

20

After nine and still no signal from Sam's mobile.

So far I'd got nowhere with the Paris Sûreté and I felt increasingly worried I wasn't going to be able to persuade the police to take her story seriously. If the killer was already on the train, it was now just a question of time before he found a way to be alone with Sam. Somehow I had to reach her first.

I rang Andrea Morelli in Florence.

A bored-sounding detective from Criminal Investigation informed me that he was out of town until tomorrow. I explained that I was Sophie Lister's father, which met with the telephonic equivalent of a blank stare. Investigator Morelli, he said, was attending a police conference in Naples. He suggested I ring back in the morning.

'I need to speak to him urgently.'

'I'm afraid that won't be possible. The officer who knows the name of the hotel where he's staying . . . has just gone off duty.'

'Then call someone else. His wife must know how to get in touch with him.'

'Ah no, no . . . at this time of night, impossible.'

'What about his mobile?' I said, doing my best to keep calm.

'I'm not authorised to give out the number . . .' He hesitated, and I thought he was about to offer to call Morelli himself. 'There's a chance the *ispettore* will ring in later. If he does I will be sure to tell him.'

It was the same story with the Austrian Bundespolizei. The desk sergeant at their GHQ in Wiener Neustadt listened politely to my concerns for the safety of a passenger on the Vienna–Paris express, but seemed more interested in asking about my connection with the young woman – how was I related to her, what was the nature of the perceived threat, and so on. I realised I had little hope of cutting through the red tape to reach the right people in time.

All the while I kept ringing Sam's mobile. Afraid I might already be too late.

As a last resort, I tried to contact the train direct. An automated helpdesk connected me eventually with a representative of the Austrian Federal Railways, who regretted he could do nothing because the sleeping cars were managed under contract by the Compagnie Internationale des Wagons-Lits. He gave me a number to call, in Paris. I began to dial the twenty-four-hour emergency hotline, but didn't complete – on the last digit I hesitated, then hung up.

Something about this didn't feel right.

Sam's own account and the mobile network evidence had convinced me that she was being followed, yet I had a small niggle that I'd pushed to the back of my mind. The problem was simply that when Sam rang me from the station, she had said nothing about Venice. Why didn't she tell me that after he'd threatened her the killer had been in touch again?

I rang Phil back. He was still at the office.

'I'm on my way out the door. Can it wait?'

'One more piece of information. Those calls Jimmy made to Sam Metcalf's mobile in Venice . . .'

'They were text messages.'

'How far apart?'

'Inside an hour.'

'Did she reply to any of them?'

'All three.'

I took a deep breath and let it out slowly. She had exchanged text messages with the man she believed was stalking her across Europe.

'Check if he *spoke* to her any time last week.'

'I already did. I have the sheet in front of me. Up until the weekend, he was calling her every day.'

'What?' It took a moment to sink in.

'They were calling each other . . . sometimes three, four times a day.'

I had to laugh, mostly with relief. 'I think I've been done.'

It seemed pretty obvious that Sam Metcalf and Jimmy Macchado were friends, possibly more than friends. Which might account for her strange behaviour.

'All right,' I said in a measured tone. 'This changes things . . .'

'Mr Lister?' Phil cut me short. 'You know what? I've been here since before breakfast. I'm off down the pub. Cheers.'

After I hung up the phone, I went over and checked my computer for message alerts then, lighting a cigarette, paced the room. It looked now as though my first instincts about Sam being unreliable were right. More than likely she was running away from some messy domestic situation, pursued by a lover who wouldn't let go rather than the man who murdered my daughter.

I decided that before raising the alarm I needed to have another talk with Sam Metcalf. As far as I was concerned, the pressure was off.

Just then a blue message tab on the taskbar of my laptop started flashing. The second I saw who was trying to reach me, everything else went out of my mind.

21

templedog: I was beginning to think you couldn't make it
adorablejoker: i'm a little late is all . . . the train was late
td: you're here. That's what matters

I said the words 'you're here' out loud as I typed them. Still wound up tight over the whole Sam business, it gave me a sense of release. I felt exhilarated, almost light-headed, I was so pleased to see Jelly. It was as if she'd just walked into the room and lit up the entire damned Ritz.

We hadn't talked since the time at the library in DC and I'd missed her. I'd been looking forward to this moment – counting the days, the hours.

td: you know, I had a dream last night that we met
aj: hmmm . . . and what happened?
td: what do you think? The room spun around, the walls and ceiling vanished, the earth melted away . . . we kissed
aj: hush . . . you know I wouldn't have stood for that kinda nonsense
td: but you did
aj: all right, Mister . . . so let's say we kiss
td: so hard it takes your breath away
aj: okkkayyyy . . . then let's say i have to hold on to you
aj: or i'll fall . . . damn you

I glanced up from the screen of my laptop, which was set out on the repro Louis XVI dressing table, and for an instant saw not my reflection in the gilded mirror but Jelly's. I had to stop myself reaching out my arms to catch her.

You can't recreate the spontaneity, the anticipatory thrill of words appearing on a laptop screen. When I read the above now, an exchange that at the time seemed full of charm, humour, even a kind of empathetic magic, I'm struck only by its banality. The beguiling sizzle of Web 'convos' doesn't survive translation to the cold medium of print. With instant messaging, not being able to see the person you're talking to (neither of us had a cam) adds mystery – it also allows plenty of scope for misunderstanding. Which, as Will warned me, is where the danger of the Net conversation lies: you fill in what's missing with what you want to believe.

aj: it isn't real, ed
td: when you went to Washington, I was afraid I'd lost you
aj: you shouldn't even be thinking like that

But I was thinking like that, and suddenly I understood that the rules of the game had changed. Maybe I was fooling myself, filling in the gaps with what I wanted to believe, but something happened with that virtual kiss that I hadn't reckoned on. I should have seen it coming, should have known in whatever region of my mind this obsession was growing that a line had been crossed.

td: what the hell is happening to me
aj: you'll figure it out
td: just now . . . I couldn't distinguish between being in my head and yours . . . like we were one for a moment. Does that make any sense to you?

She didn't answer. I waited, resisting the urge to type something more. I wanted to hear her say, yes, she felt it too. A pause stretched into a complicated silence. It was as if the distance between us had suddenly grown immense. I must have sensed what she was going to say next.

aj: eddie . . . i have to tell you something you're not gonna like
aj: i have to go
td: you have to GO? You only just got here
aj: wish i had more time to talk. But really i have to go . . . i mean like right now
td: no wait . . . wait, I need to tell *you* something
td: surely you can stay . . . just a little longer . . . hey, come back!

She'd vanished. I reached out in disbelief and touched the screen with my fingertips. How could she just take off like that? How could she do this? I felt a tide of resentment sweep over me. Didn't she realise something extraordinary and quite wonderful had just occured?

What the fuck's the matter with you, I shouted, as one might after somebody who has just walked out of a room, letting the door slam behind them, but really asking the question of myself. What had got into me? How could it possibly make the slightest difference whether I ever 'saw' Jelly again or not?

I slumped in the chair, staring at nothing. The dull ache in the pit of my stomach wouldn't let me consider that there might be an innocent explanation for her sudden departure. I was furious with her, devastated by her leaving, and at the same time I felt embarrassed by the way I'd reacted.

Here's your chance, a voice inside me said, to put an end to this nonsense: hit the delete button, forget her, walk away . . . *while you still can.*

I remembered Will's warning that internet obsessions can

be as powerfully addictive as cocaine use or compulsive gambling. But I knew that wasn't it.

I needed to get some air.

Wandering aimlessly along the Quai des Tuileries, I followed some steps down into an underpass and came out on the waterfront opposite the Musée d'Orsay. It's always a little cooler by the river and I find the old cobblestoned quays, lit at regular intervals by green-shaded lamps fixed to the embankment wall, a peaceful place to walk at night.

I stopped near the Pont des Arts to light a cigarette. Looking upstream to where the Seine divides around the prow of the Île de la Cité, I glimpsed the twin towers of Notre Dame through an arch of the bridge. The over-familiar picture-postcard view struck me as new and somehow different. Patchy swells of music drifted across from the Left Bank and suddenly the city seemed more alive, more full of beauty and interest than I'd ever known it before. When I walked on, I imagined Jelena at my side, her arm in mine, and I was showing her Paris for the first time.

There could be no mistaking these symptoms, yet the spectacle of a middle-aged Englishman mooching along the banks of the Seine obsessed with a young girl he's never laid eyes on, who doesn't in any meaningful way *exist*, escaped my usually keen sense of the absurd.

I tried to dismiss the whole thing as a patch of internal turbulence. Maybe it had to do with losing Sophie, or my decision to hunt down her murderer. But more likely I was just searching for what had gone missing from my marriage. I had to remind myself of the consequences for Laura and our family, everything I'd worked for, if I allowed this ludicrous infatuation to develop. The potential harm it could inflict on all concerned. In my head, I could hear myself sounding like my wise and provident brother-in-law. Only I lacked Dr Calloway's conviction.

On my way back to the hotel, crossing the Jardin du Carrousel in front of the Louvre, I paused for a moment under a street lamp and called Sam Metcalf.

Satisfied now she wasn't in grave danger, just running around Europe playing games with her boyfriend, I needed to be sure our meeting tomorrow morning at the Gare de l'Est was still on. I might have written Sam off as a flake, but her computer remained potentially a vital source of information.

Still no signal from her mobile. Maybe Jimmy had finally caught up with her and they were together now on the Vienna–Paris express, sorting things out over a glass of champagne. I kept walking, and then a minute later tried her number again.

This time, I heard it ringing.

22

'Listen to me!' He spoke low, enunciating the words clearly into the headset mic positioned half an inch from the corner of his mouth. He saw the little green light turn on at the toolbar. The mic had picked up the command that returned the system to recognition mode.

So far, so good. Now for the sound check.

'New paragraph.'

'Greetings,' Ward said, dictating the first thing to come into his head. *'Capitalise that, capitalise Jimmy, exclamation mark, new line, capitalise* hope you can join us for ice cream and cookies to celebrate Linda's *capitalise that* birthday *delete that* funeral on *capitalise* Friday at eleven o'clock *full stop.'*

He followed the blinking insertion point on the screen of his laptop, where after a small delay each word magically appeared. He had the technique down now, speaking naturally in continuous phrases without pausing between words. A train was hardly the ideal acoustic environment for the Talk-master, but it could have been worse, the sleeper could have been right over the wheels.

He smiled at 'funeral' which struck him as pretty funny.

You saw the slate wiped clean, the innocence come back to her face – a flash of how she must have looked as a child – you heard her asking, the way Sophie did, asking for her Mom . . .

Yes, he felt a twinge of regret, sure, but it was . . . unavoidable. He stretched his fingers inside the latex gloves, opening them, closing them.

Still a kid really, in her koala bear panties, Ward.

A sudden lurch of the train rolled one of the dead girl's limbs against his foot. He pulled it back as if he'd been scorched. He hated being stuck with her in this stinking sardine can of a bathroom; it felt now like the air con was on the fritz.

He'd searched every inch of the compartment, and found nothing. Sam must have taken the Toshiba with her. What if she'd given it to the Rivers for safekeeping? Ward knew he was taking a big risk waiting here for her. The situation was all screwed up. A lot of unpredictable factors, a lot of shit that could go wrong.

He sat on the toilet seat with his laptop perched on his knees, trying to figure out the best place to be stationed when Sam got back. He'd managed to drag her friend into the tiny shower cubicle and draw the curtain so he didn't have to look at her eyes, but those big bare legs stuck out from underneath. Something smelled bad.

He wasn't getting pool colours any more.

'*Stop listening!*' he commanded, pausing the hands-free system. He reviewed the trial text, picking up a couple of spelling errors, but nothing serious, no multiple-word misrecognitions, no gobbledygook.

Timing was the real problem.

What if they took too long over dinner? What if Sam didn't come straight back to her compartment? He looked at the screen clock: 21.53. The train would be arriving at Linz in thirty-five minutes. If Sam didn't walk through that door in the next fifteen, he would have to let it go, abort the mission.

Then Linda's sacrifice would have been for nothing.

23

'Say all goes to plan,' Balfe Rivers asked, as he signalled the waiter, 'where do you see yourself five years from now?'

'On a beach?' Sam gave him her innocent look, then broke into a grin. 'Five years . . . I'd have to think about it.'

'What kinda question is that, honey?' Fern said. 'Married with a houseful of rugrats, is that what you want her to say? Sam is going places, she'll end up curating one of our finest museums, you wait.'

'Let her answer.'

Sam thought she had answered the question. But now they were both looking at her expectantly. 'I want to go back to Italy someday. To live.'

'Back to Florence? Frenzy . . .' Fern was a little drunk.

'Yes, Florence.' Sam hesitated. After tomorrow they

wouldn't see each other again. She said simply, 'I left my heart there.'

Fern raised an eyebrow but neither one of them made any comment. The waiter brought the check and the subject of her future was dropped.

'Well, how was dinner, kiddo?' Balfe sat back and rubbed his hands.

Sam had been hungry. She'd chosen the *pâté de campagne*, then *poulet à l'estragon* followed by *tarte tatin*. Standard Paris brasserie fare, but the glamour of the first-class dining car made everything taste better.

'Wonderful, thank you.' She sighed, then shook her head. 'Listen, I want to . . . thank you both for *everything*.'

'The Orient Express,' Fern muttered, 'it sure wasn't.'

'You're more than welcome, Sam.' Balfe smiled at her, ignoring his wife's ungracious remark. 'It's been a delight having you with us.'

'He's going to miss you,' Fern said with a dangerous glint, then after a shade too long added, 'as will I.'

'We happen to be *on* the Orient Express,' Balfe said, 'the direct descendant of the original train that left Paris in eighteen eighty-three. It has a genuine pedigree, unlike the Venice-Simplon, which is just vintage rolling stock restored for the high-end tourist market. This is the real deal.'

'Well, isn't that interesting,' Fern said. 'Are we done here? I'm sure Sam's heard quite enough about the goddamn train.'

'Why don't I order another bottle of rouge?' Balfe suggested. 'Then we can hang out together till we get to Linz.'

'I don't know . . .' Sam glanced at Fern.

'Hey, it's our last night, guys, let's live a little.'

'You two can do what you want.' Fern pushed herself up from the table, the marionette lines around her mouth set in a tight little smile. 'I'm off to bed.'

Sam felt uncomfortable. She wanted to stay in the restaurant car. As long as she was with the Rivers she believed nothing could happen to her, but the last thing she needed was to get mixed up in their marital squabbles.

'I think maybe I should . . . too.' She rose with her.

'You sure?' Balfe looked up at Sam. He was sitting with one arm across the back of the banquette. 'You know, Linz was Adolf Hitler's home town.' He turned over the palm of his hand and smiled.

'For its sins.'

Andrea Morelli was in two minds about whether to wake the girl and escort her back to her room, or let her stay. She lay curled up beside him, snoring lightly, a slim bronzed arm flung across his chest.

The wine had made him drowsy. If he left it much longer he'd fall asleep himself and he didn't really want her around when he woke up in the morning. On the other hand . . . his eye followed the glinting line of white-gold hairs that divided her smooth belly. The investigator sighed.

Why would anyone choose to cram a body into a fridge?

Presumably so that it wouldn't be found for a few days . . . in hot weather, no smell. Or just to keep it fresh. Was this a gay cannibal thing, he wondered, or had Macchado interrupted a crime in progress? He couldn't get over Luca's nerve in calling him again (after being told not to disturb him) with a name that meant nothing. Lucky for him, the little *figlio di puttana*, it hadn't been at a critical moment. But maybe it wasn't all his fault. Ed Lister could be persuasive.

He was too tired now to return Lister's call. What could be so urgent that he needed to speak to him at this time of night? It could surely wait till tomorrow now.

'I need to get some sleep, baby,' he murmured, leaning

over to jog Gretchen's magnificent shoulder. But then he caught her scent, a mixture of new-mown Alpine grass and apples, and thought of a compelling reason to let her stay.

One change of mind prompted another.

He sat up against the pillows, reached for the hotel phone and dialled the number of the Hotel Ritz in Paris. As he asked, in his barely adequate French, for Edward Lister, he had a feeling he would regret both decisions.

'*Merci, monsieur . . . ne quittez pas.*'

The operator came back, told him the line was busy.

Outside the door of 21/22, they stood in the swaying corridor and chatted a while longer. Sam was in no hurry to go inside. The girl she was sharing the sleeper with was friendly but a talker, the kind who insists on telling you their life story.

'I wonder . . . could you and Fern maybe look after this for me?' She was holding the shopping bag that contained her laptop. 'Just for tonight.'

'Be glad to, Sam.' Balfe beamed at her. 'I think it says quite a lot about our friendship . . . I mean the fact that you trust us with such precious cargo.'

They were used to her lugging the computer everywhere, never letting it out of her sight. She'd told them it contained ten years of her art history research, not all of it backed up. Which wasn't far from the truth.

'It's just you hear stories, you know, about robbery on trains.'

Balfe caught her eye and nodded. She had accepted, on Fern's insistence, his offer to escort her back to her compartment. It was time now, she sensed, to call it a night.

Sam was about to hand him the bag when she heard above the clatter of the express the familiar ring of her cell phone. She put the shopping bag down, pulled her cell from her waist band and flipped it open.

She held up a hand to Balfe to wait.

'Ed?' She recognised Ed Lister's number on the screen.

'I've been trying to reach you since . . . the train . . .'

It wasn't a good connection. She thought she heard him ask if she was okay. 'I'm fine,' she answered, 'fine.'

'Somehow I expected you would be. Look, I'm not sure what's going on with you, Sam, but I don't like being messed around.'

'What are you talking about?'

'Whoever called you in Florence and threatened you . . . that is, if you really did receive such a call. He's not the person who . . .'

'You think I invented that?'

'. . .the figure in the snapshots. Can you hear me? They're not the same person.'

'How can you be sure?'

'You should've told me about your friend, Jimmy Macchado.'

'You know Jimmy? Wait, has anything happened to him?'

'Somebody *has* been following you, Sam . . . he may still be following you. He could even be on the train. If I told you it was Jimmy, what would you say?'

'*Jimmy?*' She gave a shout of laughter. 'That is so crazy. Why would Jimmy follow me, for Christ's sake? Anyway, the last time I heard of him he was lying on a beach in Porto Ercole.'

'When was that?'

'I dunno . . . day before yesterday.'

'Sunday. Well, according to my sources, on Sunday, your friend . . .'

But she never heard the rest of the sentence. There was no warning, just an implosive whoosh as the train plunged into a tunnel. The noise in the corridor grew suddenly much louder.

'I didn't get that . . . Hello?' She flattened a hand over her free ear, moving away from Balfe to the window. 'Hello?'

The connection was dead.

Her gaze fixed on the tunnel's safety lights as they rushed by in a continuous white line. She thought about Venice and wondered if Jimmy could possibly . . . no, there was no way. He'd have called first.

Sam felt a light touch on her shoulder and was conscious of Balfe standing right behind her, close enough for her to feel his breath on her neck. She shut her eyes, thinking shit, this is all I need, but saying nothing yet as she gave him another second to take his hand away.

When he didn't, she knew there was a problem.

'The tunnel's eight and a half miles long,' he said.

'It's *what*?' She turned to face him.

'I'm crazy about you, Sam.' He tried clumsily to grab her around the waist, but she stepped back out of reach.

'Jesus, Balfe.' Sam burst out laughing. 'You are kidding, right? You know, this is really really not a good idea.'

'Isn't it?' He was looking at her with shiny, hungering eyes.

'You know it isn't. And nothing's going to happen. So calm down, and let's just forget about it, okay?'

'I'm crazy about you. Have been from the first moment I saw you.'

'No, you're not,' she said firmly. 'All you are is a little frisky.'

She picked up the heavy shopping bag and went over to the door of 21/22. As she worked the card-key, her back turned, she felt apprehensive that Balfe might pounce, try to force his way in behind her.

She needn't have worried.

'What about the laptop, Sam?' he asked. 'Still want me to look after it for you?'

The resignation in his voice made her soften. He looked

134

so pitiful, standing there in his natty bowtie and blazer, she almost relented.

'Nah, that's okay. I guess I'll hang onto it. But thanks anyway.'

'We could always go back to the bar for another glass of wine . . .'

He was sweet, really, just a harmless old guy.

'G'night, Balfe.' She smiled at him.

'Yeah.' He nodded and turned away.

It was strange though, Sam thought, as she cracked open the door, worried now that she'd acted petty and ungrateful, if he had kissed her she wouldn't have minded all that much.

She hesitated, then stepped inside the darkened sleeper.

24

I wasn't thinking clearly when I finally got through to Sam Metcalf from the Jardin du Carrousel. It was reassuring to hear her voice – she sounded all right, in high spirits even – but instead of wasting precious time accusing her of playing games, I should have been asking about Jimmy Macchado.

With hindsight, I regret that I didn't try harder to find out when exactly she had last *spoken* to him. It would have revealed that something was wrong and surely led to my asking Sam whether she thought Jimmy's mobile might have been stolen, and the person following her impersonating him.

I was about to ask when we were cut off.

I sometimes wonder, if I'd caught on sooner, if I'd been more on the ball, perhaps, and not drifting around Paris in some kind of altered state, whether it would have made a difference. It might have gained a little time, I tell myself, but that's about all. I believe the outcome was always inevitable.

When Sam didn't call back, I just assumed it was because she had no interest in continuing our conversation. Walking across the Place Vendôme, I kept dialling her mobile until I reached the doors of the Ritz, then gave up. It was now a few minutes past ten. In less than half an hour, the Vienna–Paris express would be making its first halt at Linz on the German border. I decided to try again then.

As soon as I got back to my hotel room, I checked my laptop. I thought there was a chance Sam might have replied to the e-mail I'd sent earlier when I was trying to reach her urgently, when I was convinced the shadowy figure in the photographs had followed her onto the train. Then I saw the note in my system tray, and who it was from.

> I tried to tell you this before, but couldn't . . . it looks like I won't be online again for a while. Look after yourself, k?
> Jelena

Her status was 'currently offline'. The message had been sent at 21.35, ten minutes after Jelly bailed out of our last conversation and perhaps five after I left the hotel. It was a depressing little wave goodbye, but it explained the abruptness of her earlier departure and confirmed what I'd begun to suspect about Jelly's response to the new situation we found ourselves in.

If she wanted to break things off now, it was probably because she was afraid to face up to her true feelings. I sympathised, I was still busy resisting my own: I also knew she couldn't keep running from them forever.

I tried typing a casual 'see you around' reply, but failed

to get the tone right. A second attempt sounded resentful and angry. I decided to sleep on it, leave the whole thing till morning. Good plan, but not workable.

I messaged her back that we had to talk.

Oh, so the music's too loud for ya is it?

She could hear Lazlo Kaloz, her neighbour in 4B, thumping on the partition wall. Jelly reached for the volume dial, turned it down, and screamed at him to mind his business. Crazy mother*fucker*!

Then cranked it back up. Beyoncé's 'Irreplaceable'.

With a glance at the screen to see if Ed had typed anything more, she went over to open the window, letting in the roar of rush-hour traffic on Lexington Avenue. She lit up a Marlboro, puffed on it nervously a couple of times, then stubbed the cigarette out in the window box.

She felt ashamed about yelling at Lazlo. He was a fruitcake, always talking to himself, carrying on long conversations in different voices, but he meant no harm. And better the crazy you knew . . . Lazlo was a small price to pay for having her own apartment right in the middle of Manhattan, a rent-controlled studio walk-up she'd been lucky enough to inherit from a friend.

She had told Ed she lived out in Brooklyn, just to be on the safe side.

This is hopeless . . . Shaking her head, Jelly came back in the room, naked under the towelling robe hanging open. Her hair was one big mess, she hadn't showered yet and she didn't know what the fuck to do about the Ed situation.

She only knew it was getting out of hand. Why did they need to talk?

God, all they ever did was talk. TALK!

As long as they'd known each other, Jelly had never quite understood what it was he saw in their friendship. It beat the crap out of her why someone like Ed, who could have anything or anyone he wanted, would choose to spend time chatting with a nobody like her . . . on a damned computer. He was beginning to scare her.

What the hell was his problem?

She took a deep breath, sat back down at the desk and started typing.

Sam Metcalf closed the door to the compartment quietly behind her. She could just make out her companion's silhouette in the upper bunk. Mercifully, the girl seemed to be asleep. The last thing she felt like was having to listen to her gab all night.

As her eyes adjusted to the dimness – the overhead cabin and reading lights were off, leaving only the blue nightlight to see by – Sam realised that the lump under the blankets wasn't Linda. It was her whale of a backpack.

A narrow strip of white light appeared under the bathroom door. Or had the light always been on and she simply hadn't noticed? She heard plumbing noises, then the sound of water running.

The girl was in there, taking a shower.

Jeeesus . . . Sam sniffed the air and wrinkled her nose. It occurred to her that Linda could be up and down that ladder all night long.

She threw the shopping bag onto the lower berth. The bedclothes were not the way she had left them. Her first thought was that the girl had been sleeping in *her* bunk, which was not only a little weird but totally unacceptable. Then, as Sam locked the door to the corridor and hit the switch for the overhead lights, she saw something that made her almost cry out in surprise.

Suspended from a fixed coat-hanger on the back of the door was the silk Ferragamo robe she had bought for her ex-lover and then given to Jimmy as a reward for helping her get away from Florence.

Her heart leapt into her throat and, for a split second, even though she knew it made no sense at all, she wondered if it might not be her Federico who had been pursuing her across Europe.

'Jimmy?' Sam asked aloud, hoping.

25

The text of our last conversation was still onscreen, along with Jelly's photograph, and for a while after she'd gone I sat there under her sharp, amused gaze, trying to absorb what she'd just said. It had been a revelation.

I imagined her at home, still at her desk between the windows, the framed print she'd bought at a thrift shop, a Braque still-life of musical instruments (she'd described her Brooklyn apartment to me in detail) hanging on the wall above her head. I looked at her face on the screen and smiled. No, this changed *everything*.

My whole world had been turned upside down.

I kept scrolling back to that moment, as brief and unexpected as a shooting star, when Jelena admitted that I meant more to her than just a friend.

templedog: what you just . . . the loving me part. Did you mean it?
adorablejoker: no, i only said it for my health

I'd laughed out loud when I saw those words.

I tried to mask my true feelings, agreeing with her when she suggested we both needed 'distance', could use a break, should maybe '*take it easy*' (that phrase again) for a while – Jelly couldn't have made herself any clearer – but it made no difference. I was euphoric.

td: I know it's crazy . . . people are not supposed to fall in love like this

aj: you're not listening, Ed . . . i said i'm NOT in love with you

td: it's all right, it's ok . . . I understand

aj: look, let me lay it out for you so there's no confusion. i do love you, but i'm not in love with you . . . and that ain't gonna change

td: I can't explain what's happened to me. I've never felt like this about anyone

aj: do i need to remind you . . . you have a wife and son?

td: it's as if all my life I've been waiting for you

aj: will you stop with that shit! my father walked out on us when I was ten . . . I'm not going to be the reason you do the same to your family

td: you're a good sweet person, Jelly . . . how could I fail to love you

aj: ohhh . . . don't, please don't

It might take a while before she saw things exactly as I saw them. But there was no hurry, we had all the time in the world. I was ready to go along with her inclination to step back and not contact each other for a week or two, because I knew now that deep down she felt the same way.

I wasn't completely blind. Over the moon, maybe, but aware of the risks I was taking. I recognised that anyone looking at my behaviour from the outside might see it as aberrant, delusional, even leading down a dangerous path, but it really didn't feel that way – I wasn't crazy, I was simply in love.

I was considering whether I should e-mail Jelly again – just to let her know I hadn't stopped thinking about her, not for a single moment, since we signed off – when an electronic chime alerted me to incoming mail.

Due to unforseen (sic) circumstances the hour of the
Reception has been brought forward. The show is due to
begin imminently. Please join us.

The stilted, mock-formal announcement was signed 'Ward'.

I hadn't forgotten about the house on the *homebeforedark*
website, or the invitation to a live webcast at midnight. I may
have been distracted by the commotion over Sam Metcalf
and my own inner turmoil, but an ability to cut off, compart-
mentalise, switch from one subject to another with relative
ease has served me well in business and in life. The secret,
I find, is to keep the lines between things clean: I don't like
pictures that bleed into each other.

I'd put the 'Reception' to the back of my mind, but still
had hopes that it could lead to some kind of contact with
Sophie's murderer. There was no *hard* evidence of a link
between the website and the person who killed my daughter.
I knew Sophie had made sketches of the white mansion,
inspired by some vague or perhaps real dread, and then left
the web address on Sam's computer. That much was clear.
But, when I thought about it, I couldn't establish a definite
connection between Sam's first getting in touch with me and
her subsequently claiming that she was threatened, possibly
followed. Or with the coincidence of my being in Paris when
she contacted me again. There was a blurring of the lines, a
shifting of the boundaries between what was real and what
was not that made me uneasy.

Yet I couldn't help feeling, as the invitation to the
'Reception' beckoned, that somehow it *must* all tie together
and that the answers I was seeking were waiting for me inside
the white mansion. Since gaining access to its dismal interior
– apart from the discovery that one of the inhabitants was
an amateur musician, a struggling pianist – I'd really learnt
nothing more.

The difference was that now the website was aware of my existence. It didn't occur to me till later to wonder how the sender of the note knew my e-mail address.

Whoever or whatever 'Ward' was, we were in touch.

I logged on to *homebeforedark.net.kg*.

The site was slower to download than usual; or maybe it just seemed slower because the familiar setting had changed from day to night. The mansion rose up between dark trees, its picket fence and long pillared porch bone-white under the only visible source of light, a patch of stars that twinkled rather too strenuously over the slate roof.

The scene looked peaceful enough and it occurred to me that I might have been wrong about the environs of the virtual house: as a nightscape, certainly, it appeared more rural than suburban. The stillness was broken by the occasional cry of an owl.

I typed in the password, *Levelwhite*, then 'walked' up the garden path and knocked at the front door. It didn't open.

Waiting for something to happen, I wondered what time it was there. The shutters were all closed, the windows behind them dark, giving the impression that the household had retired to bed. The place couldn't have appeared less welcoming. I'd been invited to a reception, a party. Where was everybody?

Then I heard the music. As before, very faint and hesitant. I had to strain to catch the familiar notes, but someone in the house was playing 'Für Elise' on the piano. I knew it was only an effect, but it made the hair stand up on the back of my neck.

The phone began to ring. For a moment, I wasn't sure which one.

In an upstairs window a light came on behind the shutters. I saw a shadow cross the louvred casement as if somebody was going to answer it, then whoever cast the shadow turned and started pacing backwards and forwards in the room.

I snatched up the receiver. It was the hotel switchboard asking if I wanted to speak to Andrea Morelli.

26

Sam stood inside the compartment, listening for the soft patter of the shower to stop. There were other small sounds coming from the bathroom that she preferred not to try to identify. Then, whoever it was in there turned off the water. In case they hadn't heard her the first time, she repeated, louder, 'Jimmy?'

Again, no reply.

More tentatively, she said, 'Linda? You okay?'

Silence, something was wrong.

Sam started to back away slowly towards the door to the corridor, keeping her eyes on the bathroom. As she reached behind her, fumbling for the handle under the folds of the silk robe, she noticed her Toshiba lying on top of the bunk where she'd just thrown it down and hesitated.

There wasn't time.

Her hand found a switch and she cut the overhead lights. A second later she saw the seam of light around the bathroom door go out. Her heart racing, she turned down the handle and pulled. It wouldn't open, she'd engaged the lock.

'Oh Jesus, Mary, God,' Sam breathed. She was still tugging at it frantically when the door to the bathroom opened inwards.

On the threshold stood the figure of a man drenched in blue. His wet clothes made it look as if he'd been painted that colour; but the blueness came from the nightlight in the ceiling and the illuminated screen of a laptop, standing open on the wash-basin behind him, casting a livid glow over everything.

'What are you doing here?' Sam challenged him boldly, trying not to show she was frightened. She couldn't make out a face. He wore dark rimless glasses and a shower cap pulled low over his forehead and ears, held in place by headphones with mini antennae. His eyebrows were taped. He looked like an insect in a track suit.

She knew this could only be Ward.

Her voice shook. 'Where's Linda?'

The feculent smell drew her eye down to the soaked floor of the bathroom behind him. He didn't answer, but took a step forward, and she caught a glimpse of the Australian girl's bare legs sticking out from the shower stall.

Sam started to scream but the sound never left her throat.

As she turned away from him he lunged, throwing an arm around her neck from behind and clamping his other hand over her mouth. The speed and power of his assault overwhelmed her and made resistance pointless. He loosened the choke-hold long enough to tear a strip of silver duct tape from a roll he wore like a bangle on his wrist and seal her mouth, then wrap it a couple of times around her head. His face was an inch from hers, she could feel his warm breath on her ear.

'*Listen to me!*' he commanded. For a moment Sam thought he was talking to her, but then she realised he was speaking into a mic on a boom close to his lips.

'*Open quote capitalise* glad you could make it *comma* FRIEND *upper case exclamation mark close quote.*'

★ ★ ★

'How can I help you, Signor Lister?'

He sounded wearily patient, leaving me in no doubt that by returning my call at this hour he was doing me a favour.

'Thanks for getting back, Andrea. I know it's late, but there's been a development. You remember Sam Metcalf?'

'The girl from Boston who let your daughter use her computer? You were going to meet her and keep me informed.'

'She never showed up.'

'Any idea why?'

'She claims she received a warning. I heard from her again this evening.'

He sighed. 'Go on.'

I quickly told Morelli about the phone call I got from Sam in Vienna before she boarded the overnight train to Paris; how she was convinced that she was being followed by Sophie's killer. I mentioned the photos, then filled him in on the calls to her mobile which I'd had traced to a friend of hers, Jimmy Macchado.

'She could turn out to be just paranoid. In which case, I'm sorry to have bothered you. But I felt I ought to let you know.'

There was silence from the other end.

Morelli said, 'Excuse me one moment.' I heard female laughter in the background, then a muffled exchange and what sounded like a smack. He had cupped his hand over the mouthpiece, but not very effectively.

He came back. 'Signor Lister?'

'I'm still here.'

He cleared his throat and said, 'Jimmy Macchado was found murdered this afternoon in a house near the Piazza Antinori.'

'Jesus Christ,' I breathed. 'When did it happen?'

'Sometime over the weekend. Indications are he's been dead three days. I'm not in Florence, as you know, so I haven't

seen the report yet. It looks like he was killed when he interrupted an art theft.'

'You realise what this means?'

'I know what you're thinking. It doesn't necessarily follow
that whoever killed him also stole his mobile.'

'Perhaps not, but the point is somebody made the calls
from his number. And more than likely that person has been
following Sam Metcalf and is on the train with her now.'

'It's a possibility, but from here . . . there's not a lot I
can do.'

'Listen to me,' I said as calmly as I could. 'This girl has
information about whoever murdered my daughter. If he is
on the train, then he's going to kill her too. The Vienna–Paris
express stops at Linz in eleven minutes. What you can do is
contact the Austrian police now and get them to meet the
damned train.'

'I'm afraid, Signor Lister, it's not so simple.'

'Then bloody well make it simple,' I shouted.

'There are certain protocols . . . there isn't time.'

'If you do nothing, Andrea, another innocent young
woman with all her life before her will die. It's still your
case, isn't it?'

Even before I put the phone down, I started keying Sam's
number on my mobile. I could hear it ringing, but there was
no answer. I kept trying, hitting redial every thirty seconds.
My hands sweaty, shaking.

I was so tense I failed to notice there'd been a development
onscreen. What got my attention was the music; as if announc-
ing a dramatic event, the tinkling reprise of 'Für Elise'
suddenly grew louder, more insistent.

I looked up at the house. The shutters with the light behind
them swung back and, like an advent calendar, revealed a
man and woman standing at the upstairs window, locked in
what appeared to be a passionate embrace.

146

The silhouetted couple twirled slowly. I couldn't make out many details. From certain angles it looked as if they were kissing; from others, as if the woman was resisting, trying to get away.

Then, at the bottom left-hand corner of the screen, a dialogue box opened and a prompt advised that 'Ward' was typing a message.

m: glad you good make it, FREND
m: jest in time four the show . . . all live, all action
m: stay tuned, and taste the realty . . .

'Who are you?' I tried typing back, but there was no space available for a reply. It was a one-way conversation.

27

In the mirror above the wash-basin, darkly entwined, they looked like one person. Ward stood with his feet planted apart, shoulders braced against the top bunk to counter the swaying motion of the train. Sam couldn't move unless he did. Almost a foot taller, he held her tightly between his thighs with one arm around her neck and the other wrapped around her chest, pinning her arms to her sides. When he spoke (in that hoarse cadenced whisper she heard first in Florence), she felt the rise and fall of his diaphragm against her upper back. They faced the open bathroom door, Ward talking into the mic and following his utterances as they appeared after a brief delay on the screen of his laptop.

He seemed totally engrossed, not taking any notice of her.

In her terror, barely able to think, Sam knew she had to find some way to attract attention. The steward had removed her and Linda's passports so they wouldn't be disturbed in the middle of the night – he wasn't coming back, but if she could just reach the bell he'd said to use in case they needed anything.

She tried to recall its exact position on the wall above the bed; it was by the light switch. But she needed to be sure. She remembered groping for the door-handle, the silky folds of the robe she'd given Jimmy getting in the way . . . oh God, no.

A stifled sob of despair brought a flux of vomit up into her mouth. It had just struck her: Ward must have killed him too. The spew swilled against the back of her teeth and met the duct-tape barrier. Afraid of choking, she swallowed, siphoning air through her nose in panicky little snorts.

She felt Ward's hold on her neck relax, then tighten again.

Her breathing returned to normal, or near enough. She wanted to cry but then her nose would run and block her sinuses. Jimmy wouldn't have stood a chance. He only thought the best of people. Fighting back tears, knowing she should never have involved him, Sam felt a surge of anger. She was damned if she'd let this sick fuck do the same to her. She was going to get out of here, beat the odds, survive.

The train would be arriving at Linz any moment now. She just had to hang on a little longer.

'*Open quote* I want you to imagine *comma close quote*,' Ward said into the mic in a flat emotionless monotone, '*open quote* that your hands are my hands *comma* as I undress her *comma* unhooking her bra and *new line* releasing those big playful puppies *comma new line* sliding her panties over her hips *dot dot dot* damn *comma* but she's hot *exclamation mark close quote*.'

He paused and sucked his teeth.

Dislodged in the struggle, Sam's glasses were still hanging from one ear; if she tilted her head, she found she could read the text on the screen of Ward's laptop. She realised he was using voice recognition software – with limited success judging from the mangled phrases that scudded across the page – but she had no idea why, or for whose benefit he was recording this garbage, or where it was heading.

He cleared his throat and continued in the same dull tone,

'*Open quote* lower my mouth to her tits *comma* teasing the nipples *new line* mmmmm yes *comma* kneeling before her *comma new line* pressing my face into her wet kitty *new line* breathing in that musky scent *new line* oh god *dot dot dot* I don't know how long I can hold it *new paragraph open quote.*'

'*Capitalise* hard yet *comma* good buddy *question mark close quote.*'

What if this were a prelude to rape, Sam thought? It would at least buy her some time. But as she listened and watched, waiting for the ordeal to begin, she realised it wasn't going to happen. The lewd descriptions her attacker was dictating to his laptop didn't match what he was doing. Ward wasn't touching her in any sexual way. He wasn't aroused. It was just talk.

She didn't know whether to allow herself to hope, or prepare for the worst.

'*Stop listening!*' he said.

When he spoke again close to her ear, addressing her for the first time, the words did not appear on the screen.

'You wouldn't listen, Sam,' he said softly. 'I can appreciate your wanting to help Sophie, see justice done. But this isn't what it seems. I warned you not to go stirring up the past. You just wouldn't listen.'

Sam made a gagging sound, rolling her eyes and jerking

her head sideways towards the bunk where her Toshiba lay in the shopping bag.

He was watching her in the mirror.

'I know, honey,' he said, 'I know what you're trying to say. We've become close these last few days, haven't we? Friends almost. Believe me, I'd love to just take the damned thing and leave, but we're too far down the road now for turning back.'

He lifted the end of the sentence into a question.

Sam shook her head violently, made incoherent pleading noises for him to remove the gag and let her speak. He didn't react. She felt the vibration of her cell phone again against her hip and wondered if Ward had felt it too through her bones.

'Sam, I'll let you in on a little secret . . . I truly loved her. Does that surprise you? You have any idea what it's like to love someone? Her daddy can take some credit for bringing us together. But, you know, I do believe we were always intended.'

As the train leaned into a curve, the driver braked suddenly and then accelerated, throwing them off balance. Ward reached out to steady himself and for a second let go her arms. Long enough for Sam to tug her cell from her belt and press Talk.

She barely got the phone up to her taped mouth before he caught her wrist and prised it from her fingers, sending her last link to the world spinning to the floor.

She screamed. Inside her head it sounded more like a high-pitched moan. Please God, she prayed, let someone hear me.

He crashed a latex-gloved fist into her face.

Sam fell sideways onto her bunk. Her glasses came off and a gush of hot blood flooded her nose. Ward grabbed a handful of her thick hair and dragged her spluttering back up onto her feet.

She fought him, trying to get a knee to his groin, stamping

down on his foot with a kitten heel, scrabbling at his hands as they closed around her throat. He didn't flinch, but steadily pushed his thumbs deeper into the soft hollow of her trachea. She looked up at Ward's face, her frantic eyes beseeching him now, but saw only the twin blue squares reflected in his glasses. The tiny cursors blinking.

He was back in front of his laptop screen.

'*Listen to me . . .*'

I came and went from my desk, unable to stay still, my heart thumping in my chest. I was getting an intermittent signal from Sam's number, but no answer. The only hope was that she'd gone back to the restaurant car, or maybe the bar for a nightcap, and left her mobile in the sleeper compartment.

All the while I kept a watchful eye on the white house.

The reception I'd been invited to attend hadn't materialised. Not that I knew what to expect. There was nothing 'live' about the webcast. I was aware of Ward as a controlling presence at the other end of the terminal, but all the signs pointed to the show having been pre-recorded. By now I was too worried about Sam to care.

The misspelled obscenities read like dispatches from an adult chat room and barely held my attention. But the familiar, insinuating way Ward spoke to us (I assumed there were other viewers), the 'my hands are your hands' business, gave me an unpleasant feeling.

It never crossed my mind that he was speaking to a computer, or I might have guessed sooner what was really going on. I just thought the clumsy mistakes were deliberate, as if he wanted to make the subtitles for the shadow-play in the upstairs window sound authentic and urgent.

The silhouetted avatars were now engaged in lovemaking explicit enough to give spectators the frisson of virtual voyeurism. As the commentary turned into dialogue, I got the inescapable feeling from the action onscreen that something terrible was about to happen.

k: oh god, help me
k: i'm almost there
m: pushing back the hood and flicking the little pink pearl fast and hard so it feels like . . . the rush of fluttering wings
k: oh my god
k: i'm almost THERE . . . starting to tighten
m: rolling you over so now I'm on top
k: please just . . . DO IT TO ME
m: fuckkkkkkkkkkkkkkkkkkkinggg bitch i let go now and fuck you with all i've got . . . pounding into you . . . biting your tits, neck, ear . . . wild as a fox
k: oh god just a little more
m: slip my hands around your neck
m: you . . . *like* that, you little slut?
k: oh god . . . oh my god yes
m: *she's got the GLOW on her . . . eyes shut, rosy mouth hanging open, nostrils flared . . . hasn't a clue what's coming next*
m: feel my hands around your neck start to tighten . . .

I jumped up and walked away from the desk, my mobile clamped to my ear – Sam's number was ringing. I willed her to answer, but while I concentrated on the sound, faint and drowning in static, I couldn't take my eyes off the screen.

I lost the connection and hit redial.

I came back, sat down heavily in my chair and lit a cigarette. I tried to reassure myself that what I was watching was just fantasy, a game of make-believe – that it wasn't real. But the dialogue had left the comparatively innocent actions of the couple in the window far behind. I followed the subtitles onto the screen with growing revulsion and then horror because suddenly I knew that the words represented what was happening now, live, right in front of my eyes.

It was as if to read was to become complicit in the act.

Sam's number started ringing again.

Come on, pick up, I said aloud, you *must* pick up.

m: i want to see your face, look at me

m: you dare turn away . . . look at me, bitch

k: what are you *doing* . . . no, don't . . . your hurting!

m: *her sift white neck, mmmm, oh boy, lak a swans . . . I tell ya she is dee licious . . . ya smeel the **feer** in her? you kin jest tastc it . . .*

m: pressing my thumbs into your throat . . . lok in my eyes

k: please stop . . . no, I can't breathe

m: the gates of heaven . . . open . . . *taste* . . . words with an iron shape

k: NO, PLEASE . . . JESUS! WHAT ARE YOU DOING . . . **DON'T**

Sam's mobile answered.

Under the pounding and clatter of the express I heard the elusive sounds of a struggle, punctuated by a muffled whinnying squeal that sent shivers through me. I was too late.

There was a sharp thud, more scuffling, and then a dreadful sucking gurgling noise like a dentist's aspirator drawing off saliva, after which everything went quiet.

He was strangling her, strangling her to death.

I started yelling into the phone . . . I don't even know what I said, or if anyone heard me. I felt as if something precious was slipping from my grasp and nothing I could do was going to stop it hitting the floor and smashing into a thousand pieces.

I was still yelling after we were cut off. I remember thinking this is what it must have been like for Sophie.

The hotel phone rang. Morelli didn't identify himself, he just said the Austrian police would be boarding the train at Linz in two minutes. I was almost certain of what they'd find, but I couldn't tell him.

I kept hoping they might get there in time.

★　　★　　★

153

Her vision became blurred before she started to black out. Sam imagined she could feel the train slowing down. Saw the street lights of a town flicker by behind the blind at lengthening intervals, as if they were stopping, coming into a station.

Then realised it was only the darkness steadily gaining.

In the last moments of consciousness, she retrieved an eidetic memory of childhood, a colour-saturated snapshot of herself, Samantha, aged seven, standing between her parents on the sunny veranda of their vacation home near Lake Michigan . . . Mister Bluebird on her shoulder . . . everything satisfactual.

Absolutely sure this is the freest moment.

I glanced at the screen and saw the woman give her lover a tender kiss before withdrawing from the window. The man lingered, leaning out over the sill and looking up at the night sky, as if admiring the stars, then with a lifelike yawn he closed the shutters. The party was over.

A few moments later the light in the bedroom went out.

Softly, the piano (having fallen silent earlier) struck up again, this time playing the accompaniment to Brahms' 'Lullaby', a female voice singing in the original German, '*Guten Abend, Gute Nacht . . .*'

The front door of the darkened house swung open.

I moved my cursor into the entrance, double-clicked and instantly found myself in the parlour with the two armchairs in front of the cabinet TV that Sophie had drawn in her sketchbook. Only here the little screen was live and, instead of the love scene from *Breakfast at Tiffany's*, showed the interior of a sleeping car.

I watched in fascinated horror as the jumpy, grainy picture drifted in and out of focus while the video camera panned down from the top to the lower bunk. Then, as the second

154

half of the haunting lullaby filled the room, the cam pulled slowly back to reveal Sam's body sprawled on the floor of the compartment.

She was fully clothed, just as Sophie had been, lying with her head resting on her shoulder, one bare arm extended towards the window. It looked as if she'd been trying to reach her mobile, which lay under the ladder to the upper berth only inches from her outstretched fingers.

'*Morgen früh, wenn Gott will, Wirst du wieder geweckt.*'

The grotesque irony of the lyric was no doubt intentional. 'Tomorrow morning, if God is willing, you will wake again . . .' The angelic voice dipped and soared while the cam closed in on a glazed eye, the protruding tongue, then cut to a dark stain on Sam's dress. I turned away.

It was then I noticed that there was somebody in the parlour watching TV.

The only light came from the flickering screen, but it was enough to show that one of the chairs was occupied. All I could see was the back of the viewer's head and his hand on the armrest. I realised with a dazed, sickened feeling that the figure was meant to be me – sitting there, enjoying the show.

I tried to move forward but the cursor wouldn't let me. Then, as if he'd seen enough, 'Ed Lister' aimed the remote at the cabinet and switched off the TV.

My laptop screen faded to black.

28

Ward took a last look around the compartment as the night express, with a long sigh of the brakes, pulled into Linz station. He'd already tidied up, retrieved Sam's cell phone, stuffed her shoes (one of the heels had scraped his shin) along with his laptop and headset into his rucksack, then dragged her body into the bathroom. He'd had to heave it on top of Linda's before he could shut the door.

He picked up the Toshiba. He only had seconds to make up his mind.

He could slip out into the corridor, walk back along the train to the couchettes and join everyone else getting off here. The risk was someone might notice him leave the compartment, and then the CCTV cameras on the platform . . .

Or else, go out the window. It opened inwards from the top, creating an eleven-inch gap. Tight, but not impossible. He'd already checked the angles. The express was coming into the platform on the starboard side; he could see that the sleeper cars would end up overlooking the tracks out beyond the main station. He assessed the risk of sprain or injury . . . the drop was a good twelve feet.

He had the rope. If he could just get that damned tune off his brain.

He chose the window.

Ward never understood what people saw in music. The lullaby had left him with a raw, savage feeling inside . . . pale-green needles line-dancing on the cylinder of blue glass that revolved slowly inside his head. Music did things to him;

even the sweetest melodies could tear up his head with jagged shards, blinding white, sometimes red. The food of love made him want to throw up.

But he knew how to . . . hell, he could imagine the impact the soundtrack must have had on his audience. He smiled as he pulled on a pair of leather gloves over the latex ones. But there wasn't time to think about that now.

Ward lowered his rucksack and the shopping bag containing the Toshiba first. The other end of the half-inch nylon rope was tied to the middle rung of the aluminium ladder, which he'd jammed under the window. He climbed up onto the table and, with the grace of an acrobat, posted himself head-first through the opening.

The night air tasted yellow.

Outside the train, facing downwards, he descended hand over hand by the rope until his feet were clear of the window, then flipped his legs over his head in a neat somersault. But didn't complete.

Instead of abseiling to the ground, Ward pulled himself back up the rope and, clinging to the window frame, untied the hitch from the ladder; the rope slipped away between his knees, the ladder fell back inside the sleeper. As he hung there a moment longer, trying to close the hinged part of the window with his free hand, he heard knocking at the door of the compartment.

A woman's voice said, '*Polizei. Machen Sie bitte auf.*'

Ward let go and dropped straight to the track. Ed Lister must have been working the phones, his money doing the talking. He'd got out just in time.

He landed awkwardly catching his ankle bone on a timber railway tie. A sharp pain shot up his left leg, but when he stood and put weight on it the ankle didn't give way. As far as he could tell he hadn't broken or twisted anything. He didn't bother to coil the rope or detach it from the bags. Just bundled everything together under an arm and, keeping his head low, started to walk fast alongside the train.

Ahead the broad swathe of silver track and overhead cable ran through a built-up section with houses on either side. He hadn't reckoned on the station being so close to the centre of town. An area of darkness lay out beyond the front carriages.

Too far to risk without cover.

At the first gap between the carriages, Ward hunkered down and crawled forward under the coupling gear so that he could look through to the other side of the train. The end of the platform was thirty or forty yards back, but right across from where he crouched he could see some freight-cars standing in an unlit siding.

He heard a commotion in the carriage behind him; a deep-voiced man was shouting orders in German – they must have found the bodies. It wouldn't be long now before they were down on the track with dogs, searching for him. As he weighed his chances of reaching the siding without being seen, a storm of sirens and flashing blue dome lights announced the arrival of reinforcements.

Ward looked at his watch. From the train he'd called 'Willy's Reisen', a taxi company he'd found on the internet, and arranged for a cab to meet him on Klosterstrasse in fifteen minutes. He could still make it if his ankle held.

Then he saw the searchlight coming towards him. Dazzled by the beam, it took Ward a moment to realise it wasn't part of the police operation. The light was on the front of a through-train hurtling down the track on the south side of the station.

He crawled out from under the coupling and stood up. The pain in his ankle rose to another level, the adrenaline boost worn off by now. Relying on instinct to judge speed and distance, and which set of rails the train was on, Ward darted away from the shadow of the stationary express.

He could hear shouting as he ran towards the light. Hurling himself into the warm buffer of air a few yards ahead of the engine, he felt the shining rails tremble under his feet before the enormous noise of the train engulfed him.

He fell into the arms of the night, tumbling over and over until he found himself on his back looking up at the deep blue-black sky, safely through to the other side. The long goods train, still running, would give him time to seek shelter. A few stars were showing, their little fat faces, terrifyingly plump, watching him as he picked himself up and limped towards the deserted platform.

He needed to find someplace quiet where he could settle down to work on the Toshiba. Now that the laptop was in his hands, no one was ever going to find him. He thought about Ed Lister in Paris and couldn't help smiling, shaking his head at the nerve of the guy . . . *all my life I've been waiting for you*. Sounds familiar, Ed. It was up to him to make sure 'Templedog' didn't get away with it this time.

Ward already had the name and address of the girl in New York.

PART TWO

London

29

I used to know her mobile number by heart. It faded quite a few months ago, yet even now I can't bring myself to take it off my speed-dial or any of my address books. I read somewhere that it's not healthy to hold on to these empty reminders, but I like seeing her name every time I bring up the contact list on my computer.

I find the link a comfort, like keeping a candle burning.

All morning my head had been full of thoughts of Sophie. It wasn't just knowing that I'd be talking to the police later about Sam's murder and that Sophie's case was bound to come up; a host of little things kept reminding me of her. I kept seeing an image of her as a child – I'm not sure that it was a genuine memory – standing outside in the dark throwing pebbles up at the window to attract my attention.

Sometimes I 'feel' Sophie the way an amputee feels the familiar shape and weight of a phantom limb, but this was different – almost as if she were making her presence felt deliberately, at a critical moment.

'You said she was being strangled.'

'How did you know?' the other one asked.

'I didn't . . . it's what it sounded like over the phone. I could hear her choking.'

'Let me get this straight. You heard choking, then she grew quiet. Do you remember what time it was?'

I took a sip of coffee. My hand shook a little, enough for the cup to rattle when I put it back down on the saucer. 'Ten fifteen. I know because I was counting the minutes before the train was due to arrive at the station.'

There were three of them – Chief Inspector Edith Cowper, Andrea Morelli and Detective Constable Daniel Ince from the National High Tech Crime Unit. We were in the conference room of my offices on Tite Street. They sat like a tribunal on one side of the mahogany conference table; I faced them on the other.

'Investigator?' Cowper turned to Morelli, creased, unshaven, heavy-eyed from lack of sleep; the strain of the past thirty-six hours showed in his unusually subdued manner. He had flown over from Linz that morning.

'Both women were strangled.' Morelli cleared his throat and, looking down at a piece of paper on the table, read aloud, '" . . . deep bruising either side of the voice box, well-marked signs of asphyxia in the lungs and over the heart. Scratches on the neck probably made by the victim as she tried to loosen her attacker's hands."

'The autopsy notes for Linda Jack, the occupant of the upper berth in the cabin, are almost identical to Sam Metcalf's. No evidence of sexual assault . . . in either case.'

I shifted in my chair. The explicit language of the webcast had more or less convinced me that Sam was raped. I wanted to ask Morelli to elaborate, but this wasn't the moment. We exchanged a glance and he went on. 'According to the coroner's pathologist, Sam died between ten and ten twenty.'

'Which would seem to support Mr Lister's statement.' Cowper smiled, let it fade.

She was in control here, doing most of the talking. A thin snip of a woman, ash-blonde, about my age, Edith Cowper of the Wiltshire Constabulary was the senior police officer in the UK with a continuing interest in my daughter's murder. She wasn't heading a new investigation; Cowper had been instructed to look into my allegations of police negligence against the Met – an appeal for justice which hadn't won me many friends at Scotland Yard.

'Do you think you could have misinterpreted the sounds you described?'

I wasn't sure where this was leading, but there was a hostile edge to Cowper's questions which I did my best to ignore. 'I can only tell you what I heard.'

'The sounds of a struggle? Choking?'

I nodded. There was a silence.

'Did he leave any evidence this time?' I asked, wanting to bring the focus back where it belonged, on the murderer.

'They're still searching for identifiers.' Morelli made a steeple of his fingers. 'It's unlikely he left no trace. Every criminal, Signor Lister, leaves something of himself and takes something with him from the scene of the crime.'

'I seem to remember hearing that one before,' I murmured.

'If you don't mind, sir,' Cowper said crisply, 'We'll ask the questions. How did you come to know Jimmy Macchado?'

'I didn't. I already told you. Somebody using his mobile rang me in Florence. I found out it was his phone because I had the number traced.'

'Is that something you do routinely, Mr Lister? Have people's numbers traced?'

'I got an anonymous call. I thought there might have been some connection with Sophie.'

'You never had any contact with Macchado when you were in Florence?'

'No. The caller said he had a wrong number. I'm fairly certain now it was the person who murdered my daughter.'

'Any idea how this person knew your number?'

'None whatsoever.'

'You gave your mobile number to Sam Metcalf.'

'That's correct.'

'Not your e-mail address?'

I shook my head, no.

It was starting to feel like an interrogation.

In Paris, still not certain that Sam was dead, I'd sat up most of the night with a bottle of Scotch, waiting for the phone to ring. I kept going back over our last conversation. I could hear her voice, breathless, straining to be heard above the din of the train, her whoop of laughter at my suggestion that Jimmy was following her – she'd sounded lively and relaxed, happy even. If we hadn't been cut off then, I told myself, things might have turned out differently.

Around three thirty a.m. I got word from Andrea Morelli confirming that the events I'd witnessed remotely had really happened. I could give up hoping that the webcast had been a game, a sick fantasy. It was almost a relief.

Later, on the way out to the airport, numb and exhausted, I made a detour by the Gare de l'Est. I had the driver wait outside the north entrance, while I walked through the ticketing hall into the main concourse. Sam's train was still on the arrivals board – under the automated display I saw the special announcement.

Information Voyageurs: Suite à une présomption d'accident de personne à Linz le train 262, Orient Express Rapide 1er, Arrivée: 9h 48, Venant de: WIEN MUNCHEN STRASBOURG, Voie: 24 est annoncé avec du retard indéfini.'

It was the name Linz and the circumspect phrase 'indefinite delay' that made it final. I went over to Track 24 and stood looking at the empty platform, the concrete buffers, the weeds growing up between the gleaming rails . . . I hung my head.

The image of her body sprawled on the floor of the sleeper came back. Sam had died trying to bring me information about the man who killed my daughter, and I'd doubted her. Lost precious time thinking she was lying or playing games.

I knew deep down I could have done more to save her.

The story of a double murder on the EuroNight express was already breaking on CNN and Fox as I left Paris.

Two hours later, stuck in traffic on the way in from Heathrow, I rang my office and discovered the police had been trying to get in touch. I returned Edith Cowper's call from the car. When she'd finished with me, I took a few moments to think things over. Then I got on the phone to Phil at Secure Solutions.

'You want to be careful, Mr Lister,' Phil said, after listening to my account of the night's events. 'They could decide to make life difficult for you. Wouldn't say too much about live webcasts, if I were you.'

'Cowper's bringing a computer and internet crime expert, a man called Ince.'

'That's a joke. I know Dan Ince. Ginger-haired prat from Dulwich, he couldn't find bleeding Viagra on the Net. From your description, whoever's behind the snuff-house site has advanced hacking and programming skills. You need someone who can play the game at his level, an adversary.'

'You think the police can't handle this?'

'After the cock-up the Met made of your daughter's case? You're asking me?'

I didn't comment.

'You've been given another chance here, you don't want to waste it.'

'What if they ask to look at my laptop?'

I'd told Phil that I'd managed to save the text of the webcast and thought there might be other information stored on my laptop which could help trace Ward.

'We need to move fast or he'll vanish again. Sooner you get the machine into the right hands, the better. Not that I'm advising you to withhold evidence, Mr L.'

'Of course not. You have somebody in mind?' I thought he was going to offer his company's services, which would have been understandable. We already had a working relationship. 'Somebody I can trust.'

He didn't hesitate. 'Campbell Armour. He's not one of ours, but he's clever, straight, and probably the fastest gun for hire in the business.'

'So why isn't he working for you?'

'I tried to recruit him after he did a security review and another internal job for us, both highly sensitive. Didn't want to know. He's the young maverick type, but if anyone can smoke this creep out, he will.'

'Where's he based?'

'Only drawback. Tampa, Florida.'

I felt that could be an advantage. 'Anything else?'

'I'll send you his CV. He's a naturalised American, from Hong Kong originally, Scottish-Chinese background – grandfather worked for Jardine and Mathieson, married the housekeeper and stayed on. His parents came over to London in eighty-nine after Tiananmen Square, opened a restaurant in Wapping, then emigrated to San Bernardino in Southern California. Campbell won a scholarship to Stanford at sixteen, and it goes on from there summa cum laude all the way.

'One flaw. He likes to gamble, or used to. Narrowed his options for a while, but he seems to have got the problem under control. He chooses the client, by the way, not the other way around. He can be an arrogant little sod.'

'What do I have to do to qualify?'

'Don't worry, I had a quiet word. Told him what happened to your daughter. He's interested, and he's got some ideas . . .'

'You already spoke to him? When, for Christ's sake?'

'The moment I heard the girl on the train didn't make it. I knew you'd be in a hole, Mr L, so I took the liberty. What time's your meeting with the Old Bill? I'll make sure you talk to Campbell first.'

'What took you to Paris?' Edith Cowper asked.

'Business. I have an office there.'

'So you just happened to be in town when Sam called?'

I nodded.

'Do you usually stay at the Ritz?'

'I don't see how any of this is relevant, but yes.'

'When she called you from Vienna, were you surprised to hear from the victim again? After the way she stood you up before?'

'I accepted her explanation for what happened . . . she was afraid.'

'Didn't she tell you she was *still* afraid?'

'She thought she was being followed. I felt it was possible she was just imagining things. Later I became concerned . . .'

'You felt there was a connection with your daughter's death.'

'I told you,' I said quietly, 'I was approached by Sam Metcalf. She claimed Sophie had left some stuff on her laptop that could identify her killer. She was going to hand it over to me in Paris. If no computer was found in the sleeping compartment, doesn't that tell you something?'

'Assuming she had the laptop with her in the first place.'

I felt a surge of exasperation. 'I know she did—' I cut myself off just in time. 'Why do you think her friend Jimmy Macchado was killed?'

I appealed to Morelli, who was doing an impression of

Napoleon in exile, frowning at the furniture and saying nothing. 'Andrea?'

He turned up his hands and shrugged.

Cowper said, 'We only have your word for all of this. Did Sam Metcalf ever communicate with you by e-mail?'

'You already asked me that.'

'It's a slightly different question.'

'We spoke on the phone . . . that was all.'

Daniel Ince leaned forward. The only one in uniform, he had a face that was too small for his head, reddish hair and an uncomfortably direct gaze. He'd been taking notes on a yellow legal pad.

'Any objections, Mr Lister, to our forensic retrieval division examining your laptop? It's a routine procedure.'

I hesitated, though I'd been expecting the question. 'Now that my daughter's murderer has killed again,' I said, 'I imagine you'll be reactivating her case.'

Cowper answered. 'I can't comment, not in the middle of an internal enquiry.'

'If he'd been caught a year ago,' I kept on, looking at Cowper and Morelli, 'Sam Metcalf and two other innocent people would still be alive.'

'Sir, the question DC Ince asked you, ' she said, unruffled, 'was will you allow access to your computer?' She stared at me across the table. 'Or do we need to get a search warrant?'

I didn't doubt Edith Cowper's dedication and integrity, but if a civilian blows the whistle on the police in this country – and I had publicly accused the Met of gross incompetence – they close ranks faster and tighter than the teeth of a zip.

I held her gaze and said, 'That won't be necessary.'

I don't make a habit of lying to the police. I consider myself a reasonably honest, law-abiding citizen. But I couldn't just stand by and watch them screw up all over again. Sam's murder had left me shaken and angry (at myself as much as others) and I felt I owed it to her not to squander the lead she had given me. Not to accept that she died for nothing.

'I'd like to help any way I can,' I murmured, as I let Detective Constable Ince take the wrong laptop into custody, meticulously write out a receipt for a machine that I use purely for business.

Perhaps I was guilty of obstructing the course of justice, or taking the law into my own hands, but I didn't look at it that way. I saw my deception simply as a means of buying some more time; and, into the bargain, making sure that Ince didn't find out about Jelena – for her own protection as much as mine.

I trusted Phil's opinion that acting independently we could respond quicker and be more flexible than the police – I had the financial resources, and I was driven in a way that they would never be. Sworn to track down Sophie's killer, I wasn't prepared to let this one last chance, as I saw it, slip through my fingers.

30

After they'd gone, I stayed on in the conference room, staring out of the window at the river, wondering now if I'd made the right decision. After all, the police had the authority, the manpower, the wide reach. But I was still angry enough about the way they'd handled Sophie's murder to feel justified in being a little grudging with the truth. Besides, it was too late for second thoughts.

I thought about the information I'd withheld. Images of

Sam's body on the floor of the sleeper came flooding back and I wondered if Sophie's last moments had also been filmed, set to music, sent out live from the grotto at the Villa Nardini for the enjoyment of God knows what kind of audience. Watching the water pile up white against the stone piers under Albert Bridge, I pictured her lying there alone in that hellish place, and shivered.

It opened the door to a memory of when I first lived in New York, far enough in the past now for me to recall the incident more as a dream than something that actually happened. I find myself, in this New York dream, looking down at the body of a girl sprawled at the bottom of a black pit – a recurring image that because of Sophie will always haunt me now – unsure of what to do and having to decide whether or not I can trust the police. I closed my eyes and the door slammed shut.

The interview had run over by more than an hour.

'Don't ask,' I said abruptly.

'I've no intention of asking.' Audrey, my assistant, had returned from showing them out with a what-was-*that*-all-about look on her face. 'You were helping the police with their enquiries.'

'Something along those lines.'

'They took away your old laptop.'

'I lent them my *only* laptop.' I gave her a significant glance. 'In case anyone wants to know.'

'You'll be lost without it.'

I smiled. 'They didn't say anything to you?'

She shook her head. Audrey had provided loyal support when I raised my formal complaint against the Met. I didn't like involving her. I try to keep a degree of separation between business and my personal life, but where Audrey is concerned it's not so easy. We've been together too long; we know each other too well. What she had to deal with last year when

Sophie was killed went far beyond the call of duty. But then Audrey had watched Sophie grow from a small child. She adored her . . . everyone who knew her did.

'You're meeting Campbell Armour in five minutes.'

I took my time before saying, 'I won't be taking any calls.'

She set up the video link with his office in Ybor City, Tampa, then lowered the window blinds. The sun was washing over the wide plasma screen built into the conference room's only solid wall. Presently the image of an untidy desk staked out by a miniature American flag on a plastic log shimmered into view.

She waited hand on hip, one eyebrow raised. 'Cuppa?'

I thanked her no and turned my chair to face the screen. On her way out, Audrey said, 'Well, at least they didn't march you off in handcuffs.'

'Not this time.'

I could hear someone coming.

Campbell Armour entered left of the screen and stepped quickly around to the front of the desk. His back to the camera, he swept aside piles of paper to clear a space, then turned and hoisted himself up on the edge, swinging short bare muscular legs as he tore the ring-tab off a can of Mountain Dew.

I took in the oversize blue Dolphins T-shirt, baggy white trunks and sweatband with 'Search Engine' on it that pushed his thick black hair into a spiky crown. He was small, compactly built, with a wide, flattish face and, behind rimless lenses, light tawny eyes that drew your attention. He looked about fifteen years old.

He threw his head back, took a long chugging drink, then held the frosted can to his cheek and said, 'Hey.'

It struck me with some force that I was putting a lot of faith in Phil's judgement. 'You must be Campbell.'

He raised the can in greeting. Wry grin. 'Breakfast.'

'Have you looked at the material yet?' I was keen to get down to business. On the phone, last night, Campbell had asked for any information I had – names, website addresses, passwords, e-mails, documents. There wasn't much.

'All except for the photos . . .' He hesitated. 'They're gone, Ed.'

I frowned. 'Gone? Are you sure?'

Campbell took another swig of Mountain Dew. 'Just came from Sam's webpage.' He wiped his mouth. 'You didn't happen to download any?'

'I imported a couple to take a closer look on Photoshop.'

'I'd like to see them – now, if that's okay.'

I reached for my laptop – the one I'd chosen not to hand over to the police – and with a couple of clicks brought up the relevant sub-folder.

They weren't there. I felt Campbell's tawny eyes on me.

'Hold on a second.' I checked the Recycle Bin. Nothing.

Shit, I said under my breath. I looked up and saw that he'd moved to the chair behind his desk. He was rocking back and forth, hands clasped behind his neck.

'I must have scrubbed them by mistake.'

'You know what a Trojan is, dude?' Campbell asked.

He was referring to the horse, an electronic version of the original wooden stratagem dreamed up by the ancient Greeks to penetrate Troy, not the condom – I had a feeling Campbell had used the line before.

I managed a smile. He had an irritating voice, a soft Dixie drawl that didn't quite sync with the vestigial sing-song of South China.

'It's a program with a hidden agenda,' he continued. 'Once inside your computer, it runs like an ordinary server, while secretly opening a back door to your system . . .'

'I've a rough idea what it does,' I interrupted him, closing down the lid of my laptop. 'You think someone hacked into this machine and deleted those shots? That would imply Sam *did* catch him on film.'

'I'd need to check out your system to be sure.'

'If it was Ward, how would he have got access?'

'There are only two ways. Either through your floppy disk or CD drives, or via a connection to the internet.'

'I really rather doubt anyone having tampered with this.' I tapped the shell of my laptop. 'It's rarely out of my sight.'

'Then the attack most likely was remote.'

'If it happened at all . . .'

'Sure, Ed, we're just speculating. You asked me how. Okay, he could have introduced a Trojan to your computer on the back of information that you requested from a website – a website he controls. I haven't had a chance to explore the mansion yet, but it's the obvious link.'

'I take the usual precautions,' I said, sounding defensive. 'Talk to Phil.'

'You mean you run a couple of anti-virus scanners? You installed a firewall, the latest Spyware? Not much help against a player like Ward. He inhabits a world where things are almost never what they seem. It can be a dangerous place.'

'I think I'm aware of the dangers,' I said.

I hadn't hired a cyber-sleuth to tell me the internet was a murky old hall of mirrors. I remembered Will's owlish expression when he warned me that I was 'flying blind' over Jelly. I'd heard nothing from her since the night of the murders, the night I told her I was in love with her. But that was what we'd agreed.

Campbell was looking at me intently.

'You need to get your laptop swept, Ed. If it turns out to be dirty, you could be in more trouble than you know.'

'Isn't that why I'm talking to you?'

He was already starting to get on my nerves. I didn't want to give him the impression I had something to hide, but I was uncomfortable with the idea of Campbell reading my personal conversations (even if I could rely on his discretion) and no doubt asking questions about Jelena. She had nothing to do with any of this and I intended to keep it that way.

'Let's say Ward planted a Trojan inside your laptop.' He leaned forward, slowing his delivery right down as though he were talking to a child. 'Every time you go online, it sends him your temporary IP address, which allows him into your computer. He can open ports and emplace software where and when he needs it. He can read your data stores, contacts list, diary, e-mail and document folders. He can become a 'blind copy' addressee on every e-mail you send and snoop on any other internet traffic you initiate. Equally, he can examine every reply packet you receive. All undetected. He can do virtually *anything he likes* with your system, Ed, and that includes creating and deleting files.'

I nodded slowly as the implications sank in.

'He gains control over your life.' Campbell locked his eyes on mine as if he wanted to be sure I understood. 'He becomes you.'

'I think I get the picture. Thanks.'

'You bet.' He gave a lopsided grin that I didn't find particularly engaging. 'You can either send your laptop over here by courier, or take it to Phil and let his diagnostic team at Secure Solutions do the job.'

There was no contest. I'd trusted Phil before on confidential issues. He was also a man of the world. 'I'll messenger it round to him this afternoon.'

'Excellent. Just one other thing, Ed. You know how the text of the murder webcast is all garbled and misspelled? Did it occur to you the killer might have been using speech recognition software?'

'I was afraid that what I was reading onscreen was actually happening. He said the "show" was live. I only knew for sure when I finally got through to Sam on the phone and I heard her fighting for her life.'

'He strangles her, runs a commentary over the mic . . . sharing the experience. All live action. That's one sick dude.'

I shook my head. 'I use one of those dictation tools myself.'

'You never had a hope of saving her, Ed.'

There was a silence. I gestured at a row of trophies arrayed in a glass-fronted cabinet behind his head. 'What are they for?'

'Tennis,' he said. 'You play?'

'Used to, until my son started beating me.'

'We should have a game. I might even let you win a point.'

We both laughed, a little too loud. 'Let me ask you something, Campbell,' I said. 'I know about your IT skills – Phil tells me you're the best – but what is your experience of tracking cyber-stalkers in the real world?'

'I've been involved in a couple of investigations.'

'You're not licensed as a private detective. You don't carry a gun.'

He cleared his throat. 'Nope, I mostly help law enforcement agencies and legal firms find people. I don't do collars. Just get the information.'

'You're being hired to track down . . . a killer, a monster.'

'Maybe so, but he's not going to look like one, Ed. He won't be easy to recognise. He'll be as ordinary as you or me.'

'We haven't talked about money yet.'

'I get five hundred a day plus expenses.'

'Sounds reasonable. I'd like to offer you double and a bonus . . . based on results.'

Campbell grinned, then ducked out of sight behind the desk. He resurfaced holding a limbless Barbie doll. 'My daughter Amy's. Comes through like a tornado leaving her stuff every place. What kind of bonus are we talking about here?'

'A million dollars. If you bring in the man who murdered Sophie.' I'd offered rewards before, but they'd produced no leads, only raised false hope.

'A million.' The detective frowned and looked down at the Barbie torso. 'By the way, did Wimbledon start yet?'

'Monday.'

'Any chance you could throw in centre-court tickets for the men's final?'

His face broke into a smile. 'Just kidding. Later, dude.'

31

I had agreed to meet Will Calloway at a pub near Lancaster Gate. One of those anonymous watering holes that cater mostly to tourists staying in third-rate hotels overlooking the park – air-conditioned, airport lounge music, menu in five languages – it was a typical Will choice of venue. He's always had a mutinous taste for the dreary, the nondescript.

I got there around seven and found him sitting in a booth at the rear with a gin and tonic, reading the sports pages of the *Evening Standard*. Beside him on the velour banquette lay a large padded envelope.

'I expect you've seen this,' he said as I joined him, pushing the newspaper towards me. The front page ran a shot of the 'murder carriage' in a siding at Linz.

I'd skimmed the article, which included an interview with Sam's travelling companions, an American couple called Rivers. There was nothing about Sophie.

'The police here aren't even admitting a connection.'

Will shrugged. 'They may have their reasons.'

'I just want them to reopen Sophie's case.'

'You could always prime the pump.'

'And have the media crawling all over us again?'

The only other person I'd told about what happened in Paris was Laura. She had been appalled, frightened, but mostly angry with me for going over to meet Sam Metcalf without letting her know. She assumed that Sam was the reason for my trip and I didn't disillusion her. I just said: 'I was afraid you'd try to talk me out of it.'

Will was watching me. 'I understand why you might want to keep a low profile, Ed, but you can't have it both ways.'

I cleared my throat. 'That's . . . well, no longer an issue.'

'What is?' He looked blank, but he knew perfectly well.

'The person I met online I told you about. We decided to take a break and not see each other for a while.'

'Oh, you mean Island Girl.' Will chortled. 'She dump you?'

I let that go. 'You were right, it was becoming a distraction.'

'Well, I'm glad you've returned safely to your senses – for everyone's sake.'

And that was Jelly dealt with. I was relieved in one way, but also a little put out that Will didn't seem interested in asking more searching questions about her.

'So what did Dr Wass make of Sophie's drawings?'

'You ready for another?'

I looked at my watch. I didn't have to be anywhere, I just wanted him to get on with it. 'No thanks.'

'Mind if I do?' He got up and went over to the bar, came back with a fresh gin and tonic and the double whisky that I had refused.

'Will?' I was starting to get impatient.

He took his time answering. On the phone, all he'd told me was that his colleague had looked at the sketchbook and made some comments.

'You're going to be disappointed,' he said. 'Elna Wass feels the drawings have no bearing on Sophie's murder, or events leading up to it. At least, that's how I interpret her observations. I didn't tell her the story behind the sketchbook, who the artist was or what happened. I wanted an unbiased reaction.'

'Did you explain about the website?'

'I felt that would only complicate things.'

He was silent for a moment.

'So? What were her impressions?' I had to drag it out of him. 'Did she think the drawings were of a real or imaginary house?'

'She assumed it was the family home.'

'Greenside? Laura would love that.'

'But it wasn't important . . . from a diagnostic point of view.'

'She's a shrink. I suppose she took your line that Sophie was trying to express through her art what she couldn't talk about in real life.'

'Something like that.' He looked uncomfortable. 'Elna picked up on the strong, very dark feeling of oppression from the interiors, as we all did. She said that it jumped off the page at her. And the fear.'

'Fear of what? I thought you said Wass didn't get a sense from the drawings of an exterior threat.'

'She feels the threat came from within.'

'From inside the house.'

'Ed, listen, I don't want to get into the jargon.' He looked at me over the top of his glasses. 'You're not going to like this in any language. Elna believes that the exciting cause, the inspiration for the drawings, is the artist's troubled relationship with her father. He is her oppressor, the one she's afraid of . . . you.'

I took a deep breath and just sat there staring at him. Then I burst out laughing. 'For fuck's sake.'

'I know, I know what you're going to say . . .'

'No you don't.' I was still laughing, just. 'I can't believe you even pretend to take this crap seriously.' I shook my head. 'You really think that I *oppressed* Sophie? For Christ's sake, Will, my daughter, your niece, was strangled and bludgeoned to death by some lunatic and this woman is going on about father complexes?'

'I didn't say I agreed with her. But I have to respect her view as a doctor. Maybe you should think about it.'

'Think about what? You know how close Soph and I were . . . you *know* how much I loved her. All right, I may not have been the perfect father. I was away a lot, probably I didn't pay her enough attention, but we had a healthy, loving relationship. The idea that she was afraid of me is not even worth discussing.'

I took a swallow of the Glenlivet, grateful for it now.

Will held up his hands. 'Look, I'm sure you're right and the facts don't support Elna's theory. But you can see how she might have come up with the idea. The shadow over the house, the Alice-in-Wonderland tricks of perception and scale, the figure in the chair staring at the box.'

'I don't remember a figure in a chair.'

Removing the moleskin sketchbook from the envelope and placing it on the table, Will leafed through the drawings until he found the one of the gloomy lounge with the cabinet TV in the corner, *Breakfast at Tiffany's* paused on the screen, two empty chairs . . . *Only now somebody was sitting in one of them.*

Just as there was the night of the live webcast.

'What the hell is this?' I pulled the sketchbook around. I could see the back of the viewer's head, his hand on the armrest. It was the same likeness I'd encountered inside the virtual house; only here, I was more recognisable – a gaunt and somehow sinister effigy, watching Peppard and Hepburn doing their thing in the rain.

Sophie's favourite movie. I could feel Will looking at me, not saying a word.

For a moment I thought I was losing my grip. I reached out and ran my fingers over the drawing, peering closely at the pen strokes, the fine cross-hatchings in ink that in places had the density of an engraving. I wanted to make sure the figure hadn't been superimposed later, the sketch tampered with in any way.

I couldn't understand – I still can't – how I'd once seen those chairs as empty.

It's three hundred and seventy-five yards from the Pizza Express on the south side of Notting Hill Gate to the front door of our house in a cul-de-sac off Holland Park Avenue. I know because I used to take Sophie and George there when they were small and on the way home I'd make them play a game of counting footsteps. The useless number stuck in my brain.

Sometime after eleven Will and I left the restaurant. We'd gone on to another pub, then ended up having a bite together and, unavoidably, too much to drink. I steered him into a taxi and decided to walk the short distance back to the house to clear my head. It was hot for a night in June, a muggy tropical kind of heat that doesn't suit London yet. I took my jacket off and slung it over my shoulder.

About halfway home, I had to stop for turning traffic at the corner of Campden Hill Road, where the strip of shops and restaurants changes into the residential area of Holland Park and the way becomes quieter, less well-lit. When I walked on I heard a footfall some distance behind me. I didn't pay much attention.

There were still a few people about and I was too busy worrying about Campbell Armour's theory that someone had maliciously accessed my laptop. The concern was neurally wired to a bundle of other anxieties – about the police, Jelly, Laura, Dr Wass's disturbing interpretation of Sophie's sketchbook, the figure in the chair.

I paused to light a cigarette, using my jacket to shield the flame of the lighter from the warm wind gusting up Holland Park Avenue. As I continued on my way, I heard the footsteps resume, keeping pace with mine. I stopped again, they stopped. I glanced over my shoulder, back up the hill, but now there wasn't a soul in sight. I had the pavement to myself.

I started to pick up speed, staying close to the high wall on my left which protects the front gardens of a row of imposingly tall houses from the street. I heard the echo of an accelerating tread behind me, then inexplicably it faded to nothing. I ducked into a doorway let into the wall and waited while a surge of traffic coming from both directions at once drowned all other noise.

When the roar died down I walked on again. A young couple bodied up out of nowhere and overtook me in silence. I noticed they were wearing matching trainers and, for no good reason, I smiled at them as they strode past. I admit I wasn't exactly sober. But I was sure I didn't imagine those footsteps.

The barrier with the 'Private Byway No Thoroughfare' sign was in the up position as I turned into Campden Hill Place and climbed the single-track road to its hidden enclave of three detached houses. A white stucco four-bedroom with a pillared porch, ours stands at the top of the loop. When I came within range, the outside security light snapped on. Laura had gone down to the country that morning: there was nobody home.

In a pool of brightness, searching my pockets for the key to the front door, I became aware that I was being watched. I'd sensed movement, off to my right by the wooden paling that separates our house from the next door block of flats.

I turned my head and saw that the branches of a privet bush in front of the fence were trembling: I could have sworn an area of deep shadow had just been displaced by something darker. Suddenly I knew I wasn't alone in the cul-de-sac.

In my inebriated state, heart thundering in my chest, I was having difficulty getting the key into the lock, when I heard the sound of a light footfall. It came from inside the house. Before I could turn the key, the door swung open.

'What the . . . what are *you* doing here?' I almost shouted.

Standing before me in a cotton dressing gown, barefoot and holding a glass of wine in her hand, was my wife Laura.

32

'What is it now, Luca?' Investigator Morelli said, without looking up from the file on his desk. He rubbed his temples, trying to massage away a nagging headache. He wasn't in the mood for Francobaldi.

'This arrived for you.' The assistant detective sounded hesitant. 'A fax from the Sûreté in Paris. You should perhaps take a look.'

He went on reading. 'All right, all right, just leave it.'

'Anything you need to know that isn't covered by the report . . . I'll be next door. We made some good progress while you were away.'

'Is that what you call this? Progress?'

The way he felt was partly the result of too little sleep – he got in from London late last night, then had a blazing row with Maria, who claimed to have smelled a woman's scent on his clothes. She'd banished him to the living-room couch.

'With respect, Ispettore, yes. We picked up the Arcangeli kid. We're talking to the mobile phone networks, interviewing the Englishman's neighbours. The CCTV footage shows Jimmy Macchado seeing the girl off at the station and coming away with the canvas bag we found at the house.'

'For Christ's sake.' Morelli sank his head in his hands.

Luca kept going. 'The Ferragamo wrapping tissue clearly ties in with the robe that was left on the train. Originally purchased by Sam Metcalf but changed that evening by Macchado for a smaller size . . .'

'Forget all that, he wasn't killed for some poncy robe, or his mobile phone.'

The young detective shrugged. 'Unless it was just meant to look that way. You came up with cannibalism as a possible motive.'

Morelli groaned. He'd attended a meeting earlier that morning with the US consul, a humour-free zone called Avis Chance, who wanted to know what the *Questura* was doing to find the killers of Sam Metcalf and Jimmy Macchado. He'd explained to her that, though the investigation was at an early stage and they were waiting for results from the Violent Crime Analysis Unit, the Austrian police, and so on, it had top priority. Dr Chance made it clear she wasn't impressed.

Since then the day and his headache had only grown worse.

He'd just had Commissario Pisani on the line telling him he was getting heat from *his* superiors at the Ministry of the Interior. Pisani had passed on their concerns. 'Open season on Americans in Florence, *mio caro*, not good for tourism.' They seemed to have forgotten about the English girl, Sophie Lister.

Morelli felt like saying there were too many tourists in Florence, they could do with thinning out. But he kept that one to himself. He'd been asked if, in his opinion, this was the work of a serial killer. Nobody had mentioned it, but the home-grown 'monster of Florence' who terrorised the city in the 1970s and 80s still haunted the memories of police and politicians alike. A fictional Hannibal Lecter might be an exploitable visitor attraction, but the return of the real thing, real fear rising like a poisonous mist off the Arno, was not. Morelli had said no, he didn't anticipate any more deaths – not in Florence.

'I think we can drop the gay lunch angle, Luca. What else?'

'Our rent-boy thief, Gianni Arcangeli, may have seen the

murderer when he was scouting out the house Saturday evening. He recognised Jimmy Macchado talking to someone in the courtyard, but was too busy trying to stay out of sight to get a description. Gianni doesn't speak English. He said both voices sounded American.'

'All down here.' Morelli sighed. 'Tell me something I don't know.'

'You think the murderer thought Sam Metcalf's laptop was in the canvas bag?'

Morelli nodded. 'Obviously.'

'And when he discovered it wasn't?'

'He decided to ice Macchado anyway.'

'Is that another of your jokes?' Luca gave a sly grin. 'So why did he take the robe, then leave it behind on the train?'

'What is it with you and that fucking robe?' He laughed.

Morelli had never understood why his effete young *assistente* with the long hair, trendy glasses and elegant manners (he was from an old aristocratic Florentine family) wanted to be a cop in the first place. But the truth was he found Luca Francobaldi more intelligent and better company than most of his colleagues. If he was hard on him at times, it was partly for the younger detective's protection.

'Well, you're always saying that every murderer leaves something of himself at the scene of the crime and takes something away . . . Here.' Luca slid the fax from the Sûreté in Paris over the desk and stood up. '*Ispettore.*'

'On your way out, do me a favour – ask Theresa to bring some coffee.' He glanced over the sheet. 'Why didn't I get to see this right away?'

'I've no idea.' Luca shrugged and closed the door behind him.

The fax was from an Inspecteur Touchanges of the Sûreté and concerned Ed Lister's visit to Paris a week ago. What had caught his eye was a reference to the Conservatoire

National Supérieur de Musique, where the subject had spent an hour Wednesday afternoon, apparently enquiring about the eligibility of his god-daughter to study piano there. It struck Morelli as odd that Lister had left the visit out of his account of his movements the day of the train murders.

Maybe he just forgot, or possibly it was deliberate. The meeting at Lister's office in London: he remembered the way the man had reacted when he reported they'd found no evidence of sexual assault, as if it surprised him.

He'd seen something in his eyes then, something veiled.

Morelli thought for a moment, then picked up the phone and, reading his number off the fax, rang Professor Lucas Norbet, the Conservatoire's tutor for admissions.

33

Jelly glanced sideways at Mrs Cato sitting in her gold wicker chair next to the piano stool and caught 'the look' on her teacher's face. She knew how badly she was messing up; dropping notes, floundering in the fast scale runs, dampening too hard on the soft pedal; her expression sucked, her touch was elbow-heavy. She couldn't make the damned thing *flow*.

On a crash of thirds she stopped playing, the sound bouncing around the walls of the basement studio. What the hell was wrong with her?

'I know, I know, I know . . .' Jelly hung her head.

Mrs Cato hadn't said a word. A tiny, scrunched-up old lady, still glamorous in her long satin gown, silver hair twisted into a sort of conch-shell on top of her head, she didn't *have* to say anything – just give her that look.

'We can do better, Jelena dear,' it said. She felt like bursting into tears. She hadn't practised enough was all it was.

She regretted now taking on the piece she was meant to play at the Performing Arts Center next Thursday. A Chopin Nocturne, technically it was a big jump for her. But she had chosen something challenging, so that if she pulled it off it would make both her and her teacher look good.

Pleasing Mrs Cato was her highest motivation. The old lady had been telling her since high school that she saw a brilliant musical future in her stars, always on her case to audition for the Juilliard or the Brooklyn Academy. She hadn't applied because she didn't quite trust Mrs C's glowing appraisal of her talent, and was afraid that if she failed to get accepted she would never recover what confidence she had. There were days when she wasn't even sure she wanted to devote her life to a discipline so demanding it left room for little else.

Music, her teacher liked to say, should be in everything you think, feel and do. If you apply yourself through consistent practice, Jelena, you'll find the order and harmony you yearn for in your playing and in life. It'll make you strong enough to overcome every trial and difficulty. But it has to be your *whole* life, or nothing.

Lately Jelly had seen music more as a place of refuge. She just had to sit down at the piano and instantly she'd forget all the daily bullshit. Immersed in her tunes, cocooned in sound, she'd feel protected, enriched, safe from every harm.

Then there was Paris. Still the impossible dream.

'Play it over, angel,' Mrs Cato said gently. 'Only this time try to imagine you're having a conversation speaking to some-one you care about through music rather than words.' She gave an airy little flourish with a jewelled hand. 'Play as if you want passionately to connect with that person. Let them hear your heart and soul shine through the music.'

What the hell . . . was she talking about?

She loved Mrs Cato for not getting mad at her, for being the best teacher in the whole damn world, but to be told to switch on the emotional current, put more juice, more 'soul' into her music was not the advice she felt like hearing right now.

'There's somebody in your life, young lady, isn't there?'

Jelly laughed and shook her head. 'Makes you say that?'

She couldn't be picking up on *him*, surely? Ed didn't count. Besides, after the last time they talked, she had deleted his name from her Friends List, cleared her archives of their conversations, removed his photo and all associations of their virtual acquaintance from her computer. It was like a weight had lifted. The past few days he'd been on her mind, but he was starting to fade there too.

'I'm not seeing anybody,' she said truthfully.

The old lady just looked at her with her grey witchy eyes. When she wasn't giving music lessons, Mrs Cato moonlighted as the Church Street neighbourhood psychic, reading palms on Thursdays, the Tarot (by appointment only) on Fridays in her front room.

Sometimes she got her antennae crossed.

Shit, look at the *time* . . . Jelly was meant to be meeting Tachel and the others at eight fifteen. It was gone seven already.

She took a deep breath. 'I'm sorry, Mrs C, but I really gotta run.'

Morelli didn't feel like going home. He'd called his wife a while ago now and told her he was catching up on paperwork, not to wait up. He knew that meant he'd be sleeping on the couch again. His back was still aching from last night. But the investigator had another reason for being at his office after hours.

He sat staring at the telephone on his desk, debating whether or not to get in touch with Gretchen, his miracle-working Czech physiotherapist. Before him, scrawled on a napkin from the Hotel Sorrento, was her number in Marienbad encircled by the coral-pink lipstick imprint of a kiss.

He'd been thinking about her on and off all day. In the middle of the interview with the US consul, Dr Chance, he'd fallen into a lustful reverie, remembering the blonde's enthusiasm, her delicate tact, the line of little white-gold hairs marching down her firm stomach . . . *the treasure trail*. He sighed. Gretchen had only been a one-night stand, but she was a nice person – that's what made the difference.

Once upon a time Maria had been a nice person. What happened?

He looked around the walls of the tiny room, which Francobaldi insisted had been a padded cell in the days when the Questura building housed a mental institution. His eye stopped guiltily on the constellation of family photographs.

Resisting temptation, Morelli stuffed the napkin back in his jacket pocket. He booted up his computer, typed 'Ragtime' in the Google search-bar and hit the return key. Selecting one of several websites that listed Scott Joplin's compositions, he went through his oeuvre until he found 'Fig Leaf Rag' – the piece in the repertoire of Ed Lister's god-daughter that had impressed Professor Norbet.

Morelli highlighted the audio option, then leaned back in his chair, hands clasped behind his head, and listened as the syncopated piano he associated with Prohibition-era gangster movies filled the room.

The giveaway, surely, was Lister's reluctance to name his gifted American protégée. God-daughter, my ass. It was obvious he was playing around, but so what if he had a lover or kept a mistress? He could afford the luxury – even one with an expensive musical talent. Norbet had finally admitted that 'Monsieur Lister' had made a generous donation to the Conservatoire's scholarship fund.

Morelli felt exhausted suddenly, ready to go home. He yawned and stretched his arms above his head, briefly waving them in time to the music. The rag had lifted his spirits. He might be under pressure to get results but, as he'd reminded his boss, Pisani, the most promising crime scene lay outside their jurisdiction. He was pinning his hopes on the forensic results from the train – when they became available – giving them a lead, a breakthrough even.

In Linz, he'd interviewed an elderly Swiss couple who'd had the sleeper next to Sam and Linda's. The wife claimed to have heard noises of an 'amorous' nature through the partition wall, then, as the train arrived at the station, music, the sound of a piano playing – something classical, she thought it might have been Mozart.

Her husband said, never . . . Brahms.

It was a stretch, probably way off the mark, but in a case where evidence was in short supply, every little piece of information helped – Morelli wondered if piano music might be a link. He picked up the phone and dialled Marienbad.

Gretchen answered. 'Did I wake you?' he asked.

'*Andrea*? No, you didn't wake me.' She was lying, he could tell by the delicious thickness of her voice.

'I would very much like to see you again.'

She laughed and said, 'I've been waiting for you to call.'

After he put the phone down, Morelli turned up the volume on his laptop and played the 'Fig Leaf Rag' over again. The irresistible gaiety of the tune made him laugh out loud and, Gretchen on his mind, want to dance around the room. He got to his feet and tried a few steps with his eyes closed, holding his imagined partner.

'How late is late?' Tachel wanted to know, as Jelly banged open the door to her studio apartment. 'Fifteen minutes? Twenty? An hour?'

'What's wrong with you? I can't help it if the local . . . forget it.'

Cell to her ear, Jelly heeled the door shut behind her, slipped her shoes off and immediately started to strip, leaving a trail of clothes across the polished wooden floor to the bathroom.

Sitting on the edge of the tub, looking at her toenails, she laughed at Tachel's fussing and said, 'Calm down, I'll be outside at eight thirty.'

She turned on the shower, brushed her teeth while the water got hot, then climbed under the jet, worrying about what the hell she was going to wear, briefly interrupting the flow of her thoughts to remind herself to feed the cats and tidy the place before she left in case . . . *in case what?*

She was nervous about seeing Frank Stavros again after so long and not at all sure how she was going to feel or if she was doing the right thing. She tried to remember, turning her face into the needle spray, what Frank looked like without clothes on . . . a lot of body hair . . . oh hell no, there was no fucking way.

Four of them, a double date. Safety in numbers. The others were supposed to be picking her up and then driving out to Coney Island in Bernardo's car for dinner at this really great Italian place, Gargano's on Surf Avenue. The clam linguini there was out of this world. It was going to be wild, Tachel promised.

Jelly knew her friend was behind the plan to get her together with Frank. But at least he'd had the decency to call Tuesday and let her know he was back in town and wanted to meet up. They'd already had the awkward convo, so there wouldn't be issues hanging over the evening. They were ancient history anyway.

Their two-year affair hadn't survived Frank's being transferred to LA. He'd asked her to move out to the coast, but when she'd joined him for a trial weekend she discovered he was playing around. A stuck-on-himself music video producer with Warner, Frank claimed he was just lonely, the other girls meant nothing, she was the one he really loved . . . what an asshole. After Jelly got over the hurt, mostly to her pride, she'd felt nothing but relief. In the year since they broke up, she'd been on a few dates, but not with anybody she wanted to see again, let alone sleep with. Never one to put herself out there, she found she preferred being on her own. She was enjoying her new freedom and, until now, her friendship with Ed hadn't gotten in the way. Why would it? Jelly had told no one about him, apart from Tachel – and she deliberately hadn't gone into detail. It was only when Ed started acting crazy, saying he was in love with her and all that bull, that she decided her oldest friend should know the whole story.

Tachel's reaction was unexpected. She didn't laugh or even crack a smile. After hearing about the older English guy with stacks of money whose daughter had been killed by a stalker, she made it clear she thought it was a bad situation.

'Even if he's telling you the truth, which I doubt, you know nothin' about him. *He* could be the stalker . . . Why you doin' this to yourself, girl?'

Jelly was defensive. 'He just wants someone to talk to, really, he's . . . harmless.'

Tachel had rolled her big eyes and sighed. 'Please.'

She'd followed her advice, though, heeded her warning, and typed Ed Lister out of her life. But from the very first moment they met, waved to each other across a crowded chat room, she *knew*. She saw this trouble coming, she should have walked away a long time ago.

When the intercom buzzed, Jelly was dressed and ready. She had on her favourite dark blue low-rise jeans, a black baby-T with 'The Mexican Airforce is Flying Tonight' scrawled across the front in white sky-writing letters and her Old Navy flip-flops. No make-up, hair in a ponytail, minimal lip gloss. She didn't want her ex getting the idea she'd made a special effort. A quick check in the full-length mirror on the back of the door. She looked . . . well, it would have to do.

She took a last drag of her Marlboro and stubbed it out. Frank wanted to know if she'd quit. As if it was any of his damned business.

On the phone earlier Tachel had reminded her of their mission, which was for Jelly to flush 'Colin Firth' out of her system, and get laid. One hot night with her old Greek lover, Tachel totally swore, she'd feel like a new woman.

Jelly wasn't so sure, it sounded to her like a pretty desperate remedy, but in spite of her misgivings she couldn't help feeling a little tingle of excitement as she ran down the stairs.

34

A thousand miles south, Campbell Armour slapped dead a mosquito that had been feasting on his ankle while he sat out in front of the pro-shop at Cypress Lake Golf and Country Club, basking in the glow of victory.

He'd annihilated his old rival Touch Kendal in straight sets.

Towel around his neck, vaporising sweat – the temperature was still up in the high seventies – Campbell was rerunning highlights of the match (he'd asked a spectator to shoot it with his cam-corder) on the laptop perched on his bare knees.

He smiled at the way – it really did look an *im*possible return – he'd broken TK's serve in the seventh game of the opening set. Fast-forwarding to match point, he watched himself power a massive backhand into his opponent's rear right corner that made the poor guy shake his head in bewilderment. A killer shot.

'We had a battle, dude, always do,' he'd said to Kendal as they walked off court together. 'You have no idea how much I needed that.'

His euphoria didn't last. Starting to come down from the

endorphin high that had briefly helped take his mind off a frustrating day, Campbell stared gloomily at the clouds of bugs floating around the powerful court lamps, then let his gaze drift off into the stifling darkness beyond.

He was getting nowhere with the Lister case.

He'd spent the last two days fruitlessly trying to track down the website Ed had given him. His attempts to resolve the domain name *homebeforedark.net.kg* had yielded an obscure Internet Service Provider in Kirghizstan, which meant he had little hope of locating the IP address. He'd run a WHOIS on the site and come up with alternative contact details that were impractical to trace and probably false. After following looping trails of fake IDs, fictitious addresses and stolen SIM and credit cards, he'd come to a dead-end. Ward had vanished into the smoke.

He hit rewind for one more morale-boosting glimpse of his historic backhand, then pulled the virtual mansion up onscreen. It was starting to get to him that he hadn't yet succeeded in putting a foot across the threshold.

Campbell didn't like being shut out of anywhere.

Earlier he'd gotten the lab report on Ed Lister's laptop back from Secure Solutions in London. It had received a clean bill of health, which surprised him. As requested, they'd scanned the hard disk for viruses, internet worms and prevalent malware, looking out in particular for Trojan Horse programs. They'd checked the boot sector to make sure it hadn't been hijacked and found it was clear of infection. They seemed to have done a pretty thorough job.

How then did the photographs Ed claimed to have imported from Sam's webpage disappear from his laptop? There was no evidence on the deep scan that he'd ever downloaded them; maybe he just thought he had.

He wondered about his client. Somehow he got the feeling Ed wasn't telling him everything he knew. Campbell had an idea that trust might be part of the problem, which was understandable in the circumstances. Ed Lister was a wealthy man.

The million-dollar bonus wasn't the only reason Campbell had taken on the job, but he knew he'd been thrown a lifeline and it influenced his decision. He couldn't see any other way out of the deep hole he'd dug for himself.

Campbell owed money, and this time to people who didn't play around. They'd given him a week to come up with the sum, principal and interest, or he could expect a visit from 'Cholly' in debt collection. A smiley old cracker in glasses and lizard-skin cowboy boots, 'Cholly' was the most feared enforcer on the Gulf Coast.

Already depressed by his lack of success, when he thought about how much he personally had riding on this case, the detective's spirits slipped even further.

He *had* to find Ward. Seven days wasn't that long.

The virtual mansion looked deserted. The only change since his last visit a couple of hours ago was that darkness had now fallen, which supported his theory that the daylight and night-time modes on the site corresponded with the cycles of the Eastern Time Zone. It probably meant nothing, but there had been other indications that Ward might be operating somewhere on the east coast of the United States. In a global hunt, he consoled himself, it was at least a start.

He tapped in the password Ed had given him.

A gust of raucous male laughter blew across the teak decking from the clubhouse, where some of his tennis buddies were kicking back, guzzling Coors and yee-hawing like a bunch of rednecks. Campbell, who'd exiled himself to his own private Siberia out by the soda machine, found their down-home stories and jokes (often of a sexual or racist nature) not so much offensive as beneath his horizon.

'Hey, Campbell!' one of them yelled across. He'd been doing his best to ignore a suggestive discussion about the Williams sisters and their domination of the women's professional circuit.

'Y'all hear the one about the two lesbian frogs?'

'Excuse me?' He looked up from his laptop as if he hadn't caught the question. He knew they were just out to make fun of him. But the others weren't willing to wait for a punchline they'd heard a thousand times.

There was a collective groan, followed by a male chorus of: 'IT REALLY DOES TASTE LIKE CHICKEN.'

Campbell nodded and gave a bemused smile as the laughter swirled about his ears. What had this got to do with him? He held up his palms in mock surrender, then went back to his laptop. He'd already tried all the conventional ports of entry to the house – doors, windows, garage, cat-flap. Nothing. The password still didn't work; he could only assume it had been deliberately changed by Ward.

It really does taste like chicken . . . He failed to see how anyone could find that funny. He didn't consider himself a prude, but Campbell felt the comparison was vile and demeaning, as well as untrue; he'd eaten frog legs . . . and then from out of nowhere, or rather from this unlikely source, an idea came to him. The crude, pointless joke had reminded him of something.

Something Ward had said.

He brought up the text of the murder webcast and quickly scrolled down the dialogue between 'm' and 'k' until he found what he was looking for.

At the moment where he starts to strangle her.

m: i want to see your face, look at me
m: you dare turn away . . . look at me, bitch
k: what are you *doing* . . . no, don't . . . your hurting!

m: her sift white neck, mmmm, oh boy, lak a swans . . . I tell ya she is dee
licious . . . ya smeel the *feer* in her? you kin jest taste it . . .
m: pressing my thumbs into your throat . . . lok in my eyes
k: please stop . . . no, I can't breathe
m: the gates of heaven . . . open . . . *taste* . . . words with an iron shape
k: NO, PLEASE . . . JESUS! WHAT ARE YOU DOING . . . **DON'T**

It was the unusual phrase, 'words with an iron shape', that
had stuck in his mind. Was it meant to describe sexual arousal
– the musky metallic flavour arising from . . . well, the act
of cunnilingus the murderer wanted to give the *impression*
he'd performed on his victim – or the rankness of her terror?
Or both?

It could be just a mistake, a word or two left out, making
nonsense of an already garbled text. But her fear, even in
transcript, was palpable.

Campbell had to remind himself that her killer didn't molest
Sam sexually. It was only a fantasy, possibly reflecting what
he would like to have done to her, which would make sex at
least part of the motive; or maybe included simply for the
enjoyment of an audience that he knew got off on that sort
of thing.

Either way the guy was a sick one. He'd found other examples of vivid yet incoherent imagery used by the murderer
in his webcast that suggested there might be something odd
about Ward in the realm of the senses, something out of
whack.

The idea of a specific pathology would come from his wife.

Kira was still awake when Campbell got home. A light showed
under their bedroom door; he could just hear the soft rattle
of laptop keys.

He put his sports bag down quietly in the front hall, hooked
his rackets over a peg in the closet, then went straight in the

kitchen and took an ice-cold can of Mountain Dew from the refrigerator. When he'd quenched his thirst, he let out a long sigh. He still wasn't used to living in a box.

It was a year since they'd moved to 'Wild Palms Manor', an upscale gated community in the historic suburb of Ybor City, Tampa's old Latin quarter. They got a deal on an attached townhouse with a two-car garage and, the clincher, a tiny backyard for Amy to play in. Campbell still preferred the down-at-heel section of Tampa across the river where they'd rented a rambling apartment in an old Deco building until Kira started work at the hospital. But this was the first home they'd ever owned, bought with the help of a soft loan from his wife's family in San Francisco. He wasn't in any position to complain. Especially not now, when he didn't even know how much longer they could afford to live here.

He climbed the stairs barefoot. Kira was sitting up in bed propped against the pillows typing out the paper on molecular something-or-other which he knew she had to hand in by tomorrow.

'Hi hon,' he said, almost meekly.

She glanced up at him and waved but didn't speak.

After taking a shower, he looked in on Amy, who was fast asleep in her cot, one tiny arm draped around a teddy bear nearly as big as she was. Campbell stood for a moment, letting the picture of trusting innocence deepen the guilt he felt for having let his family down, compromised their security, maybe their whole future through his own stupidity. He'd lost a lot of money, all their savings, and more.

He hadn't had the nerve to tell Kira yet.

Gently removing the stuffed animal from his daughter's embrace, he bent down to kiss her forehead, then went into the master bedroom.

Kira didn't look up. A wing of black hair curtained her eyes.

In awe of her discipline, her limitless capacity for work – his wife was studying for her masters in biochemistry and psychology at USF while putting in four days a week as a research assistant in the Clinical Neurophysiology Laboratory at Tampa General – Campbell knew better than to interrupt, especially when he'd spent the evening playing tennis at the club. He sometimes felt Kira drove herself too hard.

In his own work, he valued her occasional psychological input and liked to think of them as a team. He waited until she had turned out the light before bringing up the subject of Ward, whose profile she'd helped him put together, and abnormal sexual imagery. He needed her opinion.

She listened without a word as he struggled to tone down descriptions there was really no way to sanitise. When he had finished, her prolonged silence and the regular sound of her breathing made him think she'd fallen asleep.

'You know what this reminds me of?' she said at last. 'Auras.'

'You mean like invisible colours around a person?'

'No, I'm talking about the sensations that immediately precede an attack of epilepsy. All the senses can be affected and vision, hearing, smell, taste and touch sometimes get confused. The patient may suffer from emotional disturbances too.'

'What are you saying? That this guy could be an epileptic?'

'Just a thought. Another possibility is that he's a synaesthete. You know how some people can hear colours or see sounds . . . often they're like artists or musicians? Synaesthetes' brains are cross-wired, probably due to a mutated gene, so that one sensory experience can trigger another. The weird associations, the flashes of light, confusing the taste of her vaginal secretions with a visual image, the engorgement of her clitoris with the sound of rushing wings . . . 'If you like I can mention it to the director of the programme.'

It wasn't a thing you could control – he blamed it on Kira's solemn use of the word 'engorgement' – but Campbell was dismayed to feel himself becoming aroused. He coughed, then said, 'Won't that be kind of awkward, honey?'

Kira laughed in the dark. 'Why? Because I'm a woman?'

'This is a murder investigation,' he said sternly, for no reason other than he suspected his serious-minded wife was aroused too.

35

A few minutes past six the next morning, Friday, Campbell was at his desk explaining to Ed Lister via video link with his office in London that, while he hadn't had much luck so far tracking the *homebeforedark* website, he'd managed to put together a psychological profile on Ward.

He could see Ed was not impressed.

'I've a busy day, Mr Armour,' he said in a clipped, businesslike tone the detective hadn't heard before. 'I was hoping by now we might have got beyond profiling. What happened to following the electronic trail? I thought that was your expertise. It's what I'm paying you for.'

His client was standing by the window with his back to the monitor. Wearing a dark suit, striped shirt and tie, he looked lean and important with a sheen of elegance about him that Campbell found intimidating.

'Still working on it,' he said and took a sip of his coffee. 'The website's been inactive since the train and it may turn out to be untraceable. You asked for an update. Well, this is where we're at, dude.'

'All right, all right.' Ed made an impatient gesture, a slashing motion with his left hand. 'And please don't call me that.'

Campbell shrugged. 'What little we have on Ward seems to fit the profile of the delusional stalker. A loner, most likely unmarried, low self-esteem, has had few if any sexual relationships. He yearns for intimacy, but at the same time feels threatened by it. So he picks a victim who is unattainable in some way. A likely factor in his choosing your daughter . . .'

'Look, I don't mean to be rude.' Ed cut him off, swivelling his head to look at him on the monitor. 'But I've heard all this before.'

'Just stay with me, you'll see where I'm going.' Campbell held Ed's gaze. 'He comes from a background that's an emotional wasteland, as often as not abusive, and grows up in isolation with a poor sense of his own identity. He's not crazy, but let's say predisposed to psychosis. A delusional stalker cannot by definition be reasoned with. In his mind he has created a "real" relationship with the power to transform his own lonely life – he refuses to accept that his victim is not interested in him.

'Now, here's the key, Ed. The guy believes that he and his victim are *meant for each other*. His conviction that they are destined overrides any fear he might have of consequences. Initially, he can't see that he's being threatening, or frightening. He can't appreciate that his actions are hurting others, he doesn't regard what he's doing as wrong. To him this is "true love", it's just that the object of his love doesn't recognise it yet. With enough persistence he believes he will eventually win her over.'

Campbell watched his client turn away from the window and come and sit down in a chair beside the table. He could see he had his attention now.

'The stalker,' he went on, 'who already has difficulty separating reality from fantasy, will blow up the least reaction from his victim into a delusion of intimacy. What he cannot achieve in reality he makes up for in the fantasy world he has created and it's precisely the imaginary element that makes it so hard for him to let her go. He can't understand the word "No". Why would he, since he believes it's in the stars for them to be together? When he realises finally that it's not going to happen, he may decide that if he can't have her, then no one else will either.'

'He kills her,' Ed said flatly, looking straight at him.

'And gets what he wants which is absolute control over his victim.'

'What about Sam Metcalf and the others?'

'Often with cyber-stalker cases, particularly "love obsessionals", it's not only the target who is in danger, but also those around her if the stalker perceives them to be in his way, or a threat to his own safety.'

'You think my daughter was his first victim?'

'Serial stalkers tend to be disturbed individuals who choose their victims at random. I don't think that's the case here. Ward is too smart and there's too much about him that *doesn't* fit the profile. He's different. I get the feeling that he still wants something . . . maybe from you.'

Ed frowned. 'You mean money?'

'If this was about money, he'd have been in touch before now. The fact that he's left some teasing hints and clues, while carefully covering his tracks, suggests a common sociopathic trait – he feels the need to tantalise the authorities and show how much cleverer he is than his pursuers. At some level, they all want to be caught, but in Ward's case . . . I don't know.'

'Then what does he want?'

'When you were watching the webcast, did it ever occur to you that you might be the only one – watching, I mean?'

Ed shook his head. 'I assumed I was part of an audience.'

'You didn't get a hint when you entered the house and found your effigy sitting in front of the TV? That you'd been singled out? That the whole show – leading up to the clip of the body laying on the sleeper floor – was for your eyes only?'

'At the time, no.' He glanced at his watch. 'I've wondered about it since.'

Campbell smiled a little. 'He planned it all. The second e-mail you received from Sam Metcalf on the train, the one giving you the username and password, was a forgery. I've no doubt the source was Ward. None of this proves that he put on the "show" just for your benefit, but he wanted you to be there.'

Ed leaned forward. 'All right, but why? Why me?'

'He wants to involve you. It's part of the stalker mentality. He wants you to react. I was thinking about it last night . . . I guess you've already considered the possibility that whoever killed your daughter was really trying to get at you.'

'It was one of the first questions Morelli asked me. I can't think of a single reason why anyone would want to hurt me, or my family.'

'Still, you could have missed it. You need to go back over the last ten years, maybe more, and think about people who might hold a grudge. You could've done a deal, bought a chunk of land or developed a site, and without knowing it ruined someone's life . . . that type of thing. Let somebody down.'

'I don't let people down, Mr Armour.' He stood up and reached for the control panel. 'When can I expect your next report?'

'Give me a couple of days. Just remember, Ward may turn out to be a delusional, or hiding behind the mask of a stalker to disguise his real motive. Either way it doesn't mean he's accomplished his mission.'

206

'I'll bear it in mind.' The screen faded to black.

Campbell sat for a moment. He tried to think what it was about Ed Lister that didn't quite gel. The guy was obviously sincere, but too smooth – and he had something else going on. He couldn't get past the impression his client was holding out on him. If he was right, it was going to make his job more difficult.

He let his thoughts wander, listening to the sounds of the Armour household stirring. He could hear Kira in the shower, Amy singing to herself in her cot.

He wasn't going to be able to put off telling them much longer.

Reaching out a bare arm, Jelly groped for the radio alarm on the bedside table and opened one eye. Five more minutes. She groaned, pulled the comforter over her head and lay there listening to the traffic on Lexington under her windows barrelling downtown at stop-go intervals. Last night had been a total, total disaster.

What had she *expected*? That a year in LA might by some miracle have changed Frank Stavros? He'd started pawing her in the back of the Jeep before they'd even gone half a block; and then acted loud and obnoxious all evening, reminding her why they broke up in the first place.

She'd never felt so relieved to get home and lock the door of her apartment behind her. Checking her inbox last thing, she'd discovered an e-mail from Ed saying it was important she contact him – something had happened.

Obviously just a ploy. She'd ignored it and gone to bed.

The alarm went off and Z-100 FM brought Missy Elliott bouncing into the room like sunlight. Across the hall her neighbour's door slammed. She could hear Lazlo muttering to himself out there, jangling his keys.

'You think I don't know they're watching?' he was saying,

'I seen 'em on the corner, right across from the Cuban Mission, looking up at my window.'

Then, as he lumbered past her door and down the stairs, putting on a high squeaky voice to reply, 'Why would anyone want to spy on a pathetic tub of lard like you?'

'It's a stakeout. You think I don't *know* . . .' Lost the rest.

She only ever *heard* the craziness. Whenever she bumped into him on the stairs or in the street, Lazlo was always polite and as sane-seeming as anyone. Jelly yawned and turned up the music, then got out of bed and headed straight for the bathroom.

Ten minutes later, showered and dressed, she was sitting at her desk between the windows, one of the cats, Mistigris, on her lap. Leaving her breakfast (half a toasted bagel and a glass of OJ) untouched, she lit a Marlboro and brought up the text of Ed's e-mail on her computer. She knew she should stick to her guns, but it couldn't hurt to reinforce her position, let him know she wasn't changing her mind.

She typed her answer:

OUT OF THE QUESTION.

Hesitated, then hit send. Oh shit . . . she took a furious drag of her cigarette. *What are you doing there? Waiting for me?*

She hadn't expected him to reply – at least, not instantly.

templedog: there's something you need to know

He'd gotten back to her on Messenger, which only made it worse. She debated for a second, staring at the screen as if mesmerised by his words.

td: Jelly, I wouldn't be contacting you if it wasn't serious
adorablejoker: hold on a sec . . . doorbell

She stubbed out the Marlboro she'd just lit and leaned back in her chair, raking both hands through her hair; then, lacing her fingers behind her neck, her bent arms sticking out like wings, she rocked back and forth. What the hell was going on here?

aj: back

td: are you at work

aj: on my way . . . running late

td: ok, I'll get to the point. What's happened is that a girl my daughter knew in Florence has been found murdered on a train

aj: oh my God . . . *my God*!

td: it looks like she was stalked by the same person who killed Sophie. It's dreadful news, I know. But the fact he's killed again may make this monster easier to track down. The police seem to think so. Jelly, listen, I don't believe *for a moment* that you're in any kind of danger – I wasn't even sure whether to tell you.

He couldn't possibly be making this up, could he?

aj: this is so shocking . . . i don't really know what to say. i'm sorry, it must be hard for you . . . i really have to go now

td: we may need to talk again

aj: i don't know . . . i meant what I said about taking a break

td: look, I'm not trying to scare you, I just think because of the present situation we ought to stay in touch.

aj: let me think about it, k? . . . I gotta run

It was so clear to her he just wanted an excuse to go on talking that Jelly forgot for a moment the gravity of what she'd just heard and smiled to herself.

Only later, on the LL train coming out into daylight on the elevated track at Prospect Park, did she remember that the story had been on the Fox Report . . . *two* girls, wasn't it, though, murdered on a train in Europe?

209

What exactly had Ed meant by not in any danger? What had made him think of *the opposite* of that? He wasn't trying to scare her?

Well, you could have fooled me, Mister.

36

I knew something was wrong the moment I saw Peter Jowett, our gardener and handyman, standing out in the middle of Little Meadows Lane. Just before we turned in the gates of Greenside, he stepped forward and flagged the car down.

'Hold on,' I said into the phone, and told the driver to pull over.

'Andrea, I hate to do this to you.' I was on the line to Morelli in Florence. 'It looks like we've got a problem here. Let me call you back.'

He gave an exasperated sigh. 'Signor Lister, I've been trying to have this conversation with you for two days now.'

'I'm sorry but I can't talk now.' It was Saturday morning and I'd left word for him that I could be reached on my mobile between ten and twelve, when I knew I'd be driving down to the country alone.

'I only have a few more questions. You were saying about your god-daughter . . .'

'I told you, she really has nothing to do with this business.'

'Maybe not, *signore*, but she had a bearing on your movements in Paris. A music student, I believe. She plays the piano? '

'Yes . . . I thought we'd covered the subject.'

Morelli had obviously spoken to Lucas Norbet at the Conservatoire and assumed, as any Italian male would, that I was having an affair. I felt like telling him to stop wasting his time and mine – as usual – on an irrelevance.

'What is your god-daughter's name, Signor Lister?'

'Andrea, I really have to go now.' I cut him off.

I was still thinking about what he'd said and the potential fallout if he pursued this line of enquiry as I lowered the window and Peter Jowett blurted out that Jura had been run over and killed by a vehicle that didn't stop.

I stared at him, not really taking it in.

The details followed, more or less coherently. The accident, I gathered, had happened around ten that morning. Peter's son, Andrew, who works for us as a part-time stable lad, found her lying in the ditch. Nobody saw or heard anything – no screech of brakes, no sound of an impact. The old black Lab had gone missing earlier. It was raining hard, Peter told me. I caught the smell of wet fur that still hung about his hands and waterproof jacket.

All I said was, 'How did she get out on the road?'

'Why didn't anyone think of calling my mobile?'

Laura, barely audible, mumbled something about not wanting to break the news to me over the phone; she knew I was coming home for the weekend and it seemed better to wait. George just stood.

The boy has always been closer to his mother. Although physically we look a lot alike – tall, loose-limbed, angular, eyes grey-blue, hair dark – I'm not sure how much else we have in common. We find it hard to communicate.

I couldn't get anything more out of them. They were numb, but I was not invited to share their misery. I felt like an outsider. It made me realise that they regarded my presence there as almost irrelevant.

Later that afternoon, I took my son with me to help dig Jura's grave. We chose a spot on the Downs behind the house where Sophie had liked to walk her dog when she was at home. She'd doted on the animal. George drove the body up there in a small trailer attached to his new quad bike, while I walked behind carrying the pick and spade. The hole had to be dug deep enough to deter foxes.

Jura was wrapped in a tarpaulin, but I wanted to see her before we put her in the ground. I told George to look away. Her injuries were not as gruesome as I'd feared. A flap of skin had been torn from the bow of her chest, leaving a crimson rosette that stood out against her damp black coat; a dewclaw had been ripped off and her muzzle had been lacerated, a small section cut away exposing her gums and a blood-speckled eye-tooth – it looked as if she was smiling. There was no other damage that I could find. The fatal injuries, I assumed, were internal.

When I removed her collar, I noticed Jura's name-tag was missing, but didn't attach any significance to its disappearance; she could have lost it at any time. I folded the corners of the tarp back over her like a parcel.

Digging the grave took us the best part of half an hour; we were both sweating and grimy by the time the job was done. We piled some rocks on top of the low mound of earth to mark the place and talked about a headstone and what it might say. I suggested a cairn with a simple inscription. 'It would be nice if it could be in memory of both of them, don't you think?'

George's reaction was unexpectedly vehement.

'No . . . she'd *hate* that,' he burst out. 'It's so totally *un-*Sophie. She hated any kind of sentimental . . . just because it was her bloody dog . . . sometimes I think it's like . . . you never really knew her . . . at all.'

He soon became incoherent, and then with a hoarse moan

212

his scrawny frame convulsed and he broke down. He hung his head and just stood there, heaving with sobs. Heart-breaking to witness, but I'm not sure it wasn't healthy for George to vent his feelings. He never talked about what happened, about his sister's death.

At least, not to me. I walked over to where he was standing and awkwardly tried to put an arm around his shoulders. I couldn't see his face, but his hard scarecrow body immediately stiffened, as if programmed to resist and repel any attempt at affection. He wouldn't let himself be hugged. I was the same with my own father. We weren't demonstrative either.

'It's all right, George,' I said. 'If you want to talk about her, if there's anything at all you want to ask me . . . I'm always here.'

He turned away. I thought I heard him say under his breath, 'No, you're not.' But I could have been mistaken.

It was my father who gave the dog to Sophie as a present for her ninth birthday. I'll never forget her reaction – she was just young enough to show unaffected delight. I can still see her eyes widen, still hear her laughing for joy, when he conjured the fat little puppy from his bulging coat pocket.

Everything connects, if you think about it.

My father was a stonemason, a 'gentleman' builder (although he disliked the term), who ran the family business from a small yard around the farmhouse where I grew up near Tisbury. A meticulous craftsman, specialising in the care and preservation of old buildings, Charlie Lister never approved of what I do for a living – property speculation, by his lights, was not a real job. He wasn't impressed by my material success or by my marriage to a Calloway (which raised more eyebrows among my family than hers), but he was hugely proud of his granddaughter. He died, mercifully, a year before Sophie. His last words to me in hospital, where they could do nothing to slow and little to cushion the final gallop of pancreatic cancer, were about her. He'd always believed in her talent and her future as an artist. He told me he saw Sophie as the one who would keep the flame of Lister artisanship burning.

The reality, just two years on, is that as a family our sense of who we are and where we're going has become fractured, and diminished.

In an oblique way I'm sure it was what George felt, what provoked his outburst. For all of us, Jura's death meant that a living connection with Sophie had been severed. I think he felt he was the only one left.

We cry, they say, when we feel unprotected.

I went for a walk later that afternoon, taking a route I know well that leads up onto Cranborne Chase and across the Wiltshire-Dorset border. It's wonderful striding country, a terrain of gentle swelling hills and steep-sided hollows that gradually flatten out towards the coast. On Win Green Hill you can usually see across four counties and I always get that exhilarating feeling of being on top of the world. Not today. The rain had stopped, but it was still muggy and overcast. Oblivious to landscape or weather, I tramped along head down, listening to Elgar's *Variations* on my iPod, avoiding reflection. I just wanted to wear myself out.

Sometime after six I got back to Greenside, having made a detour by the lane where the accident happened. I felt I owed it to Sophie to visit the actual spot and recreate in my mind's eye how Jura met her end. I also needed to satisfy myself that it really was an accident. Her wounds hadn't looked right somehow.

Crouching down, I examined the surface of the road. Any blood, hair or animal tissue, I realised, would have been washed away by the rain. But I thought I might find a glass splinter broken off a front-light assembly, or perhaps a flake of paint from a wing of the hit-and-run car. There was nothing, no sign of the missing name-tag, no evidence of any kind that there had been an incident. It was only when I explored the ditch that I noticed a shred of what looked like black bin-liner caught on a hawthorn stump. I retrieved it and, opening it out, saw that there was blood in the folds of the plastic.

In an instant, I went from vague suspicion to unshakable conviction that the dog was killed elsewhere, brought back here and dumped.

Whoever did this, did it deliberately.

37

Laura had prepared an elaborate dinner that we ate in the kitchen, as we always did when it was just us. It had been her way of dealing with things after Sophie died – keeping busy, observing small family rituals, putting a brave face on it. I knew how upset she really was about Jura. Nobody had much appetite. Even after my long walk, I felt only a gnawing ache in my stomach that I tried to deaden with alcohol. Sitting in grim silence, we were all relieved when the ordeal came to an end and the three of us could go our separate ways.

We didn't discuss the incident. I got the feeling that Laura wanted to believe I was somehow to blame for the dog's death – just as I'm sure that deep down she held me responsible for Sophie's. She never came out with it and said, 'This is all your fault.' But her eyes whenever they caught mine had that accusing look.

I decided not to tell her about the evidence I'd found in the ditch that indicated Jura was killed intentionally. It would have only caused more anguish. I didn't want to alarm Laura either, in case I was wrong and it had been a random, isolated incident – unconnected with the uneasy feeling I'd had last night of being followed home from Notting Hill Gate, an experience that in the end I'd put down to paranoid feelings or too much to drink.

The irony was that this miserable crisis had come at a time when the ice between Laura and me had begun to melt a little. That sounds misleadingly hopeful. We were carrying too much baggage for anything more than a short truce. But finding her at Campden Hill Place when I believed her to be in the country, once I got past the idea that Laura was checking up on me (I even wondered if she was having me tailed), had been somehow a comfort.

It's odd how a person you think you know as well as it's possible to know anyone can become such a mystery again. When we talked now it was more like a conversation between strangers than husband and wife. We stayed up late watching an old Robert Altman movie on TV, *Short Cuts*, which we first saw together in New York. The parallels in some scenes with our own slowly dissolving marriage were hard to miss, but neither of us made any comment.

In bed later, strangers there too, Laura's enthusiasm caught me by surprise; she seemed recklessly uninhibited, almost wanton. It wasn't like her and it didn't feel right: as if someone else had taken her place while the real Laura was on leave of absence. In return, I made love to my wife with the ardour of a man guilty of unfaithfulness. In the midst of all that sweaty ill-founded threshing, I had the sensation again of observing us, the Listers, from a distance.

But last night seemed an age ago now.

I took a tumbler of whisky upstairs to the library, watched the news, then went online and dealt with some e-mails. There was one from Campbell Armour with a six-page attachment titled 'Synesthesia'. I wrote back letting him know what had happened to Jura, describing her injuries and suggesting that the dog had been deliberately killed, then run over to make it look like an accident.

Since I last spoke to Campbell, I'd given careful thought to his theory that I was being targeted by somebody. I was pretty sure he would see the cruel, senseless execution of Sophie's old Labrador as part of their campaign. But I'd failed to come up with a single name.

The room felt airless. I got up from the desk, walked across to the bay windows that overlook the garden and opened one of the sashes. It was too dark out to see anything. I lit a Gauloise and stood contemplating my reflection in the panes of distorting antique glass. I decided to take a look at the synaesthesia material Campbell had sent me later. It was just an excuse really for leaving my computer on standby on the off-chance that Jelly might sign in.

I thought about her all the time. Couldn't stop myself.

Although we'd agreed to take a step back, give each other some space for a while, as she put it, I'd insisted on keeping open the link between us for her security. But the desire to talk to her and 'hear' her voice was more powerful than ever. As I turned to stub out my cigarette, the ash falling on the polished wooden floor before I could find an ashtray, I suddenly felt an overwhelming need to get in touch.

I sat back down at the computer and, just as I was about to click on her name, a dark blue message tab on the toolbar started flashing. It seemed such an extraordinary fluke – or yet another example of Jelly's powers of ESP – that I laughed aloud. It was the kind of gleeful sound nobody makes unless they are alone.

She must have sensed that I wanted to see her, and come online: I could only assume because she wanted to see me too. Then, on the point of answering her, I noticed the name that had lit up was not in fact Jelly's. I stared at the screen in disbelief, reluctant to accept my mistake until I looked more closely and realised that what I saw didn't make any sense. It *had* to be a mistake.

The letters 'ST' on the blue flashing icon stood for Stormypetrel – Sophie's screen-name. The air went out of me in a short reedy gasp.

I knew what was running through my head to be impossible, but I could hear my heart beating faster as I checked my contacts list. It showed a yellow smiley face beside the screen-name I'd never been able to bring myself to delete. It indicated that my daughter was online.

I just sat there, afraid to answer, afraid that if I didn't, the ghost in the machine would vanish. It was clearly an error, or else someone 'out there' was playing a trick on me, and yet . . .

I picked up the phone and tried Campbell's number in Tampa, but only got his voice-mail. The little girl's voice on the recording.

Then the blue flashing light went off. I hesitated for another moment before bringing up the saved messages.

Stormypetrel: DADDY?
Stormypetrel: ARE YOU THERE?

That was all.

I felt the impact of those words as a psychic attack. My gorge rose. It was like suddenly I was at sea standing on a wildly pitching deck. I knew, of course, this wasn't Sophie. For one thing, she never called me 'Daddy'.

And yet, and yet . . . *you don't stop hoping.*

'Who are you?' I typed back. The feeling of queasiness had quickly turned into anger. 'What the hell do you want?'

There was no reply.

I heard a scraping noise outside, then a small crack, like a branch or a twig snapping underfoot. I quickly turned off the desk lamp, the only light I had on in the library, and went over to the windows.

As I peered out into the garden, I couldn't help thinking, if only for a warped, gut-wrenching second, 'She's come back.' Then, glancing over at the screen behind me, I saw that whoever it was had written something more.

Stormypetrel: WHY DID YOU KILL HER?

38

I left the house quietly by the side door that leads onto the terrace and walked down the sloping lower lawn towards the lake. The sky was overcast, but I knew the way well enough and my eyes soon adjusted to the dark. I followed the path around the edge of the lake, an area of blackness that seemed to absorb what little light there was, trees and clumps of bushes barely standing out against the water.

Every ten yards or so I stopped to listen, convinced that Sophie's killer was somewhere in the grounds; nothing stirred. All I could hear was the distant mutter of the TV in George's bedroom. Under one arm I carried a loaded shotgun.

I don't know how long I stayed out there, tense and alert, waiting for the prowler to reveal himself, for something to happen. I was startled once by the loud croak of a bull-frog that came from the direction of the island, but the hush of the summer's night soon returned, deeper than before.

After a while, I gave up and wandered slowly back to Greenside, accepting that I'd probably over-reacted. The sense of threat eased but never really went away. Those messages from Stormypetrel had left me feeling shaken and exposed. Whoever sent them knew how to cause maximum anguish. 'WHY DID YOU KILL HER?' Who was I supposed to have killed? What did they mean, *why*?

Before going indoors, using a torch now, I checked the stables and the outhouses. In the garage I pulled the tarp off George's quad bike and the sight of its gleaming chrome and red bodywork made me think how easy it would be to tamper with. I decided that even if this had been a false alarm, I needed to do more to protect my family.

On the steps outside the front entrance to the house, making one last check, I swung the torch beam down the long meandering driveway. I could just make out the stone obelisks that flank the gates to Greenside. About fifty yards further along the road, where Jura had been found earlier, I saw the red tail-lights of a car winking between the hedgerows. I knew instantly it was him.

I wanted to jump in the Mercedes and drive off in pursuit, but it had been put away in the garage. The keys were in the hall. I wouldn't have had a hope in hell of catching up. In seconds, the car's lights were out of sight.

Then it struck me, as I pushed open the front door, that while I'd been searching the grounds, hunting for prowlers down by the lake, he could have been here in the house. I left the shotgun on the hall table and sprinted upstairs.

The television was off in George's room, but I could hear

water running, the sound of a bath being drawn. I spoke to him through the bathroom door, trying not to let him hear I was short of breath. I had to stop myself saying, 'Are you all right?'

When I looked in on Laura, she was sitting up in bed reading. I couldn't think of any way of asking her if she'd seen or heard anything, not without causing panic.

She glanced up from her book. 'Where have you been?'

'I had to get a breath of air,' I said, then promising I wouldn't be long, I went back downstairs. There was nothing out of place in the main rooms, no sign anywhere of an intruder. More than once I picked up the phone to call the police, but I knew there was little point. The truth was I hadn't actually seen anything. Couples often parked in the lane on a Saturday night.

In the library, I poured myself a stiff whisky and went back to my computer. I didn't touch the keyboard, just sat there staring at the screen.

The dark blue message tab for ST was flashing. I had another message.

39

'You know what gives me cause for concern?' Campbell said, talking to Ed Lister on his cell phone from a deckchair at the beach. It was Sunday.

'I'm listening.' Ed sounded a little stressed.

'Hold on a second.' Campbell adjusted the umbrella to keep the sun off Amy who was playing in the sand next to the ice box. After church he'd driven the family out to Sand Key Park, their favourite spot on the Gulf Coast, halfway between Clearwater and St Pete. His client had called him at ten to twelve by his watch.

'Don't go away, Ed.' He put a hand over the mouthpiece and said to his wife, 'Honey, you feel like taking Amy down to the water?' He didn't want the little girl to overhear anything she shouldn't.

Kira lay on her back on a mattress a few yards away. She had on a black bikini and black sunglasses. Her skin, startlingly pale, slathered with high protection sun-block, glistened like alabaster. No response. He came back to his client.

'Listen, whoever messaged you last night may or may not have known that Sophie's screen-name was still on your contacts list. What concerns me is the fact they *knew you were online*. That means either they have remote access to your computer, which we know is not the case, or they were nearby, watching you.'

There was silence the other end.

Campbell glanced at his wife, who hadn't stirred. He covered the mouthpiece again. 'Dish?' It was his pet name for her, but it didn't do the trick. He knew how tired she was and felt guilty for asking.

Amy, already on her feet, said, 'I can go swimming by myself.'

Campbell shook his head and mouthed 'No' at her.

'I got the feeling somebody was prowling around outside. I heard a noise, went out and searched the grounds. There was nobody there.'

Amy was pouting now, digging a toe in the sand and hopping around it on one leg, trying to get his attention. She looked cute in her pink and navy polka-dot swimsuit with matching ribbons on her pigtails. He signed that he would take her in a minute.

'But I could've been wrong, just imagined I heard something.'

'You were on edge, dude, it's understandable. "*Why did you have to kill her*?" That was it, nothing more? You think she was referring to the dog?'

'She? For Christ's sake, it was my daughter's screen-name. I assumed the message came from Ward and that he killed the dog.'

'A bitch, right?'

'Yes. She belonged to Sophie.'

'Well, pets and cars don't mix. We lost a dog once when I was a kid in Hong Kong, a springer spaniel called Runrun . . .' Campbell looked at Amy and tailed off. 'Why did you try to call me last night?'

'I wanted you to trace the user while he was online.'

'If it was Ward he'd have covered his tracks, but you were thinking along the right lines. Sooner or later he'll make a mistake.'

'I wish I could share your confidence.'

He smiled a little. 'So you grab a shotgun and run out of the house. After a half-hour or so you hear a car taking off. And when you get back?'

'I made sure my wife and son were all right.'

Campbell frowned. He looked over at Kira and Amy, instinctively checking on them, then let his gaze drift down the sand to a group of adults and children milling by the water's edge. Out in the Gulf two tankers and a white cruise ship stood motionless on the horizon. He wondered how many miles apart.

'No messages from Stormypetrel?'

'Nothing more, no.' He heard the slight hesitation in Ed's voice. 'I'd really like to know where you think this investigation is heading.' Getting off the subject a little too fast. 'And, by the way, I never killed anybody.'

Campbell stood up and stretched his legs. He walked over to where Kira was basking on the mattress. He could tell by the rise and fall of her chest that she was asleep. He bent down and touched her burning shoulder, still talking into his cell. 'You had a chance yet to read the stuff I sent you on synaesthesia?'

She didn't move.

'I glanced through it. Even if you're right and Ward does have the condition, I wouldn't exactly call it narrowing the field.'

'Wait till you hear this,' Campbell said, giving Kira a little nudge. He saw a frown of annoyance cloud her forehead. Wake up, Dish.

'Okay, yesterday I spoke with Claudia Derwent at Yale – she's the leading authority on synaesthesia in the US. She told me something that got my attention. It seems that when synaesthetes taste a word or feel a sound or see numbers as colours – to them it's real. These are sensed phenomena, not analogies or metaphors, okay? The theory is they've kept the extra neural connections we are all born with but most of us lose in childhood. But get this – a synaesthete's inter-sensory associations *remain constant over a lifetime*. In other words, if the word "ocean" is clocked by the subject as, say, a bunch of flowers, he or she will never experience it any other way. For a person with coloured hearing, a certain sound will *always* be blue, green or whatever. It's like a signature, dude . . . you can't fake it.'

He crouched down beside his wife, thinking now about a swim before lunch. In the cooler they had cold shrimp, marinated chicken, mixed salad and a bottle of Chablis.

'I still don't see how that reduces the odds.'

'It doesn't . . . until you find other examples of a particular signature. Sight and hearing are most commonly involved in cross-over sensory experiences. The majority of synaesthetes "see" words and numbers as colours and shapes. But there are many different permutations in the linking of the senses and a few that come close to being unique. Derwent believes our guy may belong in the last category.'

'I see.' Ed sounded doubtful. 'Did she happen to explain how she reached that conclusion? Or is she just guessing?'

Lister could be such a pompous jerk.

'It's stronger than guesswork. I sent Professor Derwent the text of Ward's webcast. She called me back yesterday evening from home to discuss the material. What she said kept me awake half the night.'

There was a pause. 'You better tell me about it then.'

The neurologist had been guarded at first, understandably perhaps, given the unsavoury nature of the webcast. Campbell had told her he was investigating a case of cyber-harassment for WHOA (Working to Halt Online Abuse) and that any information she volunteered would be treated in strictest confidence.

'There isn't enough evidence,' she'd begun hesitantly, 'to establish beyond doubt that "M" is a synaesthete. Having said that, I don't believe the examples in the text can be read as allusion or metaphor – a phrase like "words with an iron shape" is not a rhetorical trope – which to me suggests a neuropathic disorder.'

What interested Professor Derwent was that if M's brain was indeed cross-triggered so that one sense fired another, then he belonged to an unusual category of synaesthete. 'Among the various synaesthetic pairings,' she went on, 'where sight, for instance, induces the sensation of touch or sound a perception of colour, it is extremely rare for *taste* to be either a trigger or the response.'

The significance of this was not lost on Campbell.

Nationwide surveys showed the incidence of synaesthesia

in the general population to be around one in a hundred thousand – the chances of 'M' being part of any sample were no better than fair, but the fact that he'd left such a distinctive 'print' on the webcast, in theory at least, dramatically narrowed the search. In the twenty-five years since she'd started collecting data, Derwent told him, she had only come across a handful of cases where taste induced a secondary sense experience of colour and shape.

Claudia Derwent had records of just three 'tasters' in her files, two female, one male. The latter had been referred to her in the early days of her research, when she was collecting cases of synaesthesia in the northeastern United States. Her correspondent was a country physician from Norfolk, Connecticut, a village in the Berkshire foothills that was once popular with society folk as a summer resort.

The subject, unusually, was a nine-year-old boy. She'd never met the child, only receiving his case-notes in 1990, ten years after the doctor had lost touch with him. There had been no follow-up.

His mouth dry with excitement, Campbell had asked for the boy's name, which Professor Derwent had been unable to supply – her survey had been conducted anonymously – but she'd seen no reason why she shouldn't put him in touch with Dr Joel Stilwell in Norfolk.

It was possible he'd still have some record of the 'taster'.

Ed was silent for a moment.

'When do you plan to go?'

Campbell moved a little way along the beach so that Kira wouldn't hear his answer. She wasn't too happy about his taking off and leaving her with Amy at such short notice. They'd got into a big fight over the childcare issue, which made it impossible now to have that talk he needed to have with her before he left. He still hadn't told Kira about the money.

He had just five days left to come up with the full amount, before 'Cholly' would be stopping the clock. He said quietly into his cell, 'I'm booked on a Southwest flight tomorrow. I should be in Norfolk late afternoon.'

Kira propped herself up on her elbows and said, 'Where's Amy?'

'Call me when you get there.'

Campbell turned his head and took in at a glance their little encampment under the green and white shade umbrella where until a moment ago Amy had been playing.

For an instant panic surged through him as he scanned the beach, then as quickly melted into relief when he spotted a blur of fluorescent pink moving between the tan bodies down by the water's edge.

'Looking for cowry shells.'

He closed his eyes and took a deep breath, thinking he was getting jittery over nothing; then throwing a reassuring 'I got it covered' grin in Kira's direction and, still talking into his cell, he strolled towards the Gulf.

'We may not have a lot of time,' he said.

Ed had already hung up.

40

templedog: I need to talk to you
adorablejoker: why, what happened?
aj: you better make it quick. i'm at work
td: nothing happened, I just wondered . . . if you're all right
aj: look, i'm fine, okay?

td: obviously not a good moment

aj: is this hard for you, Ed?

td: only because we're talking for the first time in a week

aj: we shouldn't be talking at all . . . and it's been two days

td: don't worry, I'm not trying to pressure you

aj: i can't help worrying, mister

Ward frowned and reached for his glass of wine. It was Sunday, how could she be at work? She lied to him all the time, about almost everything – it was one way to keep him at arm's length. And the big chump is too besotted to notice.

They were something else these two.

'You just wondered if she was all right, Ed?' he jeered at the screen. 'You "just wondered" . . . hell, I bet you did.'

The guy won't let go. He's got it pretty bad, and she knows it. *'Is this hard for you?'* . . . I mean, really – she loves the hold she has over him, the little piece of work. She'd be crazy if she didn't. He took a sip of the wine, a very reasonable Sancerre, and yawned.

A wave of tiredness rolled over him.

He couldn't make up his mind whether he was hungry enough to go out for something to eat. There was nothing in the refrigerator. A walk might help him to stay awake; his body was still on Greenwich Mean Time. If he went to bed now, he'd only wake up again in a few hours and have to lie there till dawn listening to police sirens and garbage trucks painting the town every colour but red.

Seemed hard to believe that only last night he was sleeping under a hedgerow in the Wiltshire downs. He brought up the pictures he'd taken of Greenside, the leafy deer park with its six-acre lake, the magnificent old house where his Sophie was raised. Shame about her black Lab – *there it was now plodding along the lane* – but he couldn't risk the animal surprising him and barking its head off while he loaded the program.

He still had the taste in his mouth. The last bewildered look from Jura's filmy seal-pup eyes had released the flavour and texture of candy floss – it wouldn't have been so bad if he had a sweet tooth.

Out of respect for its owner, he'd kept the dog's name-tag, adding it to his key-ring for good luck. It was working already. When Ed Lister left the house, he'd successfully installed another Trojan in his laptop, replacing the program he'd ordered to self-destruct after Paris.

He liked the library at Greenside, the smell of whisky and tobacco, the worn, over-stuffed chairs, all those leather-bound books – it reminded him of his grandmother's old home. At the foot of the stairs, he'd stood and listened to the others moving around on the bedroom floor above, and thought of Sophie.

He'd been in and out of there in three minutes.

It felt good though to be back in the city. The apartment had been vacuumed while he was away; the bathroom and kitchen left spotless, which suggested Mrs Karas had been in, at least twice. The tidiness of his three featureless rooms, glazed partitions under the stamped-tin ceiling of a modest loft, was comforting to him. Everything in its place, as Grace used to say, and a place for everything.

He sat in his work-space, the horseshoe-shaped network of banked computers, monitors and electronic boxes that he called home. The custom-built set-up, which included mail and file servers, switches that routed incoming traffic to the correct ports, and an impenetrable firewall on a Linux computer with packet-filtering rules he'd written himself, all tightly screwed down, was Ward's listening post, his flight deck, his cybernaut's module – gateway to the universe.

He retrieved the text and scrolled down through a tedious section of dialogue where Ed comes on to the girl as a patron of the arts – he wants to help her study piano in Paris, no strings attached, he's doing this because he believes she has talent, etc, only she gets all fired up and righteously tells him she could *never* accept his charity. What crap! He's got the cash, she's basically a hustler . . . where's the problem?

But then they get into something a little more interesting.

In what has to be a calculated move, Jelena lets him know she's been seeing someone . . . and, surprise, surprise, Ed doesn't take it too well.

adorablejoker: remember i told you i broke up with my old lover when he relocated to LA? Well he's back in the city and we went out the other night
templedog: I see . . . how did it go?
aj: we had a lot of catching-up to do
td: you sleep with him?
aj: it's too soon for that, but who knows . . . i think there's a reasonable shot of us getting back together . . .
td: you know I still feel the same about you
aj: ed, please . . . all i'm doing is getting on with my life
td: and you feel it too, you're just pretending
aj: no, I don't. I meant what I said, it's not *real* . . . moving on, you told me i wasn't in any danger. What made you think i might've been?
td: It was only if someone was trying to get at me and it ever came out that you and I knew each other
aj: ahhh, okay . . . so it's your reputation you're worried about.
td: no, I meant they could use you

Ward leaned back and closed his eyes.

He knew what Lister was going through. He remembered the exact moment when Sophie, his princess, had told him online that she had someone she cared about back in England. The shock and hurt stayed with him, the empty feeling, the nothingness, the rage at being rejected . . . it never went away. The boyfriend, he found out later, didn't in fact exist, but that was beside the point.

It might seem strange that a person of Ed's intelligence, who stank up any room with his aura of money and power, could become infatuated with this nobody from nowhere, could be so *deluded*. A powerful man flirting with self-destruction was not an edifying sight, not even tragic. But Ward couldn't say it altogether surprised him.

Anyone could see she was playing him for a sucker – anyone but Ed, that is. He had to believe that deep down his little cyber-whore was in love with him and that in time she'd come to realise that the two of them were meant. There was only one place this was heading. He wasn't going to accept that the relationship was over. He wasn't going to take no for an answer.

What the girl didn't know was that Ed Lister had been here before.

It felt like a stroke of luck, if not entirely unexpected, when he discovered that Ed was pursuing a woman half his age on the internet. He was intrigued by the way their paths were converging. But Ward could claim at least some credit for enabling and enhancing the process. Like the ESP connection that Ed was under the impression he enjoyed with Jelly. The only reason she knew about the party at Greenside was because *he* had told her. And the next time Ed checked his archives he would find the conversation that proved her right.

YOU TOLD ME . . . yes, well, let's call it a joint effort.

If Ward looked hard at the situation there was a symmetry here, a kind of poetic justice in the range of possibilities it opened up. He wondered if Ed had any idea how much they shared, how close they were getting.

Soon, he thought, no one will be able to tell us apart.

Norfolk

44

'Mr Armour?'

A thin hunched figure reading a book on the terrace lifted a hand in greeting as Campbell pulled into the driveway of the fieldstone farmhouse and cut the engine of his rented Toyota. The old man rose and shuffled slowly forwards to meet him.

'You found the way all right. I'm so glad.' Bent nearly double from osteoporosis, Dr Stilwell was the same height sitting or standing.

It had taken Campbell an hour to drive out from Bradley airport, following the doctor's precise directions that brought him up through the samey small white towns, the rolling hills and never-ending woods of Litchfield County. Approaching Norfolk, he'd spotted a dead brown and gold bear lying curled up in the ditch like a worn couch somebody had thrown out, and suddenly felt a long way from Tampa. It was his first foray into the Yankee heartland.

'Great place you got here, doc.' Campbell said, looking around him, as he stepped from the car. The old house and its barn were set back on an oak-shaded rise in a half-acre of scrupulously tended grounds.

'On a day like this . . . well, I can't think of anywhere I'd rather be.' Stilwell spoke with a soft New England accent, squinting up sideways at Campbell through half-moon glasses perched on his nose; he was wearing, despite the heat, a heavy tweed suit and bowtie. They shook hands and the doctor led him over the terrace of uneven flagstones to a circular cast-iron table and chairs.

'Can I interest you in some iced tea?' A tray had been laid out with a pitcher, silver spoons, and two glasses filled with ice and mint. 'My wife's secret was to add a little ginger ale. She was from the south . . . like you.'

The doctor filled their glasses, letting him know that Mrs Stilwell had passed away three years ago and that he'd given up general practice soon afterwards. It occurred to Campbell he must have worked on well past retirement age. He had to be eighty, at least. There was a silence. He was wondering how to bring up the subject he'd come here to discuss, when Stilwell asked, 'What can I do for you, Mr Armour? I don't see patients any more and you don't look to me like a medical man.'

On the phone, he'd been careful not to say too much about the purpose of his visit or what he did for a living. He suspected that a private investigator nosing about up here in the backwoods would not be made to feel welcome.

'I'm a computer analyst.' Campbell cleared his throat. 'I was given your name by Claudia Derwent at Yale. I believe you sent her some notes on a patient of yours – this was way back – a boy suffering, if that's the word for it, from synaesthesia.'

Stilwell nodded slowly. 'Sure, Derwent published a letter in the *New York Times* inviting anyone with the condition to take part in a sample. I wrote her partly to have her confirm my diagnosis. But also because the case had some exceptional features.'

'The boy claimed he could "taste" music. Is that right?'

The doctor's eyes met his and held them in an open and friendly gaze. 'What exactly is your interest in the subject, Mr Armour?'

Campbell had prepared his answer. There was no sense in talking at this point about a murder investigation, when it might not even be relevant.

'It's really my wife who's interested. She's doing research in clinical neurophysiology at Tampa General. They have an epilepsy programme there and she's studying parallels between temporal lobe seizures and the synaesthetic experience.'

It wasn't so far removed from what she actually did.

'I see.' The doctor's eyes were still friendly, but the lines around his mouth had tightened. Campbell feared he could see right through him.

'I'm just running errands for her.' He gave a little grin that would have infuriated Kira. 'I thought maybe if I was able to trace your patient . . .' He tried to make it sound like a casual enterprise. 'You wouldn't happen to know what became of him, doc, would you?'

'Last time I saw him he was a little boy . . . must be twenty-five years ago, more. I wouldn't even know where to start looking.'

'What about your patient files?'

He laughed. 'No doctor keeps 'em that long.'

'Do you remember the name of the boy?'

'Of course. He was Ernest Seaton . . .' Stilwell paused, studying Campbell over the top of his reading glasses, as if waiting for his reaction. He frowned. 'I take it then you don't know the story?'

Campbell shook his head.

'I'm surprised Professor Derwent didn't warn you.'

The doctor, not to be hurried, leaned forward and took a sip of tea.

'Ernest was the sole survivor of a family tragedy, Mr Armour.' He put the glass down and went on. 'The Seatons lived out of town over towards Colebrook, big place up on the ridge called Skylands. It happened during the heatwave

234

we had here, summer of nineteen seventy-nine. One night after a drunken argument, the father cut the mother's throat, then shot himself with a twelve-gauge. Hell of a mess. Their bodies were discovered by the housekeeper when she came to work next morning.'

'Jesus.' Campbell tried to hide his excitement. 'I had no idea.'

'The level of violence was . . . extreme. Some people felt June Seaton had it coming to her, but he butchered her, literally slashed the poor woman to ribbons.'

'What about the kid? Was he there?'

'He was found alone in the house, hiding in a broom closet, his face finger-painted with his mother's blood. The murder weapon was a kitchen knife, one of those curved blades with twin handles. What do you call 'em . . . ? Italian word . . . a "mezzaluna". It's not known whether the boy witnessed the crime.'

'Oh man,' Campbell said, turning his head from side to side. He felt a pulse start up in his neck. 'He must have been . . . Jesus, I dunno.'

Stilwell gave him a look. 'Ernest was nine at the time. An only child. He didn't speak about what happened; not to the police, not to me, not to anyone.'

'Did you know his parents? Were they patients of yours?'

'This is a village, Mr Armour, everyone knows everyone. I wasn't their family doctor and we moved in different circles, but we were on friendly terms. Gary Seaton had a dental practice in Torrington. June, his wife, came from a higher social milieu – she had artistic leanings. Ran an antique clothing store here in town that kept her amused for a while. Skylands was hers. The house had always belonged to her mother's family, old-money Norfolk grandees.'

'Why did people say she had it coming?'

'I guess there were rumours she was unfaithful to him. June was quite a beauty, high-strung, with an aura of big-city glamour about her, you know – she had dash. She was on a different level to Gary. His drinking could also have been a factor. Sad business, but at least no one else was caught up in their troubles. The inquest established no third-party involvement.'

'Except for the boy.'

'Yes, of course, Ernie.' He paused. 'The reason you're here.'

Campbell said, 'What kind of a person would do that to his own kid?'

'You know, Mr Armour, the tragedy was not exactly hushed up, but it was contained locally. You might have expected the story to draw a reporter or two from New York, but luckily no. This isn't the sort of place that revels in notoriety.'

'Sure, I understand. I'm only interested in finding him.'

It was easier for Dr Stilwell to talk with his head bowed. But he made an effort now to prop himself up, resting his chin on a hand so that he could maintain eye-contact with his visitor.

'Were you called to the scene?' Campbell asked.

'As a doctor, you mean? No, I wasn't involved profession-ally. At least, not until later on. The boy's grandmother – Nancy, Mrs Calvert, was June Seaton's mother – brought him over to see me a month or two after it happened. I'd treated her husband once for depression and she wanted my opinion. She had taken Ernest to a big child psychologist in Manhattan for counselling. It was suggested to her that as well as being severely traumatised, her grandson might be schizophrenic.'

'Hard to imagine going through what he did and *not* being driven crazy.'

'Children on the whole are remarkably resilient,' Stilwell said. 'I examined the boy. He was maybe a little withdrawn,

236

but I found him pretty well-adjusted, all things considered. I saw him three or four times.'

'We sat over there, the two of us, in my summer office.'

Campbell glanced at the converted barn the doctor had pointed out to him earlier, a listing white clapboard shack with tall windows overlooking the pond and bog garden. He knew he was jumping the gun, but he felt almost certain now that this was where it all began. The emotional wasteland out of which 'Ward' had arisen.

'I remember the exact moment I realised Ernest wasn't ill, but different. I had some Mozart playing in the background and he asked me to turn it off. I was curious to know why. He said the notes tasted bad. "*Like flies when they get in your mouth.*"'

'I'm not a big fan of Mozart either, but man . . . that is harsh.'

Stilwell gave a little smile. 'I thought so too.'

'But you knew what it signified.'

'There were other signs. I got him to do some drawings. One of them, which I couldn't decipher, he explained was a drawing of the *sound* a helicopter makes. We looked at letters of the alphabet and he instantly put a colour to each of them.'

'Then you didn't share the psychologist's view?'

'I told Mrs Calvert I thought Ernest was synaesthetic and that his condition most likely had become more pronounced because of the trauma, but she just said, Oh, the boy's always been a dreamer. She looked after him for a while longer, but it was too much for her to handle. She packed him off to be raised by a cousin out West somewhere, I think it was Wyoming. He never came back.'

'Is the grandmother still alive?' Campbell asked.

'She died in New York two years ago.'

'What about the cousin who raised him? Any other relatives

or friends of the family who might know what happened to the kid?'

Stilwell shook his head. The detective, who'd been leaning forward to catch the old man's sometimes barely audible voice, sat back in his chair.

A silence grew between them, not uncomfortable this time, restoring the peaceful drowsy hum of the garden. Campbell was about to try a different approach, when he heard Stilwell say softly, 'Don't make any sudden movement, Mr Armour.'

The doctor was staring intently at something behind him.

'We have a visitor. Turn around very slowly. There's a hydrangea bush to your left. Look among the top trusses and you'll see one of our humming birds. Iridescent green with a black throat patch?'

Reluctantly, Campbell did as instructed. 'Okay, I got it.'

'Keep your eye on the black patch and watch what happens to it when he moves into the sunlight. There!'

There was a flash of deep ruby red. Campbell had never seen anything in his life so intensely red before. Then it was gone, leaving a whitish after-image that quickly faded against the sky. As always, when he experienced something new or beautiful, he thought of Kira – the experience incomplete unless he could share it with her.

The doctor beamed at his delight. 'He was a big favourite with my wife. It tickled her that only the males have that gorgeous colouring. She named him "Beau".'

Campbell sensed he was about to go into reminiscence mode, but the old man became quiet. Taking the hint, he stood up. 'It was good of you to see me.'

'Sorry I couldn't be of more help.' Stilwell held out a hand for him to shake. 'Have you a place to stay in town, Mr Armour?'

'I booked a motel online. The Mountain View.'

'Never heard of it. You'd be more than welcome to our guest room.'

Campbell smiled. 'I already used up enough of your hospitality.'

The doctor insisted on walking him back to his car. At the end of the terrace, he stopped and put a bony hand on Campbell's arm. 'You could always try talking to Grace Wilkes. She was housekeeper at Skylands. She might be able to tell you more.'

'Grace Wilkes,' he repeated, wondering what had made him change his mind.

'Had a rapport with the boy. She'll be in the book for Winsted.'

A long white strip of joined-up cabins tucked into a fold of wooded hills, the Mountain View motor inn was just across the state line into Massachusetts, twenty minutes by car from Norfolk. Campbell parked his silver Toyota Camry outside number fifteen and sat for a moment, listening to the radio.

He remembered Ed Lister saying the murder webcast had a classical music soundtrack . . . and that there was someone who played the piano in the virtual mansion. He made a note to ask him if the repertoire included any Mozart. The taste of dead flies, he guessed, would be a constant.

His room was ski-lodge basic, faux-pine panelling with an oil painting of Alpine pastures over the bed and a single window on the back that looked out on another parking lot. It would do for a night. He had a shower and changed his clothes, then called Grace Wilkes, only to learn she was out of town visiting her sister in Waterbury. Campbell left his numbers for her to call.

She'd be back Wednesday. *Three days* from now. He sat down on the king-size bed and thought about how he was going to break the news to Kira. As of this morning she

239

hadn't been able to find anyone to mind Amy while he was away, which meant she'd have to stay back from her job at the hospital all week.

On the way to the airport, he'd tried to explain to Kira how important it was that he follow up the synaesthesia lead that after all *she*'d given him. He reminded her about the huge bonus Ed Lister had promised to pay him if he found Ward. But she just said she had 'a bad feeling' about this case and begged him to drop it.

He felt sure she already sensed the storm that was about to hit them.

It was only luck that Kira hadn't found out yet about the money he owed. He'd managed to intercept the last bank statement, but if she happened to look in their joint savings account she'd know at once they were cleaned out. He decided not to call her just yet. It wasn't a conversation he wanted to have on an empty stomach.

A couple of miles back on Route 44, Campbell had seen signs for an 'authentic' diner in East Canaan. He found the old caboose without any trouble in a disused railway yard. Sitting up at the black marble and stainless steel counter (the interior had most of its original 1940s fittings) he ordered a cheeseburger deluxe with a side of chilli. They didn't have Mountain Dew so he drank Seven-Up.

When the food came he ate slowly, enjoying every mouthful. He finished off with a slice of cherry pie and coffee, and only then – not wanting to let the image of the blood-spattered mezzaluna spoil his dinner – let his thoughts drift back over the Skylands tragedy and the conversation he'd had with Joel Stilwell.

He was pretty sure the old doctor had seen through his story about epilepsy research. Maybe he'd made it too obvious that his interest in Ernest Seaton didn't stop at the boy's medical history. In a small, tight-knit community he had to assume news of his curiosity to learn what had become of him would travel. On the other hand maybe that was no bad thing.

By the time he got back to the Mountain View, it was too late London-time to get Ed Lister on the phone. Sitting on the floor in a lotus position, the TV tuned to the sports channel so he could watch the highlights from Wimbledon, Campbell wrote up his notes and e-mailed his client a cautiously optimistic progress report of his investigation. He described briefly the horrific events at Skylands and suggested that the nine-year-old Ernest Seaton's story certainly fitted the background of a delusional stalker – he could be the person they were looking for.

Campbell knew there was a strong possibility his e-mail would be intercepted and read by Ward. The recent contact the killer had made with Ed – using his daughter's screen ID to send him cryptic messages – was probably just a decoy so that he could gain access to his computer at Greenside. He suspected that Ward had always had some kind of electronic surveillance in place.

It was a risky strategy, one that for tactical reasons he couldn't share with his client, but if Ward discovered they were onto him it might just force him into making a mistake and flush him out into the open.

He reached for his cell to let Kira know he'd arrived safely. He wanted to tell her about the humming bird, the flash of red lightning at its throat. But then the thought struck him, what if the loan sharks hadn't believed him when he told them he had to leave town for a few days on a job? What if they figured he'd made a run for it, and decided to send Cholly round to Wild Palms Manor? The nice old guy in the lizard-skin boots . . . ringing their doorbell. He imagined Amy letting him in.

For a moment Campbell felt tempted. At the diner, he'd picked up a brochure for Foxwoods, 'the world's largest casino', just down the road in southeastern Connecticut – he could jump in the car, be there in an hour, hour and a half tops. 'With your credit score? They wouldn't even let you play the slots,' his Gamblers Anonymous voice mocked. 'You can eighty-six that idea, pal.' Campbell let out a groan and flipped open his cell.

He had until Friday to get the hundred thousand.

42

Ward lay in the dark with his eyes open. He heard a long screech of brakes in the distance, and imagined a car speeding downtown going through a stop light. He waited for the sound of impact that never came, trying to find a way back to sleep.

It was 4.45 a.m., the sky just starting to lighten, when he gave up. He got out of bed and pulling on a robe, made his way barefoot through the dark divisions of the loft guided by a faint ultramarine glow coming from the mail-server computer, which he kept on 24/7. He sat down at his workstation and stared for a moment at the monitor, following the procession of sea creatures across its full-size LCD screen. He watched as the manta ray swam across his screen and flapped off into the murky depths, then dismissed the graphics with a touch of the mouse. After rapidly performing the necessary functions, using keyboard shortcuts, he checked his mail.

Or rather, he checked Ed's mail. Quarter to ten in London, Monday morning. He'd be at the office by now, most likely online.

From a list of accounts, each one identified by a different username, Ward brought up the mailbox titled *pop3.homebeforedark.net.kg*, which was currently dedicated to receiving blind copies of any traffic in and out of Ed Lister's computer.

There were altogether six intercepts – three outgoing e-mails which looked like business, two website requests of little interest and one incoming from Campbell Armour, the private investigator hired by Ed to find out who killed his daughter.

No contact so far with 'Adorablejoker' – her screen-name made him cringe. He wondered if Ed realised she had others.

Ward had seen a copy of Armour's 'progress' report and on the whole it made reassuring reading. The attempt to profile him as a cyber-stalker, 'just reeking with symptoms' was laughably inept, and could only work to his advantage – the diagnosis was so wide of the mark, it meant they had to be looking for someone very different. He took exception though to one comment Armour had made. He'd described him as 'damaged goods'. Ward never liked the phrase and it irked him that some geeky *wunderkind* with no qualifications outside computing science could make that kind of assumption. He detected Kira's hand.

He opened Armour's message, sent last night at 11.01 p.m. EST, and downloaded the attached document headed 'Update'. He read the first paragraph and felt a sudden tightness at the centre of his chest. It announced the detective's safe arrival in Norfolk, Connecticut.

Ward became very still.

He had been expecting a tap on the shoulder sooner or later. But how could Armour have gone, almost overnight, from knowing nothing about him to getting so close he could feel his breath lift the hairs on the back of his neck?

The little slope had snuck up on him . . . Jesus, he hated that.

He rolled out of his seat, wincing as he put weight on the ankle he'd twisted on the railroad track at Linz, and limped over to the windows; he stood staring out at the livid sky. The rooftops thrown into silhouette, left the caustic taste of battery terminals on his tongue.

Without warning, the cloak of invisibility, which had protected him all his adult life, had been snatched from his back. How the hell had he *found* Joel Stilwell? The report didn't mention why the detective had flown up to Norfolk to see the old man, which suggested he'd already discussed the reason with Ed Lister. Yet, in his brief reply to the e-mail – 'Thrilled by your news. Congratulations on a remarkable breakthrough. Just to be able to put a name (and soon, let's hope, a face) to the monster changes everything' – Ed makes it clear this is all a revelation to him. He's never even heard of Skylands.

Well, of course the sonofabitch would deny all knowledge.

He read the note again and felt another surge of anxiety, as he realised the extent of his exposure. Doc Stilwell, Skylands, the Seatons, Grace Wilkes . . .

Relax, buddy. There's no way in the world they can bring it back to you. Ed Lister's the one walking the tightrope here. You need to assess the situation calmly, then plan your next move. Ward? Are you even listening?

He stretched his fingers, opening them, closing them.

This was the price he was always going to have to pay for rejoining the world. He took several deep breaths, went over and sat back down at his work-station. Before he could make any decision he needed to verify that the detective was where he said he was when he sent the message.

After extracting the IP address from the header on Campbell Armour's e-mail, Ward fed the numbers into a

Traceroute program, which would tell him where the message originated. In a second he had the route path, the city and country location of the servers the message had passed through on its way from Armour's computer to its destination point in the UK. The map on his screen gave him the information he needed. When he sent the e-mail, the detective had been hooked up to a network provider in the town of Stockbridge, Massachusetts, not far from the border with the northwest corner of Connecticut. Less than twenty miles from Norfolk.

The program couldn't pinpoint an address, but it only took Ward a few seconds to Google 'accommodation' in the Norfolk and Stockbridge areas and run off a list of local motels, inns and B&Bs. Then he swung around in his chair and picked up the printout of Armour's e-mail. The contact number he'd given Ed Lister matched the third motel on the list – the 'Mountain View' in Great Barrington.

A lid-muscle started to dance in Ward's left eye; he trapped it under a finger like an insect and held it till the tic stopped. It only happened when he was tired.

There were no windows in what he called his quarters. A curving wall of green-tinted glass tiles separated the sleeping area from the rest of the loft, allowing some daylight to filter through. It gave the bedroom, meagrely furnished with a chest of drawers, wooden chair and an antique press – all reclaimed from the street, out of choice rather than necessity – a permanently sickly hue. Ward slept on a narrow single bed that wouldn't have looked out of place in a monk's cell.

He tasted soot on his tongue, the bitter and indelible taste of the past.

He had misgivings about going home again, revisiting the historical location of images and events that never faded.

What happened a quarter of a century ago remained as vivid for him as if it was yesterday. Ward had the synaesthete's not-always-lucky gift of total recall. He could remember conversations he'd had as a child, prose passages he'd read only once, the precise location of objects in a room, floor plans and furniture arrangements, the order of books on a shelf, where every kitchen utensil 'lived' and had to be put away in its proper place.

He had a picture in his head of the mezzaluna lying on the draining board.

The next forty-five minutes he spent in the bathroom working out with weights until the sweat began to bead and the veins stand out on his forehead and shoulders. He doubted Ed Lister was as strong as he was in the arms. In London, Ward had watched him leave the house every morning to run in Hyde Park. Ed had looked a little stringy. But he liked the fact that the man who could have become his father-in-law kept himself in shape – it was one more thing they had in common.

Showered and shaved, Ward chose from his conservative wardrobe a faded oatmeal and rust madras shirt, tan chinos and an old pair of Timberland hiking boots – clothes that he thought would blend in with the rural Connecticut he remembered. Then he repacked the rucksack he'd taken with him to Europe.

He ate slowly a light breakfast of kefir and fruit with a book, *The Soul of the White Ant*, by Eugene Marais, propped in front of him. He'd decided to drive, hire a car and drive up there, following the Taconic Parkway north – he knew the way.

He would be home in a couple of hours.

43

Waiting for the Norfolk Library to open its doors, Campbell Armour sat across the street in his parked Toyota, observing a scene that was familiar to him mostly from watching old Hollywood movies as a boy growing up in Hong Kong. The quaint, prosperous little New England town nestled in a green bowl of hills, trees full of blossom and birdsong, smiling natives going about their day as if they had all the time and not much of a care in the world – it looked almost too good to be true.

Apart from the cars and clothes, Campbell thought, the town would have appeared much the same – just as peaceful and wholesome with its white-spired Congregational church, clapboard Colonials and old-fashioned stores – on that July day twenty-seven years ago when Ernest Seaton was found cowering in the broom closet at Skylands, his face smeared with blood as if he'd been anointed in some savage rite of initiation.

A mid-brown police cruiser with the windows down crawled past for the second time, the bulky state trooper at the wheel throwing a glance his way from behind a pair of Aviator shades and nodding. Campbell raised his can of Mountain Dew to the dude, took a sip. He could see what Dr Stilwell had meant about this being the kind of place that would have done its best to 'contain' the Seaton tragedy. It had an air of settled exclusivity that made him feel uncomfortable.

In town he'd sensed people looking at him as soon as his back was turned.

At a few minutes to ten, a battered Ford pick-up pulled into a parking space outside the ornate red barn that had been purpose-built as a library in Victorian times. A tall woman wearing blue jeans and an expensive linen jacket with a rope of grey hair hanging down her back, got out and trotted up the steps to the entrance porch, keys in hand.

Campbell gave it some time, then followed her into the building.

'How can we help you today?'

The girl with the grey plait was sitting behind the front desk. Up close she looked younger than he'd imagined. Her name-tag read Susan Mary Billetdeaux.

'You're welcome just to browse, if you like.'

He glanced around the library's lofty wooden interior with its stone fireplace and armchairs and paintings of wildlife scenes on the walls over the bookshelves; a solitary computer in an alcove the only concession to the modern age

Campbell cleared his throat. 'I dunno. You have microfiche? I'm looking for back issues of the *Litchfield County Times* for nineteen seventy-nine, July and August.'

Susan Mary smiled. 'Anything in particular you're looking for? We don't keep complete sets so you might do better searching by subject.'

He thought for a moment. He'd failed to find the archives of the local paper online. He saw no reason not to be upfront with her.

'You could try under murder or suicide,' Campbell said, watching her face for a reaction. 'The family was called Seaton. He was a dentist, killed his wife then shot himself. They lived out near Colebrook.'

'Well, that should narrow it down.' She smiled again slowly, as if she was amused by him, or by his unusual request. It was obvious she hadn't heard of the story.

'You're not from around here, Susan, are you?'

She shook her head and the plait switched. 'New York.'

'Me neither.'

'I sort of figured that.'

They both laughed. He followed her over to the reference section and watched her pull one of a dozen cloth-bound scrapbooks from the shelves and open it up on a reading table. Flipping through pages of yellowing press cuttings, she found what she was looking for and swivelled the book around. 'Here you go.'

MURDER SUICIDE VERDICT IN LOCAL TRAGEDY

'Did you know that dentists,' Campbell said, as he skimmed the text, 'have the highest suicide rate of any profession?'

Under the headline there was a photograph of Skylands. A white Colonial mansion on top of a wooded ridge. It was a distance shot taken from below and off to the side – Campbell felt the thrill of recognition.

He was looking at the house on the *homebeforedark* website.

'Dentists? Are you kidding?' Susan Mary said. 'They always seem so dull and boring. Maybe that's what it takes.'

The article added little to what Dr Stilwell had told him. He wasn't surprised that the inquest failed to offer a motive for the homicide. There was an inset picture of June and Gary Seaton; a mention, but disappointingly no photograph of the boy.

'I'd like to get this scanned . . . now, if possible.'

'Not a problem. I'd be glad to take care of that for you.'

He watched her disappear with the scrapbook through a door marked Private and couldn't help wondering what her silver-grey hair would look like loose, how far down her back it would reach.

At ten thirteen, Campbell e-mailed Ed Lister from the

library computer a copy of the article with a circle around the picture of Skylands, and a note: 'Look familiar? Let me know what you think. Taking a run up there now to check it out. C.'

As he left the building, starting to feel as if he was really getting somewhere at last, Campbell stopped at the desk to thank the librarian for her help.

'You wouldn't happen to know directions?'

'To Skylands? Sure. Take the mountain road out of Norfolk. Over the second ridge turn right up Deer Flats Road . . . last driveway on the left.'

He looked at her, bemused, as if this needed an explanation. Susan Mary smiled. 'You're not the first person to ask.'

44

adorablejoker: what are you doing here?
templedog: waiting for you
aj: don't fucking lie

I wasn't lying – I was at the office, checking my e-mails before going into a meeting. All right, I'd only logged on a few moments earlier. But lately I'd taken to loitering online in the hope of bumping into her, tormenting myself with the idea that, though invisible to me, she was there, talking to someone else.

Then I saw the little grey face beside her screen-name light up and any negative or jealous feelings I might have had instantly evaporated; it was as if the sun had burst out from behind the clouds. Was it just a chance meeting? Jelly insisted she'd deleted me, taken my name off her buddy list, and so had no way of telling when I was online, but I had my doubts. I think she'd seen that I was there and had chosen the 'I'm available' option.

She wanted to get in touch.

td: where are you?

aj: at the beach staying with friends

td: I thought you hated the ocean . . . your friends in Westhampton, right?

aj: at least it's cooler out here than Brooklyn

aj: hey, guess what? i bought this outfit for a party tonight and omg, it has *the* cutest top. it's a V-neck and a gold kinda color . . . now i just have to find a pair of shoes to go with it and . . .

td: I'm sure you'll be the belle of the ball

I glanced over the top of the screen through the door of my office into the conference room where the team had gathered. I had called an in-house meeting at two o'clock with the accounts department. It was now a quarter past.

Audrey caught my eye and raised an inquiring eyebrow.

aj: yeah, right . . . it's at a club in town called Scarlett's

td: I remember, used to be a disco . . . you want to be careful about giving out that kind of information. I could hop on a plane and be there by midnight

aj: ummm . . . maybe that wouldn't be such a great idea . . . look, i wasn't gonna tell you this . . . but there's a chance my ex might show up

td: I see . . . so rather than listen to your heart

aj: please, ed, don't do this

td: you choose to be with someone you never loved and never will

aj: oh jesus . . . do I really have to spell it out for you?

td: hold on a second

I had incoming mail from Campbell Armour.

251

I quickly opened the attachment and felt my stomach flip over as the clipping of the Skylands story filled the screen. There was no question it was the same house.

I glanced at the other photo, the one of the Seatons. In their wedding outfits, they looked like any young American couple from that graceless era, though a hint of stylishness about the bride made me look closer. It was nothing definite, but June Seaton reminded me a little of someone I met once a long time ago.

I dismissed the thought instantly.

My attention was focused on Skylands. It gave me a strange feeling to be looking at the childhood home of the person who killed Sophie. I enlarged the image and pored over the details, excited by the possibility that the old white house – clearly the model for the virtual mansion on the *homebeforedark* website and the drawings in Sophie's sketchbook – could soon lead us to him. It was a hugely significant development. I looked at my watch.

Campbell would already be on his way there.

aj: i slept with him

td: congratulations . . . what do you want me to say, I'm happy for you?

td: it means nothing and you know it

aj: why are you doing this? Why can't you just let me go?

td: because I believe we are meant to be together

aj: oh god, will you *stop*

td: i fell in love with you, Jelly . . . is that a crime?

aj: not with me, with your idea of me

td: you can go on denying it, but it's so obvious you feel the same way

aj: no, you got that wrong, mister . . . and this is the end of the line

I watched her leave – that is, I waited until the grey pop-up flag confirmed, 'Adorablejoker is now offline' – then I leaned back in my chair and closed my eyes. My chest hurt, I couldn't breathe, my stomach was tied up in knots; and yet, I felt strangely elated by the encounter.

We'd been here before. All our conversations now seemed to end with Jelly saying she didn't want to talk to me again, but this was different.

I thought about her reaction when I had suggested flying over to see her that evening. It had been surprising, hadn't it – I scrolled back to make sure I wasn't just fooling myself – that she didn't reject the idea out of hand?

In a way she seemed to be saying, come.

Why else reveal where she was going to be? She was using the boyfriend to make me jealous, to make sure I did hop on a plane. It was clear that she felt the same way I did – she just wasn't ready to admit it yet.

Then, when I least expected it, she messaged me back.

aj: could you do me a favor?
td: depends what it is
aj: could you look this way . . . look at me for a sec?
aj: just for one second before you go?

When she wrote that I felt my heart jump and beat faster for a few seconds. I pulled up Jelly's photo. Her face filled the screen and I could hear the thumping in my chest like a metronome racing ahead of the song I was listening to on my iPod – it was Stevie Wonder's 'Superstition'.

td: ok, I'm looking
aj: i lean in and kiss you softly on the lips
td: damn you
aj:. you're right. i think maybe this was a mistake, I should go
td: only after I return the favour
aj: haven't you got work to do, people to see?
td: they can wait . . .

aj: well . . . if it's just a kiss
td: you've got me confused here
aj: i'm confused my damned self
aj: i don't know if it's the heat or what
td: glad I'm not the only one feeling it
aj: yeah . . . what can you do?

'Any chance of your joining us sometime this week?' Audrey asked.

I hadn't heard her come into the room. She was standing in front of my desk, hand on hip, a few feet away from my laptop.

The picture of Jelly still filled the screen.

I quickly closed it down and removed my earpiece. 'Are we all set?'

Audrey just nodded. I could hear the guitar riff from 'Superstition' leaking tinnily from the white earphone. Then it struck me that something about that last suggestive exchange with Jelly didn't ring right. When she came back on a moment ago, I'd noticed that there was a slight delay on her side of the conversation that hadn't been there before. I wasn't a hundred per cent sure – and there could have been another explanation – but I had a suspicion (it still makes me queasy to think about) that after saying it was 'the end of the line' she'd sent no more messages.

I had been talking to someone else.

'You feeling all right?' Audrey asked. 'You look like you've seen a ghost.'

'Change of plan,' I said quietly, as the implications began to sink in. If it was Ward pretending to be Jelly, I realised, then he not only knew of her existence but almost certainly had found out her identity, her phone numbers, where she worked and lived. She was in real and immediate danger.

'I have to go to New York . . . tonight. I want you to cancel all my appointments and book me on the last flight.'

I stood up and started to clear my desk, wondering how often I'd talked to Ward under the impression that I was having a conversation with Jelly – and, vice versa, if she had ever spoken to the murderer thinking he was me.

48

'Grace?' Ward said into his cell phone. 'Grace Wilkes?'

'Who wants to know? Who *is* this?'

'You don't recognise my voice?'

Silence the other end.

'I guess it's been a while. Ernest Seaton, Grace.'

There was a wheezy intake of breath.

'Ernie? I don't believe it. Ernie . . .' she croaked, then started to cry. It was the first time they'd spoken since he left home. Ward held the phone away from his ear. 'Oh my . . . oh my Lord. Ernie, is it really you?'

'You haven't forgotten,' he said, adding, once she became halfway coherent again, 'There's no need for anyone else to know.'

'It's okay, I'm alone . . . on my own now.' She stopped the boohooing long enough to let out a heavy sigh. 'Earl passed away last year.'

'I'm sorry to hear that.' It wasn't news, but her saying it brought back memories of a tall, lean man with tired sunken eyes in a red and black plaid Woolrich shirt, sweeping leaves in the yard. 'I'll get to the point, Grace. I'm in a situation. There's this guy, some kind of a detective, trying to stick his nose where it has no business.'

'Would that be the same one called here last night asking questions? I told him I was out of town till tomorrow.'

'You always knew what to do.' He let her hear the sound of his laugh.

'Where are you, Ernie?' she asked, still snuffling.

'Up at the house.'

He was standing on the front porch, looking down at the ruin of the garden; he'd been shocked to see how far the place had gone back. The terraces were so densely overgrown he could barely distinguish the bones of the original layout. Boulders from the retaining walls had spilled out and rolled down the hill, coming to rest against the roots of trees and shrubs. The white fence had gone, the garden gate, the gravel circle where he used to set up his armies and re-enact historic battles.

Ward put everything back exactly the way he remembered it.

He didn't need to rearrange the view. You could still see for sixty miles clear across to the Berkshires, the forested ridges overlapping and getting fainter and fainter till they faded into blue mist on the horizon.

Unspoiled, the kind of view Ed Lister would have appreciated.

'I could meet you there,' Grace said.

In the distance he heard a car coming up the road. He jumped down from the porch and walked quickly to the edge of the terrace, where he knew there was a gap in the trees. Below he glimpsed the little silver Camry hesitating before it swung off Piper Hill Lane and then continued up the dirt track towards the house, towing a cloud of dust.

Ward turned and looked up at the one window on the front of the building that wasn't shuttered. The blue of the sky reflected in its panes tasted of rusty nails.

'No, there isn't time now. I'll get back to you.' He let himself in the front door with the key and locked it behind him.

It took a moment for his eyes to adjust to the gloom. The round table was still there at the end of the hall, covered in a dust sheet; beyond it the rising stairs. A shaft of light fell across the floor from the cracked door leading to the kitchen. The air felt cool on his face. Ward realised he was sweating.

His feet made no sound as he crossed the bare pine floor. He recognised a few pieces of furniture coated in thick dust, but the house had mostly been stripped of his family's possessions. Then through the door into the parlour he glimpsed the old upright his mother used to play. An indefinable smell, somewhere between dried flowers and mildew, became a sword in his hand. He had to fight off the memories that crowded in, jostling for his attention as he climbed the stairs.

On the landing, following the spore of filtered daylight, Ward entered the guest room and went over to the single unshuttered window just as the Toyota pulled up in front of the house, radio blaring. He watched Campbell Armour, wearing a red tracksuit with a double white stripe down the side, get out of the car and look around; then, satisfied he'd found the right place, lean back in to cut the ignition.

'Son of a gun, we'll have big fun . . .'

The abrupt muting of the old country standard left a silence deeper than before, stirring unwelcome echoes of his childhood and being forced to play musical statues in the front parlour. His father would always yank the needle on 'Jambalaya' just before Hank Williams sang the words '. . . *on the bayou'*, and behind the boy's pale eyes the orange lattice shapes that shivered to the beat dissolved, throwing him off balance. Saw you move, son.

Orange being his default colour for pain.

Ward drew back behind the faded chintz drapes as the detective, using his hand as a sun-visor, squinted up at the second-storey windows. He'd seen him around the village earlier, at the library and the real-estate office, overheard him asking dumb questions – the guy was an amateur. He might know computers, but he was way, way out of his depth here. Ward just hoped, for everyone's sake, that little Jackie Chan wouldn't try something stupid now like breaking into the house.

It wasn't ready for him yet.

What if he does come in, though, uninvited? You thought this through, Ernster? What you do? Hide in the broom closet again?

Short even for a Chinese, the kid had a wiry athletic build. It wasn't that Ward didn't think he could take him. Just that once he entered the premises, he couldn't let him leave. His eye fell on a lead sash-weight lying on the window ledge.

Now wait . . . wait just a goddamned minute. No, YOU pick it up . . .

Gripping the foot-long lead in one hand, Ward went quietly downstairs.

'How long will you be gone?' Laura asked. She was waiting for me in the bedroom when I came out of the shower.

'A day or two . . . I won't really know until I see what's involved. We're looking at a couple of potential sites, maybe more.'

'I don't understand. This just happened?'

I used the towel to dry my hair, rubbing vigorously. 'Al called me two hours ago from New York. He's got an inside track on a deal that could be spectacular. I have to move fast, or risk missing out.' I smiled at her. 'You know how it goes.'

'Why don't you let him handle it, or send someone else?'

'It's an old estate in Connecticut. Al said the view from the house is "America before the Fall". Not that I don't trust him, I just like to see what I'm buying.'

I dropped the towel and reached for the clean shirt I'd laid out on the bed and slipped it on. Laura stared at me for a moment, then went over to the sofa under the window and sat down. 'I suppose you've forgotten we're meant to be having dinner with the Rentons tonight. Shall I ring them and cancel, or will you?'

'Why don't you go?' I said lightly. 'It'll be fun.'

'You know I can't face dinner parties on my own.'

She frowned and looked down at the floor. There was a silence. I felt she knew that I was keeping something from her. I got dressed, selecting one of the dark blue suits I always wear when I travel on business. Betrayal hung in the air, but I could only think about Jelly and the fact that I needed to find her before Ward did.

Laura seemed lost in her own thoughts.

'There's another reason,' I said hesitantly, as if I was about to reveal the real purpose of the trip, 'in case you were wondering.' After Paris, I'd been expecting her to question my 'work' pretext for flying to America; in fact, I was almost hoping she would. 'I'm going to meet up with Campbell Armour while I'm over there . . . the private detective I told you about. It looks like he's made real progress.'

'I thought he lived in Florida.'

'He's planning to be in New York on Thursday.'

She rose and walked slowly over to the door, then turned and stood there for a moment; dressed in all white, she looked ominously serene. 'I take it I've heard all I'm going to hear from you on that subject.'

I shrugged. 'I know you disapprove, so . . . I spare you the details.'

There was another difficult silence.

'By the way, that policewoman rang . . . Edith Cowper. She must have just missed you at the office.'

With a heavy, wound-tight feeling I went on packing, folding my clothes into a small suitcase. 'I'll call her when I get back.'

'She said it was important.' I sensed Laura's eyes on me waiting for some reaction, but then she gave up. 'If you need me, I'll be downstairs.'

The front door to Skylands was locked.

Walking slowly around the porch, Campbell tested the shutters for all the ground-floor windows in case one had been left unfastened. At the back of the house he came to a glassed-in section and, behind a torn screen, another locked door. He could see into a mud room with snow shoes and an old pair of wooden ski poles hanging on the wall; beyond it lay what looked like the kitchen.

He wandered through the backyard taking pictures – he might need up-to-date evidence that the virtual mansion was a recreation of Ernest Seaton's old home.

The afternoon was hot and still and what remained of the garden gave off the rank smell of overgrown vegetation. Behind an abandoned berry patch, Campbell came on traces of enclosure wire for a tennis court that had long ago reverted to scrub. Hidden away lower down the slope, there was a pond choked by rushes and yellow iris with an old swimming platform half sunken in the weeds. A heron standing on a dead tree flapped off over the water.

Looking back up at the white house on the hill, framed by live oaks and hemlock, he could see what Skylands must have been like when the place was lived in and cared for – the sun catching its hipped slate roof, smoke rising from the end-chimneys of glazed dusty pink brick, the black-green shutters thrown wide open, and in the violet shadow under its long white-pillared porch, a suggestion of movement, the promise of a cool drink . . . it was like a house in a dream.

For a nine-year-old boy, growing up here, Campbell imagined, it must have seemed like paradise. Then, one hot summer's night, a kitchen knife snatched up in God-knows-what kind of murderous rage turns it into hell on earth, and the dream that was Skylands is gone forever. The only *true* paradises are the ones we have lost. Was there a clue there to what made Ernest Seaton tick? He wondered if there were any childhood relics, toys and other stuff in the house that might help him trace the man Ernest grew up to become.

The shrill jangling of his cell phone startled him.

Half expecting it to be Ed Lister, he glanced at the display. Unfamiliar number, but the 941 area code covered a fair chunk of Southwest Florida: the loan sharks worked out of Sarasota and Venice. Campbell hesitated, then switched off his cell and, sweat breaking out at his temples, walked slowly back towards the mansion.

The interior of Skylands, he'd learnt from a local realtor, was pretty much intact. The present owners, an elderly New York couple, bought the estate as an investment in the early '90s, then retired to Hawaii. They'd never lived there.

'Nobody knows their plans for the property,' Hersey Dodds had confided in him, loosening up once she realised that Campbell wasn't interested in moving his family to Norfolk. 'It's not on the market, hasn't been rented out or occupied for fifteen years, you can guess why . . . great potential though.'

He thought about Susan Mary at the town library: when he'd asked her who else had wanted directions to get here, she'd just said, oh, some developer from New York who seemed interested in buying the place. Even though it wasn't for sale.

Sitting on the front porch, removing tares that had become entwined in the laces of his trainers, Campbell considered his options. It would be simple enough to force his way into Skylands. The problem was half the town, including the fat deputy, had to know he was up here. Jail-time for breaking and entry – there were no-trespassing signs posted on the trees along the driveway – wouldn't look too good on his CV.

On the other hand, he might not get another chance.

A faint creaking of timbers came from somewhere deep inside the house. He kept still for a moment, but the sound wasn't repeated and he put it down to heat expansion or settlement. When he thought about the trouble he was in, the money he owed, the huge bonus his client had promised – he didn't have a choice.

He went over to examine the front door, remembering that, when searching for a hidden access to the virtual house, he'd tried the cat-flap. He hadn't noticed it before, but the bottom left-hand panel of the door had been overlaid by a thin sheet of ply secured by light nails, then painted. Hunkering down, Campbell used his pocket knife to lever off the veneer and found the cat-flap behind it, still intact.

The hinged plastic lid wasn't locked and with a squawk of resistance it swung back as he pushed his hand through the small opening and felt around inside, looking for a key. Then his arm, up to the elbow. There was nothing.

Wanting to be sure the key wasn't there but just out of reach, he changed his position and, holding the flap back with one hand, put his eye up to the hole. He could only see a few feet into the dim hall, but it was enough for him to register that the thick layer of dust covering the floorboards had been disturbed – how recently it was impossible to say. He could make out footprints going away from the door, and coming back. He tried turning his head, straining for a better view.

He let the cat-flap go and it rocked briefly on its hinges, then was still. All he could hear was his own slightly raised heartbeat.

His hands shook a little as he closed the pocket knife.

Off to the left, in the far corner of his limited field of vision, he had seen a pair of tan hiking boots . . . somebody was standing there, motionless, just inside the door.

Backing away slowly, he stepped down off the porch, then forced himself to walk not run across the terrace to his car, the katydids falling silent ahead of him, then starting up their racket again in his wake.

Campbell resisted the urge to look back at the house until he was safely behind the wheel, doors locked and the motor running.

46

'How would you feel,' I heard Laura say behind me, 'about my coming with you?'

I was standing at our bedroom door, looking around to make sure I hadn't forgotten anything. 'Coming with me?' It was so unexpected I didn't understand at first what she meant. 'You mean to New York? Tonight?'

She'd just run up the stairs and was a little out of breath. I turned to face her, a suitcase in each hand, afraid of seeing something in her eyes that said, I know.

Laura smiled. 'Don't look so stricken, Ed.'

'It's just that I'm surprised. You're not a last-minute sort of person. I mean . . . you don't have a ticket, you're not even packed.'

'Those are details.' Her voice unnaturally bright.

'Otherwise,' I recovered enough to add smoothly, 'I can't think of anything nicer.'

'We haven't been to New York together in ages.'

'I know, but why now? I'll be busy all the time.'

'I just thought it might be an opportunity to see Alice. You know how she's been on my conscience and, while you're working, I could go out to La Rochelle and spend some time with her.'

Alice, old Mrs Fielding, was Laura and Will's grandmother. In her late eighties, frail and befuddled, but with a tenacious, independent spirit she attributed to her Virginian ancestry, she lived more or less alone at Gilmans Landing on the Hudson.

'It's a wonderful idea. Just a pity you didn't think of it sooner. Laura, I have to leave now or I'll miss my plane.' Audrey had found me a seat on the 8.30, the last Virgin Atlantic flight to JFK. I had under an hour to get to Heathrow.

'I didn't know that *you* were going until an hour ago.' Laura stood there at the top of the stairs, one hand on the banister, blocking my way down.

'We'll do it another time, I promise,' I said, trying to resist the undertow of remorse, but knowing full well I was destroying the trust of someone I'd shared my life with for twenty-three years.

'You could at least suggest I get a flight tomorrow and join you.'

'Sweetheart, I was going to . . . I just don't think it'll work. We'd hardly catch a glimpse of each other. Listen, if it's any comfort to you, I'll go out and check on Alice, make sure she's all right.'

'Would you? She'd really appreciate a visit. You know how she adores you.' Laura started to smile, then bit her underlip. 'Sure you can spare the time?'

No doubt she was being ironic, but I'd talked her out of coming: that was all that mattered. I caught a look of regret, or maybe just resignation in her eyes. 'Listen, when I get back, it might be a good idea if we had a talk.'

'About?'

'I dunno . . . Sophie, our marriage, us.'

She gave a little laugh. 'What is there to discuss?'

I knew what she meant. We couldn't seem to connect any more, so why waste time talking when it could only make things worse? I'd imagined a different kind of conversation, one perhaps where we agreed amicably that we'd reached the end of the road. Only we weren't there yet. 'I've never told you this before,' I said. 'I don't think you realise how much I loved her. Sophie, I mean.'

Laura sighed. 'Still all about you, isn't it?'

'All right, if that's the way you feel . . . forget it.'

'Ed, I'm sorry.' She came forward and put her arms under my jacket around my waist. I lowered the cases. We said good-bye with a clumsy embrace, hugging each other more tightly and for longer than usual, clinging to the wreckage I suppose.

I sensed that Laura had more that she wanted to say, but I didn't really have time to listen. The Mercedes was waiting outside the front door. I could hear Michael, my driver, fidgeting in the hall below.

'If we ever find who did this to us . . . maybe then we can start to rebuild our lives.'

She pulled away and I saw she was crying. 'I don't know.'

I had no idea what was really on Laura's mind, but I suspect that at this point neither of us believed we had a future together. I just knew I was flying to New York to protect the girl I'd fallen in love with, whose life I'd unwittingly placed in danger – and, as focused as I was on tracking down Sophie's killer, I could think about nothing else. The two aims, anyway, were now intimately intertwined.

My last online conversation with Jelena, unsettling as it had been, had let me see that while she appeared to be saying 'come', it could equally well have been Ward who'd invited me over to the party at Scarlett's.

*　　*　　*

265

Somebody had a lucky escape.

What about you? Relieved? Or are we just the tiniest bit disappointed?

There you were waiting for him behind the door like some psycho in a splatter flick. Ernie, I warned you about getting a taste for this shit.

Ward closed his eyes. He'd let a whole ten minutes elapse since he heard the detective's car engine fade away at the bottom of the hill. Just to be sure he wasn't coming back. Now for the hard part. He started to climb the stairs.

On the landing, he stopped outside the third of four identical panelled oak doors, the door to his parents' bedroom. Ward reached out a hand, hesitated. He could hear it already. The banging gradually getting louder and more insistent, swelling to a relentless pounding beat. It sounded like it came from downstairs, but he'd checked the screens and shutters, they were all securely fastened, and there wasn't a breath of wind.

He'd come across his mother's packed suitcases in the hall . . .

He turned the handle and the din stopped; he cracked the door, pushed it all the way open. Before him lay the scene that had greeted him that night.

His bewildered eye had fled at first to a reproduction of the painting *Christina's World* by Andrew Wyeth hanging crooked over the bed, unable to meet the freeze-frame stillness of the devastation below – then something splashed to the floor and the room rushed out at him.

The colours, shapes and tastes flowing through him in a giddying swirl he had no way of controlling. He felt the heat rising – a night-time heat, muggy and close – as a solid obelisk he could see and touch. He heard a high-pitched whine that felt like a hand around his heart. His senses were cross-firing at will, going haywire.

266

The images that followed came with an emotional intensity he found almost unbearable: his mother's head hanging off the bed, her pearly teeth glistening through the mask of blood that had the smell of an eraser . . . her open eyes, staring at him upside down, searing his tongue with the bitter inky taste of quinine . . . the grey and pink matter of his father's brains spilled on the rug, on the ceiling . . . smoke clearing, the scent of cordite, green apples, the dry rustle of a million insect wings.

He couldn't cross the threshold, couldn't move, couldn't see who was in there with them. But there was *someone* . . .

He was sure of it now.

The vision cleared, leaving the room empty, yet when he tried to close the door, it seemed to stick halfway, as if there were an obstruction on the other side. He put his shoulder to the frame and pulled with all his strength, then the resistance suddenly gave way and he fell back. The door banged shut and for an instant, marooned on the bare, silent landing, Ward felt the rapture of complete certainty.

He knew he was justified.

Not everyone is lucky enough to find the path. You have to learn first to appreciate and accept the irony that lies at the heart of all progress, which says that in the end there's no such thing. He only discovered his life's true purpose when the past he'd been encouraged to forget finally caught up with him.

He understood now that however hard you try to become another person, you never will. You can shuffle the cards all you want and believe you have changed the hand you were dealt; you can adapt to changing circumstances and imagine that you've grown emotionally, morally, spiritually. You can chase after wealth and happiness, follow gospels of self-improvement and rebirth, you can wrap your faith in a flag – but you'll be deceiving yourself. You will remain who you are and always were from cradle to the grave.

The only goal is becoming that individual.

You know what I think? I think the need to seek revenge was always there, always part of you . . . you just couldn't admit it, not while you were someone else.

Until two years ago he had another life – a low-key, reasonably successful existence founded on a lie. He was invisible. Nobody knew his real name, or the true story of his origins. He had never spoken about what became of him in the aftermath of his parents' deaths; how he'd gone in what seemed like an instant (the break was so complete) from an idyllic boyhood in the bosom of a loving family to the guardianship of a cold, childless couple. The way his new 'folks' handled his arrival in their midst had been to make a bonfire of the past. He could bring nothing with him from his old life to the new. No photos of his former home or family, no books or letters, no toys . . . no reminiscences allowed. He was forbidden to speak about what happened, or grieve.

Something died in you that night . . . I know, buddy, I was there and I heard it all before. Now can we get the hell out of this mausoleum?

When his grandmother was dying two years ago, he'd thought about flying over to New York to say goodbye (he was living in Europe at the time), but in the end couldn't see the point. Why rake up memories that he had reassigned to someone else? He spoke to her on the phone and, after she passed, leaving him enough money to make a difference, wrote to Grace Wilkes, who posted on to him some of his grandmother's personal effects. They included an unsent letter in his mother's hand, which the old lady had kept safe all those years.

The letter changed his life.

Under the stairs, Ward shone his key-ring light inside the broom closet where he hid that night. A brush and pan, a pile of old *Life* magazines, some gap-stringed wooden tennis rackets . . . the blue cone of light threw the dusty objects into relief in turn. He placed the lead sash-weight just inside the closet, leaving the door ajar.

The letter was a wake-up call. It gave him a new sense of direction, showed him the way back to his long-lost self. It called him home.

Crossing the hall, Ward entered what used to be the lounge. The old cabinet TV in the corner was gone, but the two armchairs hadn't been moved. He stripped off a dust sheet and sat in the one nearest the door, running his hand down behind the seat cushions, searching for the remote. There was nothing there.

Hey, guess what I found out.

The schwartze mentioned a disco, Scarlett's, right? Well, according to the Westhampton Beach Chamber of Commerce, Scarlett's stopped trading way back in the 80s? I mean, really, how funny is that?

He removed his cell phone from the breast pocket of his shirt and used it to mime pointing a remote control at an imaginary screen, then turned his head sharply to his left, looking at where the playhouse had stood, under the window.

He called Grace back.

I caught a glimpse of Laura watching from the front porch as the car turned left out of Campden Hill Place and slipped into the westbound traffic on Holland Park Avenue, heading towards Shepherd's Bush. Michael said, over his shoulder, 'Marloes Road looks like our best bet.' He glanced up at the rearview mirror.

'Okay with you, Mr Lister?' Trying to catch my eye.

He pulled into the turning lane and slowed down. I removed my earphones and keyed my brother-in-law's number on my mobile.

'Mr Lister?' When I didn't respond, he threw the heavy Mercedes into a U-turn.

Will, who was expecting my call, answered on the first ring. 'Where are you?'

'On my way to the airport.'

'You sure this is wise?'

'You know why I'm going. I told you, Campbell has found the house the drawings and website are based on – Ward's old family home in Connecticut.'

'That's not what I'm talking about.'

When he first heard about the synaesthesia connection, Will was sceptical of being able to identify a psychopath though a little-understood neurological condition. But he had to give Campbell credit for the fact that in a week we'd gone from *'he could be anyone, anywhere on the planet'* to a name, a location, soon perhaps a face.

'You're right, there is something else.' I took a deep breath. 'I'm concerned about the girl. I think she could be at risk. Because of me.' I didn't elaborate. I didn't feel like going into it with him.

'All the more reason, I'd have thought, for leaving her well alone.'

There was a silence. I imagined Dr Calloway sitting back in his office chair, hands clasped behind his head, studying the ceiling.

'Okay, I know how this must sound to you.'

I'd already admitted to him that my feelings for Jelena had evolved.

'You say you're "in love" with someone you've never met, never laid eyes on? It sounds exactly like what it is, I'm afraid – an imaginary experience.'

'Maybe so, but it feels . . . like we've always known each other. We know each other's thoughts. I only have to think about her, Will, and . . .'

'Ed,' he cut me off, 'the sensation of being inside someone else's head is one of the commonest illusions in online relationships. The internet has given "soulmates" a new dimension that's entirely consistent with the nebulousness of the concept.'

I gave a rocky laugh.

'Does she feel the same way about you?'

'She won't admit it, but . . . yes, I believe she does.'

'It's easy to be misled by the strength of one's own feelings,' he said quietly. I could tell that my answer worried him. 'The less you know about the other – the person you project your idealised desires onto – the deeper the infatuation. Say you find Island Girl, the danger is you won't be able to see that you've nothing in common.' He hesitated. 'Or know when to take no for an answer.'

It was a gentle warning and the closest Will came to suggesting that my love for Jelly might be obsessive, verging on the pathological. I realised then that I didn't really want or need his advice.

Neither of us spoke for a while. Then he said in a different tone, 'You know what I think? I think this has got very little to do with the girl – it's about losing Sophie. You're still grieving for her, Ed. Go home to your wife and family and try to work things out. They are the only ones who can help you. They need your help as much as you need theirs.'

I felt a pang of guilt that would stay with me after I hung up; but it didn't change anything. I'd already made up my mind and I had complete certainty that it was the right, the only possible decision.

'I need to find her, Will,' I said grimly, 'before he does.'

271

47

Campbell Armour ignored the call-waiting signal.

Sitting with his laptop between his knees on the floor of his room at the Mountain View, he dragged the cursor through the gate and up onto the porch of the virtual mansion and clicked on the front door.

Still nothing. He tried again. He was on auto-pilot, repeating the procedure every half-minute or so while he talked to his daughter on the phone and watched live coverage of the second day at Wimbledon.

His visit to the real Skylands had left him feeling badly shaken. He'd been expected up at the old house and, when he thought about the hiking boots behind the front door – they could only have been Ward's – and how close he'd come to attempting to break in, it made him sick to his stomach. The strange part was that he even felt uneasy now about trying to access the *homebeforedark* website, as if he knew he was expected here too at the virtual house.

'Hold on, honey,' he said.

The ding-dong door-chime had startled him, drawing his attention away from the centre-court action. He saw the front door swing open.

'Yessss!' Campbell punched the air, as if he'd hit a winner.

Pointing the remote at the TV, he pressed the mute button, and said to Amy, 'Daddy has to go now, darlin'. Love you. Tell Mommy I love her too, and I'll talk to you both later. See ya tomorrow.'

He flipped his cell shut and, stuffing a handful of Doritos

into his mouth, for the first time entered the virtual Skylands.

The photos he'd taken earlier had established that the house on his screen was an exact scaled replica of Ernest Seaton's childhood home. The graphics were not just impressive, they were uncanny: confirming what Campbell had read about the synaesthete's gift for memorising spatial information. As he crossed the threshold, activating the 'footsteps' sound-effect Ed had told him about, the door closed behind him and he found himself walking down the gloomy hall that he had peered into that morning through the cat-flap. No dust here though, or hiking boots. The interior of Skylands was spotless. As it must once have been.

Not knowing how much time he had, Campbell dragged the cursor swiftly towards the back of the hall, his footsteps quickening as he did so, and positioned himself at the bottom of the staircase. The 3-D image swivelled around to meet him and there, straight ahead, rose the first flight of stairs.

The program would only permit him to climb slowly, step at a time, until he reached the first half-landing. Then, as he turned and continued upwards, the perspective changed and his impression of the rising stair in front of him was replaced by an overhead view, as if his eye had soared to the chandelier hanging from the ceiling, and he was looking down on himself from above.

There was something about the scene that was both familiar and menacing, yet he couldn't quite place it. He could hear music now – the soft tinkle of a piano drifting from another part of the house – as he climbed the second flight to a galleried landing with four doors evenly spaced around the central well.

He moved the cursor along the landing and paused outside the door nearest to the stairhead. Reaching for the bag of corn chips, he glanced over the top of his screen, watched Federer serve another ace; then, smiling at himself for feeling even mild apprehension, clicked on the handle.

The door swung back to reveal what could only have been Ernest Seaton's bedroom. As he took in the virtual contents of the narrow room – the Yankees All-Stars poster over the bed, baseball mitt on the foot-locker under the window, stacks of Marvel comics, a first generation Star Wars light-sabre propped in a corner, toy soldiers and cars, all neatly arranged – Campbell realised this was more than he could have hoped to find inside the real Skylands. But apart from the austere tidiness (another synaesthetic trait) there was nothing unusual or revealing here – it was typical of any nine-year-old boy's room from a quarter-century ago.

The detective walked on around the landing, his footsteps softened by a rug now, but here and there causing a floorboard to creak. The second and third doors were locked. He was about to try the handle of the fourth, when a light snapped on inside the room and gleamed under the sill and around the edges of the door-frame.

Campbell cracked his knuckles. He had a feeling he was about to find out *why* Ward had finally decided to admit him to the house. As he watched, intently now, a shadow darkened the strip of light under the door. It was as though someone had stepped up close to it on the other side.

He was waiting for the door to open, when his cell phone rang.

'I'm in the departure lounge at Heathrow.'

'Can I call you right back?'

'This won't take long. I'd like to meet up Thursday after-noon.'

'No problem, I should be through here by then.'

'I have to go out to my wife's grandmother's place on the Hudson for lunch, but with any luck I'll be back by two . . .'

'Ed, I'm kinda tied up right now.'

'Okay, I'll e-mail you the details. I take it you're still in Norfolk.'

'Yeah. Haven't been lynched yet. It's the house all right.'

'You're doing a really great job, Campbell.'

'Big old place, all shut up, hasn't been lived in for years. Any chance of an advance on the bonus? Just kidding.' He thought of mentioning his possible encounter with Ward at Skylands, but decided against it. Still watching the screen, Campbell asked his client. 'By the way, the Seatons look at all familiar to you?'

'No. Why would they? I thought I said that in my e-mail.'

He sounded a little defensive. 'We're still trying to find a connection, Ed.'

There was a pause. He could be lying, but what for? 'Did you talk to the housekeeper yet?' Ed asked.

'Holy . . . shit.' Campbell froze, staring at the screen.

The fourth door was slowly being inched open. 'Hold on.'

'Is everything all right?'

The door opened all the way and out of the blaze of light something emerged crawling on all fours. It lifted its head and he thought for an instant it was a burning child, then with startling speed the fiery icon scuttled across the hall and, before he could be certain what exactly he'd seen, dived into the boy's room.

Campbell jogged his cursor and from nowhere the thin black figure of 'Mrs Danvers' appeared. He watched her go forward and close the door to what he guessed was the master bedroom, turn and come gliding past him along the landing.

Campbell laughed. 'You caught me at a good moment, that's all.'

As a piece of theatre it was an anti-climax, perhaps intentionally so, but as he watched, still absorbed, the hatchet-faced avatar smoothly descended the stairs. At the half-landing she stopped, looked back up and beckoned him to follow.

'Ed, I gotta go.'

'Just be careful.'

The avatar had disappeared down the hall that led to the rear of the building. He heard the screen-door bang shut and went after her, navigating with the cursor the twists and turns of a labyrinthine kitchen region. The walls echoed the simulated clatter of his running footsteps.

He found Danvers waiting for him on the back porch, in the dark.

It had been daylight when he entered the house (in real time it was still the middle of the afternoon); now suddenly Campbell found himself looking at a sky full of stars, a slither of moon above the roof, fireflies winking from the high banks of mountain laurel.

His guide withdrew a flashlight from her pocket and, pulling a shawl over her head, set off through the grounds, taking the path between the barns that he had explored that morning. Looking back he saw that there were no lights showing in the house. She led him out of the garden and soon they were deep in the woods.

A grove of dark arrowy pines loomed above them. The beam of the flashlight shivered and dipped as Danvers' silhouette came to a halt at the gate of a small cemetery encircled by a wrought-iron fence.

He heard the cry of an owl – standard for a night-time scene, but always effective – as the beam passed over the half-dozen headstones, came back and lingered on an elaborate winged monument for June and Gary Seaton (later Campbell would learn that the Seatons were buried separately – June in the Colebrook cemetery, Gary in Danbury), then fell on two newer headstones. The first gave him an unpleasant shock;

it was inscribed with the name of Sophie Lister, her dates, nothing else.

The second stone, unmarked, stood above a freshly dug open grave.

The beam played over the pile of earth, the yawning pit . . . they were in B-movie territory now. Come on, dude, Campbell thought, you can do better than this. Then Mrs Danvers turned towards him, swinging the flashlight around, and he found himself staring into the concentric rings of a 'blinding' shaft of light.

As a crude attempt to intimidate him, it failed. The reason he'd been given access to the website wasn't so that Ward could warn him that he was slated to be his next victim. In cyber-land, his own mantra chimed in, things are never what they seem.

No, he was sure the killer had another motive . . . something he'd missed.

Campbell lifted his eyes to the TV. He reached for the remote and released the mute button. Federer was sprinting from the net to the backcourt, chasing down an unreturnable lob. He saw the champion miraculously hit the ball between his knees with his back to the net and win the point. The crowd went wild.

He watched the avatar's diminishing silhouette weave between the trees and lose itself in the darkness – nice touch. He smiled, then closed down his laptop and gave his full attention to the tennis.

He had arranged to meet Grace Wilkes up at Skylands in the morning – he would be able to ask 'Mrs Danvers' about a family plot in person.

48

'You look like you wished you weren't here.'

Jelly turned her head too fast and the dance-floor swam. She saw the blurred figure of a man standing behind her, his hand resting on the back of one of the empty chairs at the table.

'What you say?' The music was loud enough to pretend she hadn't heard.

'I said you look as if you'd rather be some place else.'

The man, in focus now, was wearing a dark blue polo shirt, chinos and loafers. Tall, not exactly good-looking, okay though . . . sort of preppy but not. If he had a type, she couldn't quite place it.

'Yeah, right. I'd rather be locked up for the night in an undertaker's parlour.' She squinted up at him. 'Do we know each other?'

'Not yet.' It was an open, friendly face. 'But I was hoping.'

'I bet you were.' She stubbed her cigarette out in an overflowing ashtray and reached for her glass.

'I'm not trying to hit on you. I just noticed you sitting alone and, well . . . you seemed a little lost.'

He got that right. The party was beyond boring – a stuffy older crowd, mostly white, nobody she knew. She'd even caught herself earlier wondering what it would be like if Ed Lister did show up.

'I don't need rescuing, mister.' Nudging the straw and little umbrella aside with her nose, she drained her fourth Long Island Iced Tea. She was ready to go home.

'No, I meant . . . I just thought . . . what the heck, you're an attractive woman, I'd like to make your acquaintance.'

'What the heck?' She arched an eyebrow and smiled. He was polite, seemed likeable enough and, after her, had to be the youngest person in the room. She was going to be stuck here another couple of hours at least.

'Mind if I sit?' This couldn't be him . . . oh my God, could it?

'I'm with friends . . . this is their table,' she said, still sounding hostile though she didn't mean to now. The others were all up dancing. She waved at Ronnie and Steve, nostalgically 'getting down' to Natalie Cole's 'This Will Be' (the party's retro theme was 70s and 80s R&B), and suddenly felt in a better mood. 'Hey, wanna dance?'

'I'm not much of a dancer,' he said. 'I could use some air though. How about we get ourselves a couple of drinks and go out on the terrace . . .'

Jelly nodded, not crazy about the idea. She stood up, and the room started to sway. She held out her arms and got her kilter back by moving with the music.

'I just have to hear the end of my song.'

Jelly came out of the washroom and with exaggerated care – even before she'd had a drink, the gold sandals with the three-inch heels she'd found at the Shoe Inn had her tottering like a newborn giraffe – made her way around the edge of the dance-floor and out onto the terrace.

He was leaning on the rail looking at the ocean.

There was no way, no way this could be Ed Lister. For one thing he was too young, early to mid-thirties. Plus she knew what Ed looked like; she had his picture. But then all she really knew about him was what he wanted her to know. What if he'd made everything up? What if Ed wasn't who he said he was? What if this guy *was* him after all? Just waiting for the right moment to declare himself?

The thought made her skin prickle.

He turned around to meet her and she noticed something about his face. It was a perfect oval – ears small and flat to his head, hair cut short like a cap – too perfect for a man. There was nothing cissy, though, about his strong jaw and brow, the deep-set eyes so pale they looked like a mistake. She was beginning to see him as almost handsome. The moonlight on the water thing going on in the background.

Jelly had never really thought Ed was serious about flying over to meet her at the party. Just to be on the safe side she'd given him the name of a disco that no longer existed (Scarlett's had gone out of business before she was born). The trouble was there were hardly any night clubs in Westhampton, and it wouldn't take much to find this place, right on the beach.

'I'm Guy, by the way . . . Guy Mallory.' He smiled and she saw how his thin lips receded until there was just face around his teeth.

'Jelena.' She held out a hand. 'Nice to meet you, Guy.'

She wasn't getting any vibes off him. No way was this Ed. She felt the surge of panic start to retreat. And another thing, Guy spoke with an American accent, a cheesy Midwestern twang that made her think he'd be calling her 'ma'am' next – Ed was English. She'd never heard his voice, but she could tell by the language he used, those quirky little phrases that it would be difficult to fake.

She said, 'When you first came up I thought you were someone else.'

He kept the smile. 'You know, I get a lot of that.'

'I was doubly wrong.' She shook her head. 'You don't remind me of them at all.' Then she asked in a tone she wouldn't normally have used with someone she'd just met, 'You ever been married, Guy?'

'No.' He looked at her. 'Have you?'

She nodded. 'Once. I got married online. You go to this website and type in stuff and then by the Law of the Internet, da-dah, you're married . . . I did it when I was like seventeen.'

'Who's the lucky guy?'

'Colin Firth. But we're legally separated. Any time I want I can go back to the site and get a divorce.'

Ed had 'laughed out loud' when she'd told him. She studied Guy's bland face for a reaction. He just smiled politely. It was obvious he hadn't heard it before, which was all she wanted to know.

She found talking to him easy. When conversation slowed, it didn't feel in the least bit awkward. They sat looking out at the summer lightning over the ocean, listening to the surf crash on the beach, the music – grooving on an old Temptations song, 'I Can't Get Next to You' – all of it good.

At some point, Guy said, 'I'll understand if you say no, but I'd like to see you again . . . I mean, after tonight.'

His voice went up at the end of the sentence, making it a question.

Jelly shrugged. 'Sure, why not?'

PART THREE

New York

49

She was all I could think about during the flight. I tried to catch up on some work, I tried to watch a movie, read – I couldn't concentrate. My mind kept slipping back to the thought that in a slowly reducing number of hours we were going to meet. Sleep was out of the question.

Looking down, as we made landfall over the northeastern tip of Long Island, I felt my heart give a lurch when I thought I had briefly identified below us the lights of Westhampton Beach. On the tarmac, as soon as they opened the cabin doors, in that first lungful of warm night air reeking of jet fuel and electricity, I could almost taste her presence she seemed so near, so nearly within reach.

By the time, though, I got through customs and immigration, any hope of catching up with Jelena that night had evaporated. After standing in line for a couple of hours (an earlier security alert at JFK had resulted in a backlog of arriving passengers), anger and frustration had curdled into weary acceptance.

'The Carlyle,' I told the driver, as I climbed into the waiting limousine. It was well after midnight now, too late to drive out to the Hamptons. The party would be over before we even got there.

Manhattan bound, I poured myself a Scotch and water and sank back into the grey leather upholstery, brooding over the likelihood I'd missed my best and perhaps only chance of tracking the girl down. As the glittering skyline rose above Forest Hills, it suddenly hit home that I'd come to this vast metropolis to find someone without an address, a telephone number or even a name – it might have seemed funny, if the stakes hadn't been so high.

But this was New York, I reminded myself, a place I knew well. I'd lived here, after all, nearly half my working life. It was where I got my first break in business, made my first million, where Laura and I met. For me it will always be the city on the hill. If you've hit rock bottom in the Big Apple (as I did a couple of times) before climbing back up and finding success, you know that nothing is impossible.

The limo driver was listening to James Brown on the radio. I asked him to turn the music up and began to make a plan of action for tomorrow.

As we dipped down into the Midtown Tunnel, I thought about Ward and the clipping Campbell had e-mailed me on the Seaton tragedy. I'd told the detective I didn't recognise the boy's parents. But since then I'd begun to wonder if something about the couple in the blurry wedding photo *didn't* seem familiar – if there might not after all be some connection there with my own past.

I couldn't be sure, but June Seaton had reminded me a little of the woman in that dreamlike incident, my New York dream, where I'm looking down on her half-naked body sprawled on the murky floor of a black pit.

It occurred to me that I never knew her name either.

Ten minutes after I got to sleep, it felt like, I was woken by the telephone.

I asked Campbell Armour to call back when I'd had some coffee, but he was in a rush, on his way to interview the housekeeper, Grace Wilkes, in a town called Torrington – at the last moment she'd changed her mind about meeting him at Skylands, told him the house brought back too many memories.

I thought of coming clean with Campbell then about Jelena. It was always my intention to share my concern that Ward knew of her existence. Even if I was wrong about his impersonating her online and I'd exaggerated or imagined the threat to her safety, I could have used the detective's help in finding her. But it wasn't something I wanted to explain over the phone. We firmed up on the plan we'd already made for getting together the next day. It would have to wait till then.

After I'd showered, and had breakfast in my room at the Carlyle – I have a similar deal there to my longstanding arrangement with the Ritz in Paris and regard the place as another home from home – I got down to business.

Without the usual credentials, I was forced to work from the little information I had about Jelly: I knew her e-mail address, I knew she took piano lessons with a teacher she called 'Mrs C', not far from where she lived in Brooklyn, and I knew she was some kind of supervisor at a local kindergarten. She'd always been careful not to say what the kindergarten was called, but the other day she had inadvertently – or maybe it was deliberate – revealed the nearest subway stop.

I went online and googled 'childcare' in the Prospect Park area of Brooklyn. It didn't take long to get a result. Using Mapquest I was able to narrow the search down to three possible nurseries within a five-minute-walk radius of the Church Avenue subway stop on the Coney Island line.

I must confess this wasn't the first time I'd tried to find her. Soon after we first met I made a half-hearted attempt to trace 'adorablejoker'. Out of curiosity, I gave her e-mail address to one of those Net detective agencies that supposedly can find anything out about a person (even their health plan details and credit rating) for a few dollars. When they failed to come up with the goods, I just let it go. I was afraid that if she discovered I'd been checking up on her, she might get the wrong idea.

The situation was very different now. I'm not sure if I was driven more by the need to see Jelly, or to protect her – but I felt a growing sense of urgency.

From the Carlyle I cabbed down to Fifth and Fifty-Third, where I caught the F train out to Brooklyn. Entering the subway station, assaulted by the familiar oven-waft of stale piss and pretzels, I felt a nostalgic twinge that carried me back twenty years to when I was Jelly's age and didn't always have the price of a cab-fare.

On the elevated section of track, as I watched the Manhattan skyline recede over a harsh, unappealingly flat cityscape of low-rise buildings, bill-boards and decaying, sun-baked streets, I began to have misgivings – not just about leaving civilisation behind. I had on an old pair of jeans, black polo shirt and dark glasses, aiming for a look that wouldn't stand out; but the thought occurred to me that in my rush to find the girl before Ward did, I could be leading him to her.

'You're wasting your time,' Grace Wilkes said. 'I haven't the first idea what became of the boy, couldn't even tell you if he's still alive.'

'I'd like to hear your side of what happened.'

'How did you get hold of my name?' Grace frowned, narrowing her eyes at Campbell Armour over her raised coffee cup.

'The local paper,' Campbell said, which was close enough to the truth. He felt it might be unwise to let her know he'd talked to Dr Stilwell. 'It said the bodies were discovered by yardman, Earl Wilkes and his wife, Grace, housekeeper . . . so I did a little investigative work, looked you up in the white pages.' He smiled.

She just stared at him.

'Mrs Wilkes,' he added solemnly, 'I'm real sorry about your recent loss.' The way it came out sounding gauche, but not insincere.

Her eyes looked as if they were drowning. An unnatural puffiness about her face, possibly the result of cortisone treatment, had erased once pretty features. A small woman, otherwise delicately trim, maybe sixty-five, seventy, she wore avocado velour sweats and trainers with pom-pom laces; a pair of crutches, gaily wrapped in tangerine and yellow chiffon scarves, lay beside her in the booth.

He found it hard to imagine a more unlikely Mrs Danvers.

She lowered the cup and stirred a sachet of sweetener into her coffee, taking her time before saying slowly, 'Earl was a good man. He had a lot of pain at the end. Never a word of complaint. Lemme ask you something, Mr Armour . . .'

He nodded. 'Sure, anything.'

'Why open this sorry business all up again? It happened a long time ago and I told the police back then everything I knew. I've put it from my mind. Had to.'

'I can appreciate that, ma'am,' Campbell said, tasting a forkful of the special – macaroni cheese with pepperoni sauce – and wishing he'd played safe and ordered the fried chicken basket. 'But I don't know where else to start. The police were no help, none at all.'

Earlier, Campbell had considered dropping by the sheriff's office in Canaan, but without an investigator's licence he knew he wouldn't get far. Just draw attention to himself. The sheriff involved in the Seaton case had died a few years back.

'You don't look to me like a private eye.'

'No?' He smiled, unsure whether it was his youth or ethnicity that was giving her a problem. 'Then I'd call this an effective disguise.'

The interview wasn't going the way he'd hoped. More comfortable talking to a plasma screen than face-to-face,

289

Campbell was reluctant to admit his lack of experience might be telling against him.

They were sharing a booth in the family section of Annie's Grill in Torrington, a run-down blue-collar town ten miles south of Norfolk. White-tiled from floor to ceiling with a magnolia trim, the coffee shop had been Grace's choice of venue.

She wasn't eating. 'I don't see how I can help you.'

'You *knew* him, Mrs Wilkes,' he said, leaning forward. 'You're the only one left who has a real connection.'

'I guess. But what exactly does your client want with Ernest?'

He sat back and waited a moment, toying with his food.

'There's a confidentiality issue.' He put on an official-sounding voice, looking at her over the top of his glasses. 'I can only reveal that it concerns a bequest.'

She thought for a moment. 'You said on the phone it might be worth my while to get in touch. How does that work?'

'My client is offering a substantial reward for any information that leads to the discovery of Ernest Seaton's whereabouts.'

There was a silence. He watched Grace reach for the pink clam-shell cell phone that lay beside her cup and move it closer to her. Then he said, 'Maybe we could begin with you telling me what happened that night?'

The receptionist at All Saints Preschool and Daycare Center, a heavily pregnant Indian woman in a sari called Joy, informed me in a hushed sing-song that they had no vacancies till next spring.

'I'm not interested in enrolling a child,' I explained patiently. 'A friend of mine works here.' I looked around. 'Where is everybody, by the way?'

The place seemed unusually quiet for a kindergarten.

'Nap time,' she said. 'Please speak softly.'

I showed her Jelly's photo, which she barely glanced at before handing it back, shaking her head. 'Haven't seen her.'

'I think she might be a supervisor. She . . . plays the piano.'

Joy cut her cow-like eyes to a roster of staff faces on the wall beside her desk, the 'All Saints' team presided over by 'mother hens', Mrs Quinn and Mrs Arbogast. I could see Jelly's was not among them.

'What did you say she was called?'

'I don't know her last name. It's really important. Look, I wonder if I could talk to some of the other members of staff?'

'She doesn't work here, I tell you.'

Her tone firmer now and not all that friendly.

It was the same story at The Leapfrog Center and Precious Littles. Nobody recognised Jelena from her photograph, the only one I had of her, or from my notional description. I spent the next hour trudging around in the heat checking with the other local kindergartens I'd marked on the map as 'possibles'. They were no help either. I realised that Jelly might've misled me about where she worked, but I couldn't give up on the idea that she was somehow connected with the area. The subway stop was all I had to go on, my only point of reference.

Disheartened, I retraced my steps through the drab tree-lined streets. A mixed, lower-middle-class neighbourhood of narrow clapboard houses, white-brick apartment buildings scarred with graffiti, the odd run-down mini-mart on a corner, it was a long way from the Hotel Carlyle. By the time I'd got back to the main intersection with Macdonald Avenue, my shirt was soaked with sweat. I began to feel the sidewalk sucking at the soles of my feet, every step becoming more difficult, as if I was wading through quicksand.

It should have been a warning.

I remember standing in front of the Astoria Federal Savings Bank, debating whether to go inside – Jelly had told me she once worked at a bank – when a jet fighter passed low overhead making the sound of tearing paper. I looked up at the pulsing white sky and suddenly my head started to spin. When I tried to walk on I could no longer see the sidewalk or feel my legs. There was a hand at my elbow.

We only just made it through the door of a Carvel's ice-cream franchise that was next to the bank before everything went black.

I thought I was going down, but the moment passed. I heard a female voice ask, 'You okay? Want me to call an ambulance?'

'I could use a glass of water,' I said.

The girl came from behind the counter and helped me to a chair. There was no one else in the ice-cream parlour. 'You don't look so good, mister.'

Had I imagined the guiding hand?

'I'll be fine. Just not used to the heat.' I shivered. I could feel the air conditioning turning the wet shirt on my back clammy.

'Yeah, you want to be careful, it's hot as balls out there.'

It seemed an odd thing to say. She was a fresh-faced high school kid, blonde and freckled, not more than sixteen. Revived by the iced water, I thanked her for 'saving my life', left her a tip that made her eyes light up, and headed for the door.

I turned and asked, 'Did somebody help me in here?'

She looked blank. I saw her remove a white earphone. 'I'm sorry?'

I repeated the question.

'I wasn't really looking. You take care now.'

50

'It was too quiet, even for a Sunday,' Grace began, nervously flicking the flap of her cell phone open and shut. 'I got a bad feeling the moment I walked in the front door . . . the house was silent, and there was this smell I didn't recognise.'

'You remember the time?' Campbell asked.

'Sunday mornings we'd get there late, like around nine.'

'You didn't live on the place?'

She shook her head. 'Moved out when I got married.'

Campbell dropped his gaze. 'Okay, you entered the premises . . . then what?'

'There was no sign of anyone, so I called Earl in from the yard and made him go up . . . just to check they were all right . . . I waited at the foot of the stairs. It was too damned quiet – little Ernie was *always* up and about.'

She paused, and he could see her trying to filter the memories, not to let them swamp her. 'I could hear the clock ticking in the hall, and then him tapping at their bedroom door, calling out their names . . .'

He steered her past the moment of discovery. 'The boy was hiding in the broom closet under the stairs?'

'We thought at first he was dead too.'

Campbell nodded. 'I read about the blood.'

'We woke him . . . he didn't know where he was, couldn't barely talk, trembling all over. I wrapped him in a blanket and gave him some hot tea.'

'You think he was hiding from someone?'

She squinted at him. 'Ernie hated it when his parents

fought. He'd crawl in there sometimes just to get away. It was like . . . his special place.'

'Where had all the blood come from, Grace?'

'There was *some* blood. You know how the papers exaggerate.'

'Yes, but how did it get there? On his face and hands. You think he witnessed what happened, or only went in the room after the event?'

'How the hell would I know?' She flared suddenly. 'I didn't want to think about it then – what that poor kid might have seen or heard – and I damned sure don't want to think about it now.'

'I understand,' he said, backing off.

Campbell pushed his plate aside. He looked at Grace's moon face that in repose gave little away and wasn't sure whether he should try to win back her confidence, or start putting on the pressure.

He shifted down a tone. 'How did he get on with his parents?'

'Ernest? He may only've been young, but he saw Gary Seaton for what he was – a small-town loser whose one idea of a good time was to get smashed at the Gin and Chowder Club. They didn't relate. He was a lot closer to his mother.'

Campbell nodded. 'I've seen her photograph. An attractive woman.'

'June had something about her . . . an energy, you know, she was full of life, made everyone feel good. She had plenty of admirers, but she was such a needy soul, always craving excitement.' She hesitated. 'It got her killed.'

'You mean she couldn't find what she wanted at home?'

'It wasn't a happy marriage . . . all they ever did was fight.' Grace gave him a distracted look, her attention somewhere else, focused on the past. 'They were fighting that night . . . I was up at the house, fixing their dinner. Gary had been

294

drinking and the two of them started screaming and hollering at each other until it got so bad I thought of calling the cops.' She gave a heavy sigh. 'In the end, well . . . I just left them to it as usual.'

'What was the fight about, do you remember?'

'Same, same old story. June had been at a party in New York City and stayed out all night – only this time she ended up in hospital down there. Nothing serious, she had a fall and knocked herself out, but Gary had to go and bring her home.'

'She was cheating on him.'

Grace nodded. 'He found a letter she'd written some fella she'd taken a shine to – I guess she forgot to mail it, or didn't have time.'

'You saw the letter?'

'He confronted her with it . . . accused her of planning to run off and leave him. June denied everything, said it was just a fantasy. Then Gary forced her to read part of the letter out loud . . . about falling in love. She started crying.'

'You don't know who it was addressed to? Was a name mentioned?'

She turned her head slowly from side to side. 'Not that I heard.'

'What happened to this letter?' Campbell asked. 'There was nothing about it at the inquest. Did you mention it to the police?'

'Gary could have tore it up, I guess, thrown it in the garbage; maybe it just got lost in all the confusion. I told them everything I knew. What does it matter now?'

A whole lot, the detective thought, but decided to let it go. A more experienced interviewer, he felt, might have pushed harder: he was afraid of losing her.

'You think June was really going to leave him?'

'She told me once she only stayed for the boy's sake. Said

she felt trapped up there in that big house, bored out of her mind, her life draining away. He kept her under kind of a curfew. Whenever she went out, Gary used to warn her, "Don't forget now, Junebug, home before dark."'

'Home before dark,' Campbell repeated.

'And June would always finish for him, you know, like mocking his authority, "Or there'll be the Devil to pay."'

'It must have been quite an ordeal for you, Grace,' he said calmly, though he could feel his heart racing. 'I mean, you were more to the family than just the housekeeper, right?'

'You could say so. June made a big deal about being friends with the help, but she never let you forget your place. There's always a line.'

She sighed. 'I was fond of her though.'

'And the boy?'

She lifted the back of a wrist to her forehead. 'Like one of my own.'

'After his grandmother took him to live in New York, did you see Ernest again?'

'I tried calling a few times,' she said. 'Then I got a note from Mrs Calvert saying that he'd gone to live with some relatives out West – I think she said Wyoming. She thanked me for my loyal service, but felt it would be best for all concerned if we let him forget the past and start a new life.'

'You never heard any news of him – like where he went to school out there, if he graduated college, got a job . . . he never tried to get in touch?'

'How often do I have to tell you? No.'

He took a long drink of his soda. 'You must have wondered, though, over the years, how the boy was getting on, what direction this new life had taken?'

She looked away, her troubled eyes scanning the parking

296

lot through the window. 'I always felt somehow he'd be all right, and after everything he'd been through the good Lord would take care of him.'

There was a silence.

'I still put flowers on June's grave every Sunday.'

In his mind, Campbell saw 'Mrs Danvers' coming out of the upstairs room in the website house, leading him down the stairs and out into the dark woods. The beam of her flashlight slashing through the trees.

'Was there a cemetery at Skylands, a family plot?'

She shook her head.

'Did somebody else . . . you think maybe someone else came to the house that night?' he asked in the same casual tone.

Observing her closely, he caught the involuntary flicker in her eyes.

'I heard Gary Seaton threaten his wife. I heard him say, if I can't have you, I'll make damn sure nobody else can. Gary killed June, then shot himself. If my husband was still here, he'd be able to tell you . . .'

She clammed up then, as if she realised she had said too much.

'Tell me what, Grace? *Did* somebody come to the house?'

In the subway, waiting for a train back to Manhattan, I thought about what had happened on the street. It was nothing really, a combination of not enough sleep and mild heatstroke. The whole incident had lasted a couple of minutes and I was now fully recovered. It was just the hand at the elbow that bothered me – a firm, intimate grip that I could still feel.

I imagined Jelly coming down here at rush hour. She must have walked along this platform thousands of times, perhaps even sat on this same bench – that is, if she really did use the Church Avenue stop, if I could trust anything she had told me.

I remembered asking her once if she'd read Truman Capote's *Breakfast at Tiffany's* and being surprised by her sharp, indignant reaction. 'You think I'm like the girl in that book? You really think I'd *lie* about important stuff?'

I wondered what the expression on her face had been when she typed that. Maybe Will was right and the only reliable assumption about the internet is that everybody tells lies all the time. A worldwide tissue of lies.

I was still thinking about Jelly when the Sixth Avenue local trundled into the southbound platform on the other side of the station. Half paying attention, I watched a dozen people get off and make for the exits. The train pulled out and then I noticed, across the tracks, a young woman left behind in the middle of the platform, lost in concentration while she fiddled with her cell phone. She was no one I'd ever seen before, and yet something about her seemed familiar.

She was standing in profile, her head slightly bowed. Tall, slim, elegant just in the way she held herself – at that distance, I couldn't be certain. Then she turned towards me, laughing into the phone.

She was taller than I'd pictured her, or it may have been that her hair looked different – it was lighter and frizzier and tied up in some elaborate sort of way. She turned and the instant I saw her face, I knew.

It was strange how it affected me, how unprepared I was for a moment I'd anticipated often enough. I was struck not so much by her appearance – though I could tell she was everything I'd dreamed – as by the simple fact that she existed, that she was really here in the world. It confirmed what I already knew in my heart to be true. I recognised her as the same person that I loved.

At the time it had the overwhelming force of revelation.

Jelena hadn't spotted me yet. I didn't know whether to

wave to her, call out her name, or run back up the stairs, cross the street and approach her on the far platform. I was mesmerised, afraid that if I made any kind of move the spell would be broken. Somebody walked through my line of sight. I saw them only as a blur.

I don't remember hearing the train until seconds before it came hurtling through on the middle track. I stood up then, Jelly looked across the rails, and for a brief instant our eyes met.

She didn't smile; as far as I could tell her face never changed its expression. I just saw her shoulders stiffen as if in shock or fright . . . that's the only way I can be sure she recognised me. The next moment we lost each other.

The train that had suddenly come between us, a Coney Island express, seemed to go on forever. I tried to keep eye-contact with her through carriage after carriage of brightly lit windows as they streaked past, but it was hopeless.

When the far platform came back into view, I was already sprinting for the Macdonald Avenue exit. Jelly had vanished.

'You said there used to be a piano up at the house.' She was protecting someone, Campbell thought, or else afraid.

Grace nodded. 'An old upright in the parlour . . . it's still there. June loved to play. She was such a talented, creative person.'

It occurred to him that Ernest Seaton might have got to her first. In which case, every word would likely find its way back. He was tempted to tell Grace about the more recent murders he was investigating and that he believed were connected with what happened at Skylands. But it was too soon. He asked her instead if the boy had inherited his mother's musical gift.

'Ernie?' Grace smiled. 'He didn't care at all for music. When he was little, if anyone so much as hummed a tune around him, he'd clap his hands over his ears and howl. They had his hearing checked, turned out to be perfect.'

He recalled Dr Stilwell's description of the orphaned boy comparing Mozart to the taste of dead flies. Grace didn't seem aware of Stilwell's diagnosis.

'He must have had difficulty coping with everyday life.'

'Some,' she said, hesitating. 'He was a solitary child. Ernie didn't make friends easy, but that's how he preferred it. The other kids just thought he was weird.'

'I meant because of the way he was affected by music.'

'I know what you meant,' she said. 'Anyone put on a record or played the radio around him, he'd get upset . . . his father'd say, "Boy's just seeking attention" and turn up the volume.'

'But you knew it caused him genuine distress.'

She nodded. 'I remember one time June was in the parlour practising, playing the same tune over and over, when all a sudden I heard this almighty crash. I ran in to find her bowed over the closed piano-lid. The notes still jangling. Ernie was standing by her, his face kind of a dusky red, glowering out from under his brow with a look that . . . well, it scared me. I could guess at what had happened, but June acted like it was an accident. She covered up for him.'

An outsider born and bred, Campbell thought, smart not crazy, yet predisposed to psychosis, unlikely to feel remorse or understand the feelings of others . . .

'Do you remember the name of the tune?'

'You've got to be kidding.'

Campbell glanced around the empty coffee shop. Then he leant forward and started to whistle for Grace, slightly off-key, the opening bars to 'Für Elise'. He saw her eyebrows crawl towards each other, her mouth fall open in disbelief.

'How in the name of Jesus did you know that?'

He didn't answer, letting her think about it for several seconds.

300

'You have to help me find him, Grace.'

Her eyes filled with tears. 'I've already told you everything I know . . . more than I should have done.'

'Does the name "Ward" mean anything to you?'

'No.' She didn't hesitate.

'I think there's a chance that the Ernest you raised and loved has become a danger to others. Grace, you'd be helping him . . .'

'I never *raised* him. Did I say that?'

She broke down then, sobbing quietly, shielding her eyes with her hands. He waited until she recovered, then he asked, 'Has he been back in touch?'

'I'm sorry, I can't . . . I have to go now.' She swept up her pink cell phone, then reached for the gaily decorated crutches and clumsily got up, her mouth set in a straight line like a stubborn old pony's as she manoeuvred her way out of the booth.

He just sat there, knowing he'd blown it, feeling a kind of pity for her.

Campbell paid the check and followed Grace Wilkes out to the parking lot. She was trying to put the key in the door of a black late-model Taurus, her hand shaking so much she was having difficulty.

'Here, let me get that for you,' he said.

She reluctantly handed over the key. 'Are you married, Mr Armour?'

He smiled and held up his left hand with the gold eternity band on the ring finger. 'Four years in August. We have a little girl, Amy.'

He opened the car door for her. She threw the crutches in first and swung herself into the driver's seat. Reaching for a pack of Newport Lites, she tapped out a cigarette and lit up. She blew a thin stream of smoke out of the corner of her mouth, directing it away from Campbell. 'Then go home,' she said, glancing back up at him, 'go home to them. Leave this alone.'

'I have to find Ernest Seaton first,' Campbell said, leaning through the car window. 'And when I do, I plan to ask him about the murders of Sophie Lister and Sam Metcalf. If you change your mind, you have my numbers, call me.'

She took another drag. 'I should have never talked to you in the first place.'

'Before somebody else gets hurt, Grace. He might listen to you.'

Staring ahead through the windshield, she exhaled noisily and then waved her hand to disperse the smoke; her face half in sunlight had an unhealthy sheen. Cigarette between her lips, she turned the key in the ignition and, without looking at Campbell, said in a small flat voice, 'He doesn't know.'

51

Investigator Morelli was standing in the middle of Sam Metcalf's empty living room, thinking about lunch. This was day three of the diet and he was looking forward to a *bistecca fiorentina* and salad at a family-run trattoria he liked near the Porta Romana. At home, the challenge of sticking to a low-carb regime was complicated by the fact he hadn't told Maria yet he was trying to lose weight.

He could expect, when he did, a narrowing of her black eyes.

He wasn't sure what had brought him back here. He just happened to be in the Oltrarno, driving past Sam's door, and decided to take another look around. He'd know it when he saw it, he told himself, as he threw open a window to let some air into the hot, stuffy apartment.

He thought about the young American woman he'd first encountered on a slab in the morgue in Linz choosing to call a dump like this home for most of her adult life. Her belongings had been shipped last week. The few remaining sticks of furniture belonged to the landlord. Even her absence had started to fade. You really had to know Sam's story, Morelli thought, to get the melancholy feeling that hung about the three bare rooms. A new tenant moving in on Saturday.

He was reminded of the painful telephone conversation he'd had with Sam's parents in Boston. His colleagues claimed it was the worst part of being a cop, informing the next of kin, and never got any easier. In Morelli's experience, talking to those who knew and loved the victim best helped him do his job. He'd hoped to give the Metcalfs positive news about the way the investigation was going, but the forensic report on the train from the Austrian police wasn't encouraging.

The murderer had left the sleeper inexplicably clean; just as he had the grotto at the Villa Nardini. Not a ghost of an identifier. When he considered what the creep had got away with on that train, he could understand the Viennese media branding him 'the Master of Death', but it really didn't help matters.

Morelli went through to the bathroom. He looked under the old-fashioned claw-foot tub and inside the medicine cabinet; then removed the top of the cistern and felt behind it before flushing the toilet. His men had crawled all over the place. They wouldn't have missed much.

He frowned at his reflection in the mirror-fronted cabinet while he washed his face and hands, going into a daydream about Gretchen. On the phone, she had suggested meeting up for a romantic weekend in Paris. Maybe it wasn't such a bad idea. If he could find a way of linking the trip to his work. He needed to have a talk with Laura Lister, which might qualify as a valid reason for foreign travel. There was a question mark over her husband and Paris.

He wandered into the kitchen and sat at the table listening to the wall-clock above the stove ticking away in the stillness. He felt depressed. Sam Metcalf had been dead a week and he had nothing, not a single lead. His suspicion that Ed Lister was having an affair with a woman half his age hardly counted as a development. Morelli sank lower in his chair, considering the Listers and the damage done to their marriage; something told him that the secret to solving the case still lay with their daughter, Sophie. He'd been looking at what happened here from Sam's perspective. He needed to go back to the beginning and try a different path – focus on Sophie Lister coming to the flat to use her friend's computer.

He had to assume that she never confided in Sam about the stranger he was convinced she was chatting to online, or Sam would surely have mentioned it to Sophie's father? Yet the drawings in the artist's sketchbook suggested that *she knew there was reason to be wary*. Maybe she was embarrassed to talk to the older girl, or afraid, or intended doing so but left it too late – Sam flew back to Boston to visit her family the week before the murder. If Sophie had been intrigued enough to meet up with the stranger in real-time, which Morelli felt sure was what happened, it made it less likely she would have spoken to anyone.

But say Sophie did agree to meet her killer, she was bound to have been somewhat concerned about safety. She might have taken precautions; left a note perhaps, or some clue to the man's identity, even a description, as insurance in case something happened to her. The trouble was that, other than his screen-name, it was unlikely she'd have known much about him – unless she saw him again.

With a gloomy sigh he looked up at the Annunciation clock, the one obvious place he hadn't checked during his perfunctory search. The Angel Gabriel's outstretched arm stirred a memory of his wife, after they got married, offering her bridal bouquet to the Madonna in the church of Santissima Annunziata for good luck.

He rose from the table and, pulling a chair over to the ancient stove, climbed onto the hob. Balancing precariously on the cast-iron grills, he reached up to the clock and felt behind the laminated panel of its long rectangular face: the angel's stubby wings, the orchard trees, the loggia where Mary sat at a lectern. Oily dust and grime stuck to his fingers; there was nothing there.

He lifted the clock away from the wall and revealed some suspect-looking electrical wiring, but that was all. He heard his stomach growl.

Time for that rare *bistecca fiorentina* and, sacrilege, a glass of water.

The investigator pulled Sam's old front door shut behind him. As he removed the yellow crime-scene tape, bundling it up and tossing it in a corner of the landing, he noticed with irritation how filthy his hands had become.

He hesitated – he could hear rock music blasting from the Iranians' apartment below that struck him, unreasonably perhaps, as disrespectful – then he unlocked the door, went back inside.

In the bathroom he washed his hands for the second time. Consulting his image again in the mirrored doors of the cabinet, he patted his cheeks and thought, Yes, maybe you do look a little thinner, Andrea.

He smiled, and then he got it.

'*Ma stai scherzando*,' he said aloud. It was staring him in the face.

He opened the cabinet, quickly removed the internal glass shelves and worked a hand behind one of the doubled-up sliding doors. Nothing. He slid the mirror shut and tried its twin from the other side.

Mother of God, he felt something there, taped to the back of the glass.

He tugged carefully and it came away in his hand – a twice-folded A4 size sheet of white Ingres sketch paper, the kind artists use.

52

They had arranged to meet at six thirty. It was nearly that now and here he was still stuck in traffic on the Brooklyn-Queens Expressway. Ward had offered to pick Jelly up at her apartment but she'd insisted on going straight to the restaurant from work.

She was being cautious, understandably. On the phone he'd caught the note of surprise in her voice at hearing from him so soon. As the line of vehicles inched forward, Ward thought about how nervous she'd sounded; but that, he suspected, had nothing to do with his asking her out to dinner. Then the southbound lanes cleared and he was off again in his rented VW Golf, on his way to their first date.

It was nearly six forty-five when he walked through the foyer of Renchers Crab Inn on Myrtle Avenue. He had chosen the place because she'd told him she loved seafood, and he'd never been there before.

'Guy Mallory. I have a reservation.'

The hostess consulted her clipboard and crossed off his name, then led him through to the bar where he spotted Jelena sitting on a stool apart from the crowd. She waved and smiled at him, looking relieved to see a friendly face.

'I was beginning to think I'd got the wrong place,' she said, as he joined her. He apologised for being late and ordered some drinks. A Sea Breeze for Jelly, a glass of the house white for himself. He noticed that her hair was different to last night, pulled back off her face into a tight chignon, and she had on less make-up. She was wearing a matching beige linen jacket and skirt with a plain white blouse. Work clothes.

'I wouldn't have recognised you,' he said.

'Well, buddy, this is the real me.'

'You're with Morgan Stanley, right?'

She laughed. 'What on earth gave you that idea? I work the phones for a shipping company in Flatbush. You heard of McCormicks?'

He shook his head. 'You look great anyway.'

'You think so?' Her face lit up for a brief second.

Almost as soon as they got the drinks, the hostess came back and told them their table was ready. He let Jelly walk in front of him and was conscious of the other diners looking admiringly at her as they passed, which made him feel both pleased and uncomfortable with the attention.

The blue rhombus was turning slowly inside his head.

You don't have to worry, I'm not gonna spoil this . . . I swear I won't breathe a word about how you spent your day. Not a word.

At the table, watching her deliberate over the menu, taking

forever to make up her mind, he smiled when finally Jelly chose the butterfly shrimp – he couldn't help smiling. She picked up on his reaction and flashed him a challenging look.

'That okay with you, mister?'

'I'm just amused because, well . . .' Ward hesitated. He was amused because he knew from eavesdropping her online conversations with Ed Lister that shrimp was her favourite food.

'Because it's right up there next to fried chicken and sex and us black folks just can't get enough of that shit?'

'No, no,' he protested, taken aback by her prickliness. 'It's just that I always have to resist choosing the shrimp myself.'

'And here I'm thinking racial slur. Shame on me.' She laughed. 'Damn, now I'm gonna have to let you taste one.'

Her face was prettiest when animated.

He had the wine list in front of him and ran his eye down the whites before selecting a decent Meursault. He was having the grilled swordfish.

Over dinner the mood changed and keeping the conversation going became an effort. Jelly grew quieter and seemed more subdued than last night. At the party, she'd been bubbly and talkative to the point where he'd wished she'd shut up. He was dealing here with a different person – like she said, the real me. He knew he'd have to tread carefully if he wanted to bring her out of her shell.

Ward had done his homework. From her high-school yearbook entries to the amount of back rent she owed her landlord, from her social security number, health insurance plan and favourite colour to the name of her mother's dog – there wasn't a whole lot he didn't know about Jelena Madison Sejour.

He got her talking about her love of music, coaxed out of her that she had a 'scholarship' to study piano at the Conservatoire in Paris.

'I'm impressed,' he said. 'They only take the best.' He was about to tell her that his mother played the piano, not very well, then decided that the less she knew about his family the better. 'When do you go?'

'I haven't decided yet if I *am* going. I've always dreamed of living there, but now . . . I dunno, it seems like a big step.'

'So what's holding you back?'

She shrugged. 'Never been abroad before. Don't know a soul in Paris. Not sure that I'm good enough musically. I'd be leaving behind two hopeless dependants, my cats, and then there's Mom . . . take your pick.'

'I spend quite a bit of time over there,' he said. 'So you'd have at least one friend, Jelena. A friend who'd love to show you Paris.'

'Always good to know.' She nodded, but didn't return his smile.

You nearly called her 'Jelly' then, didn't you? It was on the tip of your tongue. She didn't invite you to yet, or even mention that others call her that. A slip-up now, Ernster, and you could blow this whole thing clean out of the water . . .

Their desserts came and they ate in silence. He studied her without making any attempt to conceal the fact: sometimes she'd glance up and catch him looking at her, and he'd just smile. He didn't care if his gaze made her uncomfortable. He could see now that Jelly was more than pretty, she was beautiful. She had those wild-creature eyes set almost too far apart, the wide mouth and long graceful neck to go with them and a flawless honey-coloured hide. He didn't desire her. He might have done, but Ward was no slave to his sexual impulses. He considered himself lucky to have gotten that monkey off his back early on in life. He could see that the girl had at least half a brain – charm, and warmth too – which helped him to understand how someone like Ed Lister might have fallen for the package.

The perfume she was wearing, fresh and unsophisticated, had for Ward the shape and texture and heft of a glass paperweight. He let the silence between them grow beyond awkward, then asked Jelly if everything was all right.

She frowned at him and said, 'Why do you ask?'

'You don't seem quite yourself.'

'Compared to? How I was last night? It was a party, dude.'

He nodded. 'We had a good time, didn't we?'

'Not too good I hope.' She arched an eyebrow. 'I'd had a skinful.'

'You think I'd take advantage of you?' He smiled and looked down at his hands. 'You said you were drinking to forget.'

'I did? The drama queen talking.' She gave a laugh, then took a deep breath and let it out slowly. 'No, you're right. I guess I am feeling a little down . . .'

He could tell she wanted to confide in him. He'd been grooming her, using his knowledge of her likes and dislikes to make it seem like they had a lot in common. He just hadn't expected her to drop her guard so quickly. 'You feel like talking about it?'

She shook her head. 'Not really.'

'Still raw . . . I understand. You don't know me that well.' He sat back in his chair and smiled. 'Sometimes it's easier to talk to a stranger.'

He saw her hesitate, considering his offer. 'You seem like a nice person. Really you do, but . . . oh, what the hell.'

It was familiar stuff, only interesting for what she chose not to disclose. She didn't use Ed's name, but told him she'd been having trouble fending off the attentions of an older married man. If he hadn't known the truth he wouldn't have believed it possible she was talking about somebody she'd never met.

Ward was a good listener, he knew how to put her at her ease, when to ask questions, when to hold back. He told her he could relate because he'd been down a similar road himself – he was 'still getting over someone'. She showed concern.

He'd had to learn how to do empathy, but Ward found it came easily enough; it was, like an old movie star once said about the profession, just a question of reacting.

'Where did the two of you meet?'

She said, 'I know this is going to sound crazy.'

'Don't tell me.' He smiled, touching two fingers to his temple, as if the idea had just occurred to him. 'You met online.'

'What the . . . how did you guess?'

'Isn't that where you got married to Mr Darcy?'

'And divorced him.' She made a face and wiped her brow with the back of her hand. 'As from this morning, I'm a free woman.'

'May I be the first to congratulate you.' He raised his glass in a mock toast and they both laughed. Now that they had established a rapport, he felt confident that she wouldn't refuse the offer of a ride back to Manhattan.

After that, Ward decided, he'd just have to play it by ear.

53

The intermittent creak of a rusty hinge coming from his laptop was beginning to get on Campbell Armour's nerves. It reminded him of those screensavers with irritant sound effects like bubbling noises or fanfares or lonely static from outer space. The creaking – from the *homebeforedark* website – was caused by a screen-door on the back porch of the virtual Skylands swinging gently in the breeze.

The laptop was on the table under the window of his room at the Mountain View, half-hidden by the styrofoam box containing the remains of the cheeseburger deluxe he'd brought back from the diner in Canaan. It was now almost nine thirty and pitch-dark out. Campbell had tried several times during the course of the evening to get back inside the replica Seaton home, but without success. Ward must've decided to block him again, probably just for the hell of it.

A loud sudden banging startled him. He glanced around the room – he hadn't forgotten the hiking boots in the hallway of the real Skylands – as the screen-door effect on his laptop escalated to a more persistent screech, slam . . . screech, slam. He wondered how safe he was here at the motel.

Maybe Ward could read his thoughts. Shaking his head, Campbell aimed the remote at the television to kill the competing sound of Wimbledon, then went over to investigate. Since he last looked, twenty minutes ago, the *homebeforedark* graphics had caught up with real-time and gone over to nightscape mode.

Pinned to the listless screen-door was a note that said, 'COME'.

Campbell cleared the table-top of debris and sat down. He clicked on the invitation and found himself inside the dismal mansion, instantly transported to the second-floor landing. He gave a little grunt of satisfaction.

Ahead of him stood the four identical doors. He tried each of them in turn, directing the cursor by the dim light of the chandelier hanging over the stairwell. As before, only the door to Ernest Seaton's bedroom opened.

It swung back to reveal a small boy in pyjamas, curled up on the bed with his hands over his ears, tossing from side to side as though in torment. Campbell imagined at first that 'Ernie' (the boy's avatar, a generic snub-nosed, freckle-faced

312

kid) was trying to block out some loud noise or music that was odious to him.

But there was no sound – at least, not on the soundtrack.

Then Campbell noticed, seeping onto the landing from under the door of the adjacent bedroom, what looked like a wisp of fog or smoke. As he watched, the whitish mist billowed and transformed itself magically into a solid 3-D word-shape – LYING – quickly followed by another that spelled out, BITCH. He caught on that the boy was trying to escape the ugly din of his parents arguing.

The graphics floated out over the stairwell, silently filling the screen with snatches of June and Gary Seaton's venomous dialogue, their words making phrases and broken sentences that jostled and bumped against each other in a syncopated collage of hate.

YOU LYING BITCH You're
just *I NEVER* LOVED YOU
YOU CAN'T EVEN *GET IT UP*
GARY SEATON
trash . . . you little *cock-sucking* whore . . . **WHORE**
I'M LEAVING you really think I give a shit?
fucking any guy even looks at you
GOD, YOU *PATHETIC* LITTLE MAN
MR FLOPPY, HA-HA
Can't live without him? You're so in *love*?
You're planning to leave us, Junebug? Lets see how I can
NO . . . GARY, YOU'RE TOO DRUNK
help with that. Here, try some of this you cunt

It was so effectively done, seeing him bury his head under his pillow, Campbell felt almost sorry for the boy. Suddenly, as if he couldn't take it any longer, 'Ernie' jumped up off the bed and ran out onto the landing. Walking right through the floating words and coming out the other side, he tiptoed past the door to his parents' room. Then, avoiding the telltale floorboards, crept downstairs.

Looking over the banister, Campbell (grudgingly admiring of Ward's technical skills) saw the boy get down on hands and knees and crawl into the broom closet and pull the door shut behind him. He used his mouse to try to follow, but found himself barred. The fragments of dialogue dissolved, suggesting that in the master bedroom, where he had no doubt the night's traumatic events would soon unfold, things for the moment had quietened down – the house was still.

All he could hear was the ticking of the clock in the hall.

He thought of calling Ed Lister and telling him to log on to the website, so they could both witness what was about to happen. When they'd spoken earlier, he'd updated his client on the interview with Grace Wilkes and his suspicion that she was covering up, either out of loyalty or fear. Ed had seemed distracted, almost uninterested. He remembered him saying he was going out for the evening.

A whirring sound drew his attention to the hands of the hall clock. He watched them fly around the dial, the speeded-up chronology reminiscent of how they showed time passing in old black-and-white movies. The hands slowed and came into land at precisely four thirty-six. The regular ticking resumed.

Using his cursor, Campbell looked around the hall. A couple of suitcases had appeared by the front door. He could hear music, the faint ominous strains of 'Für Elise' – and, as the piano notes carried through the house, other noises now, coming from the bedroom, hard to identify at first. He recognised the sounds of furtive but urgent lovemaking, the gasps and whimpers of a man and woman approaching climax – then, in the midst of their stifled paroxysms, a sudden change.

There was a single cry, no other sound, no movement, nothing.

By the hall clock, a full sixty seconds passed before Campbell heard on the soundtrack the hysterical voice of a woman, presumably June Seaton, sobbing and pleading with someone not to hurt her and, in counterpoint, what he guessed were the incoherent mumblings of her drunken husband.

At that moment the boy, sleepy and bewildered, emerged from his hiding placc in the broom closet and, frowning at the suitcases in the hall, stood at the foot of the stairs looking up. He hears his mother begging,

NO, PLEASE . . . JESUS! WHAT ARE
YOU DOING... DON'T

DON'T

Despite knowing the effects were simulated, Campbell gave an involuntary shudder as volley after shrill volley of screams rang through the virtual mansion. Interspersed with dull thumps, loathsome slithering and scrabbling noises, he heard June's desperate pleadings grow fainter and more seldom under the onslaught of her attacker; the tearing sound of the victim's skin and flesh (like a zipper being yanked over and over) suggested repeated frenzied slashing.

There was a brief interval, an island of calm, before the hollow explosion of a gunshot in an enclosed space rocked the house. As the reverberations died away, Campbell leaned closer to the speakers on his laptop, straining to catch if that was still the soft plinking of a piano in the background, or something dripping.

A car pulled into the parking lot behind the motel. He looked up from the screen to the blue-curtained window beyond, his gut contracting in sudden alarm, saw the lights cut off and then heard the reassuring sound of doors slamming and laughter. It broke the spell. Realising how tense he'd become, Campbell joined his fingers together and turned them inside out, cracking the joints.

He found it hard to believe that a re-enactment of something that happened a quarter-century ago, an electronic puppet-show of memory, could have the power to chill an old gamer like himself. He removed his glasses and, breathing on the lenses, cleaned them on a paper napkin. He wondered what had motivated Ernest Seaton to recreate his parents' violent deaths in such . . . the phrase that came to mind was 'loving detail', but somehow it failed to capture the harrowing intensity an unsparing child's-eye view had brought to the production.

A blur of activity drew his myopic gaze back to the screen.

Hastily hooking the stems of his glasses over his ears, Campbell was just in time to see 'Ernie', who'd kept the same rigid pose all through the mayhem upstairs, turn towards him – horror and grief now crudely etched on his wooden avatar's face. Tears as fat as cartoon raindrops rolling silently down the boy's cheeks.

Then, in the oppressive stillness (he recalled the doc saying it had been an unusually hot, airless night), Campbell heard a sound that made his heart hammer in his chest. A floorboard had creaked overhead.

He didn't stop to think, but moved his cursor directly to the foot of the stairs and tried to go up. Only to find his access blocked. From where he stood, Campbell could see part of the landing above him. Below the lintel of what he judged was the door to the master bedroom, a crack of light had appeared and was slowly growing wider.

A shadow fell across the threshold.

In the hall below, the boy, whose perspective Campbell

now shared, had heard the creaking too and understood what it meant. Caught out in the open, 'Ernie' looked back with a panic-stricken expression towards the broom closet, as if undecided whether or not to return to his old hiding-place. At the sound of footsteps steadily descending the stairs, he darted across the hall and into a darkened doorway only seconds, it felt like, before the light snapped on revealing the bleakly furnished TV room. The detective, following behind, swung the cursor around the four walls – the room was empty. Then everything froze.

Campbell slowly lifted his eyes from his immobilised laptop screen to the curtained window. He'd heard something, someone moving around in the parking lot right outside his cabin.

54

Jelly said, 'Would you like to come up for some coffee?'

They were sitting in front of her building in Guy's car, parked near the corner of Thirty-ninth Street and Lexington. She was staring ahead through the windshield, impatient to get in the house so she could have a cigarette. 'And I mean coffee. Don't go getting any ideas, bub.'

She turned her head and saw him smile. 'I'm not that sort of person,' he said, then hesitated. 'Well, okay, but I can't stay long. I have to take a run out to Jersey to check on my grand-mother. She hasn't been well.'

'Oh, I'm sorry.' Her face clouded. 'I don't have decaff and I warn you the place is a mess. Is she gonna be all right?'

'She's an old lady, she gets a little confused. It's nothing serious. Half the time grandma doesn't know if it's night or day.'

As they got out of the car, Jelly looked up and down the street in case there was anyone waiting for her. She was *almost* sure that it had been Ed in the subway, staring at her across the tracks. Scared the shit out of her.

Guy offered her his arm as they crossed the street, the old-fashioned gesture somehow reassuring. When he'd called earlier, she hadn't recognised the name, Guy Mallory – she barely even remembered meeting him at the party, giving him her cell number. She'd taken a chance accepting an invitation from someone she knew almost nothing about, but the evening had turned out better than expected. They'd got on okay at dinner. She liked him – he was a bit stiff, didn't have a whole lot of personality, but he seemed kind and considerate.

If it *had* been Ed Lister she'd seen earlier, and he showed up again, she felt Guy might be some kind of protection.

'Promise not to be shocked?' she said as she opened the door to her apartment.

She had cleared a space for him on the old rattan couch, where he sat now drinking his coffee while Jelly stood by the open window that overlooked Lexington, smoking. She could tell that Guy disapproved, but who cared? Tachel was always on her to quit. Maybe she would when this business was over. She'd given Ed the impression that she didn't approve of *his* smoking . . . and why not? Why not tell him how to save his goddamned life? She smiled as she saw Mistigris jump onto Guy's lap and start purring loudly.

'Push him off if he bothers you,' she said, moving towards the stereo. 'What kind of music do you like, Guy?'

'You know something?' Guy turned his head and she saw

the muscles of his neck stand out like rope. 'Why don't we just sit and talk?'

'Sure,' she said, and for no reason she felt a mild unease about his being there, 'let me check my mail and I'll be right with you.'

Ever since walking in the door – no, before that, only she couldn't admit it to herself – she'd been itching to get to her computer. It was like the craving for nicotine only a thousand times stronger. In spite of herself, and everything she felt about the situation, she was curious to see if Ed had left a message.

She sat at her desk, a Marlboro dangling from her lips, and went to her inbox. It was empty, no e-mail from him, nothing.

She clicked on the Messenger tab and instantly felt an unwelcome fizz of excitement run through her body.

templedog: I'm at the Carlyle. We should meet.

Shit! As she watched, her stomach turning over and starting to cramp, another message flashed up on her screen. The crazy sonofabitch knew she was online. He'd been watching out for her, waiting for her to come home.

td: Jelly, we have to see each other

She hesitated, glancing over at Guy, who was leafing through one of her old *Vogue* magazines. She started typing and, at the soft chatter of the keys, he looked up with an enquiring expression.

'This won't take long,' she said.

adorablejoker: what would be the point?
td: we need to talk things over

aj: it's not gonna change anything

td: your life could be in danger. I came here to warn you.

aj: don't start with that shit again . . . anyway, i'm out of town

td: you were still here this morning. I saw you, in Brooklyn.

aj: it couldn't have been me, but if you say so

td: I know it was you, and I know you saw me too. When are you coming back?

aj: don't know

td: listen, we can't talk online. It may not be safe, here's my cell – 917 775 2998. Pick up the phone and call me now

aj: not possible. i'm with someone

td: then just say you'll meet me . . . steps of the public library, tomorrow at 10

aj: don't you listen? *i'm out of the freaking state*

td: where are you going to be tomorrow?

aj: you really want to know?

aj: ANYWHERE YOU'RE NOT

td: you have to come back sooner or later. I'll wait for you . . . I'll be waiting

Jelly couldn't breathe, her hands were shaking, she felt like she was about to cry. How could he be so goddamned stubborn? She needed to go to the bathroom, but there was no way she could with Guy sitting there and no music. Why didn't he just leave? She pressed the heels of her hands into her temples and half stood, as if to back away from the computer, the source of her misery, then sat down again.

She closed her eyes and took several slow deep breaths, the way she did before getting ready to play the piano, her fingers poised an inch over the keyboard.

Jelly knew what she had to do. It wasn't as if she hadn't been expecting this. She'd thought about it long and hard.

aj: i think you need to know the truth

She felt bad about laying this on him now, shattering Ed's

320

illusions after what had been a long and mostly positive connection, but he hadn't left her any choice.

aj: there is no Jelena, no 'Jelly', there never was

td: what do you mean? What are you talking about?

aj: i made her up, ed. she's just an invented character. the person you think you fell in love with doesn't exist

td: I don't get it

aj: it was all a game. i had a bet with Tachel that i could make you fall for me. i'm sorry. i tried to tell you before, only things . . . got out of hand.

There was a silence. It felt like an age he didn't type back.

aj: are you still there? eddie . . . I'M NOT HER

td: But I saw you . . . this morning, you were at the Church Avenue subway station, in Brooklyn. You were there.

aj: i've been in Pittsburgh since last night. the person you saw in the subway was Tachel. The snapshot i sent you of 'Jelly' was really her . . .

aj: she's beautiful, i'm not

td: but we recognised each other. I know we did

aj: Tachel said she noticed someone staring at her across the tracks. she guessed it was you from the photo you sent me – i showed it to her

td: I don't believe you . . . not one word of what you're saying

aj: look, i'm very sorry for what i've done. i started to tell you so many times . . . goodbye

td: no wait, it's not true, you can't do this

'Hey, buster, do you *mind*? This is a private conversation.' Jelly swung around in her chair. She had just become aware of Guy Mallory standing behind her watching the screen over her shoulder.

He held up both hands in a gesture of mock surrender but kept looking anyway. 'Sorry, I didn't mean to snoop . . . it was just that you seemed kinda upset.'

She turned back to the screen and with a click of the mouse closed the Messenger window. The page of dialogue disappeared. She could see the blue IM tab flashing on her toolbar, which indicated that Ed was still typing, but she ignored it and switched off the computer.

'Look, no offence, mister, but it's got nothing to do with you.'

'Was he the one you were talking about earlier? Templedog? The English guy you're trying to get away from, who won't let go?'

She nodded miserably and, as if she felt obliged to explain what she had written, said, 'I finally had to tell him . . .'

Jelly didn't finish and burst into tears. 'It was the only way I could get him to leave me the hell alone.'

'Here, don't cry. I'm sure you did the right thing.' Guy produced a folded white handkerchief from his pants pocket and handed it to her. 'I know it's none of my business, but he's obviously crazy about you.'

She blew her nose. 'Fool *thinks* he's in love with me.'

'I can imagine how that might happen,' Guy said with a little smile she didn't much care for. 'Let me guess. He told you that you were his destiny, you were meant for each other, it was written in the stars?'

Jelly didn't answer; she used Guy's handkerchief which smelt of patchouli to dab at the tears running down her cheeks.

'What about you?' he went on. 'You believe in all that baloney?'

She frowned. 'How do you know he said those things?'

'It's classic.' He smiled again at Jelly, but avoided meeting her eyes. 'Your friend may be genuine enough, but there are plenty of creeps out there who prey on innocent women online. Don't get me wrong. I just feel I should warn you that his behaviour is consistent with a stalker's. They all say the same things.'

'Look, I know him . . . pretty damned well. He's a good person. He wouldn't do anything to harm anyone. Besides, we're not talking about some nobody here, he's a respected, high-profile businessman.'

'But you've never met him, Jelena, have you?'

'Wait a minute . . . back the truck up. How do you know we haven't met? Did I tell you that?'

'Because it's obvious to me what's going on here,' Guy said quietly. 'The only thing I find hard to understand is why a smart, beautiful girl like you would let him into her life. How can you be sure this guy's who he says he is?'

'I told you he suffered a tragic loss. It was in all the papers. He was devastated by his child's death. You can't fake something like that.'

'Did you know that loss is often a trigger for stalking? Relationship termination, job loss, loss of a child – usually within seven years of the stalking behaviour – it's a common catalyst.'

She pictured Ed this morning in the subway; tall, thin . . . the faded jeans, black polo shirt and sunglasses. She'd been so shocked, so overwhelmed by all kinds of feelings that she could hardly think, but it was like she'd seen him before somewhere.

Jelly felt the first shadow of a doubt.

She asked Guy, who was putting on his jacket, getting ready to leave: 'How come you know so much about all this?'

'I did a spell once at the National Victim Center in DC . . . I was between jobs. We had to deal with a lot of harassment and stalking cases.' Guy glanced at his watch. 'Are you gonna be okay, now? I'm afraid I really have to go.'

She tried to give him back his handkerchief, but he gestured for her to keep it. 'And thanks for the coffee.'

At her front door, in the confined space of the lobby that doubled as galley kitchen, Guy turned to Jelly with a concerned look that made his light grey eyes seem soft and luminous.

'Listen, I don't want to alarm you, but what happens next is he finds out where you live. I've seen situations like the one you're in ignored until it's too late. You might want to consider contacting the police.'

Jelly shook her head. 'I could never do that.'

'I'm only thinking about your safety.'

'Thanks, appreciate it.'

He stared at her for a moment. 'Well, any trouble, you know how to reach me.'

He leaned in towards her and she awkwardly brushed her cheek against his before stepping back and unlatching the door, letting him out onto the stairs. Halfway down the first flight, Guy stopped, as if he'd forgotten something, then turned to look back up at her.

'Hey, if you're not doing anything tomorrow night, maybe we could get together again.'

'I was thinking of leaving the city for a few days,' she said.

'Wise move.' He held up a hand. 'Take it easy, Jelly.'

55

'You can't *do* this to me!' Campbell shouted at his laptop, rapidly keying commands, but getting no response. The screen was frozen solid. His connection had dropped out. Perfect timing.

He slumped back in his chair and thought for a moment. His host might suddenly have decided to put the website off limits, but that wouldn't have caused his system to crash. It had to be just coincidence the server had gone down at the same time.

His cell phone rang and he snatched it up. 'Yes?'

'Hey, it's me,' Kira said brightly.

Campbell closed his eyes and took a deep breath. He'd checked outside the window. There was nobody there. He was a little tense, that's all.

'Dish, I'm sorry, honey . . . I can't talk right now. You caught me . . . I'm right in the middle of something.'

'At this time of night?' He heard the disappointment in her voice, the crushed note she didn't try to hide that let him know she'd called hoping to make up. 'You okay? You sound kinda stressed.'

'Everything's fine, I just . . .' He realised that whatever he said now she was going to take the wrong way.

'You just felt like biting my head off. Amy's refusing to go to sleep unless you tuck her in. You have time to talk to her?'

On the phone with his daughter, cell clamped under his chin, Campbell logged off, rebooted, then tried to get back into the crashed website. He kept trying.

'Let me speak to your mom again, petal,' he said, after he'd promised her he'd be home tomorrow in time to read her a bedtime story.

He understood now why Ward had wanted him to watch the re-enactment. He wanted him to know someone else *was* in the house that night. This was his answer to the question he put earlier to Grace Wilkes – which probably meant that since their meeting she had talked to Ernest Seaton. He was getting closer.

'What is it, Campbell?'

'Nothing . . . I miss you.'

She hesitated. 'Just don't take any chances.'

'I'll make it up to you when I get home, I promise.'

'Oh really. And when's that likely to be?'

'Soon,' he murmured, as he watched the silhouette of Skylands loom up on his screen. 'I love you but I have to go now.'

He was back in.

In a dark, cramped place, peering out through the small window at a square of swirl-patterned rug, Campbell took a moment to get his bearings. The familiar graphics had dissolved, transposing him from the porch of the virtual mansion to what appeared to be an interior within an interior. By moving the cursor, he discovered that the space now on his screen was filled from floor to rafters by the pyjama-clad limbs of the boy, crouched motionless in half-shadow, a bent elbow blocking the miniature front door – he was sharing Ernie's hiding place.

When he followed him into the TV room, he'd noticed the playhouse, an old wooden model of a Cape Cod cottage, pushed up against the wall. He'd dismissed it as a possible sanctuary, thinking it too small, too delicately made. The boy must have climbed in under the shingle roof.

The soundtrack came to life with a soft footfall. The interior of the playhouse grew darker and suddenly the view was obscured as someone walked slowly across the front, very close to the house, then stopped. All Campbell could see now from the tiny window, looking through Ernie's eyes, was the flare of a light-fawn, blood-spattered pants leg breaking over an old black and white hi-top sneaker, also bloody.

It was like the foot of a giant.

Arms folded over head, head tucked between knees, the boy remained still, hardly breathing. In the tangle of limbs, Campbell detected the glitter of an eye alert with terror that listened now rather than saw. On the soundtrack he could hear Ernie's heart beating so loudly it seemed certain that it would give him away.

Presently the sneaker moved off and the view from the little window extended across the sea of carpet to a man's legs as he sat down in one of the easy chairs opposite the cabinet television.

Seconds passed and nothing happened. Campbell waited.

He knew what was coming next. He'd seen the drawings. Some of the detail might be different (the copies Ed had sent him were on file and he would check them later for artistic licence), but it was clear that the boy's taking refuge in the playhouse, the sense of being trapped in a small space while menace lurks outside, the predatory sneaker made to seem enormous by deceptions of scale, had been the source and inspiration for Sophie Lister's sketchbook.

She must have watched the re-enactment to catch the fear that permeated the drawings. He wondered if she'd known that it was based on real events and not just some dark Web fantasy. He wondered too if she'd noticed (although the view from the playhouse window was limited) that the lanky figure sitting in the armchair, the author of the boy's terror, looked like a younger version of her father.

Campbell felt a lead weight tug at his intestines.

He had never met his client in person, but the resemblance was unmistakable. He remembered Ed telling him about Sam Metcalf's murder and being invited to the TV room to watch a cam of the girl lying dead on the floor of the sleeper . . . and how shocked Ed had been to discover that *from behind* the figure in the chair had looked like him. It didn't make the revelation now onscreen any less disturbing.

He knew the dangers of letting himself be seduced by a website, but however little sense it made, one thing was certain – Ward wanted him to know that the person who came to the house that night was Ed Lister.

The figure in the chair raised his hand from the armrest, pointed the remote and the little TV came to life. Not, as

327

Campbell had anticipated, with a love scene from the movie, *Breakfast at Tiffany's*. The tranquil image showed a girl in a summer dress sprawled in the grass and looking wistfully towards a house on a hill.

A long red smear running west from above her hip.

The cam pulled back to reveal the famous Wyeth painting hanging crooked on a wall above a bed, and started to track slowly downwards. Past the splatters of blood and organic matter dripping and sliding at a slower pace. Then, as if Ward had decided that the viewer had seen enough, the picture disintegrated into static.

Campbell looked away from the screen, shaking his head.

What had Grace meant when she said, *'He doesn't know'*?

The suggestion that Ed had been at Skylands the night of the killings might be the truth, or just part of a game Ward was playing that moved between cyberspace and real-time, an elaborate attempt to throw him off the trail. Why hadn't he shown the figure in the re-enactment full-face? Was it because he wasn't sure it was him? Or did Ward have 'real' evidence to back up his version of events that he wanted to share with somebody? Was that the reason 'Ernie' had come home?

In the morning, he decided, he would take another run out to the house.

Jelly lowered the shades before getting undressed for bed. Then, turning out the lights, she walked around the apartment – as she always did on hot nights, last thing – raising the shades again to get maximum air from the wide-open windows.

She lay naked on top of the sheets listening to music through her earphones, waiting for sleep. She held out for almost an hour.

Jumping up at last, she went over to check her computer

to see if there was anything more from Ed. In the dark, the glow from the screen illuminated her body and put the notion in her head that she needed to cover herself. He wasn't online, but she felt Ed could see her through his words, as if they had been cut into the screen and he was standing on the other side peering at her through the little incisions.

He'd sent her an e-mail.

Since this morning, my world has changed and nothing in it will ever be the same. After you ran away I spent the day searching for you. I went to all the places in the city you've ever mentioned. I looked for your face in every crowd, expecting to find you again at any moment. I don't care how crazy this sounds.

Jelly, just say you'll see me. I know you're afraid of what will happen if we meet. But the love, the destiny we share, isn't just something . . .

She stopped there. Wait just a minute . . . what the hell! The way he was still going on about wanting to meet, it was as though Ed hadn't taken in a single word of what she'd told him. She was in Pittsburgh, out of the state, she didn't . . . EXIST!

She read on, shaking her head. He was making all these assumptions when he damned well knew she didn't feel that way about him.

I'm as certain as I've ever been of anything that this was meant to happen, that we are intended. I can only guess at what was going through your mind in the subway, but when our eyes met it was as if I was encountering for the first time the other half of my being. For me now . . . for both of us, Jelly, there can be no peace no rest no happiness no life until we are together.

329

Was he crazy or just being dense? Her throat felt dry. She got up and went to the refrigerator and, standing in front of the open door to get the chill on her legs, drank Tropicana straight from the carton.

When she came back to her desk, she finished reading Ed's words and felt humbled, even a little ashamed.

Even if you refuse to see me, I will never stop loving you. You say we can't be together. But if you don't take risks in life, my angel, the price can sometimes be far higher. I can't begin to describe what I feel for you, or what you mean to me.

I love you, Eddie

PS. I got back to the hotel half an hour ago. It's now nearly 8 pm. I'll wait here till I hear from you.

When she read the postscript she understood. She checked the header and saw that the message had been sent at 19.56 – an hour and a half *before* their last conversation. Jelly frowned. She was almost sure her in-box had been empty when she'd checked earlier. But she often got delays and glitches with her e-mails.

She needed to think about changing her Service Provider.

At least now she wouldn't have to reply – she did that already. She'd given him her answer. And the fact that he hadn't tried to get in touch since could only mean Ed had accepted her story about being someone else.

She sat staring wretchedly at the screen. Nobody had ever written to her like this before . . . shit, it wasn't even what people wrote or said or were supposed to feel any more. All the talk about destiny and how they were 'intended' reminded her of Guy Mallory's warning. Maybe Ed was acting a little crazy and obsessive, but his words were sad and beautiful to her. She knew that he really was in love with her. She wasn't going to take that away from him. She didn't see him as a threat now. What she felt was his pain and longing.

Later, in bed, Jelly kept turning the whole mess over in her head, trying to figure out what she should do. She hated to admit there was even a possibility that Guy could be right. But if Ed had been able to find her in Brooklyn, it was only a matter of time before he tracked her down here to Thirty-ninth Street.

Maybe she *should* leave town for a few days.

It was tearing her apart.

She said her prayers, including Ed in them as she had done for a while, asking for guidance in a situation that filled her with uncertainty. Just before she drifted off, she wondered what he'd meant by,

'If you don't take risks the price can sometimes be far higher . . .'

It reminded her of something Guy had said earlier when they were driving back into Manhattan across the Brooklyn Bridge.

Her eyelids were closing. She was floating out of her depth. What the hell was it?

She saw him on the stairs, looking back at her to wave goodbye. Some off-colour comment he'd made about the Twin Towers and then, here in the house, warning her that you couldn't risk showing a stalker – he meant someone like Ed – the slightest kindness, or he would take it as a sign his feelings were returned.

Did she just imagine he'd called her 'Jelly'?

56

Thursday morning, after checking out of the Mountain View motor inn a quarter before seven, Campbell Armour drove up to the diner he liked in Canaan, where he ordered his last Early-Bird special. He was booked on a ten thirty flight into La Guardia, New York, which meant he needed to be at Bradley Airport in Hartford by nine at the latest. He had a meeting with Ed Lister that afternoon in the city.

He doubled back into Litchfield County on the Winsted-Norfolk road – slowing down a couple of times to make sure he wasn't followed – then, keeping in his head the route he needed to take to the airport, made a detour via Skylands.

It was almost ten to eight when Campbell pulled up in front of the derelict mansion. He killed the engine and sat for a moment, weighing the situation. What had seemed like a reasonable plan last night – returning to the house to look for evidence to support the website re-enactment – struck him now as a seriously bad idea. Letting himself be lured out here into *real* B-movie territory . . . he had to be out of his mind. He glanced up through the windshield at the front door, getting the same unpleasant feeling he'd experienced before. Nothing you could pin down, but he felt almost certain Ward was watching from somewhere.

If it weren't for the money, and his inflexible friends in Sarasota, he'd have turned right around and kept driving. He knew he was pushing his luck, but as a gambling man Campbell never could resist playing one more hand, taking that final throw against dismaying odds. It got him in trouble every time, and yet . . . *you never can tell.* He got out of the car and stepped up onto the long empty porch.

He reached for the brass doorknob and gave the front door a tentative shove. He wasn't surprised when it yielded. He pushed again and the front door to Skylands swung inwards. His palms felt clammy with sweat.

He stood quite still, the morning sun throwing his shadow ahead of him across the threshold, and listened. The low-gear grindings of a truck climbing the hill rose from the valley below. There wasn't a sound from inside the house. Squinting at the dim hall beyond the front porch, Campbell noticed that the pattern of footprints in the dust he'd seen through the cat-flap had been scuffed over. Someone had been here since, tidied up and, conveniently, left the front door unlocked.

He might as well have found a welcome note.

He hesitated, turning to look behind him and out across the ridge to the distant view of the Green Mountains. After witnessing the re-enactment last night, Campbell wasn't so taken with the beauty of the place. The landscape felt haunted. He could only see it now through the dark prism of the website, and the terrible events that took place in that room upstairs. He caught the fresh summery scent of mountain laurel and wild thyme on the blue warming air.

Ignoring the thumping of his heart and a voice telling him it wasn't too late to change his mind, he entered the house and closed the door behind him.

He walked slowly down the central hallway, noting that the layout was identical to the interior of the virtual mansion. On either side of him, the rooms he could see into were empty apart from a few pieces of shrouded furniture. At the foot of the staircase, he stopped and looked up at the landing with the four doors.

333

He climbed a couple of steps, wavered, then decided first to check out the broom closet under the stairs where the boy hid that night.

A glory hole now, it contained nothing of any interest. But it gave Campbell the answer to a question that had puzzled him. The squeak of hinges when he opened and closed the closet door suddenly brought Ernie's dilemma alive. Maybe the boy couldn't go back in his old hiding-place because he knew he'd be heard.

Campbell stood for a moment, as Ernie had done, keeping his eyes on the landing above – nervously watching the lintel over the door to the master bedroom. In case the crack should suddenly widen. Then, retracing Ernie's footsteps, he crossed the hall and entered what used to be the TV room, or the parlour, as Grace had called it.

It felt strange to walk on the blue-green carpet with the swirling pattern of waves breaking that he'd seen from the little windows of the Cape Cod playhouse. In the gloom, he could make out the two bulky armchairs covered in dust sheets still facing the corner where, he supposed, the console TV had once stood.

There was no sign of a playhouse either.

The dank cheerless room had a fusty, shut-in smell. He went over to the window embrasure opposite the door and pulled open the shutters to let in more light. When he turned around, he noticed the only other piece of furniture. Against the inner wall, under a long panelled mirror with glazing bars that made it look like a second window, stood an upright piano. Drawn towards the instrument by a powerful, almost morbid curiosity, Campbell lifted the lid.

The piano reeked of mildew and, judging from its warped keys speckled with orange mould, hadn't been played in years; a few of the white notes had lost their ivory and looked like missing teeth. The empty music stand made him think of

June Seaton endlessly practising the nerve-racking 'Für Elise', never to improve.

He imagined little Ernie standing beside his beautiful mother . . . and lowered the lid again, careful not to make a sound. Then, glancing up at the mirror over the piano, the detective saw something in its darkly foxed panes that made him swing around, heart pounding. It wasn't some ghost from the past, or a trick of the low light. In the armchair nearest the window, under the folds of the dust sheet, he could discern the outline of a human form.

He waited for a moment to be sure the person slouched in the chair wasn't moving; then, approaching warily, he pulled back the cloth.

Campbell recoiled and at the same moment, somewhere around the back of the house, he heard a screen door bang shut.

For a long time I stood under a cold shower, letting the icy needles hammer down on my bowed head until I was numb all over. When I finally stepped out of the cubicle, I no longer felt allergic to daylight, but the pounding inside my skull hadn't stopped. I went over to the bathroom mirror, cleared the condensation and, razor in hand, confronted my bedraggled reflection.

Last night, I'd gone down to the hotel bar for a couple of drinks and ended up drowning my sorrows in a bottle of Jack Daniels Green Label at some dive on Second Avenue. The result was a storm-force hangover, aggravated by the imagined sound of Will's laughter as he welcomed me back to the real world

Well, what did you expect? You didn't seriously believe that she'd turn out to be the genuine article, did you? You made her up, Lister, she was just a fantasy, an invented character, an exotic figment of your imagination – the person you fell in love with never even existed. Hate to rub it in, Ed, but didn't I tell you?

There was Will Calloway peering over the top of his glasses and letting fly with the caustic comments. I'd been duped, taken for a ride, made to look a complete prat. No fool like an old fool . . . and on and on. Just count yourself lucky there was no scam involved and that Island Girl finally did you the favour of pricking your bubble. I closed my eyes. How could I have been so stupid?

I thought back to the moment, last night, when I learned the truth about Jelena. I still couldn't quite accept it. I tried to convince myself that she was lying, or in denial – afraid to meet me because she couldn't admit that she felt the same way as I did – or just playing hard to get, saying no when she meant yes.

In the mirror, while I shaved, one by one my arguments fell apart.

The only positive outcome I could see was that, since the girl only existed in my dreams, it seemed reasonable to assume she was no longer in any danger.

The way she was sitting, it looked as if Grace Wilkes had been there all night.

She had on the same clothes she'd been wearing when they met at Annie's Grill yesterday afternoon. The avocado velour sweats, the white hospital sneakers with the pom-pom laces – Campbell wondered what had happened to her crutches. She couldn't walk without them.

Ernie would have helped her, would have offered her his arm.

There was no sign of fear or other emotion in her grey bloated face. He must have struck without warning, hit her from behind with the foot-long lead sash-weight which lay now in her meagre lap, its business end encrusted with dried blood, strands of hair stuck to its surface. She wouldn't have known what was coming, he thought, wouldn't have had any reason to suspect the child she'd nurtured and loved was capable of harming her. Her skull had been split open and the matted wound, showing bone under the scalp, had bled into the headrest of the chair, leaving a dark stain the shape and size of an antimacassar.

Campbell had to fight back waves of nausea. He'd never been close to a dead person before. Grace looked smaller than he remembered, as if she'd shrunk. His revulsion was mixed with pity and fear. He felt ashamed of his failure to see this coming, convinced it was his talking to Grace – the only person perhaps who knew what really happened here that night – that got her killed.

After checking the backyard from the window, unable to see anything moving out there, his first thought had been to call the police. But then reflecting on how they might view this situation, he'd felt a cold flush of panic run through him. He understood now what Ernest Seaton's intention had been in using the website to lure him back to his old home.

He'd been set up. The cops were most likely already on their way.

Campbell started backing slowly from the room, uncertain whether he was alone in the house, or whether Ward was still nearby – he just knew he had to get out fast.

It was something about the way Grace was bent forward in the chair, the position of the old housekeeper's hands, that made him hesitate. In one hand, she was clutching her lighter and a pack of Newport Lites. The other, empty, was turned palm-up with the rigid thumb and forefinger raised in a supplicant gesture. It suggested that at the point of death she'd been asking for something, begging perhaps. Her last request, it looked like, to smoke a cigarette.

Every instinct was telling him to leave – leave *now* – but a natural stubbornness made Campbell resist the sensible course of action. What if he was wrong about Grace not knowing she was about to die? What if her killer had confronted her?

He came back and stood directly facing the chair, closer than before.

He'd no idea what he was looking for until he moved his head a fraction and something caught the light. He looked again and saw that the glint had come from a pink, metallic object stuck down the side of the chair. Crouching before her splayed arthritic knees, trying to avoid touching any part of her, he slid his hand between the upholstered arm and the chair cushion and, feeling around, retrieved a cellular phone identical to the one she'd had with her at the coffee shop.

The sweet whiff of old lady perfume, masking – or so he imagined – incipient corruption, invaded his nostrils.

Gagging, Campbell rose to his feet, slipped the girl-pink cell in his pocket and retreated towards the door of the lounge. He remembered Grace's story of coming to work that Sunday morning twenty-seven summers ago and the unfamiliar smell through the silent house sending her back out onto the porch, hollering Earl.

She didn't deserve this.

Her eyes seemed to follow him, then he turned and ran.

I called room service and asked them to send up a jug of espresso.

In an attempt to get my equilibrium back and regain a little self-respect, keeping my promise to Laura, I'd arranged to go out to Gilmans Landing and have lunch with their grandmother, Alice Fielding. The car was picking me up in half an hour. I needed to clear my head.

Waiting for the coffee, I booted up my laptop and checked

my mail. No word from 'Jelly'. I'd half-expected an apology or some kind of explanation. I still felt angry and troubled by what had happened. But mostly I just wanted to put the whole humiliating business behind me and concentrate now on what really mattered. Campbell Armour's investigation had reached a critical stage.

Before leaving for the airport, he'd sent me an e-mail confirming our meeting later that afternoon. In a brief update, he mentioned having no luck finding a photo of Ernest Seaton – apparently Grace Wilkes was unable to help – but he had managed to dig up a couple of better-quality snaps of the boy's parents at the Norfolk public library, which he wanted me to take a look at.

I opened the attachments. The photo of the father, posing in his dentist's whites with a 70s-style mop of hair and a wispy Zapata moustache, reminded me a little of the actor Bruce Dern when younger. Gary Seaton had that weak, querulous, slightly aggressive stance of the born loser. I'd never seen him before.

The other image, for some reason, took longer to download.

The doorbell rang. The maid entered, carefully placed a tray on the table under the window, then turned to me and said, 'Is there anything else I can get you?'

I didn't answer, or even look up. 'Enjoy your day, Mr Lister.'

I was riveted by the likeness that had finally appeared on my laptop.

The portrait of June Seaton, the dentist's wife – blonde China-cut hair and dark eyebrows, very pale, almost translucent skin, black captivating eyes – brought her back to life. I got a flash of full nervously kinetic lips breaking over slightly imperfect teeth and at once recalled their dangerous allure.

The photograph no longer left any room for doubt. June

Seaton didn't just look like someone I thought I once knew . . . it *was* her. Our paths had crossed only briefly in what seemed now like another life. But it had been long enough to make me wish they hadn't. A bohemian rich girl, she was as neurotic and unpredictable as that twitchy little smile promised. I felt suddenly afraid that everything was going to unravel now and in ways I couldn't foresee.

The last time I saw June Seaton she was lying unconscious in an empty cargo container down on the West Side waterfront.

Without touching the brakes, Campbell swung the silver Camry out into Deer Flats Road and accelerated downhill until the needle was nudging sixty, sixty-five. As the first curve came up, he cut his speed and, glancing in his rearview, caught a glimpse of a mid-brown police cruiser a quarter-mile behind. Emerging from a shady hollow, it appeared to hesitate before turning its nose into the Skylands driveway.

Campbell felt sweat break out over his forehead. If the patrol car hadn't been coming from the other direction, the Colebrook side, he'd have run straight into the sheriff's deputies. He'd got away just in time. Keeping an eye on his rearview – he couldn't be sure yet he hadn't been spotted – he drove on until he reached the junction with Route 44, the Winsted-Norfolk road, then turned sharp left.

Nine minutes later, neck and shoulders still rigid with tension, he came back off the highway onto the two-lane blacktop that would take him all the way out to Bradley Airport. He had a little over an hour to get there before they closed the gate for his flight. If he wasn't stopped first.

Campbell felt certain that Ward had tipped off the police, which meant that by now there'd be an APB or even a full warrant out for his arrest. Every mobile unit in Litchfield County would be looking for him. Up here in the boondocks he was going to be hard to miss. He thought about surrendering and simply telling the cops the truth. He was an amateur cyber-sleuth from Tampa, Florida investigating a string of killings . . . forget it, there was no way they'd believe him. Just throw his oriental ass in jail and that would be the end of any chance of finding Ward and claiming the million-dollar bonus his client had promised him.

He had until tomorrow to deliver the man who murdered Sophie Lister, or his own life wouldn't be worth living. He was due to meet Cholly at the Regency Hyatt in downtown Tampa at five o'clock, bringing the money – principal and interest.

The blacktop began to climb into rolling, thickly wooded hills. Campbell kept on checking his rearview and side mirrors, but couldn't tell whether he was being followed. The trees grew so close to the roadside that their branches met overhead, forming an unending twisting green tunnel that rarely let him see more than a few car-lengths back. Then the traffic thinned out and he started to breathe more easily as the empty road, after cresting a series of piny ridges, fell in gradual serpentine sweeps towards the Farmington River.

Coming down into the river gorge, he drove across a rusty iron-girder bridge and pulled into a viewpoint parking area used by local fishermen. He waited until he was satisfied that he didn't have a tail, then cut the engine. From the car he could see the anglers in their buff waders spaced out at regular intervals along the banks.

His hands shook a little, post-adrenal rush, as he took Grace's pink cell from his pocket, flipped it open and quickly ran through the phone's memory and address book. There were pathetically few numbers.

Campbell thought about the moment when she must have realised that Ernie was going to kill her. It would have been almost a reflex action, but he was convinced she had shoved her cell phone down the side of the chair on purpose, in the hope someone would find it and retrieve whatever information was stored there.

With any luck one of the numbers would be Ernest Seaton's.

She had wanted to tell him something when they met at the coffee shop in Torrington, only fear or loyalty had prevented her. Her Little Ernie clearly didn't believe in taking any chances. Campbell wondered again what Grace had meant by her parting words, 'He doesn't know.'

He frowned at the readout on the screen. It seemed almost too simple. There was a number – the last but one she had called – which looked out of place only because it wasn't local. Area code 201 fell within the state of New Jersey. He hit the redial button and, after what seemed an age, a female Hispanic voice answered,

'Fielding residence. This is Jesusita speakin', how may I help you?'

Campbell hesitated. The name Fielding sounded familiar to him, but that couldn't be right, surely? He remembered Ed mentioning that his wife's grandmother, Mrs Alice Fielding, lived in New Jersey, somewhere on the Hudson.

He tried the longshot first. 'Is Ed Lister there?'

'*Meesta Leesta*? Not yet, but we expectin' him.'

'Okay,' he said, letting the implications sink in, thinking this isn't possible, there has to be some mistake. But the proof was in his hand.

'You wanna leave a message?'

He thought of telling her he'd arranged to meet his client at the house, and asking her for directions, but then changed his mind. He'd get the address later from one of the Web directories, using Reverse Lookup.

'Thanks, I'll try his cell,' he said, and ended the call.

A shout went up from the river below. One of the anglers, a fat lug in desert camouflage, beer-gut hanging over his

342

waders, had hooked a fish. There was a flash of silver as the salmon leapt clear of the water, shaking its head to spit out the lure before it splashed back into the jade-green torrent, its dorsal fin briefly visible at the surface as it raced off upstream. The unlucky angler, reeling in his empty line, yelled something Campbell didn't catch and laughter rippled along the bank.

They'd be waiting for him at the airport, he thought. His best chance was to double back to Winsted, abandon his car and find other transport.

There was a tap at the window. Startled, he spun around in his seat.

A bandy-legged kid in a nylon T-shirt and blue-jeans was standing there with a cheap suitcase, smiling shyly at him through the glass. Letting out his breath in stages, the detective lowered the window. The kid asked him in a rough Hunanese dialect he barely understood if he was going to New York.

'Hey, man,' Campbell answered irritably in English, 'You can get yourself killed in this country creeping up on people like that. Can't you see I'm busy?'

The boy bowed apologetically, turned and moved away.

Where had he come from? They were in the middle of the goddamned wilderness. What was he doing here in Connecticut, in the USA? He looked too poor and too dumb to be a tourist. Campbell was aware that the prejudice he'd inherited from his parents against the mainland Chinese was at least a generation out of date. Kira would have been appalled.

'Wait a minute,' he called after him.

'I don't speak American,' the kid said, holding out a Bonanza Bus Line rover pass. 'I'm a stranger here. You can help me.'

'Maybe,' Campbell said in his rusty Cantonese, as it occurred to him that this peasant with the bowl-cut hair and teeth like leaning tombstones could be his ticket out of here, 'we can help each other. Hop in, dude.'

57

'It reminds me of a sculpture.'

'A bust of one of your ancestors, perhaps.' Morelli said mockingly, as he pinned the drawing he'd found in Sam Metcalf's apartment on the wall of his office. 'Anything else? You notice what he's wearing?'

'Looks like a polo shirt.'

'Ralph Lauren. What does that say to you, Luca?'

The younger detective's gaze stayed fixed on the drawing. 'American?'

'It's a global brand, copied everywhere.'

'He has an American look, though. Something about the eyes. Like a cowboy staring into the distance.'

'You know how bent that sounds? There aren't any eyes, Luca. That's why it reminds you of a statue. She didn't draw the eyes. Why do you think that is?'

Luca shrugged. 'Maybe she didn't get a good enough look at him.'

'If this is the man who murdered Sophie Lister, then she must have met him more than once. She saw him again, Luca.' He came back to his desk and sat down with a heavy sigh. 'Despite the fact . . . she was afraid.'

'It could be anybody.'

'I think that's exactly what the artist was trying to tell us. Her murderer looks like everyman. He becomes invisible in a crowd.'

'Well, you have to start somewhere.'

'Are you trying to be funny?' Morelli gestured towards the

pile of paper in front of him. 'Look at the response we're getting.'

After his discovery of the drawing yesterday afternoon, he had gone straight back to the office. No time for lunch – he'd grabbed a sandwich from a *paninoteca* on the corner of Sam's street. By three o'clock the head and shoulders sketch of a male Caucasian, aged twenty-five to thirty-five, had been copied, scanned and circulated by e-mail and fax to the relevant police departments in Italy, Austria and further afield; and then to every hotel, restaurant, pension, youth hostel and internet café in Florence.

In twenty-four hours, besides the usual crank calls, they'd received nineteen replies to their appeal for information. The most significant came from an old waiter at Garga, a trattoria in the centre, not far from the Piazza Antinori where Jimmy Macchado had been murdered. He'd served an American tourist two weeks ago who looked like the man in the drawing. Paid in cash, left a good tip, no reservation. He couldn't remember much else about him. Of the other respondents being followed up, Morelli had to admit, none of them so far sounded all that promising.

Luca said, 'If the girl was afraid, why didn't she just give the drawing to someone or post it home or leave it at the atelier?'

'She may not have had time.'

'You think the killer was aware that she'd sketched him? Maybe that's what was on Sam Metcalf's computer.'

'Unlikely since Sam was in Boston. She took her laptop with her.' Morelli tipped his chair back. He steepled his fingers under his chin. 'What else have we got?'

'A phone-in this morning from a woman who wouldn't say why she was calling. The moment I started asking questions she made some excuse and hung up.'

'You traced the call?'

345

'Jennifer Ursino. Lives at number fifty-nine Via dell'Erta Canina. You know that little street off the Viale Galileo, below San Miniato? I called her back and she finally admitted it was about the drawing.'

'She's English?'

'Yes. Speaks Italian with an atrocious accent. She's a widow, lives alone. Her husband died two years ago of a heart attack. He was a *Fiorentino*, in the leather business, had his own company. I was thinking I might look in on her tomorrow.'

Morelli asked, 'How did she come to see the drawing?'

'She takes in lodgers, but she said something about noticing our flyer at the bar of the Hotel Dante. She thinks the subject *may* have stayed with her . . . and, this is the interesting part, in the spring of last year.'

'Do we know if she was interviewed then?'

Luca shook his head. 'She's not a registered landlady. I would imagine that's why she was reluctant to contact the *Questura*.'

'What's the name of the pension?'

'Doesn't have a name. She just rents out a small flat and the occasional room when she feels like it. She said he was very quiet, she hardly ever saw him.'

'Well, what the Christ are we waiting for then?'

Morelli swung himself out of his chair and stood.

'You have a meeting with Commissario Pisani in fifteen minutes.'

'Get a dick, Luca.'

On the Westside Highway, speeding north towards Gilmans Landing, I sat back in the glare-free, air-conditioned limousine and closed my eyes, letting the waves of Beethoven's Ninth crash over what Dr Calloway would have called my bruised psyche. I still had a thumping headache and was hardly in

346

the mood for small talk with an eighty-five-year-old being gently wooed by Alzheimer's.

Don't get me wrong, I'm fond of Alice Fielding. She once played a central part in our lives and her place on the Hudson, La Rochelle, is full of memories of Sophie and George when they were young. We used to go out there in summer as a family to escape the heat of the city and swim in the pool, or Alice's husband would take us sailing on the river. They were golden days.

Looking out at the Hudson, I tried not to think about the girl, the nonexistent girl, I'd made such a fool of myself over. If I'd more or less come to terms with being taken for a ride – the bottom line is that Will did warn me about Jelly, and I'd refused to listen – I still had feelings for her. It doesn't make sense, I know, but I hadn't stopped being in love with her – or, as she put it, with my idea of her. I was beginning to see that 'Jelly' and I had *both* had a lucky escape.

There was no question of my going on trying to find her. You can't protect someone who doesn't exist and, whether or not Ward knew that Jelly was just a made-up person, I didn't feel her inventive friend was at any risk. I had to wonder now if it really had been him impersonating her online. But it was time to let go, get over my mid-life hallucination and move on.

I still hadn't replied to Campbell Armour's e-mail. I'd put off doing so partly because I didn't appreciate the way he seemed to be insinuating that I knew more about what happened at Skylands than I was telling him. I'd never heard of the place, *or* the name Seaton, until he went and dug them up in Norfolk.

He was coming to the Carlyle at six. Before we got together, I thought it best to clear up any misunderstanding by sending him an account of that chance meeting I'd had years ago with a woman I now realised must have been June Seaton.

I had nothing to hide. I felt it unlikely that our casual and fleeting liaison could explain anyone holding a long-standing grudge or wanting to hurt me or my family. But I knew there had to be some connection.

We met at a party, a society gathering I'd been swept along to by friends of friends, in a grand penthouse apartment on Fifth Avenue. I was twenty at the time, flat broke, an ambitious young Englishman on my maiden visit to New York.

Suitably enthralled, I remember going out onto a roof garden with my hostess, who had one of those letter-names like KK or CC, and being shown Central Park, a dark mysterious gulch below the diamond-studded skyline – and then suddenly, right next to us, there was this girl leaning daringly against the parapet with her back to the magical view, looking at me.

She was wearing a black cocktail dress with a string of pearls, flute of champagne in one hand, cigarette in the other – I can't trust my memory, the description would have fitted quite a few women there. But she was bewitching and, I thought, the last word in sophistication. She must have been at least seven or eight years older than I was. We got talking and ended up spending the rest of the evening together. We hit all the spots – Xenon, Studio 54, the Mudd Club . . . she paid – then wandered around Lower Manhattan, looking for after-hours joints. Just before dawn, on one of the West Side piers, we got caught in a violent rainstorm.

Forced to run for it, we found shelter in an empty cargo container that had an open hatch in its side. We were soaked to the skin, breathless and laughing. After doing a line or two of cocaine, we made love standing up in the hatchway because

348

the floor was filthy. It was exciting. The rain hammered on the roof, and didn't stop.

She told me her name – I'm quite sure it wasn't June Seaton. She was all for meeting up again the next night, and the night after; but I held back in a cautious, typically British fashion. I was flying home to London in a few days and I wasn't so green or so smitten that I couldn't sense she was trouble, possibly a little unstable. It was the decade of the crazy chick.

I suggested getting a cab and taking her home, at which point she became clinging and slightly hysterical. Then suddenly she announced she was going to leave the person she was with so that we could be together. I had no idea that she was married with a nine-year-old son and lived in rural Connecticut. She threw her arms around my neck, mapping out our future between desperate kisses. I tried to disentangle myself, gently at first and then firmly – in the end, I had to push her away. I shoved her harder than intended. She slipped and fell and, as she went down, struck her head on a steel bench.

I still feel ashamed of what I did next. I checked her pulse, and was relieved that she didn't seem that badly hurt, but I realised I had no desire to be there when she came around. She was crazy enough to charge me with assault and all I could think about was being put in jail or, worse, deported. I left her lying unconscious and walked away. I called an ambulance from a nearby payphone, told the dispatcher how to find her – and that was that.

I didn't hear from her, or of her, again. I fled back to London the following day. News never reached me of the ghastly tragedy which overtook the Seatons very soon afterwards. When I returned to New York to live a couple of years later, she was not on my list of people to look up. I never told anyone about what happened.

My memory of the encounter, like one or two others from that wilder period of my life, gradually faded, but I have no doubt the woman was June Seaton.

I started to e-mail Campbell, sharing my recollections of June for the first time with another person; then realised it was too much information and shortened the message to: 'Husband, definitely not . . . but the wife looks like someone whom I met briefly in New York, summer of '79. Can't imagine how Ernest could have known I once spent an evening with his mother, but it's a possible connection.'

I looked up and saw the towers of the George Washington Bridge looming above the highway. Just then my cell began bleeping.

'You don't know me.' It was a young voice, soft, hesitant, 'I'm Jelena's friend.'

I didn't answer for a moment. 'How did you get my number?'

'She gave it me. This was her idea to call, you know.'

'What's your name?' I was instantly suspicious.

'Tachel . . .'

'I'm sorry, what is it you want to speak to me about?'

'Look, mister, we don't have to do this.'

'Do what exactly?'

'Do shit.'

I thought she was going to hang up then. But the conversation went on in this punchy, semi-hostile vein until Tachel said that if I wanted to talk, if I had any questions I'd like to ask, she was willing to get together and try to explain things from her girlfriend's point of view.

The little speech sounded rehearsed and I thought about telling them both to go to hell. I'd accepted that I was never going to meet 'Jelly' and, frankly, I had no particular wish to now. But I was curious and, however contradictory this may seem, I couldn't resist the chance to talk about her with someone who knew her. I still felt I was owed an explanation.

It would mean putting off seeing Alice Fielding till later that afternoon, but she wasn't going to notice if I was a couple of hours or, for that matter, a couple of days behind schedule.

'All right. When are you free?' I asked, signalling the driver to pull over. She said give me fifteen minutes.

58

Luca Francobaldi pressed the bell in the peeling stucco wall of 59 Via dell'Erta Canina for the second time, then took a step back into the narrow street and looked up at the villa's shuttered windows. The sky over Fiesole was black.

'You sure she's expecting us?' Morelli said wearily, turning up his collar. It was starting to rain. 'Ah!' He could hear footsteps approaching.

'I really *have* to go now.' Jennifer Ursino was talking into her mobile as she opened the front door. She snapped the lid of her phone and apologised to the detectives for making them wait. '*Fa molto afoso,*' she murmured.

A pretty silver-haired woman in her early forties, baggy T-shirt, drainpipe black jeans, Prada loafers, she led her visitors through a dark hall into the lounge, where she'd been watching a game show on a huge plasma TV. She picked up the remote and switched it off. 'Drink anyone?'

Both men politely declined. She poured herself a gin and tonic, carried it over to the sofa and curled up among the cushions, tucking her long legs underneath her.

'So, how can I help you gentlemen?'

They sat opposite her on straight chairs. Morelli took a copy of Sophie's drawing from his pocket and spread it on the coffee table.

'I believe you can identify this face, *signora*.'

Jennifer nodded. 'It reminds me of someone – I wouldn't put it more strongly than that. David. He might have stayed here last April.'

'Is that why you hung up the phone earlier . . . because you weren't sure?'

She shrugged. 'Something like that.'

'David? What was his other name?'

'I don't remember. He was an American, living in Paris . . . I think he said he was doing academic research.'

'Don't you usually ask your guests for some kind of identification, *signora*?' Morelli frowned. 'Passport, *permesso*, driving licence?'

She gave a little laugh. 'I really should, I know. But I like to treat my guests as friends. I try to avoid bombarding them with questions.'

'Did David mention where he was from in the States? Where he called home?'

'I don't remember. Do you mind telling me what this is about?'

'We're trying to trace the subject of the sketch as part of a criminal investigation.' Morelli cleared his throat. 'Do you have any record of his stay?'

She shook her head. 'I leave a guest book in the flat, but not everyone bothers to sign it. He didn't. He paid in cash, gave me the whole amount up-front.'

Luca asked, '*Signora*, do you happen to remember his movements on the night of the twenty-seventh of April?'

'I've really no idea.' Jennifer stiffened. 'The flat has its own entrance on the back. He came and went. I hardly ever saw him. I sleep . . . very soundly.'

Morelli shot Luca an I'll-do-the-talking glance and went on. 'How do you find your guests, *signora*?'

'Word of mouth mostly. I get a lot of artistic types, fashion people and so on.'

'And this . . . David?'

'He just rang up out of the blue.'

'Did you know Sophie Lister, by any chance?'

'The girl who was murdered? No.'

'Ever think about him in connection with her murder?'

'No . . . Christ no, never. He seemed rather a shy, gentle person.'

'How else would you describe him? Did he smoke, drink? Any unusual habits? Did he have visitors?'

'I just said, he was very quiet, very neat and tidy. I never saw him with another person. In fact, I hardly heard a peep out of him. The ideal lodger.' She laughed.

'You say you like to treat your guests as friends, *signora*, yet you seem to have had very little contact with this man.'

'David was different. He made it clear that he wanted to be left alone and I went along with his wishes.'

'You never heard from him again?'

Jennifer shook her head, no. Morelli could tell she was lying. He went over to the window and stood looking out at the rain.

'We know that he was in Florence recently. You're quite sure he didn't come back here? You didn't speak to him?'

'I'm quite sure.'

'*Signora*,' he said gravely, turning to face her, 'I must warn you that if David is who we think he is then we are dealing with an exceptionally dangerous individual. You really need to tell us everything you know.'

Jennifer blinked as she reached for her glass. Her hand trembled and Morelli wondered if she had a drink problem, or was just frightened.

'Did he use a computer when he was here?' Luca asked.

'All right, all right!' she blurted. 'I didn't speak to him but he did get in touch. A couple of weeks ago, I got an e-mail from him asking if his old room was available. I replied that it was already rented.'

'Was it?'

She looked at Morelli. 'I didn't want him back.'

'Why not? I thought you said he was the ideal lodger.'

She hesitated. 'He made me uncomfortable.'

'Why are you afraid now?'

'I didn't say I was afraid.'

'*Signora*, tell me what happened.' Morelli's tone was gentle, more concerned than probing. 'Did he try to contact you when he was here?'

Jennifer looked down at her glass. 'I thought I saw him, that's all. I was out walking the dog on the *viale* one evening, and as I passed the old iron gates to the Villa Arrighetti' – Morelli glanced at his subordinate, but Luca was busy taking notes – 'I saw a man standing there among the trees, who looked like David. I felt sure he'd been watching me. By the time I could cross the road he'd vanished.'

'He might have been staying at the villa, or somewhere nearby.'

'Yes, I thought of that. I was worried in case he'd found out the flat was unoccupied and knew that I lied to him.'

Morelli didn't want to alarm her more, but he felt she probably had a narrow escape. 'Was that the only time?'

'I never saw him again.'

'I'm still not clear what made you change your opinion about him.'

'I don't know. It was just a feeling.'

'Did you happen to save the e-mail, *Signora*?'

★   ★   ★

'Think she slept with him?' Luca said as he accelerated into a hairpin curve on the Viale Galileo. 'She's a good-looking babe.'

'Babe? I know you've got a thing about older women. But that's because basically, deep down, Luca, you're a mama's boy.'

'She's young to be a widow.'

'So what does that mean? She has to be dying for it? She screws her lodgers instead of charging rent? I know how your mind works. No, she's covering up, but it's nothing like that. How long will they need to trace the URL and get an address from the e-mail header?'

'I don't know. I told Milan it was urgent.'

'You realise the Villa Arighetti was where the Listers were staying when they were here? Slow down or we're going to get stopped by some *Carabinieri* arsehole.'

Luca spun the wheel of the Fiat and shrugged. 'Coincidence.'

'You may be right. Florence is a small place.'

An hour after they got back to the office on Via Zara, the information Morelli had requested was on his desk. The Computer Crime Squad had traced the Internet Service Provider and obtained the telephone number 'David' used to make a connection when he e-mailed Jennifer Ursino.

The number had been decoded to a name and address in Paris – David Mallet, 20 rue Mabillon, Place Saint-Sulpice.

Something about the address looked familiar. Morelli picked up the phone, punched two numbers and asked for the file on the Villa Nardini murder. He opened the folder the girl brought him.

'I was afraid of this.' He leant back. 'David Mallet, it seems, lives a couple of doors down from Ed Lister's office in St-Germain.'

'What?'

'Still think it's coincidence?'

Luca laughed. 'Maybe too much of one.'

Morelli thought for a moment. 'I may need to go to Paris.'

It was only after she hung up the phone that Jelly realised she'd just heard his voice for the first time and that he didn't sound anything like Colin Firth. Every word he'd spoken had irritated her. Hard, mean, mistrustful, bossing her around. She pictured him now as some white-bread, gelled-down, corner-office geek. No more Mr Darcy. The weirdo in the subway must have been his damned ghost.

Do you know the Frick Collection? What a jerk! She was doing Ed a favour, trying to be nice and he had made her feel like she was bothering him. She'd had to take a twenty-dollar cab ride over here.

This was without doubt the dumbest idea she'd ever had, and all because the sonofabitch had made her feel guilty. She just wanted him to understand it could never have worked. She had to talk some sense into him. She had to be crazy.

Jelly was sitting on a marble bench in the garden court watching the glass doors that gave onto the south colonnade. Why had he suggested meeting here? So that she would feel intimidated? Did it mean he'd seen through her little game already? Her stomach was churning. The splashing of the damned fountain kept reminding her she needed to go to the bathroom. She was so nervous.

Oh hi, I'm Tachel . . . you must be Ed. I've heard such a lot about you.

She didn't have a hope in hell of pulling this off. She couldn't stop shaking. Suddenly she *had* to pee. She knew if she moved away from this spot now he was bound to show up and then they'd miss each other. Shit, maybe that would be the best solution. It wasn't too late.

Jelly stood up to leave at the very moment she heard footsteps behind her; she turned her head and saw that he was already there.

She gasped and started babbling like a fool. 'Hello, I'm . . . you must be . . .' She had a mental block, couldn't remember their names.

'I'm Ed,' the man said quietly. 'Sorry, I'm late.'

Oh Jesus . . . she just wanted to run away and hide.

She held out a hand. 'Tachel. Nice to meet you.'

He smiled, reached over and . . . *what the fuck?* . . . touched her face.

'Reality check,' he said.

59

'So you're her millionaire,' Tachel said with a half-smile, leaning back in her chair and looking me over.

'Was,' I corrected her.

'Unhuh.' She nodded. It was the same oblique, slightly mocking smile I knew from the photograph of 'Jelly' on my computer that I still hadn't got round to deleting. I couldn't read what was behind it.

'I didn't think money came into this.'

'You're kidding, right?' She sat forward, leaning her chin on her hand. 'Do us both a favour, Ed. You know that money comes into everything. You were her rich guy fantasy.'

'Well, if I was, she didn't exactly make the most of it. She never asked for a penny. At one point I'd have given her the world.'

'What the hell is your problem?'

'I'm sorry?'

'Forget it.' Tachel shrugged. 'Okay, tell me what you want to know.'

I turned my hands up. 'You're holding the cards.'

I'd taken her to lunch at 21, the former speakeasy and venerable New York landmark on Fifty-second Street. A haunt now of hedge-fund managers and well-heeled tourists, it's the kind of place I normally go out of my way to avoid. I chose it because I wasn't known there and I thought, patronisingly, that the girl might be amused but not overwhelmed by its mellow clubby atmosphere.

'You do realise,' she said with a frown, 'there wasn't one word of truth in anything she told you?' She paused, as if to let that sink in, biting her lower lip.

'All right.' I let out my breath slowly.

'Jelena made it all up. She lied to you about everything – the way she looks, dresses, does her hair, where she lives, about her job at the kindergarten, going to DC that time, her two cats . . . *I* have two cats. I don't know what all else she told you, but you can be damned sure she was either talking about me, or it was bullshit.'

'I don't remember hairstyles being discussed,' I said, just to see if it raised a laugh. Not a flicker. 'Why did she pretend to be you?'

'You'd have to ask her that.'

'I thought you were her deputy.'

She smiled then. I felt I'd missed the point somewhere.

'She had this dumb idea she could get anyone to fall in love with her online. When I found out Jelly was using my photo and ripping off my life – it wasn't lack of confidence, just plain theft – I got mad as hell at her. She's my best friend, but that girl's always had a tendency toward getting into drama . . . online and off.'

I thought of asking her about Jelly's old boyfriend, the one she'd told me she was sleeping with again, but it would have sent the wrong signals.

We were sitting in the Bar Room at a table hidden away behind the door. I ordered whisky sours and '21' burgers for both of us. Once the food came and she began to relax, Tachel turned out to be engaging company. I did my best to put her at her ease and keep things light. I even made her laugh a few times, but I can't pretend that it was plain sailing. There were gaps in the conversation and all through lunch the situation remained exquisitely awkward. It wasn't until the coffee stage that we really got around to talking about why we were there.

'What did she say to you about us?'

'Us?' Tachel raised an eyebrow. 'She never loved you, if that's what you mean. It was just a game to her, trying to make this super-straight, white, RICH, older English guy fall for her. She boasted that she had you crazy in love with her ass.'

I nodded, watching her face closely. I have to say I don't think of myself as 'super-straight'. But I was getting an education.

'I warned Jelly she was messing with real people's lives. I don't think she meant to let things go as far as they did. She said she lost count of the times she tried to tell you, but that you . . . you refused to listen. Then I think she got scared.'

'Scared? Scared of what?'

'That you might be, you know, a psycho or something . . . stalking her . . . stuff like that. She still worries that you could be a stalker, maybe without knowing it.'

'I see.' I felt my chest tighten. It was upsetting to hear how my feelings for her were misconstrued. I wanted to defend myself, but I just said, 'Well, I'm not.'

There was a silence.

'Jelly said to tell you she's sorry if she hurt your feelings.'

I smiled and made a brushing-aside gesture with my hand. 'I always knew at some level it wasn't real. Do I seem to you the kind of person who'd lose their head over . . . well, nothing? What it feels like is waking from a dream.'

'Sure it was just a dream,' she said slowly, looking at me with serious eyes, 'but that ain't no excuse for what she did; saying it's not real don't make a wrong right.'

'Forgiven.' I gave a laugh. 'She should forget about it now. I have.'

'All I can say is that I know she's sorry she hurt you.'

'Tell her I'll live.'

It was difficult, in fact almost impossible, for me not to think of the person sitting across the table as Jelly. In one sense it *was* her, but I was equally convinced (I'd asked Tachel a few carefully baited questions, and never caught her out) she was a complete stranger. She wore glasses. I hadn't been ready for that, but it helped.

Naturally it had occurred to me that this could be a double bluff and that Jelly could have switched identities with her friend to protect herself from the threat I seemed to represent. But, if that were the case, if she had done it to get rid of me – why was she here?

'And you just happened,' I pressed her, 'to be in that subway station yesterday when I was looking for Jelly?'

'Hey, I work in the neighborhood. It's not that big a deal. Plus, you may not have known it then, but you were really looking for me.'

We both laughed and our eyes met. Suddenly I didn't know what to believe, or how I felt about the situation. She reminded me of 'her' and how beguiled by her I had been when she was someone else and only existed in my imagination.

I looked down at her slim brown hands, the long tapering

360

fingers I'd often pictured making music, and asked if her friend played the piano.

'Nope, she based all that stuff on me,' she said modestly.

Outside the restaurant, she paused on the steps in front of the famous '21' façade with its painted jockey statues and lit up a Marlboro.

'What's wrong now?' she said, blowing a cloud of smoke. She'd caught the puzzled frown I had on my face. 'You know I get this all day long from people who suspect us smokers have a better time than they do because for one thing . . . we don't *give a shit.*'

'It's just that Jelena hated it when I smoked.'

'Yeah, well, I'm not her and I'm full of surprises.'

'So that's something she didn't base on you.'

She shook her head. 'Doesn't approve. Always on me to give up. How far is this place? I need to get back to work.'

'A couple of blocks.'

The music store I had suggested we visit, Frank & Camille's, had a showroom on Fifty-seventh Street. I'd told Tachel I was thinking of buying a piano as a gift for a friend and needed some advice. I didn't say the friend in question had been Jelly, which meant the expedition was no longer relevant, but it must have been pretty obvious.

I just wanted to hear her play.

We started wading up Fifth Avenue. The sidewalk was thronged and whatever path we took we seemed to be against the flow. We hadn't gone more than half a block when she stopped and, putting a hand on my arm, said, 'You know what, this is going to take too long. I really have to go.'

'Some other time?'

'I don't think that would work, do you?'

'No, I suppose not,' I said. 'Well, I enjoyed meeting you.

And thanks . . . I don't quite know what for, but I'm very glad you called.'

She laughed and started to back away. 'Thanks for lunch.'

'Can I get you a cab? '

She shook her head, then turned smartly and walked off.

I stood and watched her go, trying to ignore a small chafing voice inside my skull telling me that I needed to stop her. It took a moment for it to sink in that once I lost sight of her I wouldn't see her again.

'Wait a minute,' I called out, rather half-heartedly, 'I don't know how to get in touch.' But she'd already been swallowed up by the crowds. 'There was something else I wanted to ask you.'

It must have looked as if I was talking to myself. When I started to run after her, yelling at her to wait, people weren't slow to clear a path.

I caught up with her at the light. 'I was wondering,' I said too loudly, coughed, then lowered my voice as she turned her head, 'if you had plans for this evening.'

She looked less surprised than I'd expected. 'As a matter of fact I do.'

'You couldn't change them?'

'Out of the question.'

'It's just that I have a couple of tickets . . . for the ballet.' I had to think fast. 'I know this sounds pretty stupid, but I was hoping to take Jelena.'

She sighed and crossed her arms. 'That girl doesn't even like ballet.'

'I should have guessed.' I smiled. I remembered Jelly saying online that she was a huge fan of classical ballet. 'If you really want to know, I don't either.' A look came into her eyes then that made me think she might be open to persuasion. 'But what I'm asking is, do you?'

'I dunno.' She shrugged. 'It depends which one.'

'*Sleeping Beauty* . . . her favourite.' I had read somewhere that a revival of the Kenneth MacMillan staging for the American Ballet was opening at the Met.

She rolled her eyes. 'That girl.'

She started laughing but in a different way. 'Hey, I gotta jet.'

'Will I see you tonight?'

'I dunno . . . I doubt it.'

60

It was nearly four thirty when Campbell Armour walked through the arrivals hall of the New York Port Authority bus terminal keeping an eye out for anyone looking at him the wrong way. In his traffic-cop sunglasses, long Army Green shorts, a Tampa Bay Devil Rays baseball shirt and Nike Air force trainers, he could have passed for a tourist or a college kid on vacation. His fears of being hauled off the bus in handcuffs or stopped at the gate hadn't materialised.

Maybe his stratagem had worked and 'Chen' had already been picked up in his place behind the wheel of the silver Toyota. But as he crossed the busy concourse, he felt a prickly sensation between his shoulder blades that he knew wouldn't go away until he was clear of the building.

On the bus ride from Torrington, he'd had guilt issues about taking advantage of his wandering countryman. But the way he looked at it, fate had offered him a chance it would have been wrong to turn down. As well as handing over his rental car, he'd paid the kid a hundred bucks over the odds for the bus ticket. Worst case, he might have to spend the night in jail while the authorities tried to find an interpreter. What Campbell had bought was more time.

The two cops at the Eighth Avenue exit barely glanced at him as he sauntered out onto the street, chatting on his cell to his wife in Florida, and headed downtown. He hadn't eaten since breakfast and suddenly realised he was ravenous.

'What time is your flight?' Kira asked.

He hesitated. 'It's looking more like tomorrow.'

'You *promised* Amy.'

'Dish, this is really important. I'm getting close.'

There was silence the other end.

'He's starting to show himself. He made his first mistake.'

While he walked, Campbell gave his wife an update of the investigation. He told her about the re-enactment of the Seaton tragedy he'd witnessed on the *homebeforedark* website and Ward's extraordinary revelation that Ed Lister was at the house the night it happened. Then, careful to downplay the possibility that he might have been in any danger himself, he gave a brief, censored account of going back to Skylands that morning and discovering Grace's body.

Kira wasn't fooled, not for a moment.

'You call your client,' she said quietly when he was done, 'and you tell him that you've taken this as far as you can, now it's over to him and the police . . . then you catch the first plane HOME.'

'It's not that simple, honey.' He laughed and tried to make a joke of his being a murder suspect on the run. 'I need to bring him in so I can prove I was framed . . .'

'*Bring him in?* My God, Campbell, if you could just hear yourself. You think you're so smart, acting out your little private eye fantasy as if this was a movie, or one of your damn video games.'

'Before someone else gets hurt.'

364

'You're behaving like a child. Drop the case. You don't know what you're getting into . . . baby, please.'

'I have to do this.'

'Why? What for? So you can get yourself killed?'

Campbell said nothing.

'What are you trying to *prove*?'

'Have you checked our savings account lately?'

It was Kira's turn to be silent. He hadn't intended telling her until tomorrow, but he'd kept it to himself long enough and the truth just came out. Kira knew about his 'little weakness' – he'd had a gambling habit before they married. There had been a few slip-ups since, but nothing major. She didn't comment now when he confessed that he'd lost nearly $200,000 playing poker in a private online game. It was only when he told her that he owed another hundred k to some people in Sarasota that she said softly – he was sure she was crying: 'Campbell, how could you do this to us?'

He started to tell her he was going to pay it all back with the bonus Ed Lister had promised . . . all he had to do was find Ward.

With a despairing moan, she hung up on him.

'I've been trying to get in touch with your husband, *signora*.'

Investigator Morelli put her on speaker phone and looked across his desk at Luca, who mimed blocking his ears as Laura Lister's strident English voice overwhelmed the small room.

Morelli said, 'Yes, I know he's in New York. I've left messages . . .' He smiled into the transmitter. 'I was hoping you could perhaps save me from bothering him. It's a small thing.'

'I really can't talk now. I was just on my way out.' She sounded as if she'd run back to get the phone.

'This will only take a moment, *signora*. I need to find the address of your husband's office in Paris.'

'Try the phone book under Beauly-Lister.' Then, as if she'd realised how rude that sounded, she said quickly, 'It's 24 rue Mabillon, near the Boulevard St-Germain.'

He didn't write it down, but glanced at Luca. 'Thank you.'

'Is that all you wanted to know?'

Morelli cleared his throat. 'Does your husband live at that address when he goes over on business?'

'It's an office, not a flat. Ed always stays at the Ritz . . .' She hesitated. 'I thought you knew that. Didn't you speak to him there?'

'Has he ever . . . yes, I did, foolish of me . . . considered getting a pied-à-terre in Paris? Somewhere more convenient perhaps for his work?'

'He might have done. I honestly wouldn't know.'

'He's never discussed it with you?'

'We don't feel the same way about Paris. Not my favourite city.' He heard the soft clop of a hand briefly muffling the receiver. 'Look, I really have to go now.'

'Signora Lister,' Morelli said, 'there's been a development in our investigation of your daughter's murder.'

There was a pause. 'What kind of development?'

'It's too soon to speak of a suspect, but we have a promising lead.'

'Then I think you had better talk to Ed.'

'Of course. I'd just like to ask you about something.' She gave an exasperated sigh. '*Signora,* if it's inconvenient, I could call back at another time.'

'Oh, for goodness sake, get on with it.'

He'd never established a rapport with Laura Lister. She'd made it clear early on that she regarded him as incompetent and untrustworthy, probably just because he was Italian. Morelli felt belittled by those scornful blue eyes, and yet, oddly, he admired her – found her attitude brave, not unsympathetic. The last time he saw her, at the requiem mass for

366

Sophie at San Miniato, she had barely acknowledged his presence, had seemed more haughtily remote and isolated than ever, as if her grief, instead of starting to heal, had cut her adrift. The father, he suspected, had been too wrapped up in his own sorrow – or his little ragtime piano-player perhaps – to notice. Morelli had to remind himself that this was a fishing expedition.

'Your husband mentioned that you set up an arts foundation in Paris after Sophie died . . . in her memory.'

'It's a small charity, based in London.'

'Ah . . . nonetheless a wonderful idea, if I may say so, to give the talented but not so fortunate the opportunity to develop their skills.'

'We felt Sophie would have approved.'

He frowned and shook his head at Luca, who was showing signs of wanting to interrupt. 'I was wondering . . . has your charity ever helped send anyone to the Conservatoire de la Musique in Paris?'

'Not that I'm aware of.' Her voice sounded strained, or had he just imagined it? 'Try asking Ed. He looks after the music side.'

It was possible she already suspected or even knew that her husband was screwing around. But if that were not the case, he had no particular wish to drop Lister in it. Having just spoken to Gretchen in Marienbad and arranged to meet his magnificent flaxen-haired physio tomorrow in Paris, he felt inclined to be generous.

'He's a difficult man to reach.' He considered for a moment telling the *signora* about the drawing, but decided he'd already given her enough to encourage her husband to return his calls. He was looking forward to informing Ed Lister himself of the *Questura*'s breakthrough on the case; he also wanted to get his reaction in person to the coincidence of David Mallet living on the rue Mabillon.

'What did you have to say,' he asked his assistant as he put down the phone, 'that was so urgent it couldn't wait?'

'You're going to miss your plane.'

'Not if you drive, Luca.'

There was no signpost anywhere for Gilmans Landing.

A cluster of hidden-away, old-money properties overlooking the Hudson, it was the kind of time-warp community that would never have had much interest in advertising its existence. The driver turned at Dearwater Road, rolled down the steep lane under a canopy of stately trees towards the river, then spent the next five minutes crawling around the maze of narrow lanes and cul-de-sacs before they found the gates to La Rochelle.

Campbell paid the cab-fare and walked up the long private drive towards the Fielding home. A stone-built Victorian, not huge but right on the water, it reminded him of his grandfather's place in Hong Kong, which he knew only from faded family photos but regarded with mixed feelings as his imperial heritage. Startled by the hiss of lawn sprinklers coming to life, the detective looked behind him and saw, gliding between the trees, a blue triangle of sail halfway across the Hudson. He thought of Kira's silent tears, the shame he'd brought on them, as he crossed the gravel circle in front of the house.

He'd been half-expecting to find his client still here at La Rochelle – on the phone the maid had said Mr Lister was expected some time that afternoon – but it seemed unlikely now. The place was too quiet. Inside the porch, the interior stained-glass French doors stood slightly ajar. He flipped open his cell and punched in Ed's number. Before they finally got together, he needed to find out why the dead woman, Grace Wilkes, had the number of La Rochelle on her cell phone. Why she called here yesterday – he could only assume it was to talk to Ed Lister.

He felt relieved when he got his client's voice-mail. He left a message to say he couldn't make the meeting in the city and suggesting they reschedule. Then rang the doorbell. There was a television on somewhere, but nobody came.

After a minute or so, Campbell let himself in and followed the sound down a narrow wood-panelled hall. At the door to the front parlour, he cleared his throat and said tentatively, 'Mrs Fielding? Anyone home?'

61

He found her in a small flower-filled conservatory extending beyond the parlour into the garden. A screen door gave onto a flagstoned patio shaded by a wisteria arbour with views of the river. Alice Fielding was sitting on a chintz-covered recliner with a plaid lap rug over her knees watching an 'I Love Lucy' re-run.

Without looking up, she said, 'It was nice of you to come all this way. How do you find New York? Hot and dirty as ever, I imagine.'

'Yes, it is,' Campbell said. 'Mrs Fielding, I'm—'

'I hardly ever go up to town now.'

He hesitated. 'I'm sorry to barge in on you like this. I tried the bell.'

'But aren't they a riot?' she chortled, still gazing at the screen. 'You know, the Desi Arnazes were good friends of ours when we lived in Los Angeles after the war. They were so much fun.'

'Really? I'm a big fan myself.'

'Are you delivering something?'

'No, ma'am, I'm supposed to be meeting Ed Lister. I was wondering if maybe you'd seen him recently?'

With a little sigh of irritation, she aimed the remote at the TV and killed the sound, then turned and looked at him with arresting sage-green eyes. Crisply dressed in black pants and a grey silk shirt, she wore her hair cut short and pinned on the side with a mother-of-pearl barrette that gave her a girlish look. He put her in her late eighties, frail and clearly a little spaced, but not beyond reminding the world that she'd been a knock-out in her day.

'Who did you say you were?'

'Campbell Armour, ma'am. I'm doing a job for him.'

'Oh well then . . . Eddie has just gone down to the village to get some groceries. He should be back soon. You're welcome to wait.'

'Thank you.' Campbell hid his surprise. 'Was Ed Lister here last night?'

She gave him a puzzled look. 'Yes, he was here. Why do you ask?'

'It's just that . . . we've been missing each other.'

'He always was hard to pin down. A strong attractive man, though, even if he can be a bit of a stick, you know, stuffy in that buttoned-up English way.'

He nodded, but didn't say anything. Alice had a direct, personal manner that Campbell found a little disconcerting.

'And since the tragedy . . .' She sighed. 'He simply adored her.'

His eyes flickered away from hers. 'Yes.'

He wanted to give Ed the benefit of the doubt. But his client's admission that he'd known June Seaton had turned everything on its head. Why *had* Ed kept quiet about it until now? He must surely have realised, the moment the link with Skylands was established, that it had to be relevant? The fact

370

that he knew her wasn't proof of wrongdoing, but it made Ward's claim that Ed was present at the house the night his parents were killed seem a little less outlandish.

It was only a small step from there to speculating that June's love letter had been intended for Ed Lister and that he was the person she'd met and fallen in love with at a party in New York. What if Grace had lied when she told him the unsent letter was never found? It might help explain why she had spoken to Ed Lister here at his grandmother-in-law's house sometime the day before she died. It was the penultimate call she made from her cell phone.

The more he thought about it the worse things looked for his client. Campbell felt afraid suddenly that he was getting out of his depth.

'Would you like a glass of wine?' Alice enquired. 'I usually have one about this time.' She picked up the phone at her side and pressed an extension key. 'It'll be interesting to see if anyone comes. Jesusita's never around when I need her.'

'You're very kind. If I could make that a soda . . .'

'He's bringing a friend up here for supper later. A special friend he wants me to meet.' She leaned forward suddenly and then said in a low confidential voice, 'He told me he's madly in love with her.'

'I'm sorry . . . who are we talking about?'

'Who do you think? Eddie, of course.'

'Oh . . . okay.' He nodded, trying not to look bemused.

'I believe he said her name was Laura.'

Campbell felt lost. 'You mean his wife, Laura . . . your grand-daughter? '

'No, no, not *her*, stupid. I know her.'

'I haven't been working for Mr Lister very long.'

'Then you don't have a clue,' she said, mysteriously, 'do you?'

Not sure what to make of this, Campbell just kept nodding. He felt his eye drawn uneasily to a silver-framed photograph of the Listers on the mantel. A happy family group shot of Ed and Laura with the children when they were young, it looked as if it had been taken here in the grounds. There were several photos of Sophie when she was older, almost a little shrine to her on top of the writing desk. In one he found striking, she was trying to hold her hair back off her face on a windy day, laughing for or with whoever was behind the camera.

'Such a beautiful child, don't you think?' Alice Fielding said with an unreadable smile; she had caught the direction of his gaze.

'I was about to say, ma'am, there's a strong family resemblance.'

She waved away the compliment with an impatient gesture. 'Well, I guess that girl has awarded herself another night off. She's got a new boyfriend, Carlos, wouldn't you know it. Her head's permanently in the clouds. But with a name like Jesusita . . . isn't it simply too divine?'

Campbell was uncertain if she meant it as a joke. 'Where I live in Ybor City near Tampa,' he said solemnly, 'we have a large Hispanic community – it's quite a common name there.'

'Why, I'm sure it is, Mr . . . now I've gone and forgotten yours.' She gave a merry tinkle of laughter. 'One forgets every-thing at my age.'

'Campbell.'

'Campbell, would you mind going back to the kitchen and fetching the wine? You'll find what you need in the refriger-ator.'

I didn't have tickets for the ballet. That was just something I came up with on the spur of the moment because I wanted to see the girl again, whoever she was.

372

The problem took a little fixing and, yes, it helps to have money (I didn't think twice about blowing nearly two thousand dollars on tickets I wasn't even certain I could use), but I put it down to luck that I was able to score a dress-circle box for a sold-out performance at the last minute. It was tempting to regard it as a favourable omen, as I waited for her on the steps of Lincoln Center.

I'd arrived an hour early and hung about the front of the esplanade, keeping an eye on the subway exit and drop-off point for buses and taxis on Columbus Avenue. As dusk fell and curtain time crept nearer, every five minutes or so I'd walk back across the plaza, joining the streams of people converging on the Metropolitan Opera House – in case she'd come from another direction.

Wandering up and down the grand marble peristyle trying to spot her in the crowd, I got caught up in the first-night mood. I couldn't help being affected by the growing buzz of excitement. Then I'd go back to my original position on the steps and anxiously watch the traffic, the long line of tail-lights on Broadway.

Even if she did come, I told myself, and I was beginning to think it unlikely now, it would prove nothing.

The kitchen, neat and antiseptically clean, didn't look as if it saw much cooking action. At the far end there was a break-fast bay flooded with evening light from floor-to-ceiling windows. Campbell went over and stood looking out at the view, wondering if Mrs Fielding wasn't perhaps as tightly wrapped as he'd first thought and if he could rely on anything she'd told him about Ed Lister. She had got it into her head that he was coming back any moment with her groceries, but more than likely he'd long since returned to the city.

There were long shadows now stretching over the terraced lawns that stepped down at the back of the property to a wilderness area of wetlands and marshy reed-beds. On a pale sand bar that ran out from under the cliffs into the wide golden basin, he could see wading birds silhouetted against the water. Set ablaze by the low sun, the Hudson looked more like a lake or inland sea than a river. It was hard to believe they were only thirty minutes from midtown Manhattan.

He discovered where the glasses were kept and put them out on a tray. Then he filled an ice bucket from the automatic ice-dispenser. He decided he might as well wait an hour and see whether Ed showed up. If the maid had gone out, he wondered, who was going to fix supper for the old lady?

A word with Jesusita at some point might be useful.

It was only after he closed the refrigerator door, holding a bottle of Chardonnay in one hand and a can of Diet Pepsi for himself in the other, that Campbell noticed the fridge magnets. They were the usual miniature suspects – bear with a balloon, the Statue of Liberty, a classic Coca-Cola bottle, watermelon slice, the Little Mermaid and so on. Maybe a dozen in all. A few were holding memos, telephone numbers, and one, a modest shopping list. What caught his eye was the way the magnets were arranged. They'd been herded together in the centre of the fridge door to form an elongated heart shape or, seen from another angle, the Nike logo swoosh – a wing of the Greek goddess of victory.

It didn't look like something Mrs Fielding would do. Campbell wondered if Ed Lister could have been responsible for creating the pattern. It felt like it was there for a reason, as a reminder or a message perhaps. He remembered Ed telling him about the body in the fridge in Florence . . . but he was letting himself get carried away here. He decided the cluster of magnets most resembled a heart and imagined a bored Jesusita daydreaming about her Carlos. He thought no more about it as he carried the tray back to the conservatory.

374

'There you are at last, Eddie,' Alice Fielding said. 'It was *you* who gave Jesusita the night off. I remember now.'

'It's Campbell,' he said.

At eight o'clock, the time when the performance was due to begin, there was still no sign of her. I made one last sortie to the lobby of the Met which, apart from a few scurrying late arrivals, had emptied like an hourglass.

I had no right to feel disappointed; the girl said herself she doubted she would make it, and yet I felt both let down and slightly resentful. Turning away, I loosened my tie, unbuttoned my shirt collar and wandered slowly back to the steps.

I gave her another five minutes. Let that stretch out to ten. Then, finally resigned to the fact that she wasn't coming, I descended to street level, looking for a taxi back to the hotel. An elderly couple grabbed the first cab. The second that pulled into the area was still dropping off a passenger as I approached. I held up a hand to get the driver's attention. She was the passenger.

I recognised her a few seconds before she saw me. I can't say that my pulse quickened or my heart missed a beat. Mostly I just felt irritated as I watched her rummaging in her bag for the fare, until I stepped in and thrust some notes at the driver. She turned around then and with a harassed 'I know, I *know* . . . I'm late' shot me a defiant glance, as if somehow her lateness was my fault.

I let out a sound, something between a laugh and a gasp of exasperation, which masked the sense of wonder I felt – she looked so incredibly beautiful – as well as my secret delight in knowing now for certain that it was Jelly.

'What the hell kept you?' I asked.

'I'm here, aren't I?'

PART FOUR

Gilmans Landing

62

It was after eight now, dark out, still no sign of anyone.

Campbell got up from the desk in the parlour where he'd set up his laptop and went through to the kitchen to get another cold drink. Mrs Fielding had told him to make himself at home before she went upstairs to take a nap, still insisting Eddie would be back shortly from the village. That was over an hour ago.

He returned to his laptop and, taking a sip of Diet Pepsi, squinted at the screen. He scrolled back and re-read their last conversation – the one where 'Adorablejoker' politely tells 'Templedog' it's over, there's someone else; and he's not really listening, refusing to take no for an answer. She stands firm, makes it clear that she's not 'in love' with him, never has been, but he either can't or won't see it.

'*I know you feel the same way . . . you just don't realise it yet.*'
The first warning signs.

The girl seems aloof, increasingly reluctant to talk, which makes him only more persistent. The tone of his e-mails and instant messages changes, becomes not so much threatening as creepily affirmative; and, in the irrational, hopeful spin he puts on every word he writes to 'Jelly', every thought he shares with her, there's coiled aggression. The classic stalking scenario of 'the guy who can't let go'.

Campbell had seen it all before. He took off his glasses

379

and knuckled his eyes, then rolled the cold can of soda across his brow.

He'd come across the material almost by accident. Exploring the house earlier, he'd wandered into the study and out of professional nosiness had gone through the desk. In an unlocked drawer, he'd found a bunch of CDs, mostly business correspondence, with Ed Lister's name on some of the files. It was no surprise to learn that Ed looked after the old lady's affairs. One of the CDs caught his eye.

Under the general label, 'Insurance', he'd noticed a subheading titled, 'For Keeps'. Maybe it was meant to stand out, he wasn't sure, but it had made him curious enough to boot up his laptop and open the folder. The moment Campbell realised what he'd stumbled upon, he downloaded the files, carefully put the CD back where he'd found it, then took his laptop into the parlour.

Just in case Mrs Fielding was right and Ed did show up. Where he was sitting he would see the lights of a car coming up the driveway.

He'd spent the past hour and a quarter wading through the chronicle of a cyber-relationship gone bad – nearly two hundred conversations, messages and e-mails over a six-month period from the recorded instant that Ed and the girl met online, until a couple of days ago, when he arrived in New York. He understood now why his client had been reluctant to let his laptop be swept by the police. Why he'd been scathing about the profile he'd put together of Sophie's killer as a 'love obsessional'. Why he hadn't seemed in any great hurry to meet up.

He tried Ed's cell again; it was still switched off. He decided to wait until the old lady reappeared, then order a taxi back to New York. He thought about calling Kira, just to tell her he loved her, but decided to put it off till he was done here.

Campbell had no qualms about reading Ed and Jelly's secret

history. It was like discovering a cache of old letters in an attic trunk. Some of the language Ed used Campbell felt he'd seen before, recently. He cross-checked with the dialogue in the text of Ward's webcast, but could find no connection. Looking out for the vivid, incoherent runes of synaesthesia identified by Professor Derwent, he ran searches of Ed's documents for *'words with an iron shape'* and other examples of Ernest Seaton's unusual condition. They failed to yield a result.

He felt relieved, but not all that surprised. The idea that his client and Ward might be the same person Campbell had considered and rejected early on in his investigation. He was the wrong age, wrong nationality, wrong background, didn't have the IT skills. Plus, if Ed Lister was Ward, why would he have hired him? He'd thought about Sam Metcalf's murder – Ed couldn't possibly have been on that train.

And Sophie, his own daughter? Forget about it.

Either his client was being set up or the links between things were not what they seemed. Even after reading the telltale correspondence, Campbell found it hard to get his head around the idea of Ed Lister as a stalker.

Then he discovered the letter.

He was searching the folders for image format files, in case Ed had stored the girl's photo somewhere on the disc, when he came across a jpeg file named 'Casebow'. Again it happened almost by chance, but this time he felt sure someone was meant to find and open the file.

It contained a single scanned image of the letter, dated July 29, 1979, which June Seaton wrote her lover but never got to mail.

Darling dearest,

   We can't wait any longer. I'm so afraid I won't be able to hide my feelings and he'll know. Last night, when we talked about destiny bringing us together, your words lit a fire in my heart that will never go out. I realised then that you are the other half of my being as – yes, my darling – I am yours.

He had an image of June Seaton, weeping and terrified, being forced to read the passage aloud to her drunken husband.

It feels as if I've always known you, Eddie, but now that we've found each other we mustn't let go. The boy already senses change coming. You were right when you (word illegible) that if we don't take risks in life, the price can sometimes be far higher. I understand now.
I'm leaving him. Come tonight, June

The facsimile letter, written on blue Skylands notepaper in a backswept feminine scrawl, appeared authentic enough with its passionate underlinings, scorings-out, ink-smudges and what might have been bloodstains. The letter didn't prove that Ed Lister was June Seaton's lover or that he had been at the house the night of the tragedy, or that he killed her. But the arrows were all pointing one way.

What bothered Campbell was how Ed came to have a copy of a letter he supposedly never received. Did he find the original at the murder scene years ago and remove it then? Or had it been in Grace Wilkes's possession all this time? He could understand his wanting to destroy what might be seen as incriminating evidence, but why keep a copy? And then leave it lying around? Every question led on to three more. There were too many variables.

Yet there was no doubt about the similarities between what June Seaton reported Ed as saying to her in 1979 and the evangelical tone he uses with the girl, 'Jelena', when he tells her about his love for her. At one point, word for word. *'If we don't take risks in life, the price can sometimes be far higher . . .'*

Jesus. Campbell wiped the sweat from his face.

Everything in the 'For Keeps' folder made it look like Ed Lister had stalked and possibly even killed before. He thought about Jelly, and wondered if she had any idea what kind of danger she was in – it was textbook that where the victim and her stalker once had a relationship, violence was the likely outcome.

But was he on the right track here? The evidence could have been tampered with – it could *all* have been fabricated. And where did Ernest Seaton come into this now? Campbell knew he had to resist the obvious interpretation, respect his own mantra: online nothing, but nothing, is ever what it seems.

He pinched the bridge of his nose. His eyes felt tired. He could have happily closed them for a while, taken a nap, which reminded him that he didn't have a place to stay in New York. Focus.

In the moment-to-moment unfolding of the 'love story', he'd caught glimpses of a cyber-stalker at work, yet there was nothing to show Ed had been gathering information about his victim – usually a key sign of obsessive behaviour. Jelly's personal details would have been simple enough to obtain without alerting her. He had her photo, he knew what she looked like. Still, Campbell would have expected him to ask more questions about her life, work, family, friends, her activities outside their relationship – he shows interest in her musical ability and offers to help her study in Paris, but doesn't even bother to ask her her real name.

Ed seems perfectly content to keep things at the level of an online friendship, safely apart from his real life. He fails to realise he's let her under his skin until the moment he's about to lose her and, then . . . boom, he falls madly in love. She rejects him and now, suddenly, he's obsessed, he can't live without her – *at least, that's how it looks from Templedog's files* – so he comes over to New York to find the girl, track her down . . . and then what? Kill her?

It occurred to him that Ernest Seaton could have been trying to warn him about his client all along. It would explain where Skylands came into the picture, why the son might want to let him see that Ed Lister had murdered his mother – and was getting ready to repeat the performance.

This could be about some delayed form of revenge.

Campbell stood up suddenly and walked over to the window.

He'd heard a noise, a light scraping sound, coming from the terrace. He held up a hand against the room's reflection in the glass and peered out, but it was too dark to see anything. Raccoon most likely. The idea that Ed Lister could still be on his way back here was making him jumpy.

Another thought struck Campbell then: if what he'd just found out about his client was even half true, he could forget about getting paid, let alone the bonus.

He had just become expendable.

He returned to the desk, went online and quickly pulled up the *homebeforedark* website. He entered the password and, as soon as the graphics loaded, found himself on the back porch of the virtual mansion.

There were lights on in the house. Waiting for 'Mrs Danvers' to come out to meet him, he remembered poor Grace Wilkes sitting in the chair in the TV lounge with her skull split open. When the avatar failed to appear, he set off alone on the path through the woods to the graveyard.

It was a moonless night. No owl to be heard. Without a flashlight he could just make out the arrowy pines, the cast-iron ornamental fence around the cemetery, but not the graves. Looking back through the trees at Skylands, he noticed the house seemed brighter, glowing in the darkness like a ship at sea. Then he saw smoke billow from an upper

384

window and the next instant orange flames were licking the eaves of the roof. Within seconds the fire had spread and the whole mansion was ablaze. Campbell realised at once that he wasn't just witnessing a simulated disaster, the encrypted self-destruction of Skylands suggested that the murder-haunted website had finally come to the end of its useful life.

This was Ward signing off.

With a feeling of dread, the detective dragged his cursor away from the burning house and back over the little cemetery in the woods. By the lurid flickering light of the fire, he was able to confirm his fears.

A name had appeared on the third headstone.

Jelena Madison Sejour

Her dates hadn't yet been carved into the stone, and the grave was still open. But for how much longer? He had just watched his paycheck go up in smoke, and knew only too well what that meant as far as his future was concerned; but Campbell couldn't stand by and let this prediction be fulfilled.

He had to find the girl before Ed Lister did, or else she was going in the ground.

A girl who could be anyone, anywhere.

63

'You were someone else earlier,' I said. 'It made things easier.'

She took a sip of wine and looked at me over the rim of her glass. 'You really didn't know?'

'I couldn't be sure. Not until I saw you get out of that taxi.'

'I'm sorry.'

'Don't be. I enjoyed having lunch with the person in your photograph.'

Jelly smiled. 'I wasn't checking you out, you know.'

'It's okay, even if you were. We met as total strangers . . . well, maybe you had a slight advantage there.'

'It was the only way I could go through with it.'

'I understand. I'm glad you changed your mind.'

'Our souls had already met.'

'What?'

She laughed. 'It's what people say who get to know each other online before they meet in real-time. You know, like their relationship grew from the inside out.'

'I imagine it leads to a lot of disappointment.'

'Are you disappointed?'

'Not yet.'

She made a face and stuck out her tongue – I saw its glistening pointed pink tip and felt a sudden shiver of desire. 'Well, you're about to be.'

I wondered if Jelly really meant that, or if she was just teasing. She must have known it was, potentially, a dangerous statement.

I sat staring at her across the narrow table lit by a candle. We were in a restaurant downtown that's meant to have the best Italian food in New York – not that I remember what we ate. I couldn't keep my eyes off her. I tried not to make it too obvious by holding my gaze below the level of hers – focused on a shoulder or a bare arm, her hands, those long beautiful fingers, a stretch of throat. All evening her physical presence had an effect on me that was to say the least disconcerting.

I'm trying to keep this account dry and plain. Two hours of sitting beside her in the dark listening to Tchaikovsky had raised the temperature.

She wore a thrift-shop dress of black tulle – an ironic reference to the ballet, I imagined – put together cleverly with other items of inexpensive clothing and jewelry themed on the colours pink and black, so that she looked modern and old-fashioned at the same time. She had the bones and the verve to carry it off. Her hair was a frizzy cloud. The effect was original and utterly enchanting.

'I can't tell any more what you're thinking.'

'The old ESP letting you down?' I smiled. 'I'm thinking if I touched your hair I'd get an electric shock.'

'Nope, definitely not working. When we were online I always knew what was on your mind.'

'It's like blind people who recover their sight. Their other senses, which became heightened to compensate, go back to normal.'

'Is that really true?'

I shrugged and reached over suddenly and touched her hand and the shock went through us both. If we'd lost the knack of knowing what the other was going to say next, almost of being inside each other's heads, something else had taken its place. A sense of connection that I think we both found a little overwhelming.

There was no effort involved. We got along as if we'd always known each other, picking up a conversation that had been going on forever. We talked among other things about music and her place at the Conservatoire in Paris (there was still resistance there) and, of course, Sophie. She asked me if they'd caught the person who killed her and those poor girls on the train. I said, not yet.

She understood that I didn't want to discuss it and we moved on.

'You don't work in a kindergarten?'

'Nope.'

'You don't even live in Brooklyn?'

She shook her head. 'Manhattan. I work a boring job answering phones in an office in Flatbush. My mom lives near there.'

'Why did you lie about those things?'

'Why do you think? I didn't want you to find me.'

I thought for a moment and said, 'If you hadn't called me this morning I wouldn't have come looking for you. I'd given up.'

'You sure about that, mister?'

'Well, I don't really know. Now that I'm with you it's impossible for me to imagine . . . Jelly, you have to take some responsibility for this.'

She laughed. 'Let's just say we were drawn together.'

Another of those shivers ran through me. When I looked at her I could hardly avoid having certain thoughts – the chemistry was there and bubbling over – but I felt inhibited by her modesty, her seriousness. She had already said nothing was going to happen and I believed she meant it.

And yet she was the one who kept bringing up the subject.

'We were meant to find each other, ' I said.

Campbell Armour put down the phone, and listened.

He could hear movement upstairs which suggested the old lady had woken from her nap. As soon as she came down, he'd thank her for her hospitality, ask her to get Ed to contact him if he happened to show up later – then he was out of here.

He picked up the receiver and dialled his client's cell again. The concierge at the Hotel Carlyle had told him that Mr Lister was out for the evening – he had tickets for the theatre, he believed – which would explain why he hadn't been able to reach him on his cell. It was still switched off. He left another message.

Closing his laptop, Campbell went through to the kitchen. He tossed his empty soda cans in the garbage and began jotting down the number of a local taxi company on the refrigerator door, when a hot blast of salsa cascaded into the room from the floor above. It didn't sound like Mrs Fielding's kind of music.

He walked to the end of the kitchen. Beyond the breakfast nook a short passage led through an archway to the back door. On his left there were two internal doors. The first opened directly onto the garage – he glimpsed a station-wagon covered in a tarp and an empty space for another car with a dusty tennis ball dangling on a string to act as a parking guide. He remembered Mrs Fielding mentioning that she let the maid, Jesusita, have the use of her runabout.

The second door revealed a narrow wooden staircase. He hit the light switch. The music got louder as he went up. He guessed Charlie Cruz or Tito Puente.

At the top of the stairs, Campbell paused, one hand on the banister, and called out, hello. The door facing him was cracked a couple of inches. He could just see the foot of a single bed, the room in darkness.

389

A smooth male voice glided in over the music, startling him for a second before he realised it was a commercial. He called out again, this time in Spanish; then, knocking at the door, pushed it back.

Campbell cut on the light and walked over to the bedside table. The radio-alarm clock, tuned to WPAT AMOR, a 24-hour Latin station, showed the time as 07.30. He touched the snooze bar and the nerve-racking din ceased, the red display numerals stopped blinking. It made him wonder about Jesusita.

Apart from the unmade bed, the small hotel-like room was tidy enough. A black-velvet painting of the Virgin Mary in a jungle setting above the bed was the only wall decoration. There were a few personal effects: stuffed animals, a miniature licence plate with JESUSITA engraved over the New Jersey, Garden State logo, make-up and toiletries on the vanity and in the bathroom. Oddly, no photographs. He'd have expected some of her family in Guatemala or wherever – maybe one of Carlos. A maid's white housecoat, white pantyhose and slip were folded and laid out on a chair, white shoes underneath.

He looked through her modest pile of CDs. Campbell wasn't sure what he was doing here now. He tugged open the louvred doors to the closet and got a whiff of gardenia masking stale sweat. There was a spare housecoat hanging on the rack, some laundered blouses and a pair of jeans. A heap of dirty clothes in a corner showed Jesusita in a less appealing light.

The rest of the hanging space was taken up by a collection of old suits and dresses in zippered dust bags, probably belonging to Mr and Mrs Fielding. He parted them and noticed on the floor at the back of the closet, half buried under a down comforter, a black rucksack. Campbell felt his gut tighten.

He remembered his client's story of how Sam Metcalf became convinced she was being followed through Europe and had tried to photograph her elusive shadow. Campbell hadn't seen the results himself. They'd been wiped off the victim's webpage before he got the chance, but the common identifier in three of the shots according to Ed Lister had been a black rucksack.

He reached in and lifted the bag out by its straps; it was a Berghaus day pack, half full, heavier than he'd expected. He owned a similar pack himself, only made by Tekbag USA, with a special padded compartment for a laptop. He checked the side-flap first. The cushion-lined pouch contained a cell-phone charger cord and, tucked inside the flap, a name tag.

DAVID MALLET, PO BOX 117, RAPIDS CITY, SOUTH DAKOTA.

Campbell frowned. If the rucksack belonged to Sam's murderer, the name and address were probably false, but the choice of 'Mallet' was interesting. It was one of the placeholder names in the 'Alice and Bob' dramatis personae – archetypal characters used instead of letters of the alphabet in crypto-graphic protocols and computer security for the sake of clarity. More commonly known as Mallory, the 'malicious active attacker', Mallet could modify messages and substitute his own, which made securing a system against him the ultimate challenge.

There was no way that a hacker like Ward could have taken the name as an alias and been unaware of its significance. It was the kind of in-joke he seemed to enjoy. But if the rucksack belonged to him, then what was it doing here in the maid's closet at La Rochelle? Campbell withdrew the little card from its Perspex window. On the other side was the address of Ed Lister's office in Paris.

He was filled suddenly with a deep uncertainty, close to panic.

It had already occurred to him that the online conversations he'd read between his client and 'Jelly' might not be safe. It would have been simple for Ward to alter them to make it look as if Ed was stalking the girl. But that didn't mean he *wasn't* stalking her, or that she was in any less danger.

He sat back on his haunches and thought. Rapids City, South Dakota . . . Mount Rushmore. A teasing Hitchcock reference from Ward perhaps? The movie *North by Northwest* hinged on a case of mistaken identity, a man wrongly suspected, framed for something he didn't do. Or did it just seem that way?

He didn't know who or what the hell he was looking for. He felt afraid now, not just for the girl, but for himself. As he loosened the drawstring that secured the neck of the rucksack, Campbell's cell phone vibrated against his hip.

Kira said, 'Listen, I'm sorry I hung up on you before.'

'Heyyy!' He laughed out loud with relief, the warmth of her voice close to his ear flooding over him. 'I was just about to call you.'

'Where are you? Please say the airport.'

He cleared his throat. 'Dish, you're not going to believe this . . .'

The lights of a car coming down the hill off the highway flickered across the window. He watched to see if it would turn up the driveway, but the beams swung south away from La Rochelle.

It reminded Campbell that he hadn't ordered the taxi yet.

They'd been chatting for twenty minutes, mostly discussing the case. Kira had told him quietly they'd talk about the

392

money when he got home. Still trying to justify his following the trail out here to Gilmans Landing instead of calling the cops – she wasn't really buying it – he started going through the contents of the rucksack.

It contained little of interest. Light blue check cotton shirt, change of underwear, socks, an old pair of Adidas trainers, size ten; there were two books – a paperback of Thoreau's *Walden* and a cloth-bound copy of Giuseppe di Lampedusa's *The Leopard*. Inside the flyleaf of the novel was the ex libris of Greenside, Ed Lister's home in Wiltshire.

He'd asked Kira for a psychological perspective, talking motives now. She was explaining to him how fantasies of revenge sometimes conceal a darker truth, when Campbell interrupted her and said, hold on. Reaching the bottom of the rucksack, he pulled out an oblong box wrapped in a carrier bag from Bowery Kitchen Supplies, a professional cookware store on West Sixteenth Street. His eye skimmed the manufacturer's description on the label.

'*Forged from a single blank of high carbon steel, the 11"* *cambered blade echoes the moon's shape in the midpoint of its cycle . . .*'

He felt the flat white box grow heavy in his hands. He tore it open. Inside was a new single-edge mezzaluna still in its protective plastic sleeve.

'Jesus,' he breathed. 'Oh Jesus.'

It was an exact replica of the weapon used to kill June Seaton.

'What's wrong?'

He didn't answer. In the distance, he heard a truck shift gears.

'What is it . . . Campbell?'

'Nothing, honey.'

'Then why did you say that?' Kira said, 'Campbell, I know you. I have a really bad feeling about this. Please . . .'

'Relax, Dish.' He laughed as he shut the lid. 'Tell me about *your* day,' he said, though he felt a different sense of urgency now.

With his cell clamped between his cheek and shoulder, he swept the boxed mezzaluna and everything else into the rucksack, buckled the main flaps, then threw it in the back of the closet and closed the doors.

He took some comfort in the knife still being here. At least it hadn't been put to use yet. Whoever bought it was clearly planning to do more than chop up herbs.

He turned out the light and started down the stairs. He was about halfway, still talking to his wife, when he heard the front door slam.

'Honey, I have to go now. Kiss Amy for me. I love you.'

'Why are you whispering?'

He cut Kira off, flipped his cell shut and stood, listening. Another door banged, the rustle of shopping bags, a man's voice floating up from below.

'Grandma, I'm home.' He wasn't sure whether or not to feel relieved.

Then he heard the clip of confident footsteps returning to the front of the house, followed by low muffled conversation. Campbell imagined the old lady telling Ed Lister she'd had a visitor. He thought of slipping out the back door.

In the kitchen hallway, tiptoeing towards the exit, he remembered that he'd left his laptop and sportsbag in the front parlour.

'Campbell?'

He froze, then turned slowly around.

The figure standing under the arch, smiling at him as if they knew each other, wasn't anyone he'd seen before. He'd caught the look of surprise in the stranger's eyes, but it was quickly masked. A young open face, friendly and pleasant.

'Not leaving without saying hello?'

64

'What would you say if I told you I lied about sleeping with my ex?'

'I don't know. I mean, for Christ's sake, Jelly, I took you at your word.'

'Well . . . that was kinda the point.'

'Yes, but why would you lie about something like that?'

She smiled slowly, as if she was amused by my innocence. She had a deliciously sly, sweet-tempered smile that was hard to resist.

'About sleeping with Guy?'

'Guy is your old lover? You never mentioned his name.'

'Guy Mallory.'

'Okay, so you didn't sleep with Guy. Did you come close? I mean, was there a situation where you could have done, but didn't?'

'I told him I was in love with someone else.'

I felt a thud in my chest. 'Someone else. I see . . .'

'Yes.'

'I'm just taking this in.'

'It isn't the only thing I lied to you about.'

'No, I think I realise that now.'

'You feeling okay?'

'I don't know.'

'Let me ask you something.'

'Can it wait?'

She shook her head. 'No. It's the reason I'm here, Ed. I couldn't let you go away not knowing how you make me feel. You really meant those crazy things you wrote?'

'What are you talking about?'

She lowered her eyes. 'Your last e-mail. You said if we didn't meet, it would be like a denial of the reason the two of us were put on this earth . . . but that, no matter what, you would never stop loving me.'

A little surprised because, as I remembered, my last e-mail had been an emotional but rather terse affair, I said, 'I meant every word.'

There was really nothing else I could say. I could hardly tell her that I had reason to suspect Ward must have intercepted and edited what I'd written.

'Still feel the same? Now that you've had a chance to inspect the merchandise?'

'I wish we were alone right now.'

'Well, so do I.'

She put an elbow on the table and leaned her cheek on her hand, her head tilted to one side as she looked in my eyes. Hers, aslant, darkly melting, shone with that open-heart radiance we all hope to see at least once in our lives. I wanted to kiss her.

'This is it, isn't it . . . Jelly?' I could barely get the words out.

'Yes it is.'

There was a silence that I imagined the whole restaurant must have heard because it seemed for a moment the room had grown quiet too.

'Can't you say something . . . tell a joke or something?'

'I think we should go now. I need to go home.'

'No wait, I am just . . . trying to adjust to the new reality . . . I mean, I knew this all along. I knew you felt the same way.'

'I lied about Guy to put you off, mister,' she said in a low sure voice. 'Because you were . . . the whole situation was getting out of hand. I just felt I had to end things.'

396

'And look what's happened.'

I smiled and reached for her hand again across the table.

'Yeah,' she said, drawing her hand away, 'but that doesn't make a wrong right. Nothing's changed here. You're still married. You still have a family, Ed. As far as I'm concerned that makes you unavailable.'

'Circumstances change.'

Her eyes filled with tears. 'No they fucking don't.'

'I can't let you go,' I said.

'You know, for a moment I thought you were him,' Campbell said, as he followed the stranger into the kitchen, spinning a line about how he'd arranged to meet his client out here at La Rochelle.

'Mrs Fielding told me she's expecting Ed, any time now.'

Ward waited politely for him to finish, then looked at his watch. 'Ed Lister is in New York. It's getting kinda late, friend. I doubt he'll be coming up tonight.'

'New York?' Campbell echoed. 'She said it was okay for me to hang out till he got back, but I tell you I was beginning to wonder.'

'She takes a liberal view of time.'

He managed to smile. 'In fact, I already called for a taxi, about fifteen minutes ago. I was just going out there to check.'

'We'll know when it comes. They always honk. I'm Guy, by the way. Can I get you a beer or something, while we wait?'

He opened the refrigerator door and held up a couple of Millers.

'I'm good, thanks,' Campbell waved the offer aside; he could hear his heart beating faster. 'Campbell Armour.'

He hadn't liked the sound of that 'we'.

The man came forward to shake his hand, wiping his own first on his jeans; it was cold and wet from holding the chilled

397

glass bottles. He stared at him, unblinking, until the detective met his eyes.

He knew this couldn't be anyone but Ernest Seaton.

Ward pulled out one of the wooden chairs from the breakfast table and sat down. He appeared taller in the chair, and older than he'd first thought – Campbell guessed his midthirties, which would be about right. He noted the long muscled trunk and powerful shoulders under his washed-out green denim shirt. When he moved, it was with the natural economy of an athlete. Guy looked in serious shape, sitting there, relaxed, swigging beer from the bottle, acting like this was home.

'You don't mind my asking,' Campbell said easily, 'where exactly do you . . . fit in around here, Guy?'

'Where do I *fit in*?' He smiled and shook his head. 'Oh I get it, you heard me call her "grandma". Everyone calls her that. Al Fielding was one of *my* grandmother's oldest friends. They kinda grew up together in West Virginia. I look in on her from time to time, you know, see how she's doing. She's great, though, isn't she?'

Campbell hadn't heard a car pull up. He wondered if he'd been right here in the house all along. 'So that's how you know Ed Lister?'

'You could say.' He nodded slowly. 'We never actually met. Have a seat, and I'll tell you something about your "client" and me.'

Campbell saw his opportunity. 'Maybe another time. It's okay with you I'll just grab my stuff now and – I thought I'd walk up the driveway to meet the taxi.'

'I don't think so.'

Campbell laughed. 'Excuse me?'

The man set the beer down, wiping his mouth with the back of his hand.

'Campbell, let's not dick around any more. They're at the

398

restaurant now. When they leave he's going to offer her a ride back to her apartment, and then most likely she'll invite him up for a drink.'

Campbell stood and just looked at him.

'I tried to warn her.' He sighed, locked his hands behind his neck and tilted his chair back. 'She told me he's been stalking her online for months. Now the creep's turned up in New York. I advised Jelena to go the police. She wouldn't listen.'

Calmly admitting he knew the girl. Campbell felt sweat running down his temples, over his forehead. Ward/Ernest/Guy – whatever his name was – had set the whole thing up. This was all his work.

'You saying you're afraid my client might harm her?'

'I think we both know that's a real possibility.'

'Then why don't *you* call the cops?' Campbell said.

Ward smiled slightly. 'What would be the point?'

'None . . . I guess.' Campbell nodded. He didn't like the sudden turn the conversation had taken; the more Ward told him, the more he acknowledged, the harder it was going to be for him to get out.

'You realise, don't you, he's going to kill her?'

'Jesus. You really think so? He doesn't seem capable . . .'

'Just like he did my mother.'

Campbell hesitated. It was like a door slamming shut, the bolts being thrown. He swallowed, his mouth dry. 'You really believe Ed Lister had something to do with June Seaton's death?'

'You're still fucking with me,' Ward said, shaking his head. 'You saw him at the house that night, Campbell. You were *there*, or as good as. What I showed you on the website is exactly the way it happened. It may seem like a long time ago, but not to me and I don't invent.'

'Ed told me he met someone once at a party who looked

like your mother – he was twenty years old, never knew her name.'

'Is that right? She knew *his*. It was on the goddamned envelope. She wrote him a letter begging him to come for her.'

'The letter was never mailed.'

'Doesn't mean he didn't go up there.'

'But why would he want to kill someone he'd just met?'

'I don't buy that they just met. I think the affair had been going on for some time. Maybe she changed her mind about taking off with him, decided she wasn't going to leave her family after all. Maybe he got mad at her . . . the guy's a stalker, Campbell, a psychopath.'

Campbell felt the sweat stinging his eyes. He knew he couldn't appear too ready to agree, he would see right through him. 'My client insists he never went near your house, he wasn't even in this country at the time of the killings. He swears the first he heard about what happened was just a couple of days ago.'

'And you believe him?'

Campbell hesitated. 'I don't know.'

'Bullshit you don't know.'

The truth was he did still have lingering doubts about Ed Lister, but he had a feeling it didn't matter now one way or the other. His priority was to warn the girl that she was in danger from one of them. 'You know what?' A slight tremor in his voice. 'I think I'll give that dispatcher another call, see what's keeping the cab.'

'Where's the rush?' Ward said. 'I'm heading into the city later. I'll give you a ride. Sit down, for Christsakes, take the load off.'

Reluctantly he pulled out a chair across the table from him. Up close, Ward's wholesome country-boy looks – regular features, clear pale eyes, unblemished skin – seemed to radiate

400

good health and an inner calm. Campbell had to remind himself why he should feel afraid.

'You look like you're burning up, buddy, sure you won't change your mind about that cold one?'

He needed an exit strategy, not a beer. He thought about the CD he'd found so conveniently in the study, the online conversations, the copy of June Seaton's love letter . . . the contents of the black rucksack in the closet upstairs. All set up to make the murder look like a repeat.

He asked Ward about the letter, how it had led him to Ed Lister.

'Grace Wilkes sent it me after my grandmother died. I guess she thought I had a right to know.'

'So you decided to track him down.'

'He wasn't exactly hard to find.'

'You planned to avenge your parents' deaths. Was that the idea?'

'I wanted justice for them.'

'On the strength of one dubious piece of evidence.'

'I did my research.'

Campbell nodded. He could still back off, pretend to go along with Ward's purposefully warped view of the past – not that he was convinced it would guarantee his safety. Kira would never forgive him for this, but he had another idea.

'Is that why you beat and strangled Sophie Lister to death?'

There was a long silence. Ward just looked at him with a little fixed smile. Campbell could hear the hum of the refrigerator. A distant peak of canned laughter rose from the TV the old lady had turned on in the lounge. He knew that if Ward confessed to the murder, he was dead.

'I was in Florence,' he began. 'I planned to use her as leverage on her father, but then . . . let's just say, things didn't work out.'

'What happened? You fell in love with her?'

He shrugged. 'I don't feel the need to discuss it.'

'She reject you? Tell you to get lost?'

He didn't answer. The little smile faded.

'You know what occurs to me? I don't think you really believe Ed Lister had anything to do with your parents' deaths. I think you made up this whole thing.'

Ward sat very still, staring at him.

'Grace was the only one who knew what really happened that night at Skylands. Isn't that why you killed her? Because she told you something you didn't want to hear? Couldn't *bear* to hear?'

He just kept on looking at him, expressionless.

'What is it you can't handle? She tell you what she told me – that your mother was a spoiled, neurotic brat, who'd go with any man looked at her twice? Your daddy just a pathetic drunk? You couldn't stand the way they argued and fought all the time, was that it? How they tore pieces out of each other?'

He paused, wanting him to get angry. 'Or is there something else?'

He saw into the blankness of Ward's eyes then. It was as if some basic human constituent was missing. It could be he was in denial, or just unaware – Campbell wondered if this was what Grace had meant by 'he doesn't know' – but what he sensed above all was a flat chilling absence.

He tried to reason with Ward, told him he was sick, he needed help.

'Do I look like someone who needs help to you?'

Campbell insisted, 'You don't have to do this.'

All he got back was that long cold empty stare. He saw no way of reaching him.

'Have you eaten yet?' Ward asked, getting up and going over to the counter, where he'd left the shopping bags. He pulled out a head of celery, tore off a stick and started crunching it. It was as though the conversation had never happened.

'I was gonna fix supper, but . . . what the heck? I know this pizza joint near the bridge where they do a great pepperoni pie. We can pick up a couple of slices on our way into town.'

Campbell's mouth dried. He was staring at Ward's hands. He hadn't noticed before how unnaturally pale they looked. The cuffs of his western shirt covered the wrists. It was only where the rubber flattened the hairs on the backs of his hands that it was obvious. They were sheathed in surgical gloves so fine the latex seemed transparent. He must have been wearing them earlier when they shook hands, only they were wet and cold from holding the beers and he hadn't noticed.

Ward caught the direction of his gaze and smiled. He stretched his fingers, opening and closing them.

'I have a skin condition. Relax, it's not catching.'

'You go ahead, friend. I'll get the light,' he said.

Instinctively Campbell braced himself as he stepped down into the unlit garage, Ward following right behind him. A static dread hovered about his unprotected neck and shoulders. He heard a click as Ward pulled the string light switch and a fluorescent strip flickered on overhead. He had to fight the urge just to run.

He quickly scanned the room, taking in the shrouded wagon, the bay for a second car, the automatic garage door; and, over the workbench that ran one side of the garage, a rack of tools nobody had touched in years. There was a dusty Weber barbecue in a corner, an old set of golf clubs hanging from a hook, oars and canoe paddles among the rafters – he was looking for any kind of weapon.

He knew he hadn't got a prayer against Ward's strength, but his tennis training had made him quick-footed – over a short distance he might have the advantage. He didn't think Ward was carrying a gun.

His eye travelled back along the workbench and stopped at what he guessed was the wall switch for the door opener. It was a screw-drive Chamberlain, wall-mounted; same model as the one he had in Tampa. He knew exactly how long the garage door would take to open.

He'd noticed that Ward hadn't touched the switch when they came down the steps. Either he had a remote on his key-ring, or he wasn't planning on leaving just yet.

'How do you like this beauty?' Ward said, as he pulled the tarp off the station-wagon, a vintage Buick Electra Estate, white with wood-effect panels. Campbell hadn't a clue what year. Before he was born.

'Does it run?' he asked, glancing inside the passenger window. On the back seat there was a rucksack identical to the one he'd just seen in the closet up the back stairs. He felt like he wanted to vomit.

'Like a bird,' Ward said, dropping the bundled tarp at his feet.

Then, in the trunk space, Campbell saw the roll of garden refuse sacks, the pick and shovel. 'We're not going to New York, are we?'

Ward stepped around the front of the wagon, holding a rope.

Campbell didn't hesitate. He'd been planning his move since they entered the garage. He spun on his heel, ran back to the workbench, hit the wall switch then darted towards the garage door. He started to dive even before he heard the whine of the electrical door opener, throwing himself flat and as soon as the space was wide enough rolling under the door and out into the night.

65

We were walking uptown, crossing Washington Square, when I stopped to point out a building on the north side where I used to live back in the 80s, my first New York apartment that wasn't a sublet. Jelly made some remark, then carelessly slipped her arm through mine and said she was in the mood for dancing. She knew this place, a Cuban cafe in Hoboken where the music was so hot everyone had to get up.

'Don't worry, mister.' She saw the way I reacted and smiled. 'Half the people there are at least twice your age . . . at *least*.'

'Thanks.' I laughed, conscious of her warmth, her slim body suddenly so close to mine. 'I don't care about making a fool of myself. I'm just not much of a dancer.'

'Never expected you to be. I still wanna dance with you.'

'You don't think that would be asking for trouble?' I said stiffly.

'I'm not ready to go home yet, that's all.'

I suggested finding some quiet place where we could sit and talk. I didn't trust myself. 'I'd rather spend the time we have left alone with you.'

She frowned. 'Do you need to be somewhere?'

I shook my head.

'You make everything sound so serious . . . so, I dunno, life or death.'

She seemed very young then. I said, a little sharply, 'You've obviously forgotten what you said earlier in the restaurant . . .'

She cut me off. 'What the hell's the matter with you?'

'You said, nothing's going to happen.'

'What *exactly* is it you want from me, mister?'

'What do I want, Jelena?'

She withdrew her arm to look for a cigarette. I stood and watched her light up, then I took the cigarette from her lips and kissed her.

Fresh air filled his lungs and suddenly Campbell felt there was hope.

He came out of the body-roll running. He didn't even glance back. His heart pounding, fear pistoning his legs, he sprinted for the sheltering darkness at the end of the driveway. He must have put thirty yards between him and the house before he realised he should have run the other way, into the grounds.

Just as he decided to change course, Campbell became aware of an unfamiliar swishing sound rising on the air. The next instant he felt an explosion of pain, as though a gigantic fist had struck him in the small of the back. The breath went out of him in a single whoosh that he heard as the roar of a crowd. His knees buckled under him and he fell forward.

Then only numbness.

Campbell tried to get up. His legs wouldn't respond. No feeling at all below the waist. He groped for his glasses that had come off when he hit the ground and hooked them back over his ears. Almost useless now, one lens out, the other shattered by the fall, they let him see what had brought him down. The head of a heavy ball-peen hammer gleamed at him from where it had spun off its target and landed in the ditch a couple of yards away. There wasn't time to reach it.

He worked his cell phone out of his pocket.

He could see Ward walking purposefully towards him, head lowered. The strip of light from the garage seesawing between his legs. He flipped the cell open and hit 7, Kira's speed-dial number. He needed to tell her to get in touch with Ed Lister, call the police. He heard it ringing.

C'mon, Dish, pick up. Still ringing as he dragged himself towards the hammer. He crawled forward on his elbows and made a lunge for it, letting go his cell as Ward's boot came down hard on the wooden handle, trapping his fingers underneath.

Ward bent down, picked up the hammer.

'Hello?' Amy's voice.

What was she doing up this late? Let me speak to Mom, sweetheart.

He tried to answer her, but all that came out was a feeble croak as Ward stomped the cell phone into the tarmac. Then he put his foot on the back of the detective's neck, pinning his head to the ground.

Out of his right eye, Campbell saw him heft the hammer a couple of times, tapping the head against his palm as if he was making up his mind about something.

'Jesus, no, wait . . . don't do this,' he gasped. 'I already talked to the cops. They know who you are. They're on their way here.'

'Campbell, Campbell,' Ward said, shaking his head.

'You left some . . . they found skin cells on the train.' He was making it up as he went along, sounding frantic now. 'They'll be able to match the DNA samples.'

'With what? They need to find me first.'

'The *Questura* in Florence . . .'

Ward gave a little snort. 'Morelli? That jerk-off. Do me a favour.'

'There's a warrant out for your arrest.' His chest hurt every breath he took. 'Jesus, I think you broke my back.'

'You'll be all right. No tennis for a while. But you'll be just fine.'

'An international warrant . . .'

'Sure it is. Under what name? After they fish the girl out of the river the cops may want to talk to somebody. My guess is they'll be looking for the guy who's been stalking her, who wouldn't take no for an answer – your client, Ed Lister.'

'You don't have to kill her,' Campbell wheezed. 'Why you doing this? You got to like the way it feels, is that it? You can't even see how fucked up you are, you crazy sick sonofabitch.'

'I stay with the programme, buddy. If that makes me resolute – a man of courage and independent spirit, you might say – well, so be it. I may not have a forgiving nature, but disturbed? Crazy? *I don't think so.*'

'You're not really looking for revenge . . . you know it's just a fantasy.'

'Dish put that one in your head?' Ward laughed. 'Out of interest, how did you find me? It wasn't through my network, or the website, was it?'

He could think of no good reason to tell him. He wouldn't be willing to trade for the information. He just said, 'You made it too easy.'

He wasn't ashamed to ask Ward to spare his life, remind him that he had a family, a wife who loved him, a young daughter. He could plead for them more easily than himself. He just knew he'd be wasting his breath.

But he said it anyway. 'Please, I have a family.'

'You weren't meant to come here, Campbell.'

'I know . . . I see that now.'

He wasn't afraid of dying, but the timing . . . Campbell wanted to explain to someone: look, I think there's been a mistake, you got the wrong person, I'm not done with the world yet. There's this money I have to find by tomorrow . . . oh God.

Ward said, bending over him. 'Campbell, I guess your luck just ran out. As you know, better than most, there's not a lot anyone can do about that.'

408

The detective struggled and the pressure from the boot increased.

He lifted an arm to fend off what couldn't be escaped as he saw the hammer rise, the blunt ball-peen end coming down in a flashing arc.

The first hammer blow didn't kill him.

We walked on a few blocks without saying much. She had broken away, slipped quickly out of my arms, and now it was as if the kiss had never happened. The tension was still there, though, not very far below the surface. I found it difficult to accept that after tonight we weren't going to see each other again.

Maybe that's why I started talking about Sophie. I just let go and poured out my heart to Jelena. I told her things that I'd never said to anybody, not even Laura. We crossed over to Park Avenue and stopped at a bar in the twenties with tables outside.

After I'd ordered drinks, I said, 'I'm sorry, that was a real downer.'

'No, I always wanted you to tell me about her.'

'The last time I was in Florence,' I said, holding her gaze, 'I lit a candle for Sophie in a church near where she died called Santa Maria del Carmine. Then I wrote *our* names in the visitors book . . . yours and mine.'

Jelena looked away. 'You must have loved her very much.'

'I don't know why I did it. I just realised that I missed you.'

'It's not because I remind you of her, is it?'

'No. You don't remind me of anyone.'

She didn't say anything. I heard her stomach rumble. It seemed a curiously intimate and endearing response. Jelena arched both eyebrows. She laughed and a wisp of hair fell across her face.

I said, 'I'm going to arrange things so that we can be together.'

'We can't be together, so don't talk foolishness.'

There was a silence that lasted several seconds.

'How about another drink?'

'You know something?' Jelena said. 'It isn't the difference in our ages or even the fact that you have another life . . . it's because you're hurt, Ed, you've been through the worst thing that can happen to a person. That's what separates us. Around you I feel I don't even exist.'

When she said that it felt like she was surrendering herself.

66

Aiming for the temple where Campbell's hair grew unusually thick, Ward struck lightly again and again. He didn't want blood all over the driveway, and nothing bleeds quite like a head wound. He kept tapping the same spot until he saw the whites of the little Chinese's eyes craze over as the capillaries burst and a red glaze lacquered the corneas. He shone his key-ring light into a dying pupil and got back his own reflection, a face peering over the edge of a well.

In the singular way Ward experienced the world there were no correspondences, no analogies, no metaphor, things weren't 'like' each other – they *were* each other. He was afraid that seeing the image of his face in the well might have a deeper unwished-for meaning. He was afraid it meant some change in him.

Picking up Campbell's shattered cell phone, he hurled it into the bushes.

Then he slid the sticky shaft of the hammer through his belt, and looped the rope he was carrying under the detective's shoulders. Dragging the body back to the house, he had to stop to retrieve a Nike Air Force trainer he hadn't noticed had slipped off one of Campbell's heels. Rather than attempt to put the shoe back on, he removed its pair, tied the laces and slung them both around his neck.

It was a reflection in an untenanted eye . . . *not his face at the bottom of a goddamned well.* He banished the image with its hidden potential to dilute his sense of purpose, subvert the course of justice.

Let's just get the job done.

Ward backed the Buick estate out of the garage and ran it back a short distance past the fork in the driveway. Then he rolled forward and, taking the rougher track that led around the rear of the property, drove down to the river.

Earlier, when he was scouting for somewhere to bring the girl (in case things didn't go according to plan), he'd discovered an old 1930s boathouse on a marshy backwater. The building was overgrown with trees and too dilapidated for what he had in mind, but he could see another use for it now.

He stopped opposite the walkway and cut the engine.

He made no move to get out of the wagon. Just sat and let things settle, hands at ten to two on the steering wheel, staring out at nothing. The far side of the boathouse he could hear the river go by in a silver rush.

Find that one a little tougher than the others, Wardo? With the young wife and kid down in Florida? This isn't the time for regrets. We're falling behind schedule.

He wasn't meant to be here that was all.

There was always a risk that Campbell would find Grace's body before the Caanan sheriff's department got a patrol car out to the house, but his turning up at La Rochelle had caught him off guard. He *had* no regrets about what he'd done. The detective might have been more useful to him alive, as a witness turned against his client; on the other hand, his murder would be seen now as Ed Lister's work.

The taste lingered, acrid as asparagus water, a blue-green triangle with spike-sharp corners. Was that how Campbell found him? Had he revealed some aspect of his synaesthesia online? If there'd been more time, he'd have got it out of the little slope exactly how he traced him to Skylands. He wasn't too worried about the police. That was just desperation talk.

It niggled him, though, that he could have let something slip.

His fingernails splayed on the wheel were giving him harsh, disapproving looks. *So now what's your problem?* Ward resented their smug critical personalities.

He opened the Buick's tail-gate and pulled Campbell out onto the dirt track. The ground was softer here. Ward had put on an old pair of deck shoes he'd found in the house belonging to Ed Lister; they pinched a little, but at least he didn't have to worry about footprints. He dragged the detective's body across the planked walkway to the boathouse. A derelict wooden structure with a swayback roof and gaping holes in its walls where sections of the clapboard siding had collapsed, it leaned alarmingly out of true.

You know, before she came out to the house, Grace had her hair done at First Impressions, finest salon in Norfolk, specially for you . . . her little Ernie.

Spare me the violins. I was there, remember? Told her how nice she looked – she appreciated the fact someone had noticed.

The door had settled on its hinges. Ward had to shoulder it open, then pull the body after him. Inside, the blackness seemed at first impenetrable; he stood still for a moment, getting used to the dark and the brackish smell, listening to the hollow, restless slapping of confined water against the piers.

He could just make out the outline of an opening the far end.

Ward heaved on the rope. He heard the joists groan and felt the floor shift under his feet. He'd gone far enough. Not trusting the wooden platform to support their combined weight, he decided against his plan of dumping Campbell in one of the boat slips. He left the body where it lay, head propped against a fallen beam, staring out through the framed inlet at open river.

He wasn't sorry to get back to the station-wagon.

'I have to go into New York,' he told Alice Fielding after they'd eaten. 'I'll take the Buick, if it's okay with you.' He'd found some soup in the refrigerator – Jesusita's home-made gazpacho – which he'd poured into bowls and brought through to the lounge on a tray with Ritz crackers and the open bottle of Chardonnay.

'You look nice, dear,' she said, as if she was his mother.

He'd cleaned up and was wearing one of Ed's old suits, which he'd borrowed from the closet in the guest room. He'd helped himself to a shirt and tie too.

'I have a date with a beautiful girl. I'm going to show her the town, then I thought maybe I'd bring her back out here to the Rock.'

'There was a man earlier asking for you. What kept you so long?'

'I'm sorry,' he hesitated. 'We caught up with each other in the end.'

She nodded. 'Does this beautiful girl have a name?'

'Jelena.'

'You know what you're doing isn't right, Eddie. One of the last royal princesses of Montenegro was called Jelena. Do you love her?'

'We love each other,' Ward said distractedly. He was looking at the collection of framed photos of Sophie Lister on top of the desk, getting the sweet chalky taste of candy cigarettes. 'Until she came along, I was nobody.'

She smiled. 'How romantic.'

'You're nobody till somebody loves you.'

'Did I ever tell you Dean Martin sang that for me once? Do you plan to marry?'.

'I'm already married . . . remember?'

'Oh Eddie,' the old lady chuckled reprovingly.

The phone beside her rang. She reached out for it with a shaky hand.

'*Don't answer that!*' The tone of his voice made her shrink back.

He strode over and put a hand on the receiver. She looked up at him with bewildered eyes while he waited for the ringing to stop. When it did, she said, 'You're not really Eddie, are you?'

Ward smiled. 'What makes you say that?'

'You think I don't know?'

She lay back in her rattan recliner and closed her eyes.

'I think you may be a little confused that's all.'

'Yes, possibly.' She gave a sigh. 'You're *very* alike.'

He watched her nod off, then after a few moments startle awake as if alarmed by her own involuntary absence. He hadn't decided yet what to do about Alice.

A perfect edge does not reflect light.

Ward held the curved blade of the mezzaluna up to the fluorescent strip above the workbench. He tilted it back and forth and saw how the polished arc scintillated. Like any new knife it had come out of the box factory-sharp, which for his purposes was nowhere near sharp enough.

With a felt-tip pen he drew a quarter-inch black stripe

414

along the blade's convex edge, then clamped the mezzaluna in the bench vice. Holding the steel in both hands at a twenty-degree angle and using a circular motion, he worked methodically from one end of the crescent blade to the other, keeping the angle of his stroke constant by watching the ink dwindle evenly up to the edge. Once the ink was rubbed away, he turned the blade around in the vice and repeated the process on the other side. Then he concentrated on smoothing the cutting edge . . .

You know better than to interrupt when I'm busy.

I realise this may not be the best time to bring it up, Ernie, but memory reconciliation is something we really need to address.

Memory reconciliation? What are you, my head doctor now?

The butcher's steel, bonded with a fine diamond abrasive, both sharpened and honed at the same time. As the edge became thinner, he could see it bend away from the steel leaving a long metal feather. It was a sign he was getting close. He flattened the angle of the steel to about ten degrees and, using a lighter down-stroke, removed the burr. When he was satisfied it was smooth as he could possibly get it, Ward held the blade up again to the fluorescent strip, looking for reflections from the edge.

This time there were none.

He slipped the plastic sleeve back onto the blade, wrapped the mezzaluna in a cloth and placed it in his rucksack. He was all set. With the pack slung over one shoulder, he hit the door-closer switch and walked out of the garage to the parked station-wagon. The sweet night scent of nicotiana plants growing around the porch swarmed up his nostrils. He touched the car door-handle and the contact sparked off a high-resolution memory of the parlour at Skylands.

He saw Grace sit slightly forward in the armchair to keep her candy-floss hair-do from flattening against the dusty headrest as he walked up behind her. Grace telling him, her Lil' Ernie, that he didn't need to worry, his secret would always be safe with her. Well, it would now . . . whatever 'his secret' was.

You shoulda let her finish, buddy. You shoulda let her finish. You shoulda . . .

Should I? Ward stood motionless, staring out across the river towards Wave Hill. In the distance he could see the cable lights of the George Washington Bridge glinting through the tops of the trees. He looked at his watch: 11.42. They'd have left the restaurant by now. He wasn't counting on them going on somewhere else before returning to her place, but it would help if they took their time.

He couldn't imagine Ed inviting her back to the Carlyle.

He glanced up at the house. The old lady's bedroom was dark. He'd reminded Alice before they said goodnight to be sure to take her sleeping pills. She was on two 2mg tabs of Lunesta – he'd checked the prescription notes on the label – which was a strong enough dose to put out Mike Tyson's lights. In the morning, all she'd remember would be that her grandson-in-law came to supper, then drove into town, saying he'd be returning later with some girl. Her last words to him were, 'I promise I won't tell, Eddie. Not a soul.'

If she got things muddled, her wires a little crossed, Ward thought, as he swung the Buick around and headed down the driveway, it couldn't do much harm.

67

They were so natural with each other, that was really the thing.

Her feet hurt like hell, her favourite pair of Jimmy Choos that cost her a month's pay were as good as ruined, but any time Ed suggested getting a cab, Jelly insisted, no, no, she was fine, she loved to walk.

All she was doing was delaying the moment when they would reach the corner of her street. She kept thinking ahead to what she was going to say when it came to crunch time: there was no way she could risk inviting him up.

They were on Third Avenue, a couple of blocks from home now, talking as they went along, the pace getting slower and slower the closer they got to Thirty-ninth Street. Ed was busy telling her he'd decided he wanted to change his life – give away his money, help the poor, save the planet and all that hilarious bullshit. He explained how his feelings for her had made him see the world in a new wonderful light.

Then he started going on about leaving his wife and coming back for her.

'It'll take me a month to arrange things, maybe less.'

God, the fool really was *serious*.

'Why even say shit like that when you know you won't do it and if you did that I wouldn't be able to love you? You're not free, you have a family who need you . . .'

He halted middle of the sidewalk and swung her around by the arm, forcing her to look at him. 'I can't live without you, Jelly,' he said.

'You're crazy, you know that? We've known each other for how long, five hours? And you want to give up everything for . . . you haven't a fucking clue!'

People passing by were giving them odd looks.

'Seven, if you include lunch. I'm going to cancel my flight, stay over a couple more days. We can get to know each other better.'

'Oh Jesus.' She pulled free, twisting her head away. 'Why do you have to be so goddamn stubborn? You know something? You're really starting to scare me.'

Jelly marched on ahead and then, wiping her eyes, turned to him. 'Anyway, I won't be around this weekend. I'm going down the Jersey shore with Guy . . .'

'Guy? What do you mean?'

'Some friends of his have a rental right on the water. It'll be fun, you know, just hanging out . . . He's got tickets for a Mary J. Blige concert in Asbury Park.'

'I thought you told him you were in love with someone else.'

'Yeah, well, we're still friends. We're cool around each other.' She was afraid he'd see through her attempt to pass Guy Mallory off as her old boyfriend. But how could Ed possibly know? She wasn't even sure why she'd mentioned Guy's name at the restaurant. Maybe she thought of him as a kind of insurance. A safeguard. Guy had turned up at the right time, they seemed to get on okay, but she had no idea if she wanted to see him again. 'I just want to move on with my life.'

'You think maybe if you do decide to go to Paris . . . ?'

'Eddie, we have to give this up,' she said gently, taking his hand as they turned into her street. 'We both know I'm not what you really need.' It was a line she remembered from some movie.

He nodded slowly, working his frown into a solemn little

smile as he said, 'I think it's more a case of I'm not what *you* need.'

'I'm sorry, Eddie.' She couldn't look at him.

Ward pulled into the kerb on the south side of Thirty-eighth Street and Lexington Avenue, a block away and diagonally across from Jelena Sejour's apartment building. An old Murray Hill walk-up, it was one of the last hold-outs against the flashy high-rises that had overwhelmed the once sedate residential neighbourhood.

He was driving his Golf rental, having left the more conspicuous and less reliable Buick station-wagon across the river at the Huyler's Inn parking lot in Alpine, NJ – he planned to collect it on the way back after picking up his passenger. He looked through the windshield at the fourth-floor windows. No lights were showing.

Still out gallivanting, as Alice would say.

He turned on the car stereo, tuned it to a wide band of static between stations, then cranked up the volume – the way he used to when he was a kid to drown out the sound of his parents arguing.

Then he settled down to wait.

On the stoop of her apartment building, I stood and watched Jelly fumbling for her keys, angling her open purse to catch the light over the door. I could see how badly her hands were shaking.

'Can I help you with that?' I offered.

'Thanks. I got it.' She snapped her purse shut and held up the keys.

'Well then.' I stuffed my hands in my pockets, took a step back onto the sidewalk. 'I don't suppose we'll meet again.'

'You understand I can't invite you up,' she said.

'No, I understand.' She was busy fitting the key to the lock.

'You take care, Eddie.'

I bowed my head, not trusting myself to speak, then turned away.

The next second I heard her keys clatter to the ground. I swung around and ran up the steps and caught Jelly as she turned to face me, her arms already open. I held her tight and she gave a weird little cry, part sigh, part whimper. Then our lips touched and almost immediately I felt the tip of her tongue seeking mine and when they met I felt a warm electric shock that became a series of warm electric shocks.

I don't know how long we stood there, as deeply entwined as it's possible for two people to become with clothes on. It was a kiss that carried a lot of dubious freight and belonged in some way to another age. But was probably none the worse for it.

After a while, she pushed me away. I stumbled down the steps. I don't remember seeing her bend down to pick up her keys or run inside. Suddenly she was gone and the door had banged shut behind her.

Ward couldn't quite believe his luck.

He watched Ed Lister come to the corner of Thirty-ninth Street and walk slowly out into the traffic holding up a hand for a taxi. He wasn't sure what had gone down, but the display he'd just witnessed on the doorstep was clearly a farewell scene.

He might have had to wait all night.

A yellow cab screeched to a halt at the Englishman's feet.

Ward slid low in his seat, then opened a window. He was pretty sure he overheard Ed say to the driver, 'Hotel Carlyle.' The radio was off now.

He waited ten minutes: in case either one of them had a change of heart. Then he started the engine and drove around the block, crawling up Thirty-ninth Street. He gave a 'yesss' of satisfaction when he found an empty parking space right outside her front door, things still going his way.

In the outer lobby, he looked down the list of names beside the mailboxes and rang the bell for SEJOUR. There was no reply. He hit it again impatiently.

The intercom crackled. 'Jelena?'

'Go away, Ed,' she said, '*please* just go away.' Her voice cracking with emotion reminded him of half-melted sugar crystals at the bottom of a coffee cup.

'Hey, it's me, Guy . . . Guy Mallory?' The CCTV obviously was broken.

'Guy?' He heard her confusion. 'What you doin' here?'

'I was in the neighbourhood, I just thought I'd see if you wanted to go out for a nightcap . . . if you're not busy.'

'It's kinda late, isn't it? I'm sorry, I've a really bad headache.'

'Can I get you something? Would you like me to come up?'

'No, I'll be fine.'

'Have it your own way.'

'What?'

'Nothing. Get some sleep.'

She let it go. 'Listen, call me, okay?'

She hung up before he got the chance to say goodnight.

Ward stood there, head lowered. He felt his face getting hot. He was a little disappointed in Jelly not wanting him to come up. She sounded pretty upset. He would have offered her his shoulder to cry on.

In a sudden eruption of rage, he kicked at the door and cursed loudly and viciously enough for a couple walking past to turn their heads.

Then he took off the rucksack, swung it to the ground by the straps and hunkered down beside it. He found a way to sit on his heels without getting Ed's suit dirty, resting his back against the tiled wall under the mailboxes.

Ward knew he could easily force the lock and get into the building, but he preferred to wait for one of the other residents to come in or out. He wanted to be seen heading up to Jelly's apartment by someone who would remember him.

He'd give it twenty . . . half an hour max.

70

The telephone in my hotel room was ringing when I got off the elevator.

I was so certain it was Jelly, I began rehearsing what I was going to say to her as I hurriedly swiped the lock, pushed open the door, then ran to pick up the extension on the bedside table.

'You're a hard man to find, Signor Lister.'

'Andrea.' I fell back to earth. 'It's you.'

'Did you receive my e-mail?'

'Hold on.' I went back and kicked the door shut. 'What e-mail? I'm sorry, I just walked in.'

'Then you haven't heard from your wife?'

'No.' I felt my insides tighten, afraid he was going to tell me something had happened to Laura, or George. 'Is everything all right?'

'She sounded in good spirits when we spoke earlier. I asked her to pass on a message, in case she found you first.'

'I've been out a lot. I had my mobile switched off.'

'My spies tell me you were at the opera.'

I didn't bother correcting him. Still in another world, I wasn't in the mood for Morelli' s suave, easy-going banter.

'Andrea, it's late here. I need to get some sleep. What can I do for you?'

'We have a suspect.' He cleared his throat importantly. 'I want you to open the attachment I sent you. Can you look at it now?'

I put the phone down and went over to the desk; it took seconds to boot up my laptop and retrieve Morelli's e-mail from my inbox. The attached image file downloaded as I carried the laptop back to the bed.

'You know the face?' the investigator asked.

It was a pen and ink portrait of a man, head and shoulders, no one I'd ever seen before – at least that was my first impression.

'Where did you get this?' I demanded, my heart beating faster. The portrait was in the same intense, meticulous style as Sophie's drawings.

'Sam Metcalf's apartment. I found it in the bathroom, tucked behind the doors of the medicine cabinet.' He sounded pleased with himself. 'I believe your daughter may have hidden it there.'

The missing page cut from her sketchbook.

'I don't recognise him,' I said, still staring at the screen. 'You think this is the person who killed her? Sophie actually *drew* her murderer?'

He didn't answer.

I looked closer at the head. A Roman bust – the kind students at the atelier are encouraged to draw – wearing a Ralph Lauren shirt. I could see the little polo player emblem on the breast pocket. The effect was smooth, bland, sinister – I had no doubt that was what Sophie had intended. She must have done the sketch from memory (it seemed unlikely he'd have sat for her, or let himself be photographed) as a kind of predictive Identikit. She knew.

I felt proud of her and at the same time devastated.

It was a good-looking face, instantly forgettable. I was determined to memorise every loathsome feature.

Morelli said, 'We've been trying to get in touch with her art teacher. Bailey Grant is in Tunisia and not contactable. I was hoping you might have an opinion . . .'

'Yes, it's her work,' I said impatiently. 'And if you'd followed up the connection with Sam Metcalf when I told you about her . . .' I stopped myself. It was pointless getting angry. 'You said you had a suspect.'

'Your daughter's drawing has led us to someone we are very interested in talking to . . . *Un secondo.*' In the background I could hear a disembodied Italian voice squawking over a PA system. 'Forgive me, Signor Lister. They finally announced my flight. Does the name David Mallet mean anything to you?'

'Mallet? No.'

'He was staying in rented accommodation near San Miniato on the night your daughter was killed. The landlady recognised him from the drawing as one of her lodgers. He was there for a few weeks, very quiet, kept himself to himself, doing some kind of research; she thought he might have been writing a book.'

I was stunned into silence.

'She was pretty sure it was him,' Morelli said. 'He's American, lives or was living in Paris. It could be a false trail, or just coincidence, but the address David Mallet has been linked with is interesting – 20 rue Mabillon, I believe, is a couple of doors away from your office.'

'What the hell does that mean?

'I don't know. But my advice is be careful. I'll be in Paris in a couple of hours. I've asked the Sûreté to run some checks. When do you get back to London?'

'Tomorrow . . . maybe.'

'By then I may have more.'

There was nothing from Laura on my voice-mail, which didn't altogether surprise me; she wouldn't have paid much attention to anything Morelli said and she hated leaving messages. But still, I thought, she must have realised this could be important.

Campbell Armour had called twice – at 5.47 p.m., to say he couldn't make the meeting; then again at 10.38 p.m., leaving word that he needed to talk to me urgently.

It was now after one. I called him back at the number he'd left; dialled it without thinking. There was no reply. Five rings, then the recording cut in and I recognised my own voice on the tape. I'd reached Laura's grandmother's house, La Rochelle. I checked the number again, it was right. Just didn't make any sense.

I wasn't worried about Alice Fielding. I wouldn't have expected her to answer the phone this late – the old lady was usually in bed and asleep by ten. But I couldn't understand what the detective had been doing at her house. Why on earth would Campbell have gone out there? How did he get the number, the address?

It had to be some kind of mistake. I tried Campbell's cell, then I called his home number in Tampa and left a message.

I fixed myself a large Scotch and water, drank it down and poured another.

The discovery of Sophie's drawing, leading so swiftly to the identifying of a suspect, should have raised my spirits, but it had left me feeling depressed and uneasy. I wasn't sure what to make of Ward living near my office in Paris. It sickened me to think I must have passed him on the street and not known.

I couldn't stop thinking about Jelena.

Her scent was on my hands and face, my clothes. I could still taste her, feel the warmth of her skin. I kept going back to the moment at dinner when she admitted she felt the same way I did. Maybe I was still wrong, but it seemed to me obvious that she didn't really want me to leave. I had to force myself to walk away. I just knew it was up to me to do the right thing, and that meant thinking about what was best for her. I so nearly went back and rang her doorbell.

I carried my drink to the desk and sat down with my laptop to study the sketch of 'David Mallet' more closely. I made an effort to imagine the man's face in different guises, different contexts. I pulled up the photos of Ernest Seaton's parents and looked for some family resemblance. I couldn't see it, couldn't see either Gary or June in those neutral features; yet there was *something* about him.

I began to wonder if I hadn't caught a glimpse of the face recently – possibly even tonight, here in New York. It was just a vague impression, the memory of it lodged at the back of my mind like an itch I couldn't reach. But I felt there was a chance, if it had happened this evening while we were out together, that Jelly might have noticed whatever it was I'd missed.

I dialled her cell.

Wake up, Wardo, company.

Ward rose to his feet. A young mother, maybe not so young, pushing a baby in a Maclaren stroller and dragging a four-year-old, turned in at the entrance to the building. What was she was doing out with the kids this late? As if it was any of his business. With a friendly smile he went to her assistance.

'Here, let me give you a hand with that.'

She let him, didn't even question what was he doing there, hanging about the lobby after midnight. As he helped her up the steps with the stroller, Ward explained: he'd left his front-door key in his girlfriend's apartment and she wasn't back yet. He charmed her with the little story he'd prepared.

'I'm Eddie, by the way. Eddie Lister.' He hesitated. 'Jelena's friend?'

He looked neat and respectable enough in Ed's dark blue suit from Brooks Brothers. Ward had been waiting three quarters of an hour.

She gave him a blank look.

'Jelena Sejour in 4A . . . the coloured girl?' He used the non-PC label to give her something to remember.

'Oh . . . oh, yes. Sure, I know who you mean.'

He held the front door wide open for them, then picked up his rucksack and followed mother and children into the building. Outside their ground-floor apartment, he said good-night and started to climb the stairs.

71

Jelly hadn't moved from the bed where she'd thrown herself down when she came home. She'd kicked off her shoes, what was left of them, then couldn't be bothered to change out of her clothes. She always predicted that if they ever met it would be a total shambles. Now her only satisfaction was knowing she was right.

The apartment was as she'd left it when she ran out – make-up, underwear, rejected clothes, towels everywhere, like it had been hit by a hurricane. The look she'd taken so much trouble putting together seemed stupid and pointless now. The ashtray on the glass coffee table beside her was choked with half-smoked butts, various shades of lipstick on the filters. World go away, she thought.

Mistigris was glaring at her from his favourite spot on the top shelf of the closet. She couldn't see Minou, her other cat. She needed to pee, but wasn't ready yet for any alteration to the state his kiss had left her in. She still had

427

that dumb schmalzy waltz from the ballet twirling in her head.

Jelly didn't recognise the number when it came up in the display window of her cell. She just knew it was him. She removed her earphone, waited till the fourth ring, then with a sigh hit Talk. 'Yes?'

Ed said quietly, 'Whatever you do, don't hang up. Just listen . . .'

'Why are you calling? You got three seconds.'

'It's not about us, Jelly. Check your e-mail. I've sent you a drawing of somebody. It's important you look carefully at his face. If you remember seeing him anywhere tonight, maybe at the Met, or walking back from the restaurant . . .'

'Oh my God! How *dare* you pull this shit on me?'

'It's not what you think. I'm not trying to scare you, really I'm not.'

'Eddie, don't do this to me, please. PLEASE . . . just leave me alone.'

She switched the cell off and threw it down, then with a loud wail burst into tears. After a while, she got up from the bed and walked over to her computer. The little envelope was laying there in her intray. If she opened it, she'd feel bound to answer and that was exactly what he wanted. She highlighted Ed's e-mail and moved the cursor to the delete option, then hesitated.

What if he wasn't messing with her?

She heard a sound outside her door. Her eyes swivelled to the kitchen and entrance hall a second before the doorbell rang.

A little drunk, I poured myself another whisky, then went over to the corner windows and stood gazing out at the East River. I was thinking about Jelly, the way she'd reacted just now. She'd more or less accused me of using the threat of Ward as an excuse to keep talking to her, as a way of holding on. Maybe she was right. If we were followed tonight, the truth is, I hadn't noticed. But still . . . I still needed her to look at the face in the drawing. Just to be sure.

The phone rang. I walked unsteadily across to the desk and picked up.

'Where's Campbell?' The detective's wife, Kira, returning my call. 'I haven't heard from him and I'm worried.'

'If I knew where he was, Mrs Armour, I wouldn't have troubled you, but I'm sure he'll be in touch,' I said, trying to sound more confident than I felt.

'He called me from some place in Jersey. That was over two hours ago.'

'Did Campbell say what he was doing there?'

'Waiting for you.'

'Mrs Armour,' it was an effort to speak without slurring my words, 'I never told your husband or anyone that I was going out to La Rochelle.'

'He got the number off Grace's cell phone.'

My head swam. 'Grace Wilkes? The housekeeper at Skylands?'

I heard her hesitate. 'Campbell didn't tell you?'

A tremor of alarm ran through me.

'He went back out to the house this morning before he left Norfolk and found her dead. She'd been murdered.' I sat down heavily in the chair.

'Jesus.' I was sobering up fast. 'Are you sure?'

'Am I sure?'

'I'm sorry, I'm just taking this in.'

I heard her stifle a sob. 'Oh God.'

I felt at a loss. 'Look, I'm sure he'll be okay.'

'Then why am I getting nothing from his cell?' she asked, her voice rising and shrill. 'I warned him. I tried to stop him getting involved with this case. He knows about computers . . . not psychopaths.'

There was a silence. I thought I could hear her weeping.

'It's all your fault. You got Campbell into this. He would never have taken the risks, if you hadn't offered him . . . so much. He didn't tell me was in trouble, he had debts he needed to pay. Oh God, I just know something's happened to him.'

'Mrs Armour, I promise you your husband has more than earned—'

'I don't care about *money!*' she screamed.

'You have to help me,' I said quietly. 'You'll be helping Campbell. It could even save his life.' I paused. 'I need to understand what's going on inside Ward's head right now, what he thinks I did to him.'

There was another longer silence.

'His head is the website. He believes you came to the real Skylands . . . came for June. He wants the world to know you killed her, and his father.'

'I've never even been near the place. Look, I met June Seaton once at a party in New York. We spent an evening together. That was it. I never saw her again.'

'Maybe, but in his mind you were there.' She hesitated. 'He may have blocked out what really happened that night.'

I thought about the boy's face and hands covered in his mother's blood.

'What are you saying? *My God* . . . he was nine years old.'

'Campbell asked me if I thought Ernest could have murdered his parents and suppressed the memory. There are precedents. If he had reason to fear his mother was going to run away, abandoning him to an abusive father – it's possible.'

'But what's this got to do with me? With my family?'

'June Seaton wrote you a love letter she never mailed. When

430

it came to light two years ago, the letter could have triggered a response in Ward. Awakened feelings of remorse he can never admit to himself. So he transfers his guilt onto you . . .'

'Then why didn't he come after me? Why Sophie?'

'To make you suffer. He wanted to "avenge" his parents' deaths and destroy your life. He used your daughter, but wouldn't have bargained on falling in love with her . . . which, I suspect, only created more unresolved conflict.'

'Love? Didn't you just tell me the guy's a psychopath?'

'I think he's going through a psychological purge that he doesn't fully understand – or rather it's going on in him.' She paused. 'It's not over yet.'

'What do you mean?'

'Campbell found evidence that Ward may be getting ready to kill again. We were on the phone, he was going through a closet, I think he said it was in the maid's room, when he came across . . . a computer bag or rucksack.'

'Jesus Christ.'

'I don't know if I should be telling you this. There was a name on the pack with an address Campbell said looked the same as your Paris office. He thought *you* might have been Ward . . . only he wasn't sure you weren't being set up. I called the police. I didn't know what else to do.'

'You did the right thing. What was the name?'

'He read it out to me. David something or other.'

'Was it David Mallet?'

'Mallet . . . Mallory. Mallet, yeah that's it. He knew it was made up because it's one of the placeholder names we both use in our work.'

I heard myself ask, 'Did you say Mallory?'

I rang Jelly back on her cell. It was switched off. I tried her landline and got a recorded message – she had Call Intercept.

A female robot asked me to identify myself before the call

431

could continue. I gave my name and added (before I remembered the system wasn't designed to recognise a message) that this was a matter of life and death.

'Thank you. Please hold.'

After what seemed an eternity, measured out on an instrumental version of 'Mr Bojangles', I heard the same recorded voice say, 'The person you are calling is not available. Thank you. Good bye.'

I cursed, waited a moment, then punched the redial button.

72

Jelly walked over to the door, her bare feet making no sound on the stripped pine floor. She eased the tiny security flap over the peep-hole to one side and put her eye to the fish-eye lens. Guy Mallory was standing in the hall, his back half turned, looking down the stairwell.

He swung around then, as if he'd heard something, and she saw he was wearing a suit and tie, which looked odd with the rucksack slung over one shoulder. He took a step closer to her door and she straightened up, thinking fast.

'Jelena, I know you're there.'

Too late to pretend otherwise. 'Guy? What are you doing here?' She tried to sound groggy, as if he'd just woken her. 'I told you, I don't feel like seeing nobody.'

She peered out again. His face, distorted by the wide-angled lens, had a wooden, almost mask-like expression. 'Are you all right?'

'Yeah, I'm fine,' she said. 'I took some Tylenol. Now please go away. Lemme get back to sleep.'

'I had to make sure you were safe.'

'Safe? I'm okay, really.'

'It was just that when you wouldn't let me up before, I thought maybe it was because your stalker friend was there with you. And you couldn't talk, you know? I just wanted to check you were okay.'

'He's not here, Guy. I'm fine, thanks.'

'You haven't heard from him then?'

She hesitated. 'Not really . . . he . . . well, okay, I did see him briefly. He took me out to lunch, we discussed the situation and that was it. No plans to meet again.'

'I find that hard to believe. Stalkers are very persistent.'

'Look, if there's one thing I'm sure about . . . I'm sure he's not a stalker.' But she didn't sound sure.

Jelly thought about Ed calling her, e-mailing her, calling her back again – she'd refused to take his last call . . . maybe it was her fault for giving him the wrong idea. The next thing he'd be round here. Now he knew where she lived.

'It's just that I saw this guy earlier hanging out in the lobby downstairs, he looked a little crazed.'

'Yeah? So what else is new? This is New York, Guy.'

'He could come back. All I'm trying to do here is protect you.'

Behind her the phone started ringing. Jelly let the flap fall, turned and leaned her back against the door. Shit. She raked her fingers through her hair and closed her eyes, uncertain what to do.

'Are you going to get that?' she heard Guy say through the door.

Oh what the fuck. She twisted the lock.

Brushing past the girl as she held open the door to her apartment, Ward made straight for the telephone on the glass table and picked up.

He stood listening, looking back at Jelly, taking in her barefoot deshabille, the disordered room, the bleak ammoniac smell of cat-litter – a pewter rectangle with blunted edges. He had to close off his senses.

'You know an Ed Lister?'

She nodded miserably.

'You want to talk to him?'

Jelly shook her head. 'I don't want to talk to him.'

He pressed the number two key, declining the call. 'Didn't I tell you? This guy's just not gonna let go.'

He watched her open a pack of Marlboro and light up a cigarette as she came back into the room. She sank down onto the edge of the bed and he saw the tears.

'Hey, it's okay. As long as I'm around, I won't let him hurt you.'

'You don't understand,' she said, exhaling smoke.

'You have feelings, I know,' he said gently, 'but they're not real. You don't even know him. Jelena, none of it's *real*. Mind if I sit?'

Ward slipped his rucksack off his shoulder and lowered it onto the rattan couch, then cleared a space and sat down.

'A stalker,' he went on, same soft voice, 'however sincere he may seem, is a natural liar. All that sweet talk he laid on you about true love and destiny, it's written in the stars – all lies. The fact he was hanging around downstairs, don't be surprised if he tries to come back now and "rescue" you from danger.'

She frowned. 'Why would he think I'm in danger?'

'You're not in any danger . . . except from him. It's a common stalking fantasy. He dreams of proving his love for you by an act of chivalry. Another one is turning the tables, where he'll claim he's the victim and that *you* are stalking *him*, the stalker stalked. You see what we're up against? If you don't give him what he wants your friend is going to turn violent. You need to tell the authorities about Ed Lister, report him to the police or the FBI. Don't wait.'

She laughed. 'Go to the cops? Are you kidding?'

'It happens very fast. With someone like Ed, love can turn in the blink of an eye to a deep hatred that's every bit as consuming. If he can't have you, believe me, he's going to make sure no one else can either.'

He lifted that straight from his own 'profile', the one Campbell wrote, with a little help – no doubt – from his widow, Kira.

'What's up, Mistigris?' Jelly smiled. 'He only goes to people he knows don't like cats. His name means "joker" in French.'

'I like his name.' He kept a neutral expression as the animal jumped up on his lap and started purring. 'You need to call somebody.'

She shook her head. 'I couldn't do that to Ed. Anyway, I happen to know he's flying back to London tomorrow.'

'You forgive my saying so,' he leaned back, stroking the cat's ears, 'but you don't know that. You don't know squat about Ed. It's not *safe* for you to stay.'

'Hey now, wait just a minute . . .'

'When I leave here I'm driving out to my grandmother's house in New Jersey.' He spoke with an urgency he needed her to feel. 'There's plenty of room. If you want it, you got a bed for the night. No strings.'

'Thanks, I'll be fine.'

Still acting stubborn. Dumb of her, but only to be expected. He could see she was rattled now, trying to put on a brave face.

'Your life is in danger, Jelly. Where else can you go?'

She took a deep drag on her cigarette, screwing up her

eyes and choking a little on the smoke, then stubbed it out in a full ashtray that he couldn't look at without seeing a dark tunnel, widest at this end and narrowing down to nothing.

'You said Jelly just then.'

'Other people call you that?'

She glanced at him. 'Yeah, it's my nickname.'

He shrugged. 'We don't have a lot of time.'

'Okay, okay.' She sighed. 'There's my girlfriend, Tachel. I guess I can stay at her place tonight. You could drop me off there. She lives not far from the expressway – you know Woodside?'

Ward smiled. 'Not a problem.'

'I need to change out of these clothes.'

'You want I'll wait outside.'

'Stay there. I'll use the bathroom.'

As soon as he heard Jelly lock the door behind her, Ward opened a side pocket on his backpack and took out a small pair of pliers. He gave her thirty seconds, then rose from the couch, spilling the cat off his lap, and went over to the window where the phone line came into the apartment. He cut the wires.

Then, using a pair of Jelly's discarded pantyhose, he picked up the telephone receiver and wiped it clean of potential prints. Just to be sure, he polished the cradle too and the surface of the glass table.

He sat back down, undid the top flap of the backpack and brought out an oil-cloth bundle. He unwrapped the mezzaluna and laid it carefully across his knees; then, holding the knife by one of its handles, peeled off the plastic shield that guarded the edge. He shoved the cloth and shield back in his pack, unzipped a long side-pocket and placed the naked blade inside it with the handles facing outwards. Instead of the zipper, he used alternative Velcro fasteners to close the pocket again, so that when he wore the backpack the weapon would be easy to get at.

He had practised the 'draw' – left hand reaching across the body and under his right armpit – until he was satisfied he could respond to any given situation in about a second and a half.

Ward donned a fresh pair of rubber gloves. He blew into the fingers of each hand before pulling it on, then stretched and snapped the latex to get rid of any air bubbles. He heard the thick doggerel rhythms of rap music coming from behind the locked bathroom door and guessed the girl had switched on the radio because she wanted privacy. He found her modesty becoming.

73

Jelly sat on the toilet, hunched forward, holding onto the edge of the tub with one hand, the other clamped over her mouth to stop herself from crying out. A minute ago, less, she'd called Tachel and heard the number ringing and then suddenly the line had gone dead.

She'd understood at once what that meant.

Something had felt wrong the moment she let Guy in the apartment. She should have run then, when she got that first bad vibe, when she had the chance. What could have possessed her to open the door to him? She stared at the wall-phone slowly unwinding at the end of its corkscrew cord.

She grabbed the receiver and tried again, this time dialling 911, just to be sure. Nothing. He must have cut the line. Her cell was in the other room. She'd meant to bring it with her but couldn't find the damned thing and then Guy had said hurry, they needed to hurry. He must have took it. Oh Jesus God.

Why was he doing this? What did he want with her? She thought about Ed's e-mail attachment, the one she'd deliberately neglected to open, and felt a sick rush of fear. She hadn't seen anyone following them tonight, had she? Anyone that looked like Guy? How could she have been such a fool, almost letting him convince her that Ed was the danger? It was Guy . . . who killed people. But she couldn't think on that now. She had to try to stay calm, focused, find some way out of this situation.

The bathroom window was not an option: too small to climb through, too high above the street to call for help. And, if she started yelling and screaming, he could just bust down the door. It was ridiculous how badly her hands were shaking. She joined them, closed her eyes. Then, through the fear, an idea came to her.

There was one person she could contact – her next-door neighbour, the weirdo in 4B. He never went out. She hadn't thought of him before because he was crazy and they weren't speaking on account of the music issue. But if Lazlo wasn't asleep – and even if he was – she knew how to get his attention.

Jelly climbed into the tub and turned on the shower-radio. She put an ear flat to the tiles under the nozzle and listened. She could hear someone moving about in there – thank God, he was still up. Then the muttering started. Two voices, one high and whiny complaining about the noise, the other getting angry.

She heard Lazlo lumber into his bathroom, still talking to himself, and start banging on the party wall.

She cranked the volume for Jay-Zee as loud as it would go.

★   ★   ★

438

'I wouldn't be speaking to you if this wasn't an emergency.'

'I'm sorry, sir, but without knowing the subscriber's over-ride code I have no way of reaching them. I cannot over-ride Call Intercept.'

'Then do me a favour, operator, try the number yourself. Maybe they'll accept your call.'

'Please hold.'

Several moments later the operator came back and said she'd been unable to get through because there was a fault on the line. I knew then for certain that Jelly was in immediate danger. It meant 'Guy Mallory' was already there.

'He's going to kill her.'

'Sir, I suggest you call emergency services.'

'There isn't time,' I shouted.

'The number is ringing for you now,' she said wearily and signed off with a meaningless 'Thank you for using AT&T.'

I slammed the receiver down, stunned by the enormous urgency of the situation.

In the ten minutes or so I'd wasted on the phone getting nowhere, I could have been halfway to Thirty-ninth Street. I grabbed my jacket and was already out in the lobby, waiting for an elevator to come, when the phone rang again.

I hesitated, then ran back for it.

'Mr Lister?' It was Eve-Louise on the front desk. 'There's two detectives here from the NYPD would like to talk to you.'

'Tell them I'm on my way down.'

Ward knocked on the bathroom door. 'Time to go, sugar.'

She didn't reply. He could hear the loud music, the banging on the wall – he knew now what she was up to in there. 'Let's go, Jell.'

'Jelena?' He tried the handle, then stood back, ready to kick in the door, when the noise stopped – she'd turned off the radio. He heard the toilet flush, then the door opened and Jelly emerged carrying an old Lord & Taylor shopping bag stuffed with her overnight things. She'd changed into jeans and a T-shirt and Ward caught a whiff of the perfume she'd worn for him the other night at dinner.

A green glass paper-weight, smooth and cool against his cheek.

'I'm ready,' Jelly said. He noticed her hands were trembling. 'I just have to leave some dry food and water out for the cats.'

'All right, but we don't have all day.'

While she was taking care of the menagerie, Ward looked through the peep-hole into the hallway. The coast was clear.

Nobody else lived on their floor apart from her and Lazlo. As she turned from locking the door to her apartment, down the hall on the right Jelly saw 4B's crack open and her neighbour's glittering eye appear above the door chain. Then the eye withdrew and she heard Lazlo talking to someone at his back. She recognised his other voice, the high-pitched one that sounded like a woman nagging.

'I can't take another minute of this. You know what time it is? You gotta do something, you gotta shut that bitch up.'

'Enough, already,' Lazlo bellowed.

Then he hollered through the crack at Jelly, 'This time you went too far. You little cock-sucking whore. Yeah, you heard me, slut. I'm gonna put a stop to your dirty little game once and for all.'

He'd pulled this crazy shit before, but never to her face. Jelly shouted back at him across the hall, 'You don't like it, why don't you call the cops, asshole?' She felt Ward put an arm around her shoulder and guide her towards the stairs.

'We don't need to get involved here.'

'You crazy motherfucker,' she kept going, 'you should be in Bellevue. If you don't call Emergency Services, I will.'

The door slammed shut. Jelly prayed Lazlo had got the message, but she didn't hold out much hope. She heard the rattle of a chain and the next moment a flab mountain in matching royal blue robe and pyjamas shunted into the hallway. Lazlo looked huge, but hardly intimidating.

'I've had just about as much as I can *take*,' he roared, his distended jowls pink and wobbling with fury.

'Back off, bozo,' Guy warned him.

'Who the fuck are you?' He advanced on them. 'Who the fuck are you to tell me jack-shit? You fuck.'

Then abruptly, as if some switch had been thrown in his head, the rage seemed to pass. Without a flicker Lazlo changed modes, reverting to the way she'd seen him act in public – polite, considerate, harmless.

'Are you all right, Miss Sejour?'

Guy answered for her, 'I never say anything twice.'

'Is this man bothering you?' He took another step.

It was only now that Jelly understood what she had done, the danger she had put him in, involving him in her troubles. She gestured frantically at Lazlo to leave it alone, go back inside. But he kept coming.

Guy said quietly, 'You just crossed the line, fats.'

The menace in his tone made Jelly glance down. Some kind of curved blade had materialised in Guy's hand. A gleaming metal extension of his arm which he held straight out and close to his side.

She screamed, 'He's got a knife.'

Guy let go her shoulder to concentrate on the big lunk bearing down on them. This was her chance to create a diversion, her one shot at breaking free. Jelly ducked behind him as he swung the knife in a rising backstroke aimed at Lazlo's unprotected throat, then launched herself off the top of the stairs.

441

She levitated, taking three steps at a time, stumbled and fell at the bottom of the first flight. A retching noise from above, something between a cough and a gasping, choked-off cry, made her convulse with fresh horror. She kept going, though, afraid that if she looked back and saw Guy coming she would freeze. Jelly got to the second-floor landing before she heard him behind her – the few heavy thumps made it sound like he was leaping whole flights – easily gaining.

He caught up with her as she reached ground level.

'I'm parked right outside,' Guy said calmly, taking her arm as if nothing had happened. 'We're going to walk out of here together.'

He wasn't even breathing hard.

Something splashed on the tiled floor. Jelly looked up. He covered her mouth, catching the scream before it left her throat. Blood was dripping . . . gushing now down the narrow shaft of the stairwell. She felt a warm whip lick across her bare toes, unprotected by her Old Navy flip-flops, and grew faint.

'If you're smart,' Guy said, tightening his grip on her upper arm, 'you'll just get in the car and not say a word.'

The elevator had passed the tenth floor, halfway to the lobby where the detectives were waiting, when my cell rang.

'Yes?' I could hear a car engine, traffic.

A man's voice said, 'Tell him we're going for a ride.'

'Who is this?'

'Tell him we're taking a run out to the house, he knows the way. Oh I'm sorry, sugar, you can't talk with my dick in your mouth.' There was a sound of tearing tape and then a cry I recognised. 'That better?'

I heard Jelly sobbing.

'Tell him if he calls the cops, I'll kill you.'

I knew the voice. Last time I heard it was in the garden

442

of the Villa Nardini in Florence, standing over the grotto where Sophie died – a husky, lilting Midwestern drawl that signed off with, 'Take it easy, Ed.'

She burst out, 'Please don't hurt me, oh God . . .'

Then they were gone.

74

About halfway across the George Washington Bridge, I leaned forward and told the cab driver I'd changed my mind, when we got to the New Jersey side I wanted him to turn right around and take me back to the city.

He caught my eye in his rearview, but didn't say anything.

We were on the bridge's lower level, heading out to the house at Gilmans Landing, where I could only guess Ward had taken Jelly. The last couple of miles I'd started to have doubts. I knew how to get there, of course – *he knows the way* – but what if it wasn't the house? Could he have meant Skylands? What if this was some kind of trick? I could hear the tyres singing out: bad call, wrong decision.

My mobile rang. The phone lay beside me on the back seat of the taxi where I'd just thrown it down. I'd been speed-dialling Jelly every few minutes.

I snatched it up and hit the answer button. 'Ed Lister.'

Nothing. I could hear some kind of faint background music, the brassy fanfares of a Mariachi band it sounded like, but nobody spoke. I glanced at the display screen and saw the message alert for an incoming video feed.

The little screen lit up, went black, then an image formed

of an unmade bed, tangled sheets, pillows piled against the headboard. Slowly the camera tracked to a picture on the wall. I recognised it from Jelly's description, a Braque still-life of musical instruments. It had to be her room, her studio apartment on Thirty-ninth Street.

The picture froze. I thought, no, Jesus no, they're still there. I'd fallen right into the trap. He was going to kill her right there in the apartment . . . if he hadn't already. The video was probably a recording of her murder, which he wanted me to witness.

I waited for it to restart, sick with apprehension, trying to prepare myself for the horror I believed was about to unfold. We'd been here before, only this time I'd let it happen. My mind raced back to my headlong exit from the Carlyle, bailing out of the elevator on the fifth floor and taking the service stairs down to the hotel's side entrance, giving the detectives the slip – then, for ages, not being able to find a cab. In the end I'd decided against checking Jelly's place first. I'd calculated Ward was fifteen to twenty minutes ahead of me, I didn't have a moment to lose.

The screen on my mobile came back to life.

Different picture. In place of the Braque still-life I was looking at a gaudy painting on black velvet of the Virgin of Guadeloupe. Different room. It was like an instant reprieve. I'd only ever glanced in the door but I recognised the maid's quarters at La Rochelle. They were already at the house. Then the camera panned down and I knew the feed was live. At the foot of the bed, I saw a hunched figure on a chair, arms and legs roped together, head wrapped like a mummy's in silver duct tape (the eyes and nostrils alone were visible). As far as I could tell, Jelly was still conscious. It wasn't too late, I told myself.

A flurry of movement in front of the lens briefly obscured my view. When the image cleared, the camera had closed in on her masked face and I caught the look of sleepy terror in her eyes. Jelly was reacting to something coming towards her – I couldn't see what it was, only the twin arcs of light reflected in her dilated pupils. Then the screen went black.

I said into the phone, 'How much do you want?'

'You *know* this isn't about money.'

'We can work something out . . . whatever it is, I'll do anything.'

Ward laughed. 'You still don't get it, Ed, do you?'

'Just let her go. You can explain when I get there, but killing another innocent person won't help you.'

'Help me? Land sakes alive, Ed, they're gonna say *you* killed her. That's the whole idea. And, you know what? They'll be right. I'm going to hang up now.'

'Wait, there's one thing you should know—' But he'd already cut me off.

I looked out of the window and saw that we were coming into the bridge's toll plaza. The driver went through the E-Z Pass and I told him to take a right onto Pallisades Parkway – I'd changed my mind back.

He squinted at me in the rearview and I held up a couple of hundred-dollar bills, then pushed them under the plastic grille. 'How fast can you get there?'

'I could lose my licence,' he said.

I showed him two more.

It was hot and stuffy in the wheel-well of the station-wagon. Jelly lay curled up like a question mark, unable to move, the floor of the trunk above her weighted down by the displaced spare wheel. Every breath she took she had to suppress a panicky, claustrophobic fear something could prevent her from taking the next one. What if she sneezed and her nasal passages became blocked? What if her nose started bleeding, spontaneously, which it sometimes did? As a teenager she

445

used to worry that her nostrils were too big. Now she wished they were the size of Ohio.

She lay in the seamless dark, feeling faint and dizzy, afraid of losing her balance even though she had nowhere to fall. Some instinct told her she must at all costs stay awake. She tried to remember poems, lyrics, jokes; anything to keep her mind active. She had to fight a deep longing to close her eyes.

She switched to music. In her head, she played the Chopin Nocturne she'd been practising for the recital, and drifted off into a daydream that was about people having a conversation, talking and arguing in musical phrases. Her attention began to wander. Perhaps this was all a dream. In his car, something happened . . . she had an idea that Guy had put a needle in her arm. But she could have dreamt that too.

She had no clue where they were, except it felt like a long way from Manhattan. *A needle!* It was too quiet for the city. She remembered a sign that said, Atrium of Tenafly . . . what the fuck was that? A deserted parking lot. Guy helping her out of the Golf and making her lie down in the back end of an old station-wagon. Was that the plan? Maybe he'd given her a roofie shot, the forget-me pill . . . She must have blacked out. Did he do it yet?

Jelly couldn't remember, couldn't think straight.

She made another attempt to move her arms and legs. Nothing happened. It wasn't just because they were tightly bound, or because the shape of the wheel-well forced her to lie a certain way, her muscles weren't responding. The smell of gas and oil made her want to throw up. Then, out of nowhere, the image of a curved blade flashed before her eyes and she felt Lazlo's warm blood splash her foot. She gagged, sucking air in through her nose. What had happened to Guy? She'd heard the wagon door slam shut, a while ago now, or was it only a minute – she'd lost all sense of time. She didn't have a sound picture of him coming back.

Jelly listened, straining to hear. Her ears were covered by the tape he'd wrapped round and around her head. It was like listening to the roar of the ocean inside a shell. Beyond the constant surf, she imagined she could hear the sound of lapping water.

The station-wagon was at a slant. Maybe that was why she felt like she was falling all the time. It must be parked on a slope.

I went slowly up, one step at a time, not even trying to keep quiet. If they were here, then Ward was bound to have heard the taxi in the driveway, seen the headlights. I just kept my eye on the door to the maid's room on the landing above me, wishing now I had a gun or some kind of weapon.

I still didn't know if I'd made the right decision. Arriving at La Rochelle a couple of minutes earlier, I hadn't noticed any vehicle parked outside. The house was all lit up, which gave me some encouragement, but there was no sign of anyone. I'd walked straight through the kitchen, down the back hallway and stopped at the foot of the stairs and listened.

The door to Jesusita's room was locked. Picking up a fire-extinguisher that stood on the landing, I smashed the door-handle, then used the heavy canister to batter the door open. I took in at a glance the unmade bed, the empty wooden chair, the length of rope tangled up in its legs. They'd been here and gone. Light was coming from the bathroom. A pool of water glistened on the threshold under the half-open bath-room door. I shouldered it all the way back.

Nothing looked out of the ordinary. The tiled floor was wet, as if somebody had taken a shower recently. A pile of used towels and a sodden bathmat lay under the wash-basin. The plug had been left in the bathtub and an inch or so of soapy water. I felt the temperature, cold.

I turned off the light, came back into the room and threw

the fire-extinguisher down on Jesusita's bed. I stood for a moment, trying to think. Why had Ward sent me the live video feed, then taken Jelly and locked the door to an empty room? Why go to all the trouble? Unless he needed to delay me for some reason. He must surely want me to find them? I wouldn't have been invited out to La Rochelle unless his plan depended on my being here.

Then I saw how this was supposed to work. The empty chair, the rope, the twisted sheets, I realised now – if Kira Armour was right in her analysis of Ward's motives, his crazy insistence that I killed his parents – would become part of the evidence against me, the trail I left behind as I prepared to kill again. My fingerprints were sure to be everywhere.

It was all a set-up. I remembered the drowsy frightened look I'd seen in Jelly's eyes, and felt a rush of anger at the thought of anyone wanting to hurt her, and because of me. I was the one Ward really wanted to destroy. I closed my eyes and saw his mother sprawled on the floor of the cargo container, soaked to the skin, a trickle of blood at the corner of her mouth. If it hadn't been for that single ill-fated night I spent with June Seaton, none of this would have happened.

The past had come back to haunt me, and in retributive ways that seemed out of all proportion to anything I did wrong. The irony was that my determination to avenge Sophie's murder had blinded me to the possibility that I had set the desperate sequence of events in motion. That it was my fault she died.

If true, if only even partly true, it was pretty hard to bear.

But I had to let that go now. There was no time to waste on regretting what couldn't be changed. I thought about Jelly and the obsessive love I felt for her that had put her life in danger and, unless I could find her before Ward carried out his sick threats, was about to become the cause of her death.

'They're gonna say you killed her . . . And, you know what? They'll be right.'

He didn't really need my help to execute his plan, make her *my* victim. I was afraid Ward would decide not to wait, just go ahead without me, and I would be unable to prevent the horror from repeating itself.

It took only a minute to search the other rooms and establish that they were no longer in the house. Relieved to find Alice Fielding unharmed – the old lady was in bed, propped up against the pillows, sound asleep – I looked in the garage and saw that her Subaru and the vintage Buick station-wagon were both missing. They might have driven off in either one of them, but something told me that Ward and the girl hadn't left the grounds.

There weren't many places he could have taken her. I grabbed a flashlight from the table in the front porch and ran down through the garden, across the terraces towards the pool area. Without a key to the enclosure, I could only shine the beam through the chain-link fence into the changing pavilion and pool house. Nothing stirred among the fugitive shadows. The pool itself, empty and overgrown with weeds, had been fenced off to prevent accidents. A memory surfaced of one blazing August weekend years ago when I first taught Sophie how to dive and swim lengths underwater. The area was deserted.

I switched off the light and stood for a moment in darkness, listening. I could hear the distant hum of city traffic, but closer by the only sound and movement came from the Hudson, which I could see glinting between the trees in changing patterns of black and silver. A foreboding, some sense of the inevitable, drew me to the river.

I started jogging along the shore road, swinging the beam of the flashlight up and down the riverbank, calling Jelena's name – afraid now that I'd got there too late. It was the kind of trick Ward would enjoy playing, offering false hope, letting me believe she was still alive, when the worst had already happened. It would give him a sense of ultimate control. I thought about phoning the police. He'd warned me not to, but I couldn't see now it making much difference.

Drawing level with the boathouse, I stopped to get my breath. I called out to Jelly again, if only to let Ward know I hadn't given up looking for them, and waited. The darkness gave nothing back. Then I heard a noise from the trees and bushes growing at the river's edge that sounded like the cry of a bird, a night heron, perhaps. I heard it again. Only this time the cry registered as human.

Very faint but quite distinct – a cry for help.

It was a man's voice, coming from somewhere nearby. I turned the light on the derelict boathouse, which loomed above me narrow and gaunt against the starless sky, and brought the beam down to the open door, letting it play into the inky interior, then back along the walkway that crossed the marshy ground between the boathouse and the track.

Halfway over I spotted a figure crawling towards dry land.

Campbell Armour didn't look up or react when the light fell on him. He didn't stop either. His glasses had gone, his face and hair and sweatshirt were caked with blood, but he kept inching forward elbow over elbow, dragging his short crippled legs behind him. I knelt down and put a hand on his shoulder.

'Campbell,' I said close to his ear. 'This is Ed Lister.'

He flinched at the sound of my voice, then turned his head and I saw his eyes were full of blood. 'He's got the girl, Campbell. Do you know where they went?'

'I thought you were . . . him.' There was a long silence. He barely had enough strength to speak. 'I need you to call my wife, tell her . . .' He faded.

'I'm going to get help, then you can talk to her yourself. Where are they?'

He didn't answer and I was afraid I wouldn't get anything more out of him. 'Campbell, he's planning to kill her . . . we don't have much time.'

'I heard the wagon go past . . . other side of the bay.'

I knew where he meant. The shore road winds around a pocket wilderness area of wetlands and tidal shallows to a stony point that juts out far enough to catch the main currents of the river. The track ends in a private launch ramp, where we used to put the Fieldings' sail-boat in the water every summer. It wasn't hard to imagine why Ward might have taken her there.

I pulled out my mobile, punched 911 for emergency services and after I'd spoken to the dispatcher, handed the phone to Campbell.

'Stay where you are. They'll find you.'

'I'm not going anyplace,' Campbell said. I caught the flicker of a smile. 'This wasn't in the plan, dude.'

'You brought him in, Campbell . . . you'll make it,' I said, though I couldn't tell how badly hurt he was. 'The million dollars will be in your account tomorrow.'

'In case I don't . . .' He asked me then, agonisingly slowly, to do him a favour – it was a business matter, which I promised to take care of for him. I gave his shoulder a squeeze, got up to leave.

'Ed, wait. He's got a knife . . . it'll look like you used it on her.'

'I know,' I said and started to run.

After a short distance, I turned off the track and plunged into the reed-beds, parting the dense bulrushes that rose like a solid wall before me. When I sank down into the muddy water they reached well over my head.

As the crow flies the boat ramp lay only a couple of hundred yards across the marsh. The way round by road is a lot longer.

75

Ward stood on the slipway close to the water's edge watching the river take on the changing mood and temper of the night sky. The cloud cover had broken over the cliffs of the Palisades and a handful of stars were showing on the smooth gliding surface of the deep-water channel out in midstream.

The light-speckled river flowed through him and he saw it twist and turn into the single continuous plane of a Mobius strip. On his tongue it had a silky texture and tasted bitter, metallic, thick – somewhere between dandelion milk and blood – the taste of perpetual sorrow.

He was thinking about the girl in the trunk of the wagon and decided that he couldn't wait any longer. It didn't really matter whether Ed Lister was there to witness the end or not. Either way this was going to destroy him. He would have liked to share the moment, but now he just wanted to get it over with.

Wait a minute . . . 'get it over with'? Do I detect a certain reluctance? Don't tell me you got feelings for the chocolata, Ward. Ward??? Oh hecko, you do, don't you? My advice is stick with the programme, bud, wait until he gets here. Listen . . .

There were crackling sounds coming from the marsh.

No, he felt nothing for Jelly. She'd been pleasant enough to him, she was cute enough, in another life they might even have become friends, but so what? He felt calm about what he had to do.

He returned to the Buick, opened the tail-gate door and pulled the spare wheel out onto the concrete ramp. He gave it a shove that sent it trundling down towards the river. He watched the tyre jink as it hit the water and topple over on its side with a splash; then lost sight of it as the longshore current bore it swiftly away.

He shouldered his rucksack.

Where's the rush? Ed shouldn't be long now. Why not wait?

Ward lifted the flooring of the cargo bay. In the dark he could just make out Jelly's form curled up in the wheel-well. He took his key-light from a pocket (the wagon's interior lights were disabled) and shone the sapphire beam in her face. She blinked and he smiled down at her.

'Don't be afraid, Jelena. I won't let anyone hurt you.'

You want to give Lister the treatment, the full wax, don't you? It'll stay with him longer if he's a witness, if he takes part. Maybe forever. Cm'on, man . . .

He tried not to let her see the blade in his other hand, but she had to know what was coming. She started to squirm and shake her head, making a moaning, gagging noise as she attempted to wriggle up out of the well. He saw the frantic pleading in her eyes, showing too much white now as they rolled around in her skull. He grabbed an arm and pulled her upper body out onto the tail-gate so that her head was hanging off the edge, her throat exposed.

'Make it easy on yourself, sugar. Lay still for me.'

She wouldn't though, and she wouldn't stop the moaning either, which got on his nerves. Ward placed a hand over Jelly's eyes so he didn't have to deal with her looking at him, beseeching him. He could feel her wet eyelashes tickling his palm as he raised the gleaming mezzaluna above his head, gripping one of its horn-like steel handles in his fist.

He was about to do it, swing the curved blade – in his mind it had already begun its downward flashing trajectory – when he met resistance. He wasn't getting the usual 'this is it' feeling, no ecstatic sense of revelation, no deep conviction of his own higher authority. Yes, well . . . *didn't I try to warn you?*

He found himself back at Skylands, waiting outside the half-open door to his parents' bedroom. He could see the mirror on the vanity, reflecting a detail from the painting over the bed. He moved and the door swung back to reveal the wider tableau, life stilled by carnage . . . his mother's upside-down eyes staring at him, bitter-tasting as quinine . . . the grey pink ooze of his daddy's brains on the walls, the ceiling . . . the dry rustle of a million insect wings.

It never changed. He heard the high-pitched whine that felt like icy fingers closing around his heart. Then the eraser smell hit him . . . the blood.

He couldn't step across the threshold into the bedroom, couldn't see who was in there with them. In the medullar centre of his brain he felt a sudden blaze of heat as if some synaptic or neural circuit had shorted out. But there was someone . . . in the mirror, bloodied, small of stature. The mirror never lies.

Grace's voice calling you, 'Ernie, Ernie.'

Like smoke the picture cleared; the bedroom, the dusty landing, Grace's sobs echoing through the silent house, all evaporated; leaving him raw and trembling, glad to be reunited at last with his family, with himself. Glad to be home.

He could hear Ed blundering through the darkness.

Ward lowered his weapon and looked up at the sky, the cluster of stars. Their little fat faces, terrifyingly plump, watching him. All right, all *right*. He pushed the girl back into the wheel-well. Then slammed the tail-gate shut. He walked around to the driver's door, leaned in to pull the gear shift into neutral.

'When the water reaches you, don't struggle,' he said softly, coaching her over the back seats. 'Just let yourself be one with the spirit of the river.'

454

Then he released the handbrake and closed the door.

The station-wagon rolled down the slope, the heavy vehicle slowly gathering momentum. Ward could see already that it wasn't going to be enough. The surface of the single-width boat ramp had crumbled in places leaving pitted sections of concrete and gravel which impeded its progress. The Buick's front wheels caught in a rut and the wagon had barely entered the water before it came to a standstill.

He could hear the splashing getting closer. He looked over towards the reed-beds, expecting Ed to appear at any moment, and felt the blood rise to his face.

A furious agitation, almost panic, seized him.

He thought about going under the hood and adjusting the throttle cable, but there wasn't time. Ward jumped down off the launch ramp and searched the beach for a decent-sized rock. He found one right away close to some old pilings – it felt heavy enough and was the right shape.

He carried it back to the wagon, climbed into the driver's seat and started the engine. The big V-8 turned over but wouldn't catch. The whirring getting weaker, the battery dying on him. Ward cursed and switched off, then twisted the key in the ignition. Nothing. He repeated the process, trying it again and again until the engine suddenly gave a cough and spluttered into life.

He pinned the accelerator pedal to the floor with the rock, jamming it so it wouldn't budge, then put the automatic shift in drive and jumped clear as the old Buick lurched forward. The wagon planed along like a hovercraft, the water up to its wood-grained side panels, then swung around with the current and sank.

Ward stood and watched it go down. He thought he saw the girl's head framed for a moment in the tail-gate window, but it was too dark to be sure.

The going was harder and slower than I'd expected. Wading through the marsh, I could see little beyond the high wall of rushes immediately ahead. I had to keep stopping to realign myself by the city-glow of Yonkers on the further shore or the lights of the George Washington Bridge behind me. I could hear the river flowing off to my right, but it was easy to become disoriented.

About halfway across, turning inland to avoid a ring of deeper water, I heard a car engine come to life, then high engine revs, followed by a heavy splash. I knew at once what it meant. I raced on, praying I would get there in time.

Emerging at last from the reed-beds, I ran barefoot – I'd lost shoes and socks in the marsh – along the pebble beach towards the slipway. I couldn't see anyone, but the beam of my flashlight soon picked up the station-wagon lying ten maybe twenty yards offshore, half-submerged. There was still hope.

It had beached itself on a sandbank that at low tide sometimes gives boats trouble along that stretch of the Hudson. I knew that the deep-water channel lay just a little further out and that the current would want to drag the wagon that way. I took it as given that Jelly was on board. Stripping off my jacket, I plunged back in the water and started to make for the Buick, when I heard a voice behind me call my name. It could only be Ward.

I thought of ignoring him and carrying on, but I realised I wouldn't get far. I looked back and saw a figure standing motionless on the edge of the ramp, the glimmer of a curved blade swinging rhythmically from his left hand.

I switched off the flashlight as Ward jumped down off the ramp and came loping towards me, splashing through the shallows. I could feel the sweat rapidly cooling along the length of my spine.

He was on me so fast I had no time to think how I was

456

going to defend myself. Instinctively I ducked and heard the mezzaluna whistle past my head as Ward's shoulder rammed into my chest and knocked me over. I scrambled up at once, before he got his balance back, and grabbed his arm, the one holding the blade, from behind. He hit me with the back of his free hand hard across the mouth, but I clung to his arm as he swung around. He was in better shape than I was, and much stronger. It was just luck that I was able to stay close; I knew if I let go now I wouldn't get another chance. He hit me again in the head, this time with his fist, and I went down.

I felt my grip on his knife arm loosen and then I was on my knees in the water and he was standing over me with the mezzaluna raised above his head. I struggled to get up. He kicked me in the ribs and I felt a jagging pain in my side and collapsed.

I waited for Ward to deliver the *coup de grâce*. But instead he let the blade fall to his side. I was still holding the flashlight and I swung the beam up into the eyes of Sophie's murderer. If I'd been thinking clearly I'd have realised that he had no interest in killing me, he just wanted to stop me from reaching the station-wagon.

'Go ahead, take a good look.' He was smiling down at me. 'You see a family resemblance? I've been told I have a lot of June in me.'

'I met your mother once, a long time ago,' I wheezed, as I got up on all fours. 'I really don't remember much about her.'

'Well, ain't that a shame. Because you seem to have made quite an impression on her. I like hearing about my mother, Ed. By all accounts June – Junebug, my pa used to call her – was a charming and intelligent woman.'

'I do remember her as being pretty fucking crazy. There's a trait you may have inherited.'

He laughed. 'You took advantage of her then.'

457

'I didn't kill her.'

He was silent for a moment.

'What would you say, Ed, if I told you I don't believe you did . . . kill her? I got it wrong.' He lifted his shoulders. 'Hey, we all make mistakes.'

He wanted me to react, get angry with him. I shone the light at the Buick lying offshore like a stranded whale. I could see it moving a little now as the strong current tugged at its hidden bulk.

'Are you trying to say that Sophie died for no reason, for nothing?'

'Someone has to pay.' He smiled, shaking his head. 'If it's any comfort, your daughter never knew what was coming. I followed her into the garden, and you know those sheds where they keep the lemon trees in winter? I snuck up behind her . . . she felt no pain. None at all.

'I loved her, Ed. She just didn't feel the same way about me.'

'You're the one who's going to pay,' I shouted at him.

'You know what Dante has Virgil say in the *Purgatorio*? "Love is the seed in you of every virtue and *of all acts deserving of punishment*."'

'What the hell's that supposed to mean?'

'You still owe me, buddy.' Ward shrugged. 'See, it doesn't matter whether you came to the house that night or not. June was planning to forsake her family, dump us . . . for you. You were the one.'

'You think I knew anything about that?'

'We all do things in our lives, Ed, that have unforeseen consequences or repercussions we never intended and mostly never even get to know about. You may not have killed my ma, but you damn sure caused her death, you were the catalyst – you kindled the fire inside her wayward heart – and that makes you as guilty as if you'd wielded the knife.'

'But I *didn't* wield the knife . . . somebody else did.'

He went right on. 'You probably think I'm being too hard on you because you were young, strange to the city, out of your depth? Well, just consider the mayhem that resulted from your night of passion with June Seaton.'

'Oh, I've thought about it.'

'I blame you for the damage you did, Ed, for wrecking my life, for taking everything that was mine, everything I loved.'

'You need to turn that around,' I said quietly. 'You're the one who wrecked our lives. When you murdered that beautiful innocent child . . . it *was* for nothing. You just couldn't face up to what you did . . . you knew damn well, you always knew, what really happened to your mother and father.'

He gave a short puzzled laugh. 'Help me out, Eddie.'

'You killed them, you sick bastard.'

Ward was silent a moment.

'Let's try to be rational here. I don't remember everything that went down that night, but a nine-year-old kid slaughtering his parents, *the two people he loved most in the world? In cold blood?* Now does that make *any* kind of sense?'

'I thought your kind never forgot.'

'My "kind"? You learn that from Dish Armour too?'

I could hear the station-wagon bumping and scraping along the bottom. I shouted, 'We need to get the girl out of there.'

'You're a little late, hotshot. But let me tell you, for the record, Jelena was one sweet piece of ass . . . man, was she ever up for it.'

He waited a beat. 'Just messin with ya, *Mister*.'

Without warning he lashed out with his left foot, aiming a kick at my head that missed but caught the flashlight and sent it spinning from my hand. I grabbed his foot and at the same time stood up fast. Ward toppled back and went down in the darkness. I sprang on top of him and, forgetting he

459

still had the knife, hit him as hard as I could, connecting with what felt like nose and cheekbone.

I got up and tried to wade back out to the wagon.

I'd hit him nowhere near hard enough. Already on his feet and, out for blood now, he came after me with a low roar. I could hear him surfing my wake, steadily gaining. Imagining at any moment the mezzaluna splitting open my back, I weaved and changed course, then suddenly swung back towards land. A dark shadow shot past me. I heard a curse followed by a heavy splash. Then silence.

I didn't see what happened, but guessed he must have slipped and smacked his head on a submerged rock. I put my hand down in the water and felt around in the mud and shingle and almost at once came on an arm, a shoulder. He was still semi-conscious and groaning as I pulled him up onto the beach.

I wrenched the mezzaluna from his grip and, kneeling over him, brought the razor-sharp blade up under his chin. I couldn't see Ward's face, or know how badly he was hurt, but it occurred to me that I'd only saved his miserable life in order to kill him. This was the moment I'd dreamt about, lived for. Here at last I had my chance to avenge Sophie's death.

I held him by the throat, enjoying the voluptuous feeling of my fingers digging into the cold stringy muscles of his neck. All I had to do now was draw the blade swiftly across his windpipe. It should have been simple.

But it wasn't. I needed more than this. I needed to hear Ward say he was sorry and mean it, I needed him to confess and then beg my forgiveness for what he did to Sophie. He started to choke and for a second I eased the pressure. I don't know what made me relent, whether it was because his own crazy sense of grievance had stolen my appetite for revenge, or because I had come to understand that whatever he'd done, however horrific his crimes, he was still a human being. Or maybe I just wasn't capable of deliberately killing anyone. In the moment I hesitated a slow grinding sucking sound from the river brought Jelly's plight urgently back into focus.

I looked up and saw the bone-pale outline of the station-wagon stand on its front end and slide beneath the water. I hurled the knife away and, leaving Ward semi-conscious on the beach, waded and then swam out to where I thought the wagon had gone down.

76

In the river, treading water, it was more difficult to judge distances than from dry land. I quickly scanned the surface for a vortex or stream of bubbles from the submerged vehicle, but there was nothing. Then, taking several short breaths, followed by a deep one, I dived down and kept kicking hard until I touched bottom. I wasn't afraid, I've had plenty of scuba experience, and I knew what to do. I set about trying to locate the station-wagon, staying close to the dive point at first, then gradually expanding the area of search by swimming in ever-widening circles. It was so dark it made no difference whether I kept my eyes open or shut. I had to feel my way over the shifting riverbed. Very soon I lost my bearings.

After forty seconds or so, unable to find any trace of the sunken Buick, I came back up for air and, again treading water, looked about for some kind of turbulence. In every direction all I could see was the dark gliding mirror of the Hudson. It added to a growing sense of desperation. I could feel the strong current bearing me downstream and suddenly my hopes of finding the wagon and reaching the girl in time seemed negligible. I knew I had to concentrate on the task, not the person I was trying to rescue; yet it was only the thought of Jelly and how terrified she must be right now that gave me strength.

I'd convinced myself she was still alive down there, still conscious; but with every passing second I was aware of that becoming less and less likely. Then, a few feet away from me, as I turned my head towards the shore, I noticed a telltale eruption of bubbles troubling an otherwise smooth stretch of water.

I took another deep breath and plunged again.

One thing I've learnt from years of diving is the importance of staying calm underwater. I knew that from the moment the Buick went down, unless the windows were open, it would take at least three minutes – maybe more – to become fully submerged. It didn't necessarily mean the person trapped inside had that long. But panic is *the* enemy. I estimated Jelly had been down there just over a minute.

I made two more dives before I found the station-wagon lying on its side in about fifteen feet of water. Moving quickly over the top of the front wing and windshield, I pulled myself along by the roof rack until I reached the rear passenger door. I got the door open and managed to hold it against the current long enough to swim inside before gravity and the weight of the water swung it shut behind me.

The interior was already flooded. One of the windows resting on the riverbed could have been open or shattered, but whatever the cause it reduced the odds of Jelly's having survived. I felt around the cabin, methodically sweeping the front and back seats in case she was trapped by a seat-belt. There was no sign of a body.

By now I'd used up most of my air supply. My lungs felt

ready to implode (Ward's kick in the ribs hadn't helped) and I was resorting to every trick I knew for conserving breath, releasing little bubble streams of air and working my jaw at the same time. Soon, I realised, I wasn't going have enough juice left to get out. I scrambled through into the trunk space, ignoring the small sensible voice that was urging me to leave now, immediately – while I still could.

Then the wagon made a sudden lurch, slid a few feet and settled at an angle with the front end lower than the back. I wasn't sure how far we'd drifted from the shore, but I guessed the Buick was lying close to the edge of a deep channel where the water at high tide runs forty to fifty feet. If the current took it over the ridge, I knew the chances of anyone surviving would be minimal. On the plus side, the tipping of the wagon had given me an idea – it was really my last hope. I kicked upwards and, in the highest corner of the cargo bay, found what I was looking for – a small triangular pocket of trapped air.

I broke the surface, mouth and nose first, and after the relief of that first violent intake of breath, gulped several lungfuls of what tasted like pure oxygen. It took a moment before I realised in the pitch dark that the rapid effortful breathing I could hear wasn't my own. I felt something move against my side underwater and knew I was sharing the trunk space. I couldn't tell what state she was in.

All that mattered was that she was alive.

I touched Jelly's face and discovered her mouth was still sealed with duct tape. She moaned as I felt around the back of her head, trying to find some way to loosen the tape. There wasn't time. I could feel the water in our temporary air cave rising. A voice inside my skull, frantic sounding, was saying we had to get out *now*.

'You'll be okay,' I shouted at Jelly, holding her chin up to keep her nose above the surface. Her arms were tied behind her back. 'We're going to stay calm and swim out of here together . . .'

The water had reached my mouth.

I had planned to go back out the same way I came in, but realised that manoeuvring a disabled person through the gap between the top of the back seats and roof with zero visibility would be impossible. I felt for the lever that opened the Buick's tail-gate on the inside (remembered from when Sophie and George were little and liked to ride in the back), found it and pushed the heavy door down with my feet. The hinges were on the bottom so it stayed open. I instructed Jelly to take several short breaths, followed by a deep one, then linking one of my arms through hers, pulled her back under the water.

As we swam out through the open door, I kicked down for both of us and pushed off hard from the tail-gate to get clear of the wagon. I shot upwards, but Jelly stayed behind. I swam back and tugged at her arm, tried again to drag her with me, but she didn't come. Something was keeping her there, preventing our escape.

I could only think that her feet had become entangled, or that Ward had tied them in some way to the frame of the Buick. I knew I had just seconds to free her. Letting go Jelly's arm I dived down and felt around her legs for any obstruction.

Reaching under the floating hem of her jeans, I ran my hand down her bare calf, finding nothing until I touched a familiar shape that for a second didn't register because it had no business being there. I touched it again, felt the contours of bony limpet fingers clamped to her flesh and realised that it was a hand – a hand around her ankle, holding her fast.

The shock went through me and I reared back, hitting my head on the Buick's bumper. I opened my eyes into the murk and for a moment all around me was light, a sparkling turquoise blaze, as if I was staring at a swimming pool on a

464

summer's day. I had no idea where I was, or which way was up or down; it occurred to me I'd started to swallow water and was hallucinating. I knew the hand belonged to Ward and that he must have followed me down here, willing to go to insane lengths to make sure the girl drowned. I thought of him then not as human but as some kind of implacable monster pursuing us into the abyss.

I should have killed him when I had the chance.

In a frenzy of rage and loathing I lashed out with my bare feet at where I thought Ward's head would be. I couldn't see him at all, not even a darker shadow. I just felt my heel connect with something that yielded and that could have been a face and I stomped on it again. I had an arm around Jelly's legs, still trying to pull her free, but there was no give. Ward must have attached himself to the wagon somehow. I imagined him holding the trailer hitch with one hand, his lower body wrapped around a back wheel, the way a Moray eel winds its tail around a projecting rock or part of a wreck to keep its prey until it drowns.

As I kicked down again and again, desperation set in and I started to black out. I remember thinking it was all over, we were both going to die, when I became aware of a change in the water around us. I could feel the current eddying strongly on the downstream side of the Buick and then, suddenly, the wagon started to move.

I don't know if Ward felt it too, but something made him let go his grip on Jelly's ankle. I had just enough strength left to grab her arm and swim her out of the way as the heavy car flipped over on its roof and, tyres up, fell off the edge of the underwater ridge and slithered away towards the bottom of the deep channel.

We rose to the surface. I don't remember the relief of my first swallow of fresh air or rejoicing at seeing the night sky again or feeling grateful to be alive – only an irrational primitive fear that Ward could still attack us from beneath as I turned on my back and struck out for the shore, struggling to keep Jelly's head above water.

I knew even before I carried her up onto the beach and lay her on her side that she'd stopped breathing. I went through the procedure, placing my cheek close to her face, checking for airflow; looking for the rise and fall of her diaphragm. Nothing. I grabbed a wrist to feel her pulse, gave up and slammed my ear to her chest. There was a faint heartbeat. She was alive, it seemed, but only just.

There wasn't time to unwrap her head. I scrabbled at the duct tape that covered her mouth, got my fingernails under a seam and tore it away, making a slit of an opening. Then I tilted her head back and, pinching her nostrils shut, took a deep breath and blew it slowly and gently into her mouth. After a couple of seconds I broke away, counting one thousand, two thousand . . . On five thousand, I bent down again to repeat the kiss of life, when she made a choking sound, river water came up, she started coughing and then her eyes opened.

It was a while before she could speak.

We sat up on the launch ramp, exhausted and shivering, arms around each other just trying to get warm. I could hear the sound of sirens in the distance and saw to my relief the blue flashes of rotating dome lights right across the bay, making their way slowly towards us along the shore road from the old boathouse.

The approaching police and emergency services meant that Campbell had been found alive and in a fit enough state to have pointed them in our direction. Although she seemed all right now, I knew Jelly would also need medical attention.

'This doesn't change anything,' she murmured.

'What are you talking about?'

There was a silence. I said, 'I came back for you, didn't I?'

466

She laughed. 'Yeah, took your time about it too.'

Earlier, soon after we scrambled ashore, I'd heard faint splashing out on the river. There was no way of knowing if it was Ward, but it made me wonder what had persuaded him to come after us in the water. Perhaps he realised there was a chance I might succeed in rescuing Jelly from the submerged station-wagon; and decided it was too risky for him to wait on the beach.

The police report concluded that he probably drowned in the Hudson that night and his body was swept out to sea. I went along with the theory, if only to give Jelly some peace of mind, but no trace of Ward was ever found.

'He's gone now,' I said quietly, 'gone for good.'

'But what if—' she began.

'Jelly, from now on I promise—'

'Don't.' She put a finger across my lips. 'Just because you saved my damned life . . . oh Jesus, Ed, I let him in.' She started crying. 'I let *him* in.'

'It's all over now.'

'Is it?'

'Try not to talk,' I shushed her.

Paris

I waited until the recital had begun and the ensemble had almost completed the Chopin section of the programme before quietly opening the door near the top of the auditorium and stepping inside.

It was early evening and the Salle de l'Orgue was dark enough for the back rows to be almost invisible from the stage. I found a pillar to lean against and partly conceal myself behind – there were plenty of empty seats in the small subterranean amphitheatre (it was an informal concert by the students), but I didn't want her to know I was in the audience.

On stage, sitting very straight at the concert grand, Jelly looked thinner and older, a little more drawn about the face, than I remembered, but still just as beautiful. Since we last saw each other in New York we'd stayed loosely in touch, but had let the old connection between us drop. She'd e-mailed me that she'd taken up her place at the Conservatoire and I was pleased to know that at least something good had come out of the nightmare I'd put her through.

After I got back from the States, I gave Laura a full uncensored account of everything that had happened. I was honest and open with her because, frankly, I had no reason not to be. Her reaction was unexpected. When I'd finished, she just smiled sadly and said, 'This doesn't make it any easier to say what I have to say to you, Ed.' Then she broke the news that there was someone else in her life, and that it had been going on for some time – from even before Sophie was murdered. Laura wanted an annulment, the Catholic way of divorce, on the basis of clandestinity – which strikes me now as a little ironic – meaning that our union was invalid because we were not married before a priest.

I am still coming to terms with all that that entails.

The ensemble reached the end of a Chopin Polonaise, the strings pulling back to let the last gliding notes of the piano hang on the air. The audience showed its appreciation as the violinist and cellist stepped forward to take a bow. Jelly remained seated while the applause died down and the other two musicians left the stage.

She waited for the audience to settle, then began her solo piece. It was a Schubert Impromptu, slow and melancholy, with a flowing melody line that soared high above the darker, more passionate phrases, which she played with such delicacy of touch and feeling, it was impossible not to be moved. I listened more or less spellbound until I realised I'd lost track of time and was going to be late for another engagement. I slipped out, closing the door soundlessly behind me.

I lingered for a moment in the dark hallway. A tightness rose up through my chest and formed a hard knot at the back of my throat. I thought of waiting till the end of the concert and just saying hello, perhaps asking her out for a drink.

It would have been simple to change my plans. But something in me resisted. I felt a reluctance to get involved again, even though my feelings for her hadn't really changed, even though the situation at home had. Irrevocably. I don't know why, I just decided it was best to leave things as they were.

I could hear muted but enthusiastic clapping from the auditorium. For an encore she struck up a bright Scott Joplin rag – one I hadn't heard before. The tumbling, relentlessly cheerful barrelhouse sound made me smile. I turned then and began to climb the shallow stairs that curved upwards between walls of black slate and exited into the main hall. I'd almost reached the top when I noticed someone standing there, a tall familiar figure.

The clothes he was wearing – suit, shirt, tie, even the shoes – were either mine or identical to mine. Then I saw his hand reach for the rail at the same moment I did and realised my mistake; there was no one there. I was simply walking towards my own reflection in a full-length mirror on the back of the half-open door.

I sent letters of condolence to Sam Metcalf's parents and the family of Linda Jack, the other girl on the train. I found it easier to write now that I could tell them that justice of a kind had been done, the murder of their children avenged.

Vengeance stirs primitive emotions. I'm not proud of the satisfaction it has given me, but I can't pretend that I don't rejoice in the removal of Ernest 'Ward' Seaton from the face of the earth. The person who best understands and shares that sentiment (he told me once he had a Sicilian grand-mother) is Andrea Morelli. I underestimated Morelli. If it hadn't been for his quiet perseverance and a tough but compassionate nature, the outcome might have been very different. He received a citation for his role in tracking down the murderer of three foreign residents of Florence and I've heard is in line for a promotion.

I also found a way privately to express my gratitude.

Campbell Armour made a full recovery from his injuries. He was lucky and, when it really mattered, his luck held. The beating he took from Ward's hammer left him with a fractured skull and an epidural haematoma (an accumulation of blood in the lining of the brain), which required emergency surgery. His wife and daughter flew up from Tampa and I arranged for them to stay at La Rochelle so they could be near the hospital in Englewood. The other day I received an e-mail

471

from Campbell saying it felt good to be home, debt-free and hoping to be playing tennis again by Christmas. His claim to have been permanently cured of his gambling habit I found less convincing.

I still have dreams about Sophie's murder. I haven't stopped grieving for my daughter and doubt that I ever will. Just as I don't expect to get past the idea that I was in some way responsible for what happened. But life goes on, and the fact that it does seems less cruel, less unfair now. I can't say I'm at peace with myself, I neither expect nor want 'closure', but I have at least found a degree of acceptance.

I'm sure that Jelena with her 'get over it, move on' philosophy has been a positive influence – I have her to thank for helping me find the way to a new life.

The night of the concert, when I got back to the hotel, there was a note from her in my system tray. She had spotted me at the back of the Salle de l'Orgue, lurking in the shadows, as she put it, and was furious that I'd had the nerve to drop by and then sneak away *without even telling her*. She said that she'd looked everywhere for me after the recital but I'd already left. I replied with a brief apology, explaining that I'd had other plans.

When I returned to Paris a week later I called Jelly up, and the next evening took her out to dinner at a restaurant called L'Ami Louis.

It felt a little uncomfortable at first being together again. Maybe it had something to do with finding ourselves at last in circumstances that could be described as nearly normal. Strangers but not strangers, we weren't so much awkward with each other as reserved and a little wary. It was like picking up the old conversation where we'd left off, and yet at the same time starting over from scratch. We didn't mention Ward during dinner, or at any point that evening.

After leaving the restaurant, I had the taxi drop us off at

the Pont de la Concorde and we walked back to the Ritz along the banks of the Seine. More or less as I had once imagined. We stopped at the same spot where months ago I'd stood and, looking upriver at the illuminated towers of Notre Dame through an arch of the Pont des Arts, wished Jelly could have been at my side. Now she was.

I walked on, taking her arm, and maybe fifty yards further along the riverbank paused again. It was then something occurred that I have no explanation for.

We were standing on the quayside by an empty landing stage, sharing a cigarette (she had switched to smoking Gauloises) and talking. I have to say it was neither peaceful by the water's edge nor particularly romantic. It had just started to rain and we could hardly make ourselves heard over the blaring tourist commentary from a passing Bateau Mouche; but then, as the river grew quiet again, cutting through the slapping of the boat's wash against the quayside, I detected a faint thin sound that sent a shiver through me.

It was impossible to tell where the music was coming from. I looked around but we were between bridges and there was no sign of anyone on the embankment above. The quay was deserted.

'Is that your cell?' Jelly asked with a frown.

I shook my head, unsure whether it was a ring-tone I could hear or another kind of recording or just somebody whistling the tune, but we'd both recognised the first limpid seesawing notes of 'Für Elise'.

It didn't last more than a few seconds. As the melody began to pick up the pace and swell into the graceful flourish of arpeggios that modulate back to the main theme, the music suddenly cut out.

I could feel my heart hammering against my ribs as I stood very still, gripping Jelly's arm, determined not to over-react. I wanted to run up the stone steps to the Tuileries in case he was there somewhere, watching us, but it would only have scared her. She was unaware of the significance of what we'd just heard and I couldn't possibly enlighten her now. I made some flippant remark about how in Iran garbage trucks play the tune to warn people to bring out their trash.

There was nothing more. And there's been nothing since. I'm not a great believer in coincidence, but it was almost certainly just that. Nevertheless, I've had to accept that as far as Ward's demise is concerned there will always be the shadow of a doubt.

Jelly and I see quite a bit of each other now, mostly when I'm in Paris. I don't know what the future holds for us. She believes in taking life a day at a time. I have plans to take my life in new directions that I can't easily envisage her fitting in with. There's a lot to work through, and we may never resolve our differences, but it seems at least possible that I wasn't wrong when I told her that this was always 'meant to happen'.

In fact it was Ward who wrote those words, as Jelly was quick to point out. But then she smiled and said it didn't make them any less true. Which made me think about the moment when I saw her step out of that taxi at Lincoln Center and knew somehow that it was really her.